Praise for Lauren Smith's
Wicked Designs

"Smith's fast-paced historical keeps readers on their toes as they're taken hostage by a whirlwind of characters and an unforgettable romance."

~ *RT Book Reviews*

"Lauren Smith's debut *League of Rogues* novel is a fun, clever and wonderfully sympathetic read that will no doubt earn her a number of fans."

~ *The Romance Reviews*

"The best thing for me was the quality of Lauren Smith's writing. I will read her again. She is a fresh voice to watch out for."

~ *Romantic Historical Reviews*

"I really enjoyed *Wicked Designs*, Lauren Smith's debut Regency historical novel. This witty and entertaining romance features an emotionally scarred hero, a smart heroine and a loveable group of rogues..."

~ *Rakes and Rascals*

"This story was the best of romance, friendship, and love. It was a quick, easy read that put a smile on my face."

~ *Cocktails and Books*

Wicked Designs

Lauren Smith

SAMHAIN
PUBLISHING

Samhain Publishing, Ltd.
11821 Mason Montgomery Road, 4B
Cincinnati, OH 45249
www.samhainpublishing.com

Wicked Designs
Copyright © 2014 by Lauren Smith
Print ISBN: 978-1-61922-315-8
Digital ISBN: 978-1-61921-745-4

Editing by Noah Chinn
Cover by Kim Killion

First Samhain Publishing, Ltd. electronic publication: January 2014
First Samhain Publishing, Ltd. print publication: January 2015

Dedication

To Amanda who changed my destiny when she sat down next to me in Torts law class. To my grandmother who taught me to love romance novels and made sure I went home with a stack every Christmas. To my parents, for their love, support and enduring hours of writing "shoptalk".

Acknowledgments

There are so many people I'd like to thank who offered support and encouragement. To Nadia and Rohit, who were the first to set me on the path of pursuing writing as a career. To Henry C. for being a wonderful muse when I wrote my hero Godric. I have to thank my parents who are always supportive of my desire to write and offer sage advice on working towards success. I want to give a special shout out to my brother who has supported me and even composed beautiful theme music for my Godric and Emily. Thanks to all my teachers who saw the spark of the writer in me, especially Joy Edwards, who gave out candy awards at the end of every year. She gave me the Oh Henry! candy bar and proclaimed I'd be a writer. I also want to thank the lovely people in my Regency Romance Critique group. They've read countless drafts and offered endless suggestions and support on my manuscripts. I couldn't ask for a better group of writers and friends. Last but certainly not least, a special thanks goes to my editor Noah. He made me laugh more times than I could count during our revisions and most importantly he inspired me to be a better writer. Thank you Noah, from the bottom of my heart.

League Rule 4

When seducing a lady, any member of the League may pursue her until she has declared her interest in a particular member, and at such time, all pursuits of the lady by others must cease.

Excerpt from *The Quizzing Glass Gazette*, April 3, 1820, The Lady Society Column:

Lady Society was quite entertained earlier this week, when she was witness to yet another wicked scheme perpetuated by a member of London's notorious League of Rogues. His Grace, the Duke of Essex, was seen to have been seducing a most attractive widow in the midst of a musicale hosted by Viscount Sheridan.

It seems the duke has truly broken with his long time paramour Miss Evangeline Mirabeau. For all marriage minded mamas, there is a collective sigh of sadness that His Grace is a determined bachelor with no intent to marry. Shame upon His Grace for not being a gentleman that mothers could safely marry their daughters to and indulging in his wicked lifestyle.

Lady Society will continue to watch the League with the keenest interest...

Chapter One

Something wasn't right. Emily Parr allowed the elderly coachman to help her into the town coach, and the queer look he gave her made her skin crawl. Peering into the dark interior of the vehicle, she was surprised to find it empty. Uncle Albert was supposed to accompany her to social engagements and if not him, certainly a chaperone. Why then was the coach empty?

She settled into the back seat, her hands clutching her reticule tight enough that the beadwork dug into her palms through her gloves. Perhaps her uncle was meeting with his business partner, Mr. Blankenship. She'd seen Blankenship arrive just before she'd gone upstairs to prepare for the ball. A shudder rippled through her. The man was a lecherous creature with beetle-black eyes and hands that tended to wander too freely whenever he was near her. Emily was not worldly, having only just turned eighteen a few months earlier, but this last year with her uncle had enlightened her to a new side of life and none of it had been good.

Her first London Little Season should have been a wonderful experience. Instead it had begun with the death of her parents at sea and ended with her new life in the dusty tomb of her uncle's townhouse. With an insubstantial library, no pianoforte and no friends, Emily had started to slide into a melancholy haze. It was crucial she make a good match and fast. She had to escape Uncle Albert's world, and the only way she could do that was to legally obtain her father's fortune.

A distant cousin of her mother's held the money in trust. It was a frustrating thing to have a man she'd never met hold the purse strings on her life. Uncle Albert despised the situation as well. As her guardian he was forced to give an accounting to her mother's cousin, which thankfully kept him from delving too deeply into her accounts for his own needs. The small fortune was the best bargaining chip she had to entice potential suitors. Though the money would go to her husband, she hoped to find a man who would respect her enough not to squander what was rightfully hers. But arriving at the ball without a chaperone would damage her chances in husband hunting, it simply wasn't done to show up alone. It spoke lowly of her uncle as well as their financial situation.

As relieved as she was to not have her uncle or Mr. Blankenship escorting her, her stomach still clenched. She recalled the cold way the elderly driver smiled at her just before she'd climbed inside. The slickness of that grin made her feel a little uneasy, like he knew something she didn't and it amused him. It was silly—the old man wasn't a threat. But she couldn't shake the wariness that rippled through her. She would have been thankful for Uncle Albert's presence, even if it meant another lecture on how costly she was to provide for and how kind he'd been in taking her in after her parents' ship was lost.

The driver was engaged to bring her to Chessley House for the ball, and nothing would go wrong. If she kept saying it over and over, she might believe it. Emily focused her thoughts on what tonight would bring, hoping to ease her worry. She would join her new friend, Anne Chessley, as well as Mrs. Judith Pratchet, an old friend of Anne's mother, who'd kindly agreed to sponsor Emily for the Little Season. There was every possibility she would meet a man and catch his interest enough that he would approach her uncle for permission to court her.

Emily almost smiled. Perhaps tonight she would dance with the Earl of Pembroke.

Last night, the handsome earl had smiled at her during their introduction and asked her to dance. Emily had nearly wept with disappointment when she informed him that Mrs. Pratchet had already filled her dance card.

The earl had replied, "Another time, then?" and Emily nodded eagerly, hoping he would remember her.

Perhaps tonight I shall have a spot of luck. She desperately hoped so. Emily wasn't so foolish as to believe she had any real chance of marrying a man like the Earl of Pembroke, but it was nice to be noticed by a man of his standing. Sometimes that attention was noticed by others.

The coach halted sharply a moment later, and she nearly toppled out of her seat, her thoughts interrupted, her daydreams fleeing.

"Ho there, my good man!" a man shouted from nearby.

Emily moved toward the door, but the vehicle rocked as someone climbed onto the driver's seat, and she fell back in her seat again.

"Twenty pounds is yours if you follow those two riders ahead and do as we ask," the newly-arrived man said.

Having regained control of her balance, she flung the coach curtains back. Two riders occupied the darkened street, their backs to her. What was going on? A sense of ill-ease settled deep in her stomach. The coach jerked and moved again. As she had feared, the driver didn't stop at Chessley House. He followed the riders ahead.

What was this? A kidnapping? A robbery? Should she stick her head out of the window and ask them to stop? If robbing her was their intent, asking them what they were doing might be a bad idea... Why would they take her when there were so many other heiresses, ones more lovely than her, having their first come out this year? Surely this wasn't an abduction. Her mind reeled as she struggled to cope with the situation. What would her father have done in this situation? Load a pistol and fight them off. Having no pistol, she'd have to think of something clever. Could these men be reasoned with? *Unlikely.*

Emily worried her bottom lip as she debated her options. She could scream for help, but such a reaction could worsen matters. She could open the door and throw herself out onto the street, but the clatter of hooves behind the coach erased that idea. She'd be lucky to survive the fall if she tried, and the horses behind were too close. She'd likely be killed. Emily fell back against the seat with a shaky sigh, her heart racing. She'd have to wait until the driver stopped.

For what seemed like an hour she kept nervously glancing out the windows to assess what direction the coach was going. By now London was far behind her. Only open country stretched on both sides of the road. A rumble of hooves heralded an approaching rider, and a man astride a sleek black gelding galloped past the window. He was too close and the horse too tall for her to get a good view of him. The moonlight rippled off the horse's shiny coat as it rode past.

She knew by the close proximity of the rider and the determined way he rode in the saddle that he was involved with this business. Who in their right mind, except perhaps that foul old man, Blankenship, would kidnap her? He'd be the sort to engage in such a nefarious activity.

The other evening he'd come to dinner at her uncle's house and when her uncle had turned away for only a second, Blankenship had twined one of this thick, stubby fingers around a lock of her hair, tugging it hard until she'd nearly cried out. He'd whispered horrible things in her ear, nasty things that made her sick as he told her he planned to marry her as soon as her uncle had approved. Emily had stared back at him, stating she'd never marry him. He'd only laughed and said, "We'll see, my sweet. We shall see."

Well, she wouldn't back down. She wasn't some pawn to be captured and held at someone's mercy. They'd have to fight to take her.

Emily looked out the window on the other side to count the riders. Two led the party at the front, mere yards ahead. Another two flanked the coach on either side. One of them rode with a second horse roped to his saddle, likely for the man who rode now with the driver. Not the best of odds. Perhaps she could outsmart them.

The coach slowed, then gently creaked to a stop. Emily took stock of her situation. She fought for composure, each breath slower than the one before. If she panicked, she might not survive. She had to hide. But she could not physically escape *five* men.

Her eyes fell to the seat across from her.

Maybe—

Godric St. Laurent, the twelfth Duke of Essex, leaned back in his saddle watching the abduction he'd orchestrated unfold. Covering his mouth with a gloved hand, he stifled a yawn. Things were going smoothly. In fact, this entire kidnapping bordered on the point of tedious. They'd intercepted the coach ten minutes before it reached Chessley House. No one witnessed the escort of riders or the driver changing his route. Oddly enough, the young woman hadn't shown any signs of resistance or concern from inside the coach. Wouldn't she have made some protestations when she realized what was happening? A thought stopped him dead. Had she somehow slipped out of the coach when they'd slowed on a corner before they'd left town? Surely not, they would have seen her. Most likely she was too terrified to do anything, hence the silence from inside. Not that she had anything to fear, she would not be harmed.

He nodded to his friend Charles who was perched next to the driver. A bag of coins jingled as Charles dropped it into the jarvey's waiting hands.

11

They had reached the halfway point between London and Godric's ancestral estate. They would go the rest of the way on horseback, with the girl sharing a horse with either him or one of his friends. The driver would return to London with a message for Albert Parr and a wild story that exonerated himself from blame.

"Ashton, stay here with me." Godric waved his friend over while the others rode the horses a good distance away to wait for his signal. Abductions were tricky things, and having only himself and one other man take hold of the girl would be better. She might have a fit of hysterics if she saw the other three men too close.

He rode up to the coach, curious to see whether the woman inside matched his memory. He'd seen her once before from a window overlooking the gardens when he'd visited her uncle. She'd been kneeling in the flowerbeds, her dress soiled as she weeded. A job more suited to a servant than a lady of quality. He'd been ready to dismiss her from his mind when she'd turned and glanced about the garden, a smudge of dirt on the tip of her upturned nose. A butterfly from a nearby flower had fluttered above her head. She hadn't noticed it, even as it settled on her long, coiling auburn hair. Something in his chest gave a funny little flip, and his body had stirred with desire. Any other woman so innocent would not have caught his interest, but he'd glimpsed a keenness in her eyes, a hidden intelligence as she dug into the soil. Miss Emily Parr was different. And different was intriguing.

Ashton handed the driver the ransom letter for Parr and took up a position near the front of the coach. Taking hold of the door, Godric opened it up, waiting for the screaming to start.

None came.

"My deepest apologies, Miss Parr—" Still no screaming. "Miss Parr?" Godric thrust his head into the coach.

It was empty. Not even a fire-breathing dragon of a chaperone, not that he'd expected one. His sources had assured him she would be alone tonight.

Godric looked over his shoulder. "Ash? You're sure this is Parr's coach?"

"Of course. Why?" Ashton jumped off his horse, marched over and thrust his head into the empty coach. He was silent a long moment before he withdrew. Ashton put his finger against his lips and motioned to the inside. A tuft of pink muslin peeped out from the wooden seat. He gestured for Godric to step away from the coach.

Ashton lowered his voice. "It seems that our little rabbit chase has turned into a fox hunt. She's hidden in the hollow space of the seat, clever girl."

"Hiding under the seat?" Godric shook his head, bewildered. He didn't know one woman of his acquaintance who would do something so clever. Perhaps Evangeline, but then if anything could be said of that woman, it was that she was far from ordinary. A prickling of excitement coursed through his veins, into his chest. He loved a challenge.

"Let's wait a few minutes and see if she emerges."

Godric looked back at the coach, impatience prickling inside him. "I don't want to wait here all night."

"She'll come out soon enough. Allow me." Ashton walked back to the coach and called out to Godric in a carrying voice. "Blast and damnation! She must have slipped out before we took charge of the coach. Just leave it. We'll take the driver back to London tomorrow." Ashton shut the door with a loud slam and motioned for Godric to join him.

"Now we wait," Ashton whispered. He indicated that he would guard the left coach door while Godric stationed himself at the right.

Emily listened to the drum of retreating hooves and silently counted to one hundred. Her heart jolted in her chest as she considered what the men would do if they caught her. Highwaymen could be cruel and murderous, especially if their quarry offered little. She had no access to her father's fortune, which left only her body.

Icy dread gripped Emily's spine, paralyzing her limbs. She drew a breath as anxiety spiraled through her.

I must be brave. Fight them until I can fight no more. With trembling hands, she pushed at the roof of the seat, wincing as it popped open. Once she climbed out, she brushed dirt from her gown, noticing some tears from the rough wood on the inside of the seat. But the tears held no importance. All that mattered was survival.

Emily looked out the coach window. Nothing stood out in the darkness. Only the faint glimmer of moonlight touched the road with milky tendrils. Stars winked and flickered overhead, pale lights, distant and cold. A shudder wracked her frame, and Emily hugged herself, wanting so much to be at home. She missed her warm bed and her parents' murmurs from down the hall. It was a comfort she'd taken for

13

granted. But she couldn't afford to think about them, not when she was in danger.

Were the men truly gone? Could it really be this easy?

She opened the coach door, and stepped down onto the dirt road. Strong arms locked about her waist and yanked her backward. The collision with a hard body knocked the breath from her lungs. Terror spiked her blood as she struggled against the arms that held her.

"Good evening, my darling," a low voice murmured.

Emily screamed once, before she bit down on the hand that covered her mouth. She tasted the smooth leather of fine riding gloves.

The man roared and nearly dropped her. "Damn!"

Emily rammed an elbow backwards into her attacker's stomach and began to wrestle free until he grabbed her arm. She swung about, striking him across the face with a balled fist. The man staggered back, leaving her free to dive inside the coach.

If she could get to the other side and run, she might stand a chance. She scrabbled towards the door, but never made it. The devil surged into the coach after her. Turning to face him, she was knocked flat onto her back.

She screamed again as his body settled over hers.

The dim moonlight revealed his bright eyes and strong features.

He caught her flailing wrists, pinning them above her head. "Quiet!"

Emily wanted to rake his eyes out, but the man was relentless. His hips ground against hers and panic drove her to a new level of terror. Her fears of being forcibly taken surfaced as his warm breath fanned over her face and neck. She shrieked, and he reared back away from her, as though the sound confused him.

"I'm not going to hurt you." His voice vibrated with a low growl, ruining any promise his words might carry.

"You're hurting me now!" She yanked her arms uselessly against his hold.

The man eased off her somewhat, and Emily took her chance. She tucked her knees up, and with all the power she could summon, she kicked. Her attacker stumbled out the open door and fell onto his back. Emily barely registered that he was winded before she turned and exited the other side of the coach.

The moment she emerged, another man lunged for her. To escape him, Emily fell back against the side of the coach. Rather than grab her, he held his arms wide to keep her from slipping by him, like he was corralling livestock.

"Easy, easy," he purred.

Emily whipped her head to the left and pleaded with her mind to think, but the man she'd bitten rounded the corner and pounced, pinning her against the coach, his arms caging her in. His solid muscular body towered over her. His jaw clenched as though one move from her would trigger something dark and wild. Emily's breath caught, and her heart pounded violently against her ribs.

The man was panting and angry. The intensity of his eyes mesmerized her, but the second he blinked, the spell broke and she fought with every bit of strength she could muster.

"Cedric, I need you!" The man shouted over his shoulder.

One of the riders trotted over holding a silver flask in one hand. Emily redoubled her efforts to escape and stamped on the instep of her captor's boot. But it was too late. The man held the flask to her lips and, when she didn't open her mouth, he pinched her nose, and she was forced to part her lips for breath. Vile, bitter liquid streamed down her throat. She gagged but swallowed.

The bitter taste in her mouth made her shudder violently, and a wave of dizziness swept through her, blurring her vision. The ground beneath her feet seemed to spin. A frightening deadness stole through her arms and legs, and she weakened against the man who still held her. Perhaps if she feigned unconsciousness here for a moment, got her breath back and cleared her head she could fight...

The man with the flask stepped back and Emily let her body go limp. Her captor kept his arms around her waist and shoulder, locking her to his body. Emily drew a breath, slow and shallow so as to not attract attention. The man who held her waited as someone dropped a cloak onto the grass before he gently set her down on it. Then he stepped away to talk to his companions. She had counted five all together before she'd had to shut her eyes.

Emily did her best to lay still and breathe shallowly as she listened, but it was hard to fight the panic that rioted within her and the fog that slowly descended on her vision. Every instinct screamed for her to flee, but she remained still, praying they'd turn their attention away from her just long enough for her to rise and run.

She heard a man's voice above her. "Well, that wasn't too hard."

15

"I say, is that a gypsy child? I thought we were abducting a fine young lady of the *ton?*" Another laughed.

Emily fought the urge to snarl, despite the lethargy of her body. *Bloody, arrogant popinjays!* The anger felt better than the fear and it gave her a little more energy.

What had been in that flask she'd drunk from? *A poison?* No...that made no sense. She'd read of this bitter taste before... *Laudanum!* New anger sparked inside her. She let it flow from her head to her toes, and the illusion of strength built in her bones.

Yet another voice spoke up. "Charles, pay the driver an extra fee for his silence, and Lucien and I will see to the girl." This voice she recognized. It was the man she'd bitten. He and the others appeared to be gentlemen, if you could call them that at all.

After moving in with her uncle, she learned never to trust a man's appearance again. A fine set of clothes did not make someone a good man.

What confused her more was what these rogues wanted with her. Certainly Blankenship hadn't hired them to take her. He would have chosen men of lower standing. The riding glove she'd bitten had been of a fine quality, too fine for common henchmen.

"How long will she be out?" one of the men asked.

"Hard to say...probably a good hour." She recognized the voice as the one called Cedric. "One of us will carry her back to the manor."

A gentle hand swept Emily's hair back from her face. That same hand drifted down to her neck, caressing her skin before it touched her arm then slid along her waist. Tingles of fear traveled beneath her skin. She fought to keep her breath from quickening, but her heart fluttered wildly. When the hand brushed along her waist, Emily's breath sped up. She was highly sensitive in that particular area, and the feather light dance of fingertips along her body, through the muslin, made her stifle a giggle. She cursed her ticklishness.

The hand withdrew. Then just as suddenly the hand was back, brushing along her waist, still as gently, until she burst into fit of gasping hysterics.

"She's awake!" the captor who had just touched her called out, his voice breathless as though he was fighting off his own laughter.

Emily scrambled to her hands and knees. She'd barely moved when a body tackled her from behind, knocking her back to the ground. What little strength she had left deserted her. His knees

16

trapped her hips, pinning her to the ground. Emily cried out as his weight settled on her. He loosened his grasp enough to let her breathe but not to allow her any freedom.

"Have you got hold of her, Godric?"

Emily lashed out, legs flailing, back arching. "Please! Don't do this, I beg you!" She hated begging, but it was her last chance.

"We won't hurt you, darling." The man on top of her, Godric, ran a large palm along her side, stroking soothingly.

"Liar!"

He tightened his hold as Emily kicked and fought. "I've got her, but be quick, Cedric! She's bucking pretty madly."

Cedric knelt by her head and tilted the flask against her lips, forcing laudanum down her throat. Emily tried to whip her head to the side, but Cedric's other hand covered her mouth, preventing her from spitting out the vile liquid. It was useless to battle against her fate. She let her eyes plead where her mouth could not.

"Sorry, my dear. Truly, I am." The sincerity in Cedric's voice surprised her.

How could sincerity follow such brutality?

He kept the flask at her lips. She swallowed hard and then coughed as it the liquid burned a path through her insides.

Her last sight was of Cedric, his brows creased above his eyes. Her fingers left tracts in the gritty earth of the dark, empty road as she struggled to stay conscious. The musty aroma of soil clouded her nose, mixing with the heavy warmth of the masculine body that pinned her down. Her limbs were heavy. Her eyelids fluttered and she knew she couldn't hold out much longer. Godric gently caressed her body, as though to comfort her, but only confusion and fear followed her into the encompassing blackness.

Cedric, Viscount Sheridan, cupped the girl's chin and tilted her face to examine her. "Is she really out?"

The moonlight bathed her body, affording the men a decent look at their victim. Long, dark lashes lay against porcelain cheeks, which were tinted with a rosy blush.

"There's one way to find out." Godric's hands swept over her body, returning several times to her waist where he'd discovered she was ticklish.

17

She remained limp and unresponsive to his exploration. "She is definitely out." He climbed off her.

Charles and Lucien sauntered over on their horses.

Charles chuckled. "How many lords did you say it would take to subdue this little hellion?"

Lucien Russell, the Marquess of Rochester, bit back a grin.

"More than we guessed," Ashton replied in amusement, gazing down at Emily.

Godric took in the dirty, but stunning little captive at his feet. "She's not at all like her uncle."

Heat pooled deep inside him. His brief memory of her had not done justice to the puzzle of Miss Emily Parr. He could not forget the way she'd fought him, even in fear. But knowing he'd scared her left a hollowness in his chest. He had expected to ignore her protestations and carry her off. What he hadn't expected was for Emily to fight valiantly against him and leave him feeling every inch the villain.

Cedric stuffed the bottle of laudanum back into his waistcoat pocket. "Having second thoughts?"

Godric barked out a laugh and shrugged off his guilt. "Lord, no. You know me better than that, Cedric. She's mine now." He glanced at Emily again.

He felt oddly possessive of Emily, not that he had any right to. Still, the sudden urge to deposit the girl in a walled garden appealed greatly. Trap her in a tower like a princess from a fairy tale.

"The girl's intrigued him," Lucien said to his friends.

Godric gathered Emily into his arms.

He knew he must look a strange sight to his friends, taking such care with Emily. But something about her called to him. He ached for sensual touches, the slide of satin sheets against his skin, her silky body beneath his own. He hadn't planned to seduce her, but the little hellion's bravery had aroused him. She'd make for a wild bed partner. His lips curved into a smile at the thought.

"She can ride with me," Charles offered hopefully.

"I'd sooner trust her with a drunken sailor." With reluctance, his hands lingering, Godric handed Emily to Ashton instead.

Godric mounted his horse, then leaned down to retrieve her.

He cradled Emily sideways across his lap, one arm tightly about her waist, tucking her head under his chin to keep her steady.

The mere memory that Emily had almost outwitted him twice left Godric smiling. He'd not had such fun in ages. If he hadn't given in to his urge to touch her, he'd never have found that ticklish spot at her waist, and she might have crept off while he and the others talked. Ashton was right; she was cunning—a trait she must have inherited from that uncle of hers. But her beauty? It amazed him. She bore not a single resemblance to the reedy Albert Parr.

The ride back to Godric's country estate took an hour. They stopped once to dose Emily again with laudanum when she stirred like a sleepy kitten. The rub of her curled fists against his chest and her face burrowed against his throat, sent a thrill of pleasure through him.

He tried not to think about Emily or whether her lips tasted as sweet as they looked. He focused on the road ahead of them and his home, which lay just beyond.

The St. Laurent estate consisted of an extensive Georgian manor that rivaled the beauty of Chiswick House. His father and the Duke of Devonshire once had a friendly rivalry on the matter.

He studied the estate with new eyes, trying to imagine how Emily would perceive it.

The architect had styled the house, with six ivory columns in the front, like many of the greater Palladian homes in England. Godric's ancestors built the upper parts of the manor with lovely ashlar stone, while the lower was rusticated, lending a lacing of texture to the manor, like a woman's dress embroidered at the hem. Godric was surprised to find he was eager for Emily's approval. If she was going to stay here for a while, he wanted her to find pleasure in her surroundings.

As soon as Godric rode up to his manor's steps, a weary footman appeared and called for a groom. The elderly butler, Simkins, came to the door a moment later, escorting all the men into the hall once he assured care of their horses.

"Your Grace, we were not expecting visitors." Simkins eyed Godric's sleeping captive with open curiosity.

"Simkins, this is Miss Emily Parr. She will be my guest here for a while. Have Mrs. Downing assign her an upstairs maid to help her dress. See to her every need, but do not allow her to leave."

"Of course, Your Grace. She shall be treated like a princess."

"Don't spoil her, Simkins," Godric said, reconsidering. She was to be kept in a cage, so to speak, and it would be wise not to gild that

19

cage, at least until she understood he was in control.

A sudden thought occurred to him. His valet, Jonathan Helprin, would need to be kept away from Emily. She was a temptation to any man, and young Helprin was not a typical valet. Having been born and raised under Godric's roof, the younger man had a keen eye for the ladies, rather than clothes, where a good valet's interests should be. "Oh, and Simkins," Godric caught the butler's attention. "Reassign Mr. Helprin to duties that keep him far away from my chambers. The house, if possible. Have one of the footman see to my needs in the interim."

The older man hesitated, clearly confused. "Uh...yes, Your Grace. I will see Mr. Helprin is occupied elsewhere while your guest is in residence."

"Thank you."

Simkins then greeted the other four men who had followed Godric into the main hall. "My lords."

"Simkins, you devil, how are you?" Charles laughed. "Miss me?"

Simkins almost smiled, but kept his controlled demeanor. "I am fine, Lord Lonsdale. The house has been much quieter since your last visit and I have slept well knowing that I did not need a fleet of footmen to scrub port stains out of the carpet in the drawing room."

"Hmm, port sounds delightful. Bring me a glass when you have a chance?" Charles grinned at Simkins, who shook his head, muttering as he took his leave of the gentlemen.

Cedric pointed the way down the hall with the silver lion's head of his cane. "Come on, Lucien. Let's go warm ourselves by the fire." They left, Charles tramping along after them.

Ashton followed Godric up the staircase, Emily still in his arms. Godric chose the room next to his, the one most often inhabited by a mistress. Unlike other gentlemen, he brazenly kept his mistresses at his estate, heedless of the gossip that might result.

Godric nodded his head to the door, indicating for Ashton to open it.

"Er...you mean to keep her so close to you?" Ashton politely inquired.

"Yes. She'll likely keep trying to run off. I'll be able to hear her better if she's this close."

Ashton swung the door open to reveal a four-poster bed adorned with a blue coverlet and lilac curtains. He set Emily down, lifted her head and placed a pillow under the gleaming coils of her hair. The pins from her coiffure had come loose during the struggle and he found he liked the wild disarray.

Ashton eyed the small door disguised as part of the wall, and Godric grinned.

"I know what you're thinking, Ash..." The door led directly to his bedchamber.

"What you do with her is none of my business." Despite his constant attempts to keep his close-knit group of friends under control, Ashton was no saint.

With a nod, Ashton excused himself and Godric remained behind. His eyes drifted over the helpless young woman on the bed. Mud and grit had stained the muslin of her gown. Smudges of dust colored her nose and cheeks. At first glance, she looked like a wild little orphan but the curves of her body left Godric painfully aware she was a woman. Unable to resist, he cupped her face in his hands, running the pads of his thumbs across her cheeks to rub the dirt away. Her skin was soft, and Emily stirred slightly at his touch, her body shifting against his right hip where he'd sat down next to her.

Emotions he'd long buried welled up, tightening his throat and burning in his chest. He was a lad again, mesmerized by the allure of a young woman. A time he could never reclaim, an innocence ripped from his bleeding soul years ago.

Standing up, he retreated to the doorway. He lingered there, his eyes tracing the shape of her body. An acute sense of longing struck him. He wanted to bind her to him, but she would slip through his fingers like grains of sand.

How would she react to him come morning? With resentment and disgust, no doubt. He'd dragged her from the coach, manhandled her and drugged her. He was no hero, and a woman like her deserved a knight astride a white charger.

He ruined everything he touched.

Godric's head dropped as he closed the door and went to join his friends below.

Chapter Two

Early morning light danced through the lilac curtains, casting purpled shadows across the counterpane. Emily woke, aching and sore. The sensations puzzled her. As she sat up in the massive bed, her gaze skimmed a room elegant enough for a queen. For a brief moment, as the beauty of the furnishings sank in, she reveled in the strange fairy tale surroundings.

She slid from the bed and approached the wood and gold-filigreed dresser, tugging gently on the handle of one drawer. It slid open to reveal a collection of chemises as thin as spider-spun silk. Emily fingered the finery, sighed and turned away, only to catch sight of herself in the dressing-table mirror. A loud gasp escaped her lips as she slapped a hand to her mouth. Her gaze fell on the set of reflected eyes, open wide as they took in the sight of her dirty and disheveled dress.

Memories flooded through her while terror gripped her anew, fraying her self-control. Where was she? Where had they taken her? Emily's hands shook as she tried to tame her hair. She grimaced.

What am I going to do?

She could barely think as the dull throb of a headache pounded behind her eyes, an aftereffect of the laudanum, she supposed. She had the vaguest sense that they'd knocked her out a second time, when she'd started to wake from all the rough jostling.

Her dress was beyond repair, but that didn't matter. She needed to escape.

Emily stumbled across the room, but paused when she noticed a sky blue muslin day gown laid out on a chair, alongside three petticoats and dark blue slippers and hair ribbons. A little note was pinned to the gown.

Dear Miss Parr,
I hope you slept well.

*I took the liberty of having this gown altered this morning after Mrs.
Downing obtained your measurements. Please come down for breakfast
at your leisure.*

Sincerely,

*Mr. Simkins, butler, and Mrs. Downing, housekeeper
for His Grace, Godric St. Laurent, the Duke of Essex*

Emily stared at the note.

The Duke of Essex? Her devilish captor was none other than
Godric St. Laurent? At least she wasn't in danger as she had first
worried. These men were peers of the realm and would not murder her
or otherwise harm her like the highwaymen she'd first believed last
night.

Her friend Anne Chessley had told her quite a bit about Godric
and his friends. She'd called them the League of Rogues, a name she'd
whispered half afraid and half fascinated. They were men without rules
and morals as far as she knew, if one could trust gossip and stories
printed in *The Quizzing Glass Gazette.*

She'd also heard the name Ash last night, most likely Ashton
Lennox, a wealthy baron. The other two men were no doubt Lucien
Russell, the Marquess of Rochester, and Charles Humphrey, the Earl
of Lonsdale. Emily swallowed down a bitter laugh. What young
debutante wouldn't dream of such a romantic experience as being
abducted by the five most handsome, rich, influential and eligible men
in all of England?

Emily, however, wanted nothing more than to escape, not
entertain notions of marriage to any of them. They weren't the type of
men to marry. Still, she wondered what sort of husband the Duke of
Essex would make. A good lover if whispers were true, but more likely
to marry for purpose rather than love.

After a decent wash with the fresh water from the basin, she
donned the gown Mr. Simkins provided, a lovely, simple design that
buttoned up the front. The skirts had been cut high enough to display
the tips of her slippers, and the sleeves puffed out slightly at the
shoulders.

Emily yanked at the door handle. It didn't budge. How on earth
was she to get to out? She was locked inside. *Trapped.* Her body tensed

as a wave of panic swept through her. She ran to the windows and pulled at the sill but it wouldn't lift. To her horror, she noted a pair of nails embedded deep in the wood, sealing it. She frantically scanned the room, noticing a narrow, barely identifiable door to the left of her bed.

Where on earth does this lead to? A discrete servant's entrance, perhaps? "Might as well try it."

The handle gave way and swung inward to a second room.

A massive four-poster bed stood against one wall. Her eyes latched onto the body tangled in the sheets. She caught a wide view of a sun-kissed muscular back and a head of dark hair...*the duke.* He'd put her in an adjoining chamber. Emily padded softly to his door. It too was locked. She rushed over to his window and, like in her room, it refused to open.

She returned to his door, pressing herself against the wood, and debated screaming for help. Her lips parted, a shout on the tip of her tongue, then stopped. She was in his house, with his servants. There would be no help here, not for a captive of the duke. Anger replaced part of her fear, at least temporarily.

"Oh, for heaven's sake," she growled under her breath and turned back to face Godric.

The distant gleam of gold on the opposite side of the bed, near the wall, caught Emily's eye. She tiptoed across the wooden floor, toward him. His breathing was soft and slow; still fast asleep.

"Ah, yes." A small set of brass keys, secured to Godric's wrist by a leather string, gleamed underneath the sunlight. Emily debated: wait until he woke on his own, or try to escape now and chance waking him in her attempt to snatch the keys.

The hand with the keys lay on the opposite side of the bed, which was a little too close to the wall for her to get to. To reach them, Emily had to crawl over him. Her pulse beat wildly and her blood roared in her ears as she tried to accept what she would have to do. She'd have to touch him, the man who'd kidnapped and drugged her. Not just touch him...but crawl over the length of his body...in his bed. Could she do this? Her father had always called her brave. But being so close to a man, alone and locked inside with him in a bedroom, was she brave enough to get the keys?

Her eyes closed and she summoned the courage she'd called upon so easily the night before.

I can do this. I must do this.

She lifted her skirts past her knees and put one foot on the oak bed frame as she climbed. Hands and knees far apart, she dispersed her weight. The last thing she needed was to dip the bed and waken the devil.

Godric was so big, she had to reach with much care to grab the keys without falling. Emily held her breath and leaned over, her breasts inches from skimming over his back as she sought the tools to her freedom. She looped one finger under the leather strap around his wrist, and pulled it toward her, but the leather stuck to his skin.

She would have to touch him. For a moment, she couldn't breathe. The air in her lungs burned and she tried in vain to find an alternative. There wasn't one. She needed the keys and they were attached to the man in the bed.

Emily used her thumb and forefinger to lift his wrist an inch off the bed as her other hand dragged the keys from under his arm.

The fabric around her knees started to slide. Gravity worked against her precarious position. Another second and she'd—

Thump!

Emily fell onto Godric's back lying perpendicular to him. He groaned softly, rolling onto his back beneath her and she shifted over him to stay on top. His right hand—the keys still laced there—settled on her lower back, patting it.

Emily inhaled sharply. She was stretched out across his stomach and groin. He was still asleep. She shifted, trying to reach his hand without alerting him.

"Hmm...you naughty girl." Godric's face broke into a dreamy smile. "Evangeline, now don't squirm."

Evangeline? Probably his mistress. Emily scowled and reached for his hand again, but her movement was pointless. Godric's hand drifted over her backside and struck her bottom in a playful spank.

She wrenched her body free. "How dare you!" Her feet tangled in the covers and she tripped onto the floor, trying to escape the bed.

Godric blinked at her. "What the—Miss Parr? What in God's name are you doing in my bedchamber?" He shot up but fell back down against the pillows, slinging his forearm over his eyes with a groan.

Emily fled to the far corner of the room, heart beating against her ribs like a caged bird. His muscles flexed as he moved, like a large, sleek panther. For a second, she imagined the protection he could offer—his body cast before her as a shield, his muscles taut and forearms tense. Then she remembered how he'd taken her from the coach and the violence of the battle between them.

"Let me go at once!"

"I'm not holding you," he said in an irritated growl.

"I meant, let me leave. My chamber is locked." She stamped her slippered foot and glared, but the force was lost on him because he remained flat on his back, his eyes shut. "I demand to be released!"

"I demand peace and quiet in the morning," Godric muttered under his breath.

"Well?" Emily stamped the ground again, rather annoyed that she had no other means to get his attention. She didn't dare go closer. The memory of his body overpowering hers the previous night left her quaking anew with fear, but she was determined to maintain a brave front.

He cast off his bed sheet and sat up. She nearly swooned upon the glimpse of his bare chest. He smiled and took his time reaching for the sheet to recover himself. Emily struggled to breathe, her face afire. Was that what a half-clothed man looked like? He looked...fierce. Every strip of muscle and corded steel beneath his flesh whispered of violence and danger. Her throat went dry and she licked her lips as she tried to calm her racing heart.

"Care to join me, Miss Parr?" He patted the bed.

Emily took an involuntary step back, her shoulder blades hitting the door behind her.

"I was only joking." A slight frown wilted his lips, as though her reaction unsettled him.

"A joke? Please, Your Grace, enlighten me as to how this situation is remotely amusing. I must get back to London immediately and try to repair the damage you've wrought to my reputation." *To my life.* She wrung her hands together, trying anything to ease the anxiety that rippled just beneath her skin.

"I'm afraid that's not possible." His reply didn't make sense at first, because she hadn't expected him to deny her the right to leave.

"What? Why not?"

"Because I brought you here to ruin you."

She studied the stubborn angle of his chin and his frosted-green eyes, looking for any signs of his intentions.

"Well, at least you are direct. Or is this another joke?" She couldn't imagine how she'd save her reputation, even if this was a joke.

Then she spied the slight purple bruise that marked his cheek. The blow she'd dealt the previous night had been as strong as she'd hoped. She'd never hurt anyone before, but he deserved that and much more if he dared touch her again.

Her situation had suddenly become clear and she didn't like it one bit. When she returned to London, only the most desperate sort of fortune hunters would take her on. After such a scandal, she'd be lucky to be received anywhere socially, let alone find a decent man to marry. But then again...her eyes flicked to Godric's face. Would he do the honorable thing after whatever part of his plan that required ruination had been fulfilled? *Can I convince him to own up to his actions and marry me?* It was him or fortune hunters. She refused to consider Blankenship as an option.

With a sigh, Godric climbed out of bed to get dressed. Emily danced back, well out of his immediate reach, her face a cherry red as she pretended to look away from his naked body. It was charming, her innocent belief that if she stayed out of his way she would be safe. If he truly wanted to, he could haul her to the bed and take her. But there was little fun in that. The journey of the seduction was half of the pleasure in bedding a woman.

She stopped fidgeting and met his eyes with a strong glare.

"Why ruin me? There are many other young heiresses with more money. Do you plan to marry me?" She raised a golden-brown brow at him, a silent challenge that he found amusing. Emily was a forward and brash little creature, he would give her credit for that.

"Revenge is my only interest in you. Is that a simple enough answer? Your uncle is to blame." Godric crossed the room to wash his face.

"My uncle?" Emily's brows drew together and her lips parted as though deep in thought over the revelation of being leverage.

Godric bent, washed his face in the basin at the bedside table and then toweled himself dry. Then he pulled on a robe.

"Your uncle acquired a great sum of money from me, and I have it on good authority he's paid off his other creditors with it rather than invest it. My money is gone."

27

"That still doesn't explain why *I'm* here." She bit her lower lip, an expression of keen intelligence in her eyes. It had been ages since he'd really looked at a woman's face and found intelligence attractive. Emily was certainly both.

"What is your intention towards me?" Despair laced her tone in such a way that she drew Godric's attention.

Emily sat down on the edge of his bed, her eyes wide in disbelief. Abandoning his quest for proper clothes, Godric crossed the room, caught her chin in his hand and tilted her head back so she was forced to look up at him.

"I must keep you here a while until I see your uncle thoroughly destroyed, then perhaps I'll return you to London. While you're here, you're welcome to share my bed." He tapped her nose with a fingertip, attempting to tease her, but his words only drew a deeper frown from her. He knelt in front of her. "No harm will come to you, Miss Parr. You have my word as a gentleman."

"Gentleman?" she scoffed. "Some gentleman you are. Dragging women from carriages, drugging them. You have not one ounce of honor. I don't even see what this has to do with my uncle. Men like you ruin women like me and never look back. I dare you to deny it."

He laughed. "I wouldn't dream of denying it. I do however insist you understand I only ruin women for a purpose, not for sport." He leaned one hip against the dresser, watching her intently. "I'm sure you know how easy it would be for your uncle to sell you to a man in marriage to settle his debts. Well, no one will take you if I've been there first."

Emily's eyes darkened. "So you hurt me to strike out at my uncle?" Her voice rose in pitch but it wasn't shrill. "Have you not considered me? I am an innocent party in this. My uncle will demand you marry me, and then we'll be stuck together."

Godric gave a bark of laughter. "Ash said you were clever. I hadn't realized you had a sense of humor as well."

"Humor? I see nothing amusing in this at all. I had aspirations for marriage, yes, but it didn't include marrying someone like you." Emily crossed her arms over her chest.

"Miss Parr, I'm not sure if you know exactly who I am."

Godric saw a flash of pain in her eyes. "I know who you are. The Duke of Essex. A veritable devil, or so the ladies say. You bring ruination upon a woman with one look."

"Just a look? I thought I had to at least say a lady's name..." he chuckled, but she did not laugh.

A splash of pink blossomed on her cheeks. Her lips parted further, and her bosom began to rise and fall with her quickened breaths. It reminded him of a startled sparrow that had flown into his study once. He had to help it escape out the window before it hurt itself by striking something in its terror.

"Let me be clear, Miss Parr. I have never let society and its rules dictate my life. Your uncle could attempt to wage a social war against me in order to leg shackle me to you, but we shall never set foot inside a church together. Do you understand? Now don't look so put out, my dear. I am a generous lover. If I find that you and I suit, I shall take you as my mistress. I'm not inclined to permanent relationships, but I would keep you well cared for the rest of your life. It wouldn't be so horrible to be the lover of a duke."

Her violet eyes reflected a place far away, but were still resigned, a quality echoed in her voice. "Are all men as heartless as you? Don't you understand what you've taken from me? I *need* to marry. My parents are dead. I had but one chance at happiness and peace, and you destroyed it the moment you took control of my coach." Her eyes misted over with tears, and a second later, she keened, a quiet, small sound, before her body quaked in repressed, silent sobs.

Godric blinked in horror. Everything in his body clenched. It wasn't the first time he had made a woman cry, but these tears weren't from an angry mistress, but a young lady, a veritable innocent.

Without a second thought, he pulled her into his arms. A fierce need to protect her rose up in him, and he couldn't seem to rid himself of it. Her body trembled against his, her hands exploring his bare chest, arms, and hands. A faint tug followed on his right wrist; he jerked back, amazed to see her clutching the leather band of keys. He extracted the keys from her fingers, prying them open one by one.

Godric burst into laughter at her furious glare. "Miss Parr, you have remarkably nimble hands. Oh, the things I could teach you..." He started to embrace her again, but she ducked.

Emily sidled back a few steps, eyes wary. Gone was the woman who'd been crying in his arms. Quite a believable ruse. *Clever girl.*

"I seriously doubt you have anything useful to teach me, Your Grace." She dipped into a shallow mocking curtsey before she darted back into her room, slamming the door in her wake. The scraping sound of a vanity table being dragged in front of the door followed seconds later. He grinned and then started to whistle softly.

Let her wait. He certainly needed a few minutes to regain control, especially below his waistline.

"What do you mean, abducted?"

Albert Parr's townhouse echoed with Thomas Blankenship's fury. Albert sat at his desk, forefinger and thumb rubbing his eyes as he did his best to remain calm in front of his business partner, a man he was still heavily indebted to.

"It's all in the letter." He pushed the paper toward Blankenship, who snapped it up. The man stood before Albert with his chest heaving, his double chin wobbly against his jugular, a sight that should have lessened Albert's fear—but didn't. Quite the opposite. Blankenship had revealed the demon inside him with claws, salivating teeth and cold fire churning in his black eyes.

Albert sighed. Last night he'd arrived at Chessley House to retrieve Emily. The baron's daughter, Anne, informed him that Emily never arrived. Albert had been concerned immediately. He hadn't thought she would miss out on an occasion to see her friend, but maybe he'd been mistaken and Emily had decided to become difficult.

Perhaps she'd decided to avoid Blankenship and sought refuge with a friend. Not that she had many, at least none of whom he knew.

It wasn't until he arrived home, exhausted and irritated at Emily's stunt, that he had learned the truth. His butler handed him the letter left by the jarvey he'd hired to drive Emily to the ball. The weary driver confirmed that five men had abducted her, but refused to part with any more details unless he received some reward. Albert grimaced and slapped several coins into the driver's wrinkled palm.

The story the coachman told was fantastical. His innocent niece had managed to trick the rogues and nearly escape twice. As he heard the tale, Albert imagined Emily as some sort of heroine in a grand adventure. It seemed she had more strength of character than he'd credited her with, but once the notion ceased to be amusing, apprehension set in.

He'd recognized the sloping cursive style of the letter at once, even though the letter was vague in its details and unsigned. After several dealings with the Duke of Essex, Albert had become intimately familiar with his unusual penmanship. But it was the letter's contents that were most upsetting. Essex had stated that he knew about the money Albert had stolen and that he had taken "repayment" of a kind. He meant Emily of course.

Albert's brow furrowed as he studied the note again, ignoring Blankenship, who paced back and forth like a caged lion. If Essex sullied her reputation, she would have every right to demand marriage and that would mean... Dread filled his limbs. If Essex became an in-law, Albert would forever be at the man's mercy. That was assuming he could even get the Duke within a mile of the nearest church.

No, the duke wouldn't marry Emily. Albert had no way of forcing him, and Essex knew it. Emily was ruined, and without her he had no way to repay Blankenship. Albert struggled for breath as he fought off panic. "Dear God."

"What?" Blankenship growled.

"Nothing. I'm weary and this abduction has upset me." The last thing he would do would be to confess his fears to Blankenship. Everything depended on getting Emily married to him. The side deal they had arranged would ensure that Emily's inheritance, money tied up in Albert's brother's shipping company, would go to Blankenship and all of Albert's debts would disappear.

Blankenship stopped his pacing. "How positive are you that it is the Duke of Essex who holds her?"

Albert looked down at his desk, avoiding the gleam in the other man's eyes.

"I would recognize this handwriting anywhere."

Blankenship digested this before replying. "What would cause him to take the girl?"

"I owe Essex twenty thousand pounds. He invested it with me, but the investment fell short. I used his funds to repay you for part of the debt I owe. He's discovered his money is gone." Albert fought the urge to set his head on the desk and remain still until he died. "The man has a violent temper and now he's taken Emily as revenge."

Blankenship studied the letter, his nose and cheeks reddened with irritation. "Why would a duke risk the rumors of the *ton* over such a meager amount? He has ten times that tucked away in investments, and his annual income makes this amount laughable."

"It is just the sort of thing he would do. He's one of those rogues, that group that meets at the Berkley's club every month."

31

"Yes, yes, the League of Rogues, or whoever they are. Spoiled paramours and nothing more. They do not matter. I want the girl returned to me. She is mine!" Blankenship snarled with such venom that Albert slid back a foot in his chair.

"How do you propose I get her back? The duke has taken her. Her reputation is ruined, even if he hasn't yet touched her."

"Demand he send her back at once." Blankenship then tossed the letter onto Albert's desk.

"Even if I challenged him to a duel, he'd probably laugh it off. He has what he wants now, and he won't give her back—not until he's satisfied she's beyond redemption in the eyes of the *ton.*"

"You don't want to have her back?" The deadly chill in Blankenship's eyes unsettled Albert. "What about our bargain? Your debts to me would be satisfied when the girl is mine."

Albert had not regretted the uneasy partnership between them, until now. Something evil, something black and cruel, floated in the other man's gaze and put him on edge.

While Essex was rumored to be a grand seducer, Blankenship's reputation soiled the walls of London's brothels as the nastiest man alive. Women came away from his bed with bruises and shattered souls. Albert wasn't a man to judge others about their bed sport, but knowing that Emily would be one of Blankenship's permanent victims had unsettled his stomach to the point of queasiness. Still what was he to do? The debts he owed could have both him and Emily out on the streets in minutes if their owners demanded payment. At least her marriage to Blankenship would keep a roof over both their heads.

If Essex had her, perhaps it was for the best for everyone, including his own soul.

"I have no interest in her return. I was willing to sell her to you, wasn't I? As I see it, now she has a chance of catching a duke's eye, either as wife or mistress, and I will soon be rid of her." It was the truth. Keeping that girl fed and clothed had been a costly endeavor for an indebted man. It wasn't that he disliked her, but he had little choice if he was to keep the creditors at bay.

"So you won't contact the authorities? Surely someone will notice she's gone missing. Servants talk, Parr."

"Not mine. And no, I shan't go to the authorities. The last thing I wish to do is call attention to myself."

"Allow me to act in your stead. Let me use the authorities at your *request* to confront Essex and demand the girl be returned. Once I've brought her back, she'll be mine."

"And if she comes to your marriage bed no longer a maiden?"

"Then she'll not bear my name, but she'll still warm my bed."

Albert shivered with revulsion at Blankenship's lecherous smile. He would no doubt treat her the same as he would any doxy off the street. Albert cared about his niece's fate, but his own problems far outweighed hers. Blankenship had a reputation for making men disappear, sometimes reappearing face down in the Thames. The last thing Albert wanted was to end up dead because of his debts. Emily being used as a bargaining tool was the best purpose she could serve. May God forgive him.

"Fine, she is your problem." Albert rose from his seat with a grimace, and looked at Blankenship with a direct stare, wishing the man would be off—to heaven, to hell, it mattered not. "Now, will you excuse me? I have matters to attend to."

Blankenship stood stock-still, then curved one end of his lips. "If I don't get her, your debt remains unpaid, Parr. You know what happens to men who don't pay." His face set, the older man turned on his heel and vanished out the door. The ominous threat clouded the air like smoke.

Chapter Three

Emily collapsed on her bed, and her whole body shook. Her face burned.

"Abducted by a duke."

Emily rubbed her temples, her headache returning. This was a nightmare. What would her mother have done in such a situation? Acknowledge the facts. First, in the eyes of society she was as good as ruined. Second, she was at the mercy of a man who wanted to actually ruin her. Third, she needed to figure out what to do about the first and second facts.

Emily drew in a deep breath. She had to make a choice: escape and return to her uncle and Blankenship, remain here with Godric or hope she could make a match with some man desperate to get access to her fortune regardless of her tainted state. Only one of these options held real appeal.

Godric. The idea half terrified, half thrilled her. Did she want to be with someone though who infuriated her with his arrogance, despite his pleasing form?

Emily's shoulders sagged. All she wanted was to have the freedom to travel and live her life, hopefully with a man who loved her at her side. She wanted to be in control of her own fate and her own fortune. Even though her inheritance would be under her husband's control, if she was lucky, she might have some say in its use.

If she stayed with Godric, she'd be at his mercy. He claimed he would take her as a mistress...*if* they suited. Emily snorted. She doubted that he was the sort of man who would do right by a woman. He and his friends had abducted her after all, and this morning's encounter hadn't exactly reassured her of his good character. Instead it had reinforced her of his ill intentions. Perhaps if she could get back to London, she could seek refuge with Anne and figure out what to do and how she might still find a husband. It was a slim chance. Even ruined, she might stand a small chance of enticing one of them to marry her. But what about her uncle? He'd prefer to sell her off to pay his debts, as Godric said. Whatever man she could find would have to be willing to go to Gretna Green with her and then face her mother's cousin and pray he wouldn't prove troublesome in handing over her inheritance. The entire idea gave her a headache.

She jumped as the door to her room opened. Godric waited, keys in hand, wearing far more clothes than when she'd last encountered him. The sudden memory of him in his bed sent her heart skipping. Were all ruined women this easily distracted by the sight of a handsome man? It irritated her that she was so affected by him when he'd only caused trouble for her.

"Hungry?" Godric offered her his arm.

Emily grimaced. How could he stand there and pretend they hadn't been discussing her being his mistress and with him only half-clothed just minutes ago? With a defiant lift of her chin, she marched towards the stairs, ignoring him. She halted abruptly when she reached the bottom. She hadn't a clue where to go. She wanted to dash for the nearest door, but Emily suspected she wouldn't make it ten feet before Godric pounced on her.

Godric's lip's quirked slightly, too lazy to complete the smile. "I wouldn't try to run, Miss Parr. My servants have strict instructions to keep you in this house by any means necessary."

As if to prove his point, a footman exited a nearby door and paused at seeing his master. When Godric nodded slightly, the footman took a moment to study Emily, as though assessing her strengths and weaknesses, before he continued on his way and entered the door down the hall.

Emily sighed and waved a hand. "Please lead the way then, Your Grace."

Godric grinned and strode away without a backward glance, expecting her to follow.

It was now or never. Seizing what might be her only chance, Emily whirled to the left, toward a large door not twenty feet away that might lead outside. Clutching her skirts, she sprinted towards it, blood pounding in her ears. Suddenly she pitched forward, falling flat on her stomach.

The cold stone bit into her hands as she sought to brace her fall. Something had latched onto her right ankle. Panting for breath, she looked over her shoulder. Godric crouched behind her, a feral glint in his eyes. "I thought I advised against running, Miss Parr." Godric smiled as though they were playing some game. It infuriated her. This was her life, her freedom.

"Let me go! You have no right to keep me here." Emily kicked at his hand with her free foot, but he caught it, then slid her along the floor on her stomach until she lay beneath his crouched body. He released her ankle and rested one forearm on the floor next to her head, and his other hand gripped her hip.

Emily lay still as a doe in the glen catching the scent of man, then focused on her counterattack. She tensed and flipped onto her back, backhanding him with a sharp crack across the face.

The fingers on her hip tightened. "The time you spend here can be civil or not. I shall leave it up to you, but know that for every act of defiance, I will demand something of you in return." He growled. "You may not like the price."

His face loomed above hers with the terrible beauty of a vengeful god. With aching slowness he caged her in using his body to trap her. She shuddered at the heavy contact as his limbs matched hers. Ice warred with fire along her skin as she fought tremors of fear. It was as though she faced a lion—raw beauty, extreme power and a posed threat—yet she couldn't look away. He would devour her.

Reality struck her, reminding her to fight him. His chest was a wall of steel, however. Immovable as a mountain. Left gasping after her efforts, Emily's eyes burned with tears. She couldn't free herself, not from him, not from this place.

Godric cupped her cheek with one hand, rubbing the pad of his thumb lightly over the curve of her lower lip. The warmth of his breath and the hint of his scent tangled her senses and rationality until she was a jumbled mess. Fear sparked inside her, like flashes of lightning hidden behind black clouds.

Godric could very easily take her, brutally and completely, and she had no way to defend herself. She had to say something, something to placate him and protect herself.

"I'm sorry, I didn't mean to—"

Without warning, his hands were at her waist, his fingers moving teasingly at the right spot to make her burst into a fit of giggles. She kicked out of pure instinct, trying to cease his the fiendish attack at her weak spot.

"Stop! Please!" she gasped. "Please, I beg you!"

Only when tears where burning in her eyes and she was all but hysterical with laughter, did he stop. The whole time he had hovered over her with a wolfish grin, torturing her with those featherlight touches.

"I did warn you about exacting a price. I won't hesitate to use such weapons again." He wiggled his fingertips. If he was going to resort to such weaponry when dealing with her, she would have to keep her distance. It was impossible to maintain her dignity and insist he treat her like the lady she was when she was too busy laughing and gasping for breath like some helpless peahen.

He eased off her and helped her to her feet.

"Shall we try this again?" His voice was low and husky.

Did he have to be so tall and...and intense? Her instincts still screamed for her to run.

Dazed, Emily managed a shaky nod. Her body still trembled from the aftermath of his tickling.

"Would you like to accompany me to breakfast, Miss Parr?"

When she nodded again, he tucked her arm in his and led her to the dining room.

If she couldn't outrun him, perhaps she could try a different tactic. Emily believed in the power of good, solid conversation. Maybe she could convince him to see reason, though that seemed as likely as convincing an angry bull not to charge. She frowned and worried her lower lip with her teeth.

"What on earth are you frowning about?"

Emily ducked her head, hoping to hide her face from him. "Nothing, Your Grace. I am weary from last night's exertions, that is all."

She could have sworn he muttered something about a different kind of exertion last night, but she hadn't a clue what he meant. Before she could speak again, they reached the dining room.

Morning sunlight illuminated a large room with a table that could easily seat twelve. The bottom half of the walls consisted of cherry wood panels, and the upper half was painted a warm butter yellow. Massive portraits hung from them, where dark-haired men from various eras stared back at Emily, each of them hiding a hint of a smile in their eyes.

This room was different than the rest of the house. It felt more intimate and oddly rustic given the tall, wide windows that covered the wall opposite the sideboard. A wealth of Forsythia shrubs reached halfway up each one, the vivid yellow a bright contrast against the tangling emerald ivy that laced the windows' edges. Emily felt as though she had walked into an enchanted world surrounded by flowers.

Rather than seem out of place, Godric ruled his lands like a god of nature. He did not swagger. Rather, his stride was graceful, almost feline, when he led her into the dining room.

Emily suffered a strange moment of pride at the thought that a man like him had offered her to join him in bed. He'd slept with scores of women, that's what rakes did, but still...he'd declared his interest in her. As foolish as it was, she relished being wanted, until she reminded herself that she must stand strong against him and his merry band of rogues.

On the sideboard behind the table someone had spread out an array of fruits, ham, beef and eggs. Three men sat near one end of the table. A handsome man with red hair and hazel eyes read a newspaper and offered a calculated smile as Emily and Godric entered.

She glanced down at herself and realized how wrinkled her dress had become. Did he know that just outside the door, Godric had tickled her into submission? It still upset her that his means at subduing her were so effective.

The man holding the paper rose along with the other two men. They all bowed politely when Godric pressed her down into a seat across from the man who resumed his perusal of *The Morning Post*. Godric's hands lingered heavily on her shoulders, the pressure a clear message to keep her bottom planted in her chair or suffer the consequences.

The red-haired man set his paper down and held a rack of toast out to her. "Good morning, Miss Parr. Did you sleep well?" Emily kept her head declined as she took a piece, her hand shaking as she set it on her plate. The three men exchanged glances. A silent conversation hummed in the air between them.

"Yes, thank you. I slept quite well."

Emily became increasingly self-conscious of the fact she sat in a room alone with four powerful lords. The pale blond man on her right was Lord Ashton Lennox, a wealthy baron. She'd caught a glimpse of him two nights before, at her first come out when Anne Chessley had pointed to him. He'd been near the refreshments, drinking a glass of wine and speaking to a lovely young lady, a girl whose father was one of the owners of Drummond's Bank.

Godric chose the seat on her left, while the third man, Cedric, sat down next to the man with the paper. The seating arrangements had her entirely boxed in.

Her hands fisted in her lap.

Breathe, Emily. Breathe. She drew in the scented air and forced her body into calmness. If she couldn't flee the room, she would learn as much about her captors as she could. "Pardon me, but are you the Marquess of Rochester or the Earl of Lonsdale?" she asked quietly of the fourth man.

He raised a brow.

Emily blushed as all eyes descended upon her.

"Last night I heard the names: The Duke of Essex and Viscount Sheridan. Since I'm acquainted with Miss Chessley, I've heard those names in connection with three more: the Marquess of Rochester; the Earl of Lonsdale; and Baron Lennox. I apologize if I was mistaken in my assumption," she said hastily, but the man's hazel eyes twinkled.

"Don't apologize, Miss Parr, you are quite right. I am the Marquess of Rochester Please address me as Lucien. None of us are overly fond of titles, especially in the company of such a lovely lady. That gentleman over there is Baron Lennox." Lucien pointed to the man who had cornered her by the coach the night before. "Lonsdale has yet to grace us with his presence. Speaking of which, Ash, would you go and rouse him? Best to get him up and walking, or last night's port will make him disagreeable the rest of the day."

Ashton smiled pleasantly at Emily before he departed. There was something kind in the man's face, a sympathetic look to his bright blue eyes that gave her a flash of hope. However, she couldn't help but wonder why he needed to wake Charles when a servant could have done so.

"You're a friend of Anne Chessley's?" Cedric asked.

"Yes. She's been so kind to me since I moved to London, my lord."

"Oh, I insist you call me Cedric. I can't stand that 'lord' nonsense. Now, tell me, does she mention me often?" He waggled his eyebrows and Emily almost grinned. *This is the man who drugged you, don't forget.*

Setting aside Godric's arrogance and veiled threats, the others did not *seem* all that villainous. But she knew of their reputations thanks to *The Quizzing Glass Gazette.* They'd willingly gone along with Godric's scheme to abduct her. Yet she felt safer in their presence than with a man like Blankenship. Perhaps it was because they were all naturally charming. A quality that no doubt furthered their schemes to ruin women all over London.

It was obvious that Godric was in charge, but it seemed that the other men did not bow to him in every decision. With some persuasion, perhaps a tear or two and begging, she could get the others to see what Godric had done was wrong and she should be set free. Even rogues had to have hearts...didn't they?

Lucien returned to his newspaper. "By the way, Godric, *The Gazette* mentioned our time in Covent Garden last week."

"Oh? I am almost afraid to ask how our evening was relayed." Godric collected the tray of coffee and hot chocolate from the sideboard. Emily watched him pour his coffee, taking it black. Lucien flicked his eyes back to the paper, scanning some article. "They heard about the incident with the stolen swans...but they got the number of ladies involved wrong. Underestimated our appeal to the fairer sex again."

The men at the table all laughed at whatever antics they had been up to. Emily was certain she didn't want to know the details. Whatever swans, ladies and Covent Garden had in common was likely to shock her.

Undeterred by this change in topic, Cedric once more demanded to know of Anne's interest in him.

"Anne has certainly mentioned you quite often." It was true. Anne complained constantly about Cedric, but Emily knew she rather liked the attention.

Cedric reached for the plate of fruit. "What does she say?"

"You can't expect me to break the vows of friendship?" she asked, widening her eyes in mock innocence.

"Expect? Miss Parr, I quite demand it."

Emily imagined no one ever refused Cedric anything.

Rather than answer him immediately, she looked back to Godric. She justified her fascination by telling herself he was like a wolf. One must always keep an eye on the creature that could do one the most harm.

Godric poured a cup of chocolate for her. Her stomach rumbled at the dark liquid that swirled in her cup. He took a tiny porcelain pot and opened it to pinch at the ground cinnamon, which he sprinkled on top. It was perhaps the strangest and sweetest gesture a man had ever made for her, as though seeing to her needs and pleasures were a natural instinct.

Emily turned back to Cedric, who still waited for an answer.

"Your attentions on Anne have been duly noted."

"So I'm successful in my pursuit?"

"I would not go so far as to say that, but she is thankful that your attentiveness has discouraged others."

"In other words," Lucien chimed in, "she'd rather fight you off than half the men in London."

A little laugh escaped Emily, and Lucien winked. She'd been under the impression he'd been reading his newspaper, and she decided she liked him. Villain or not, she admired his humor.

The thought stopped her cold. She didn't *want* to like Lucien, nor did she want her only moments of joy in this life to be with the men who had abducted her.

"At least I'm not resigned to bachelorhood, like someone I know." Cedric whipped his head pointedly in Lucien's direction. "I am simply very selective."

Godric took Emily's plate and filled it with a little bit of everything before he sat down and replaced it before her.

"Thank you, Your Grace," she said demurely.

"Oh, come now, if you call Cedric by his name you must call me Godric." The seductive glint in his eyes flushed her with heat. How could this be the same man that minutes ago growled at her and pulled her fully beneath him? Emily's face flamed with embarrassment, but no one noticed.

The Marquess then chimed in. "And call me Lucien. I don't like to 'lord' myself over my new friends."

"Perish the thought." Ashton sniggered as he and Charles walked in. Charles's face was drawn with weariness, but he was still as handsome as the others with his golden hair and gray eyes.

"Morning, all," Charles mumbled as he plopped down on Godric's other side.

A flicker of concern washed through Emily as she took in the man's appearance. His clothes were immaculate, his tan breeches snug on his muscled thighs, and his silver satin vest sparkled faintly in the morning sun. But his sleep-tousled hair was unkempt, the wild halo of a rogue angel about his brow. Strain laced his eyes and his voice sounded rough, like a man who'd screamed until hoarse. Something wasn't right about this...she could sense it.

The room seemed filled with companionship, and an air of intimacy between them that struck Emily as beautiful in the way only true friendships could be. For a brief moment she forgot the dangerous circumstances that brought her here and lost herself in the shared smiles and teasing banter of the rogues.

What would it be like to be counted among their friends? As their captive, she was very alone, like a hungry dog that looked through a butcher's window on a winter's night. The chill of this position stung deep inside her soul. Emily ducked her head and took a bite of her breakfast.

In the span of a few short minutes, she'd come to understand them better. They were reasonable men, even if they had wickedly seductive tendencies where women were concerned. If she approached them with logic, and argued her case for freedom...

Maybe if I tell Godric I could produce Uncle Albert's account books, he could take it up with the magistrate. Then justice would be meted out and she could go back to London.

"Coffee, Charles?" Before the man answered, Godric poured him a cup.

"Can someone pass the toast?" Charles asked.

Cedric slid the toast rack in his direction. Emily at first only nibbled on her food, but soon hunger overtook her, and she dug into her well laden plate.

Emily discovered what was so oddly comforting about this meal. The five men were so at ease with one another. They were almost like a family. What could have drawn these five men together so?

Charles spread liberal amounts of raspberry jam on his toast, gleeful as a boy stealing cherry tarts from the kitchen.

"Charles, you had better eat more than just toast. Have some fruit." Ashton slid the tray of pears, apples and plums past Emily and Godric.

"Fine, fine."

It amused Emily to watch them mother Charles. Her tiny smile caught Charles's attention.

"I expected them all to fret over you, Miss Parr, allowing me to escape their coddling for a few days, but you've failed me," he teased. "Shame on you." The earl's eyes were a sharp grey, clear and deep in their intensity.

Emily's cheeks flamed when Charles's gaze slid along her body.

Lucien's voice broke the tension that settled because of Charles's wandering gaze. "Would you like us to fret over you, Miss Parr? Perhaps that ought to be your job, Charles." Lucien ducked behind his newspaper, narrowly avoiding sliver of pear that looked suspiciously like the one Charles had begun to eat.

"Please, I would have no one fret over me," said Emily

"Well, fret we shall, Miss Parr, because I fear you will attempt a third escape," Godric said.

Emily returned her attention to Godric. She had begun to appreciate the other men and enjoy their company, circumstances aside. Godric however... The man deserved another well placed slap. It was just her luck that marriage to him would mitigate her ruination, assuming she could even convince him to such a course of action. She narrowed her gaze and pursed her lips. To her sheer frustration, the duke laughed.

Ashton spoke up, his blue eyes fixed on her. "Third? As in, she tried a second time?"

Emily stared down at her plate. She was to be mocked now? The merriment that came at her expense spurred them on.

"She tried to escape through my bedchamber, practically stole the keys right off my wrist." He jangled the keys she'd fought for over the table. Emily nearly sagged in relief when Godric failed to mention that he'd tackled her to the floor in the hallway outside.

Charles smirked into his coffee cup. "Bet you woke him right up doing that."

Godric pretended to stretch and thumped Charles soundly on the back. He spilled his coffee, and his eyes cast daggers at Godric.

"Manners, Charles, manners," Ashton intoned in a schoolmaster's voice. "Now, Miss Parr, could we beseech you to refrain from any further attempts at escape? I assume you know why you were brought here, and that leaving now would only create more scandal. Best to ride out the storm and let Godric see to your needs while you remain here."

Emily ground her teeth in frustration. The men had pretended to use reason and good sense in taking her and would likely not listen to her pleas. *Abandon my original plan of persuasion, and prepare for war,* she thought, then raised her chin. "I apologize, Lord Lennox, but it is my duty to escape your clutches and return to my uncle." There, she'd done it. Whatever might come, she had to free herself from Godric and his friends.

"Our clutches? You really think us villains, don't you?" Godric leaned forward, resting one elbow on the table as he stared at her. "I suppose we are, aren't we?" The idea seemed to amuse him and he laughed, the sound low and rich.

Emily dropped her eyes to the snowy tablecloth and did her best not to shout. She wanted her life back, her freedom.

"Please...just let me go." Emily bit her lip as Godric caught her chin and turned her face towards his. The others watched her and Godric with interest. Her cheeks flamed.

"It isn't that simple, darling."

"How is it not?" Emily slapped his hand away from her face, and jumped up from the chair. With lightning speed every man in the room was on his feet, watching, waiting for her to run. Godric put his hands on her shoulders and gently pushed her back into her seat.

"Come now, sweetheart. You'll enjoy being here. I promise that you will like us."

They were trying to appease her, but she would not be so easily controlled. The dam that had kept her volatile emotions at bay burst. "*Like* you? How can I like any of you? You've abducted me! Am I to be grateful? Laugh as though it is some joke? Just by bringing me here, you've compromised me! Do you really have nothing better to do with yourselves?" Emily gasped and buried her face in her napkin.

Tears of rage escaped her eyes. All her life she'd been well behaved, yet these men reduced her to shouts.

I am not a child. I am a grown woman. She stilled her shaking and dabbed her napkin at the stray tears that coated her cheeks. She had to master her wrath before the situation worsened. Crying, even out of fury, would do her no good.

"Don't blame them. Blame me," Godric said. The weight of his hands eased a little.

"I am sorry, my lords." She brushed a palm against her cheek to wipe the tears. "But you must understand—I will not be cowed into complacency. You've done me a great wrong and I will not make it easy for you. You've destroyed my reputation and blackened my name with scandal. I will not sit back and let you dictate the rest of my life."

Her vow was met with shocked silence, as it should have been. Emily was more than aware she was naïve and innocent of many things, but she wasn't a fool. There would be no way to survive the scandal untainted, and she had to make these men compensate her for the loss of her future.

No one would ever break her, especially not an arrogant duke.

Chapter Four

The silence that followed Emily's words lasted for several unpleasant minutes. When Cedric stood up from the table, she was relieved for the opportunity to think of something other than her current situation.

"The sun is out. Fair weather for riding." Cedric sidestepped around a pair of footmen removing plates from the breakfast table. "Mind if I borrow a horse? Mine was favoring his left foreleg last night."

Emily stood as Ashton and Lucien took their leave. Charles vanished, but only after casting her a particularly wicked grin.

"The stables are always open to you, Cedric."

Emily rose excitedly at the prospect of riding. "May I go with him, Your Grace? It has been ages since I've been riding." The memory of her last ride was still bittersweet. Uncle Albert had sold her horse to pay off a debt her first week at his house. She still remembered the well-oiled leather saddle and the rough hair of her gelding's mane. She missed riding, missed her old life.

Godric's green eyes narrowed. Emily did her best not to show defiance. He had to suspect she would try and escape. She'd said as much only a moment ago.

"My temper may improve if I felt less like a prisoner and had some fresh air," she added.

"Is that an apology for your outburst?" asked Godric.

"It is the closest you will receive if I am kept confined to this house."

"I suppose you can go riding, but I am coming as well." Godric put a firm hand on her shoulder.

Emily hid her disappointment. It would be next to impossible to escape with even one of them around, but with two? Still, opportunities only arose if one sought them out.

"May I have a moment to change my clothes?"

Godric assented and escorted her back to her chamber, waiting outside. Emily dug through the armoire, and decided on a lovely light blue Glengarry riding habit. Lace, braids and embroidered frogs trimmed the jacket. She draped the train over one arm and rejoined Godric in the hall. His gaze swept over her approvingly. Though she didn't *want* his approval, she raised her chin a little with pride.

As Godric offered his arm, Emily took note of the beauty of the house. Statues of men and women in Grecian garb adorned the alcoves along the hall, like silent watchers.

Emily gazed up at the face of a beautiful marble woman. *I wonder what you've seen.* The statue clutched at the edge of a robe ready to slip off her breast. The seductive shyness in its eyes entranced her.

Godric's Hessian boots echoed against the marble floors, and his laughter joined in. It laced his tone as he tugged her along. "What are you looking at?"

Emily pointed at the statue. "Her."

Godric glanced over his shoulder at the statue and grinned. "I used to look at her and dream of women when I was a boy. This was before I realized that the flesh and blood variety were infinitely better." His eyes swept down her face, lingered on her breasts. A prickle of indignation tingled along her skin. She wasn't naturally violent, but everything Godric did made her want to slap him.

At least a dozen horses dwelled in the Essex stable, all fine beasts, glossy-coated and eager. She'd grown up on horseback, but did not mention this. If Godric knew of her accomplished skill, he might refuse her. She'd have to be careful.

The roan gelding was a beautiful beast, with slender ankles and strong muscles that twitched beneath his skin. This wasn't the horse Godric rode the night before. That had been a black monolith against the waning moonlight, like a fierce charger from the Middle Ages. The gelding in front of her possessed the springing, playful steps of youth. It bent forward, stretched its back, tossed its head to and fro, as it might in the fields beneath the sun's warmth. Godric had fine taste in horseflesh, she could give him that.

Emily feigned shyness as she reached out to stroke the horse. He was a curious creature, but like all thoroughbreds, the gelding showed his arrogance. His dark, cinnamon eyes fixed on her reproachfully, yet he couldn't resist bumping his nose against her palm. She jumped back theatrically when he jerked his head up and huffed.

Godric stood so close that she collided with his hard chest. His hands wound around her waist in an instant. Emily gulped as she realized how small she was in comparison to the man behind her. His grip tightened when she wriggled. Her bottom brushed against him. Startled, she jumped, but his grip kept her prisoner.

His fingertips slid up her ribcage towards her breasts. They swelled, and her nipples pebbled then rasped against the fabric of her gown. They were sensitive and aching and she didn't understand the cause of the sensation. *I hate this man. He's ruined me.* Why then was her breath quickening? Godric's fingers rubbed the underside of her breasts, exciting her further. His touch drew her in, the lure of his passion was a flame but when she drew too close it burned her back to awareness. They had an audience. He was attempting to seduce her here in the stables, in front of his friend. She trembled in anger, but also to a foreign, unfamiliar sensation, not unlike excitement.

His rakehell ways are already corrupting me. She summoned her nerve to defy him and his touch as she slipped from his grip.

Frustrated, Godric stared at Emily. Did his touch have no affect on her? He caught Cedric watching him out of the corner of his eye; no doubt he'd seen it all. They exchanged silent looks and Cedric shrugged as though to commiserate with him. True, it had been six months since his last mistress. When the bloom of that particular relationship had worn off, it had cured him of the fairer sex for a time. Evangeline had been wild in bed, but of out it her personality had been abrasive. She'd treated their relationship like a game, which was fair enough, but she had also treated the staff with contempt, which was not. She'd acted cruelly towards Simkins, whom she believed was far too familiar with Godric for someone of his station. That was unforgiveable. Simkins was like a favorite uncle, and anyone who treated him harshly suffered Godric's wrath.

Emily was nothing like Evangeline. She wasn't spoiled, which shouldn't have surprised him. He recalled too well the irritation Parr expressed at being stuck with his niece and the way Parr racked up debts, it seemed unlikely he would see to Emily's care and comfort first. Godric bristled at the thought that Parr had deprived Emily of anything.

I must be careful. She'll catch me in her enchanting web, and I'll never be free.

It was true. Godric had never felt the slightest inclination to care for a woman aside from his mother, and definitely not in the way he wanted to care for Emily. *No.* Buying pretty jewels and gowns for his mistress secured physical favors, not comfort and care for the lady. But with Emily, he already acted differently, being harsh with her was not proper behavior if he desired her complacency.

He wanted to make sure her chocolate was the right temperature. He wanted her to wear the finest silk gowns, sleep in the softest bed. He wanted her safe, warm, content.

Perhaps if she were happy, she'd come to him, let him introduce her to the passion she buried deep inside herself. He wanted to know her, possess her. All that fire flashing in her eyes when she thought he didn't see, needed to be unleashed.

I'm a bloody fool. I don't deserve such sweetness.

The black thought oozed inside his chest, pooling deep somewhere in the bottom of his heart. He hadn't realized he could feel pain there, but he felt it now.

"May I ride her?" Emily pointed to the gelding.

Godric fought off a smile. "You may ride him."

Emily blushed and hid her face in her hands. Cedric merely shook his head with silent mirth.

Women...they know so little.

The grooms pulled out the roan gelding for Emily. Godric and Cedric each saddled their own horses. He liked being self-sufficient, at least in a few ways. He had never asked for the pampered life of a duke and his grooms knew to let him see to the saddling of his own horse unless he requested otherwise.

Godric demonstrated saddling the gelding, and Emily watched with rapt attention.

"Watch closely, Miss Parr. The saddle faces this way. You must make sure that this girth, the belt of the saddle, is tight. Give it a good hearty tug, and don't worry about hurting the horse. You won't." His lower body jerked at the sight of her nibbling her lush bottom lip.

"How do I mount him?" The moment the words left her mouth, Godric saw himself mount Emily in bed...*No!* He mustn't let himself get carried away, but God, she made it so easy to lose his head.

"Here," he said, gruffly. He caught her by the waist and lifted her onto the saddle. "You must put one leg on each side, since I do not have a sidesaddle."

Lauren Smith

"Oh, yes, how silly of me." She straddled the horse, which required lifting her skirt out of the way as she settled into the saddle, revealing her bare legs. Rational thought plummeted from his brain to that annoyingly persistent spot below his waist. All he could wonder about was how she'd gotten sun on her legs. What could a young woman do so often that would require the lifting of her skirts? Godric bit back a groan.

"Um...Miss Parr, forgive my impertinence, but you lack certain undergarments." His eyes were on that smooth skin so close to his hands. Perhaps if he accidentally brushed against her leg, she wouldn't notice. Humor glinted in Emily's violet eyes, but then it was gone, masked behind that wide-eyed expression.

"Oh, I do apologize. My stockings were ruined last night."

Cedric laughed as he rode up beside them, openly admiring her legs to Godric's annoyance. "Never apologize to two bachelors for daring to show a fine pair of bare legs."

Godric shot his friend a scowl. One more comment like that, and Cedric would be in trouble.

The September sun was warm and the sky cloudless. The insects chirped, and the sound eased away the silence. It was a fine day for riding, for living. Away from the stuffy drawing rooms and evening engagements, Emily breathed again. She belonged here in the country with its green sloping hills and endless blue skies.

A light breeze tumbled along her skin and riding habit as the trio trotted along the edge of Godric's lands. Emily looked back and saw just how far they'd ridden. The manor was a stone dot in the distance. Godric caught her admiring the view, and she smiled.

"Your lands are extensive, my lord." She sighed at the enchanting sight of the English countryside.

"That's not the only thing that's extens—" Cedric began.

Godric smacked the butt of his riding crop on Cedric's horse's flank. The beast shot off at a mad gallop with Cedric shouting curses, leaving Emily wondering what he had been about to say.

Fifty feet ahead of them, Cedric slowed down and glowered childishly in their direction. He stayed a good ways ahead, leaving Emily and Godric alone.

"How long have you lived with your uncle, Miss Parr?"

"I...I don't think I would mind so much if you called me Emily, Your Grace. I dislike being called Miss Parr." It was improper, of course but with everything between them, propriety was the least of her worries.

"If you wish, Emily, but then I must insist you stop 'Your Gracing' me." The sun paled against the bright shine of his eyes and Emily's heartbeat fluttered in response.

"I moved in with Uncle Albert a year ago, after my parents died."

"I heard they were deceased. May I ask how?" Godric guided his black gelding closer to her. Her mount playfully nipped at his horse's front flank.

"They were lost at sea. My father was headed to New York to see his shipping company there. My mother insisted on accompanying him." The pain of her parents' loss was deep, one she'd buried only a short time ago. "I had been staying with family friends when I received word. The next day my uncle came to collect me."

"What were their names?"

Emily's throat constricted. "Clara and Robert."

"And you have no other siblings?"

She shook her head. "None. My mother miscarried twice after me. They stopped trying after that. Too much pain." Why she was sharing such intimate details with a man she barely knew was beyond her.

Godric looked away from her. "My mother died in childbirth when I was a boy. The babe died with her."

There were no words that could ease the hurt of losing a loved one, especially a parent. One felt lost, with no chance of salvation. Nothing could replace the sheltering warmth and security of a parent. To be robbed of that was akin to losing one's innocence.

Godric spoke again. "You have not really grieved, have you?"

It was less a question and more an observation. How odd that talking to Godric about her tragedy should be so easy. He was a stranger, yet already few barriers stood between them.

"No, I haven't." They stopped their horses. She let her reins loosen in her fingers as her horse ducked his head to steal a bite of grass.

"I think that a part of me will never really accept that they're gone. It is as though I expect them to roll up in a carriage at Uncle Albert's any day now to take me home." Emily's voice wavered a little.

Godric's eyes darkened. Emily noticed the faint shadows beneath his eyes. Out here, beneath the sun, without the pace of the day, he looked bone weary. "You must have loved your mother very much."

"I loved her the way I've never loved anyone else." He spoke so softly, it passed as more of a shared thought.

A desire flipped in Emily's heart. Before, she'd wanted to hurt him the way she'd been hurt by his cold, calculated kidnapping. But now...now she saw a man who life had wounded deeply and she wanted to erase the worries that creased his brow. It reminded her of an injured badger she and her father had found in the garden a few years before. It had broken its leg and when they'd tried to help it, it had bitten him, drawing blood. Godric was very much like that animal. Hurt and blindly striking out in his own defense.

"I imagine she loved you just as much."

"Thank you, Emily. I'm sure wherever they are, your family must be missing you just the same."

He meant it. His sincerity manifested in the glimmer of his eyes and the lift of his lips into a grim smile. A man weighed down by countless sins, believed in heaven and an afterlife. For the briefest second she couldn't help but wonder perhaps if rogues could be redeemed?

Godric reached over the small space between them and slipped his hand around hers. Neither had bothered to wear riding gloves. His bare hand enveloped hers. The warmth of his hand, so much larger than her own, offered a comfort she didn't expect—a state of peace she recalled from evenings with her parents before the fire, settled on the floor as they laughed at the humor columns in the paper. Godric's thumb stroked the sensitive plane of her palm, yet the seemingly innocent contact teased her body with a desire for something she did not understand. With that simple truth, all thoughts of her uncle and her parents evaporated. His touch made her want to follow him to the ends of the earth to see where it might lead.

But she couldn't let him win this game by wooing her into submission with tender words and caresses. Emily couldn't afford to fall for this man. They were worlds apart. He was unlikely to marry for love and she wanted someone who could love as strongly as she did. She couldn't stay, couldn't take the risk of falling for him. Her parents would've wanted her to survive, and that required escaping the duke and finding someone to marry.

Emily studied the surrounding lands. A low stone wall, about five feet in height, rose from the ground a few hundred yards off.

"What is beyond that wall?" she asked casually.

"A pond and a meadow or two, beyond that the village of Blackbriar."

A village? The fool might as well have drawn her a map to escape.

Godric kept his attention on Cedric, who raced his horse back and forth in the field, stretching the horse's stride into a beautiful gallop.

Emily's hand was still locked firmly in Godric's grasp, complicating matters. Carefully, she extricated her hand from his, and he turned to see the reason she tugged free. Emily leaned forward to pat her horse's neck.

"He's a lovely creature." She threaded her fingers through the thick mane of her gelding. She didn't even have to look up to know that Godric smiled at her.

"Are you finding that you like horses?"

"Oh, yes. They are a bit frightening, but this one is ever so sweet." She resisted the urge to laugh. She'd never been scared of horses in her life—the occasional goat, maybe, when the awful things nipped at the hems of her skirts—but never horses. Godric was in for quite a surprise.

She raised her head as though to follow Cedric's progress across the field. She waited for the moment at which Cedric swung to the right, back toward the home.

She painted a look of shock and alarm on her face and pointed frantically in Cedric's direction.

"Godric, look out! Highwaymen!"

Godric tensed, bracing for trouble and reared his horse around.

Emily dug her heels into her horse's flanks and took off at a breakneck speed, straight for the wall, praying her horse could clear it. Blackbriar lay beyond the wall. She would seek help or hide until she found her way to London.

It took Godric several seconds to realize what had happened. Highwaymen, indeed.

Emily flew across the golden field, a warrior maiden at the apex of battle. Her lowered posture and natural control over the horse were evident. The girl was cleverer than he'd thought and he had been a fool by telling her about Blackbriar.

"Emily!" he roared.

She headed right for the wall and if she didn't stop, the horse would throw her. She'd land in the lake on the other side, break her neck or drown.

He dug his boots into his horse's sides, forcing it into action.

Moments later Godric was close on her heels, only twenty feet behind, his black gelding the fastest in the stables. He nearly shut his eyes as her horse reached the wall.

In one graceful arc, she cleared it, and a few seconds later, so did he.

Emily controlled her horse better than he expected, which had landed in perfect balance. She'd jerked her mount to the side, narrowly escaping a messy end in the shallows of the lake.

Godric was not so lucky. His horse panicked as its hooves landed in the soft muddy grass of the lake's edge, and it balked, sending him head first into the water.

Emily slowed her horse when she heard another shout, this time one of fear. She turned just in time to see Godric clear the fence but get thrown from his horse. His body hit the surface of the lake in a loud splash and sank out of sight. She held her breath, waiting for him to break the surface. Any moment he'd come up sputtering and humiliated.

Only he didn't.

A thread of fear moved through her, whispering with guilt for letting a man like him die. He couldn't die because of her reckless plan, he couldn't. She was beginning, just a little, to understand him and she didn't want his death on her conscience.

Emily cast a panicked look in the direction of Blackbriar, cursed under her breath and headed back to the lake. She refused to consider why—she owed Godric nothing.

She flung herself out of the saddle and plunged into the water nearest his entry. The lake was shallow near the edge but murky. She barely pinpointed the contours of Godric's white shirt. She wrapped her arms about his chest and kicked hard, propelling them to the surface. He sagged heavily against her, unconscious, but she kept kicking, never more thankful that she was a strong swimmer. When she reached the shore, she was sucking in air as she clawed her way up the muddy embankment with Godric in tow. Her riding habit weighted her down as though she were dragging a boulder in addition to Godric's body back to shore.

She rolled him onto his back and pressed her head against his chest. He wasn't breathing.

"Oh, God, please don't be dead." Blood roared in her ears. She could barely think as panic swept through her. She had to focus.

There was one thing she could try. She'd seen a servant do it once, to a boy who fell in a pond.

Lifting Godric's chin, she pinched his nose with one hand and cupped his chin with the other. Her mouth covered his as she breathed into him, praying it would revive him. She pulled back, waited a second, then tried again and again. The fourth time he stirred, and she nearly wept with relief. He was alive.

A hand caught her wet hair, and held her, keeping their lips locked together. Godric's other arm snagged her waist and dragged her on top of him. He kissed her deeply before he rolled over to pin her beneath him.

Emily balled her fists and beat at his chest as his firm but soft lips explored hers. The taste of him blacked out all awareness beyond the satin of his lips. It was heated, but tempered with a seductiveness she hadn't expected.

A moment of lucidity shocked her into awareness. She tried to kick out and free her legs and Godric pulled back a breathless moment.

"Easy, darling. I only wish to thank my rescuer." Godric abandoned words and kissed her ruthlessly. She couldn't let him do this. He couldn't…couldn't… Emily gasped against his mouth when his hand took hold of the underside of her right knee and caressed the bare skin of her thigh while he pushed his hips deeper into the cradle of hers. Shots of pleasurable pain danced up her legs. They needed to stop, yet she found herself wanting to experience the sensations his lips and hands were creating.

Waves of heat crested through her body, the power of it terrifying. Her body quaked as confusion warred with desire. She may not like the man, but his kisses, his caresses were starting to have an entirely wanton affect on her. The realization drew a tiny whimper from her and an answering growl of desire from the man on top.

The world winked out of existence, except for the rush of blood in her ears and the panting breaths. In. Out. In. Out. The symphony of sighs and gasps that danced between each breath in an endless waltz terrified her. The temptation to let go, to abandon herself and follow Eve's footsteps. One taste, a mighty fall, and she would be lost forever.

Godric's chest shook with silent laughter as he drank in her sweet taste—innocence like fine brandy, addictive and intoxicating. Joy heated his blood and warmed his heart. She'd come back for him, rescued him.

Her hands clenched his biceps, fingers digging into him the more he kissed her. By the time he'd lifted his head to gaze down at her, she was panting, and her hips rubbed instinctively against his own.

He was transfixed by the delicate blush of her cheeks, and the slightly upturned nose that created an impish charm.

Yet he sensed she feared him a little.

Emily had never been with a man, never been kissed until he'd captured her. A more practiced woman would have known what to do. He enjoyed the little instruction he'd given her. The temptation she presented was too much to resist. He moved one hand up to cup her cheek, his thumb stroking the line of her jaw. Raw desire churned in the violet pools of her eyes, a hint of frustration added a shimmer that made him smile. She didn't like that she enjoyed kissing him.

He found her reaction to him fascinating. Other women would gaze at him with slumberous eyes, and leisurely return his kisses, or in Evangeline's case, bite him back. Emily's eyes were bright and full of wonder tinged with anger. There was an eagerness in her lips, a searching in her hands as she stroked his shoulders. It was as though she was determined to enjoy herself, even if she didn't like him. He liked the rebellious spirit in her. She was taking what she wanted from him. If she demanded he stop he would, even if it killed him. But until then he'd steal as many kisses as he could.

Godric wanted to spend days with her, explore her soft curves and find new ticklish spots. He wanted to bow down and worship at the altar of her sensual innocence. She was every bit the wanton, wild creature for which he'd spent years searching. He'd finally found her, and he would have her beneath him, atop him, against the wall, bent over the bed... Oh, the possibilities.

He hadn't known a woman could taste like this, feel like this. He felt like a damned villain, having faked his drowning, but he'd wanted to see if she would return. His friends could have found her in Blackbriar easily enough, none of the shopkeepers would keep her presence a secret from him had he been searching for her.

But she had come back. The second she'd dragged him from the lake, he'd wanted to kiss her more than he'd ever wanted to kiss any woman. Right on the muddy bank, soaking and cold. He would warm her with his passion and his gratitude. The wet skin of her thigh was smooth. The muscles there stretched against him as she tightened her leg. She had the legs of a rider. Lord, how he wanted those legs wrapped around him the same way.

Soon. He promised himself he would take her a thousand times, in every way, ride her until she couldn't walk, yet leave her begging for more.

Her touch, her taste, was all-consuming. The rhythm of her breaths and the feel of her curves cushioned him and then, through the haze of his desire, he heard Cedric's distant shout of concern.

It took every ounce of willpower to release Emily. She gazed up at him with dewy-eyed desire, surely stunned by the assault on her senses. She blinked slowly, as though still lost in the wake of a fading dream. Her lashes were long, and they curved up slightly at the ends, perfectly framing the most expressive eyes he'd ever seen.

For years now he'd only ever looked at a woman's eyes to see if they invited him to her bed and to tell if he was pleasing her. But this woman beneath him was different. Her eyes held a different invitation: to enter her heart and stay.

Like a boxer's uppercut, Godric flinched at the painful truth. Men like him didn't settle down, didn't care for women beyond the pleasures of the bed.

He was doing wrong by this young woman, ruining her body and her future. She'd expect him to marry her after, but he couldn't. Marriage was for fools who believed in love. He had even saved his friends from the folly of matrimony and now they were all enjoying bachelordom. Those in society married for political or financial gain, it was expected. But he refused to tie himself to a woman forever unless he cared about her. He was a hardened, jaded fool who avoided love. He knew how weak it made him.

Emily's bravery and quick wit were admirable, but she deserved a man who would be a worthy husband. He couldn't give her anything else but his body.

The strangest urge to justify his behavior had him stumbling for an excuse. "As I said, you saved my life, Emily. I simply wanted to show my thanks," he said, rather apologetically, as he lifted her to her feet.

She swayed slightly, and Godric threw an arm out to catch her around the waist. He tried not to look down at the lush breasts that jutted out against the thin wet fabric, or her hips, amply displayed by the wet riding habit molded to her body. Cedric rode up to the wall, staring at them both with a shocked expression.

"What happened, Godric? I heard shouting and then saw you go over." His friend's eyes drifted to Emily's body and heated in an expression Godric recognized all too well.

"Cedric, could you lend Emily your coat?" Godric's tone broke Cedric's improper attentions. The man tore off his coat and flung it over the wall where Godric caught it and wrapped it about Emily's shoulders.

"Wait here. I'll take our horses and jump them back over," Godric ordered. He knew by her wide-eyed look that she would obey.

Cedric trotted down the length of the wall to assist Godric, and when the two stood alone, he demanded to know what had happened.

"She distracted me and bolted for the wall. I didn't think she would clear it but she did—by God, she did—and better than I did. Bloody horse threw me right in the water."

"Are you all right? I lost sight of you both."

"I was fine. Poor Emily. She thought I'd drowned and was trying to bring me back to life with those sweet lips of hers." Godric laughed softly.

"You aren't going to tell her you are an excellent swimmer?"

"The water was shallow, she thought I'd been knocked senseless. Besides, I'd rather have her believe that she saved me. Otherwise, what I did to her afterwards will get me slapped."

"Oh, Godric, you didn't! That poor girl. She'll never save your worthless hide again. Tell me you didn't take it too far."

"A few harmless kisses... Maybe a few not-so-harmless caresses," he admitted. But he had no regrets. He could never regret each kiss, each second that Emily's touch reawakened the ghost of the man he used to be.

He used to treasure kisses, count them like a young man, waiting breathlessly to see again the woman who'd inspired such romantic notions in him. His first love, a miller's daughter from Blackbriar, Annabelle, had taught him how to savor kisses. She'd seduced him, introduced him to the world of sensual delights, but she'd done it slowly, the chase and challenge perfect. Since then, anything rushed hadn't been worth it.

He wanted that with Emily, the patient chase, the steady pursuit. Each kiss he'd take from her willing lips would be a sweet victory. Love seemed but a thin veil away from him now, instead of locked away inside himself as he'd always believed.

Emily leaned against the stone wall, shivering as the light breeze chilled her wet skin.

She shivered for other reasons too. When Godric had put his hands on her, his mouth on hers, his body on hers, she had lost herself. For a brief few moments she'd forgotten how angry she was and how worried she was about rescuing her crumbling life.

There was more to his embrace and kiss than the tender affection she'd witnessed between her parents. No, this was a bonfire, a blaze that drew her in to burn her to ashes. When he kissed her, they were man and woman, not lord and lady.

This dangerous game of escape and chase had awakened her most primal instincts of survival. If Cedric hadn't shown up, Godric might have taken her, there on the grassy embankment. The thought made her blush.

The men returned with the horses, and she masked her emotions with the expression of innocence she'd mastered during life with her uncle.

The thought stopped her cold.

What had her uncle done upon discovering her missing? Had he thanked the heavens, or run to Bow Street in panic? Emily couldn't picture either option.

Tears burned in the corners of her eyes. She didn't want to admit how much she'd suffered the past year, but she had, as life with a disinterested uncle hurt terribly. No one deserved to live with family who didn't love or care about them.

Emily rushed to rid herself of her tears as the men drew up on the opposite side of the wall. Godric stretched out both hands to her, and she clasped them, surprised at the ease with which he pulled her up over the wall and onto his lap.

"Here, let me get over to my—" She reached for her horse, but Godric's grip tightened around her waist.

"If you think I'm letting you back on any horse by yourself after your little adventure, you're mistaken."

"But..."

Godric's iron grip kept her firmly on his lap as he urged his horse onward.

"I think it's time we set some ground rules for your future escape attempts. Everything you try and fail will be removed as a privilege, ergo no more horseback riding and no escapes after dark. Too dangerous for you." His condescending tone made her feel like a misbehaving child. *Why didn't I just let him drown?*

"Godric." She squirmed irritably against his chest as they headed for the manor. "I will walk if I must, thank you. There is no need for this." The hand that held her waist slid lower to sharply pinch her bottom. She froze, her eyes lit with fire.

"Ow!"

"You nearly got my bloody neck broken, and I almost drowned."

"*You* didn't have to chase me," Emily shot back.

"If I want to spank you clear until next Sunday, I'll do it and not a man here will raise a hand to spare you," Godric growled.

Emily surrendered to silence after that. She'd never been prone to pout or sulk, but today was as good a day as any to start.

She continued to pout in royal fashion until the horses reached the front steps of the manor. Godric seemed oblivious to the dark scowl she aimed his way. He merely reached up to drag her off the horse and threw her over his shoulder like a sack of grain. He stifled a laugh at her squeak of surprise.

The remainder of Godric's barbaric treatment she took with a queenly silence, even when the laughter and jeers of the others threatened to shame her a hundredfold over.

"What the deuce happened, Godric? You're both wet!" Lucien's voice rang out.

"Emily made another attempt to flee."

Lucien scowled and fished out a sovereign from his pocket, handing it to Charles.

"Well played, Miss Parr, you're easier to bet on than the races."

Charles bowed as he pocketed the coin. "If you could arrange for another escape after supper, I'd be most grateful."

Emily opened her mouth to respond but Godric patted her bottom twice, his hand lingering too long. She kicked out, but it didn't dislodge that offending hand.

"She's not going to oblige you, not after she nearly drowned me."

"Ooh, let me guess—she tried to swim to France?" Smug speculation peppered Charles's voice.

"Don't give her any ideas, Charles." Godric kept walking. The others' steps joined his.

Emily was tired of watching the parade of boots upside down. She put her hands on Godric's back and tried to push up a little. Ashton and Charles strutted directly behind her, both smirking. Charles's eyes lingered on the wet clothes around her breasts.

Charles laughed at the fiery glare she sent him. "Tell us, Emily. What was your plan this time?"

The sudden urge to sock the golden-haired earl on the jaw flamed inside her. So she did—a loose swing of her fist, an easy duck by Charles, followed by more laughter at her expense.

"Don't rile her. The dear girl was brave enough to jump the bloody wall." Cedric spoke from ahead of Godric.

"You're joking! The last time I tried that jump, I fell into the lake." Charles's tone softened with admiration. Emily refused to let that sway her. She'd get her revenge on the earl for his leering.

"That's exactly what happened to me, but not our dear Emily. Oh no, she only bothered to come back and save me when I fell in and nearly drowned."

"But you're a go—" Charles began before someone stomped down on his foot and he cried out in pain.

What? Curiosity broke through Emily's mood. If she had to hazard a guess it seemed like Charles had been about to say Godric was a good swimmer. If that was true... She balled a fist and struck Godric's bottom. He rewarded her with a flinch and then he smacked her own bottom in response. Emily wanted to crack each and every one of their heads together. Her wounded pride almost crippled her ability to manage and hide her emotions. She didn't like the others to laugh at her, not when she fought for her freedom.

Ashton smiled at her. "Emily, I commend you on your courage.

Were it not for my loyalty to Godric, I would wish you luck on your future escape attempts. May they be as cunning as your previous ones."

No hint of mockery reflected in his tone—rather, a soft-hearted kindness exuded his words. *It doesn't matter. He's one of them. None of them can be trusted.*

"And for the sake of my purse, perhaps it could be before supper rather than after," Lucien added, as if proving her point.

Godric proceeded into one of the many rooms on the ground level and slid her off his shoulder into a large armchair. She clung to Cedric's overcoat to shield her damp body from so many male gazes. It intimidated her to have them all ring around her chair, staring down from their formidable heights. She slunk down an inch or two, then tucked her knees under up under her chin and turned her face away. Her wet clothes left her clammy and uncomfortable.

"Don't sulk, Emily." Ashton stroked her damp hair back from her face. "You are far too pretty for that."

Humiliation clawed through her, tearing her confidence to shreds. What did she think escaping would have accomplished? Returning to London now would not have fixed anything. Only the desperation to do something, anything to regain control of her situation, drove her to it.

She flattened against the back of the chair, eyeing Godric. He'd promised she would be safe. But trusting him was hard when he merely stood there, watching her with hooded eyes that seemed to transform into a different shade of green each time his mood changed. Reluctantly, she admitted that little fact about him intrigued her.

"We did warn you that these escapes were futile. Don't be angry at us for being proved right." Godric rotated her chair so that it faced the fireplace. The others left him alone with her as they took seats at a table on the opposite side of the room.

"I *had* escaped. You tricked me into returning." Emily glowered at him.

"There. Now, warm yourself up. I will notify Mrs. Downing you'll need a fresh change of clothes laid out." He reached over the back of her chair and rubbed her arms up and down, warming her up a little. This touch was different from the others he'd given. It entailed no heady rush of desire, nor did it infuriate or frighten her. He was simply offering her warmth and security in a single unobtrusive touch.

It was the sort of act a good husband would do, give of himself until his wife was well cared for. Emily shut her eyes, unable to fight the daydream of marriage to Godric. Yet as she reached for that kaleidoscope of light that manifested in her mind, reality shattered it. Marriage to him would be a disaster. He was so hot one minute and cold the next, his mood swings gave her a headache and he was far too arrogant. She couldn't marry a man who thought of himself so highly, it was not an irritation easily borne.

Emily relaxed and sank deeper into the chair, trying to control her shivers. Glass tinkling, and the splash of liquid, caught her attention. Godric had his back to her as he prepared a drink. Exhausted, Emily put up little resistance when he returned to her and held the glass to her lips.

"Drink this."

"What is it?" she mumbled around the rim of the glass.

"Just a bit of brandy. It will warm your insides."

Emily looked up at him through her dark lashes, seeking any sign that he meant her harm. But she could not navigate the fathomless depths of his eyes.

"Come on, darling. Drink it for me," he encouraged as he bent low over her chair. His knuckles stroked her cheek, pushing back a wet wayward strand of hair.

Emily drank, sputtered in shock at the sudden burning in her throat, and downed the rest of the glass with a gasp. Godric patted her back lightly as she choked down a cough.

"Good heavens, is this what brandy tastes like?" She'd never tried it before and found it far too bitter. She gagged and wrinkled her nose as she thought, groggily that it had an all too familiar aftertaste.

"There's a good girl." He bent and brushed his lips on her forehead.

Emily sighed heavily. Lethargy crept along her limbs as Godric joined the other men at the table. Lucien spoke about their various friends back in London. The warmth of the fire and Cedric's coat around her made her relax. Her eyelids wavered then fell. She hoped she wouldn't dream of Godric, but she knew she would when soft lips brushed her forehead again and sleep claimed her.

Chapter Five

A momentary twinge of guilt had sparked in Godric when he poured laudanum in Emily's brandy. He wanted to trust her, give back her freedom, but she'd run. He couldn't let her go, not until his revenge was complete. Even then, Godric wasn't ready to set his fascinating little captive free. It amused him to see her discovering her own sensuality, though he knew that this did not cast him in an angelic light. He had to persuade Emily to take him, not force himself upon her, and none of it had to do with his revenge on Albert Parr.

Once she succumbed to sleep, he called to the other side of the room where his friends were gathered. "Ash, could you help me?"

"What do you need?" Ashton rose from the table and came over.

Godric touched the woman's cheek, her skin was baby soft. "Emily?"

She didn't stir.

Ashton raised a brow. "Did you give her something?"

"A little laudanum in her brandy. Please find Mrs. Downing and have her bring a clean change of clothes for Emily and my robe and slippers."

Ashton left and soon returned with Mrs. Downing, who held Godric's large red velvet evening robe and warm house slippers. The elderly housekeeper was more like a beloved old nanny to him, and her sharp gaze of disapproval always made him feel like a misbehaved youth. Still, she said nothing as she handed over the fresh clothes.

"Thank you, Mrs. Downing." Godric took the items and he and the housekeeper got to work.

Godric lifted Emily away from the seat while Mrs. Downing peeled off the wet clothes.

Godric's heart stilled at Emily's beautifully sculpted curves. He hardened instantly at the thought of licking every inch of her, nibbling her hips and nuzzling the creamy swells of her breasts. Exploring the slopes and curves of her luscious—

A loud cough and Mrs. Downing's reproachful scowl broke into Godric's daydream. Recovering himself, he slipped a night rail over her and tucked her arms through the sleeves before putting his robe around Emily. The housekeeper took Emily's muddied riding boots off and slipped her feet into Godric's evening slippers which were as big as chamber pots on her dainty feet. At least they would keep her feet warm.

"Will you be needing anything else, Your Grace?" Mrs. Downing asked.

"No, thank you."

She nodded and took her leave.

Emily didn't stir until Godric tucked a blanket around her. Even then, she only sighed and snuggled deeper into the armchair. He hadn't expected to enjoy Emily's abduction this much. Nor had he expected to be quite so taken with her. His original intention had been to spoil her uncle's ability to sell her off to settle his debts. But now Emily's seduction was infinitely more personal. Lust was winning out over revenge, even if both desires led to the same end.

Godric feared he might become as much Emily's captive as she was his. Already his companions showed signs; her rebellious nature charmed them. He didn't want to think about what would happen if they decided they wanted Emily as much as he.

She could never find out how much power she wielded, enough to tear the League of Rogues apart with its sweetness and vitality.

Emily awoke, surprised to find herself back in her chamber clad only in a night rail, a huge robe and too-large slippers. She jumped when a full-figured maid with red curls that escaped her cap bustled through the doorway and started to draw a bath.

Soon Emily was ducking under the hot surface of the bathwater. The maid, Libba, was shy to talk at first, but Emily had a talent for earning trust. She listened with excitement to Emily's description of her abduction.

"How romantic!" Libba sighed, lashes fluttering.

Emily only laughed. "Romantic? I've been abducted! It was dreadful for all those men to manhandle me like a misbehaving child."

"I wouldn't be complaining of that, Miss. I'd give my soul to be manhandled by that dashing Lord Lonsdale. I started working for His Grace when I was but sixteen. When I first saw the earl—" Libba giggled before she covered her flushed cheeks. "Let's just say I would have loved for him to take such a notice in me."

"You say that now. We'll see how you feel when five men have ruined your reputation just because one of them desired revenge for something you had nothing to do with." Emily rose from the bath and wrapped a towel around herself. "It's aggravating!"

"His Grace treats you fondly, doesn't he?"

"What do you mean?" Emily could only think of that savage embrace by the lake, and the cruel pinch to her bottom, and the threat of a spanking. Fond? Godric was anything but fond.

Libba pointed to the robe and slippers that Emily had shed near the bed. "His Grace put those on you while you slept. They are His Grace's personal night clothes." Libba's bright countenance relayed an extra implication.

Emily sank onto the vanity table chair, feeling suddenly very small, in a way unfamiliar to her.

Godric had stripped her naked? He saw her body while she'd been defenseless? Did the blasted man think he had some right to her, merely because he'd kissed her a few times? Well, more than a few, and they had been most thorough kisses, Emily reflected grimly.

"Do you think... He wouldn't expect me to... I'm no haymarket ware!"

Libba paled at the implication. "He would never force himself on you, Miss. I swear it. He's a good man."

"Would a good man abduct a young woman and destroy her future, Libba?" She tried to forget how easily she responded to his touch, his kiss.

The maid chattered about how she surely had nothing to worry about, and how things would turn out right in the end, oblivious to the realities of the world. Emily dressed in one of the new gowns Simkins had ordered from London. She'd laid out a new pair of white stockings among fresh petticoats and a chemise, all sewed of expensive muslin and less modest than the gown.

The feeling of fresh undergarments and a new blue dress made all the difference. It restored her confidence from its fragile state back to a more stable one. Rather than put her hair up, she directed Libba to gather her hair at the nape of her neck and secure it with ribbon. Her eyes glittered, like a pair of lilac gemstones, as she gazed with satisfaction at herself in the vanity mirror.

"A vision you are, Miss!" Libba smiled. "You wear blue, His Grace's favorite color, very well. He will be most pleased!"

Emily frowned. She didn't want to wear Godric's favorite color. The last thing he needed was to see her behavior as encouragement.

Charles burst into her room, against all propriety and reason, causing both Emily and her maid to shriek in protest.

"You about done yet, Em—" He stopped and his eyes widened. "Bloody hell! What I wouldn't give to drag you off to my room. What say you, Emily? Care for a noonday tumble? I'll make it worth your while!"

He crossed the room and caught her in his arms, like a mad whirlwind in human form.

Emily regained her wits for a brief moment and freed one hand, slapping him. "Unhand me!"

Despite the red blotch that grew on the right side of his face, Charles continued to grin at her. "If you think I'll surrender you to anyone else downstairs, you're wrong. I want to kiss you, Emily," Charles declared. "I tend to get what I want."

Beneath his teasing, Emily sensed competition. This is just what I need—to become a trophy for these grown boys to fight over. Then again...if she could use that desire to her advantage, she might find a way to pit them against each other. Now that reality had recalled Charles, his cheeks rosied with a boyish bashfulness, and his gray eyes sank to the floor.

"Um, Emily, you'll be a good girl and not tell Godric I asked to kiss you?"

She touched her chin thoughtfully. "I wonder how he'd react to that? He does seem to have a bit of a temper."

He flinched. "Most women adore, err...my attentions."

Libba seemed to swoon next to the earl. Sometimes Emily wondered if there was any hope at all for her sex.

"As I keep trying to tell all of you blasted men, I'm *not* like other women!" She brushed past him and walked out the door, ignoring Libba's flutter of giggles.

Emily found her way to the dining room, Charles on her heels. She hoped her veiled threat to expose him to Godric had chastened him.

Ashton and Lucien stood by the windows, engaged in a fluid conversation. They frowned at her for some reason, then glared at Charles. Lucien opened his mouth to speak, but stopped when Godric and Cedric joined them in the room.

Godric took one look at Emily then threw Charles a glower that could have melted stone. Charles defiantly raised his chin.

Ashton cut into this silent war. "Emily, may I ask you a rather odd question?"

She nodded.

"Do you, perchance, speak Greek?"

Emily managed to mask her face to hide the truth, that she was indeed fluent in that particular language, as well as Latin.

"No." she lied. Ashton turned to his friends and broke into fluent Greek. She followed the resulting discussion with ease. "Charles, what did you do to her?"

Charles looked guiltily at Godric then at the floor.

"I asked to kiss her. She slapped me. I swear it won't happen again."

"Sounds like you're losing your touch," Lucien joked.

"I got a little carried away with my earnestness, but no harm was done."

Godric pounded the table with his fist. "No harm? You can't demand such things and not expect it to affect her!"

Emily's teacup clattered sharply and tea spilled onto the table. *Hypocrite.* She shot Godric a worried look. But none of the others paid attention.

Cedric spoke in a low voice. "Godric... Not to play devil's advocate, but you did more than demand a few kisses this morning, if I recall."

Exactly. Heat rose in Emily's face, but they didn't notice.

"If I want her, Cedric, then she's mine!" Godric shouted. "It's my money her uncle stole, so I can steal back in kind!"

"But Emily didn't steal your money," Lucien said sharply. "You've ruined her just by bringing her here, you don't actually have to seduce her. We aren't Arab sheikhs keeping her as a slave for our harems."

Ashton cleared his throat, silencing the room. "It's evident we all have taken an interest in Emily that goes beyond captors and captive. I advise we consider our actions more carefully and try to think with our upper heads, not our lower ones. If possible." He shot a glance at

Charles. "It's time we abided by Rule Four of our code. If any man here wishes to have Emily he must convince her to take him. Once claimed, no others may try for her. There will be no more forcibly stolen kisses, not even from you, Godric. I am putting my foot down."

His command left Emily to wonder if perhaps he really was the group's secret leader. Perhaps peerage did not actually affect the League's inner politics.

"But, Ash," Charles protested, "you can't expect us not to touch her. She's so—"

"Irresistible?" Godric said darkly. "Who the devil is in control, you or your loins?"

"Yes, she has enchanted us all, but if she knew that she could use it against us. So again I say: if any man wants her, he'll have to seduce her properly. If she resists that man's advances, he has a duty to stop paying court to her."

"And any further discussions on the matter," Lucien added, "shall be conducted in Greek."

"Excuse me, gentlemen," Emily said in English, drawing all eyes back to her. "Is everything all right? I feel as though I've caused some trouble." The tension in the room eased somewhat.

"Not at all, Emily," Lucien replied. "We were merely telling Charles he could not repeat his actions...unless you wish it, of course."

Charles grinned.

"I..." Her face heated and she turned away in embarrassment. "I am not sure what I wish. I've never had such attentions paid to me until being brought here. I find it all overwhelming." The guilty looks on their faces proved they believed her. *Excellent.* She stood a chance of escaping after all.

She'd never realized how persuasive feminine wiles could be until she'd had these five men struggling to figure her out and woo her. *Fools.*

"Then I must apologize for my forward conduct, Emily." Charles bowed his head respectfully.

"Apology accepted." She allowed Godric and Charles serve her a late luncheon from either side of her, pretending to ignore how even that had become a competition. How funny it was that, two days before, she could not have imagined she would have five roguish lords to eat out of the palm of her hand. Emily smiled as she ate, and watched.

She belongs to me. I will have her.

Thomas Blankenship ascended the steps to his townhouse, seething. He knew what that fool Parr was up to. *He means to play me against Essex in a secret bidding war. Well, I won't play that game. She's mine.*

He pounded his fist on the door rather than use the knocker.

His wizened butler, Baltus, appeared at the door. "Welcome back, sir."

Blankenship only growled and stamped past him into the hall. He shrugged out of his coat and threw it at the footman who waited by the stairs.

"Bring me brandy in my study, Baltus."

The dimly-lit study reflected the remainder of the house. Years of grime coated the windows and fireplace. Dust layered the books on the shelves and ink stains splotched the worn carpet beneath his desk. He had more than enough money to keep his house clean and in good repair, but he rather liked the symbolic decay of his living quarters. It reminded him of his own life, and urged him to fight harder to claim what he desired. Emily Parr.

Blankenship threw himself into his chair and closed his eyes. His anger was a living, breathing creature, burrowed deep in his chest. Its bloody claws raked his insides and its beady black eyes fixed on his soul. He challenged the beast, pinning it inside the dark place in his head. He still had control, for a while yet.

The butler entered with a decanter of brandy and poured a glass, setting it on the counter.

"Will there be anything else?" Baltus wheezed.

"No."

Blankenship wrapped a fist around the crystal and swirled the amber contents around. The rich color was like Emily's hair. His thoughts drifted back to the girl. He had to possess her. Her mother had escaped his grasp, but Emily would not.

Nineteen years ago, when he'd been in his late thirties, he'd still made social rounds in pursuit of a bride. The simpering, delicate flowers of the *ton* hadn't impressed him until he met Clara.

Clara Belarmy. Witty, intelligent and a true diamond of the first water. With auburn gold hair, eyes the color of succulent plums. She was an original.

He had loved her, like every other man. He spent a fortune in bouquets on her, danced more than one of those dreadful quadrilles with her. Yet she never turned her gaze his way. She always slipped off in the middle of balls to be with that young, idealistic fool, Robert Parr.

Yet Blankenship had held out hope she might consider him for a husband, given his wealth. He'd shown up on her doorstop, his mother's ring fitted just for her. Clara hadn't been available for visitors, and the butler turned him away. As he passed the window that faced the street, he caught a glimpse of Clara tucked in Robert's arms, kissing him with wild abandon.

He knew what sort of woman gave her charms to the first willing man. A harlot.

After that he abandoned London's ballrooms altogether. He focused on his business deals and harmed any investments Robert Parr made, forcing the young wedded couple to relocate to the country, where living expenses weren't so high.

But it hadn't been enough. He needed to wound Clara as much as she'd wounded him.

The news of her and Robert's deaths left him cold inside. He ground his teeth at the memory. Without the fires of hatred to fuel him, he'd kept a loaded pistol in his study, ready to fill his mouth.

Then he learned of Emily.

How Clara kept the girl a secret he didn't know. But, once he heard the girl had moved in with her uncle, he had to see her.

He began to visit Albert at his club, talking him into taking loans for investment opportunities. It was only too easy to convince Albert to invest with him and even easier to see that such schemes failed miserably. Parr had been forced to offer Emily up as a potential bride in order to settle debts. In a matter of days he secured an invitation to Parr's residence.

Finally, Blankenship caught a glimpse of her, seated at a table in the small library, her hair undressed so that it hung in riotous waves the color of evening sunlight about her shoulders. She looked every inch the wanton creature he craved beneath him in his bed.

For a second, his youthful longing flared up, like a distant star, before night fell heavy in his hardened heart.

She was just like her mother. A tease.

Women like her belonged on their knees.

In his study, Blankenship's lips curved in a lazy smile. Soon she would be his. Emily would wear the loveliest gowns, the most expensive jewels. The *ton* would know he was her master, and with her by his side, he would put those aristocrats in their place.

Each night, he would rip the clothes from Emily's body, bend her over the nearest hard surface and plow her until she begged for mercy. He'd let her maintain a fiery spirit, just to keep things interesting. Punishing her rebelliousness would be intensely arousing. Having Emily under his control would ease the ache of losing her mother. It was only fair.

He palmed his aching arousal, groaning at the thought of digging his hands into Emily's hair to force himself into her mouth. Her body would be a haven for his own longings and would make up for the years of dissatisfaction he'd had with other women when all he'd wanted had been Clara. If he pretended hard enough, Emily would be Clara, Clara would be Emily, they would be one and the same and his hunger for pleasure and for Clara would be sated.

Visions of Clara still haunted his closed eyes. He hadn't always craved to hurt, to punish. If only he'd had Clara for his own, he would have been gentle, taken care of her. But she'd refused him, married that young buck, and dashed every dream Blankenship had.

Emily was the price of revenge for his shattered dreams. She would pay for her mother's betrayal. She would bear his brats, secure his line and curry favor with the *ton* so that he could line his pockets with their wealth.

He sipped his glass of brandy and leaned back in his chair.

Luncheon was a much quieter affair than breakfast.

Charles's desire to kiss her had brought an issue to the forefront, and the gentlemen were still coming to terms with the danger that she presented to them. She was contemplating this amusing form of karma when a hand settled on her knee under cover of the table, heavy and possessive as it tightened then coasted up her thigh, gently pulling her dress up with it.

A rising blush on her face mimicked the heat that rose between her legs.

Her lowered gaze drifted in Godric's direction. His right hand was conspicuously absent from the table.

"Are you all right, Emily?" Lucian asked. "You look a bit flushed."

Emily shoved her bowl of soup away.

"I think the soup has overheated me." She tried not to look at Godric.

The hand, which had paused while she answered Lucien, began to move back and forth along her thigh, fingers digging into the rumpled fabric of her dress, seeking bare skin. The sensation was so overpowering that she barely held her teacup without shaking. She dared not try to remove his hand.

Her only thought was of Godric's body on hers, and his mouth on hers, kissing in sweet agony as he had at the lake that morning. Would she ever be free of such memories? Did she want to be?

The moment luncheon was over, Emily jumped out of her seat. All of the men looked up at her with concern.

"Excuse me!" She ran to her room. It was the only place in which she felt safe enough to hide as she fought off the unwelcome desire she held for her captor.

She climbed onto the massive bed and curled up on her side near the headboard, clutching a pillow to her chest. The heat had spread to her whole body, and she needed a moment alone to regain control.

Ashton appeared in the doorway, his broad shoulders filling the frame.

"Am I not to have a moment's peace?" she asked.

The room seemed to shrink as he strode in. Every movement he made was graceful, yet she sensed he calculated every action. He approached her vanity table, pausing to let a finger trail over the wood surface before it bumped into a silver hairbrush. Lifting the brush up, he studied it intensely.

He was the most polished of the rogues, yet for all of his barely concealed strength, a weakness shimmered in him. In his eyes, the way they softened on her when he looked up.

As though sensing her thoughts, Ashton set the brush down, and leaned casually on the bed post at the foot of the bed. He crossed his arms and stared at her, a silent challenge, not a threat.

"I'm not going to run," she said. *Not right now.*

A corner of Ashton's mouth curved up. "You're too clever for that." But he remained all the same. She sighed heavily.

"I am surprised you haven't asked me about him yet," Ashton said cryptically.

"Asked about whom?"

"Godric."

"Oh, you must pardon me." Her tone was light but sarcastic. "My usual curiosity has a way of waning when I'm held against my will."

Ashton ignored the sarcasm. "Would you like to know about him?"

"Yes." She wished she hadn't replied. The last thing she needed was for Ashton to think she was interested in Godric, for if he told Godric, she'd fight even harder against his amorous advances.

"Godric has had a hard life, despite being a duke. His mother died when he was barely six years old."

"He told me." Emily said.

"I doubt he told you all." A pause followed, as if Ashton felt Godric's pain. "The deaths devastated his father so that he turned to drink. He was a harsh man when deep in his cups."

"Did he hurt Godric?" Emily rolled over to face Ashton, her frustration and confusion gone. Godric's tragic life wrapped her up as it unfolded.

"Often. Godric was more familiar with the cane than any other young man I knew at Eton. He used to laugh when his professors threatened to thrash him."

"But I've seen Godric's back. He has no scars."

"Caning, if done well, does not break the skin but leaves only bruises and broken bones. Godric's father was a master."

She shuddered with sympathetic pain at Ashton's words. She'd never been caned or even spanked. She'd been a well-behaved child, for the most part. But when she was nine she'd witnessed the canning of a neighbor boy and his screams still echoed in her nightmares. She couldn't imagine the tall, muscled duke brutalized as a tiny boy. What had it been like for him? To have his only remaining parent strike out in despair and fury at the loss of the woman who held them together?

Emily had been fortunate to never know such abuse, and to discover that pain and torture marked Godric's childhood was like breathing in smoke. She hated that Godric had suffered the way no child should.

"How is it possible that he is gentle, at least most of the time?" Emily asked.

"He has much of his mother in him, more compassion than cruelty. He could have become a brute like his father, but instead he became a champion for those who are abused. You've witnessed his tenderness first hand."

She ignored that and tried to change the subject. "Then, why abduct me? Where was his compassion when you were all grabbing me and tackling me to the ground, drugging me with that awful laudanum! That was cruel, very cruel. Why didn't he just confront my uncle?"

"He has no proof of your uncle's crime except the loss of money. The way I understand it, he gave your uncle authority to access the investment account."

"Dare I ask in what capacity these funds were given?"

Ashton gave her a devilish smile born of amusement. "It is nothing as horrible as you might have imagined. He invested money with your uncle in a silver mine that doesn't exist."

"Can't he prove that then? Show that no such mine exists?"

"There is a plot of land that once was mined for silver, but it no longer is profitable. The investment papers are tied to that land. The only proof lies in the sum of money Godric paid your uncle and how it disappeared entirely."

Emily bolted upright on her bed. The vision of her uncle's ledgers flashed through her mind. She'd seen the figures herself, the very crime Ashton spoke of. He watched her closely now, blue eyes searching for meaning behind her reaction. "You wouldn't happen to know more about this than we thought?"

The problem was Emily didn't know if her knowledge would help her cause or hinder it. "I am a woman, Ashton. I've no head for figures or business, but I do remember my uncle mention the mine once in passing to a friend of his. I was shocked by the coincidence, that was all."

"It has often been my experience that women make excellent men of business. Your sex can often be far more competitive when pitched into battles of markets and money schemes." There was a strange look on his face as he said this. A calculating gleam heightening his already vibrant blue eyes. Did he have a woman in mind, someone other than her?

Emily smiled inwardly. *Lord Lennox, you have secrets too.*

"Ashton, if Godric had proof of my uncle's embezzling...would he let me go?"

Before Ashton replied, Lucien and Cedric burst into the room.

"Quick, grab Emily! We've got to hide her!" Cedric said, panting.

Emily took in the sight of their heaving chests. They'd been running to get here. Had something happened? If they wished to hide her, someone must have arrived at the estate and they didn't wish for her to be seen.

I have to find whoever's come and get help!

She scrambled off the bed and over to the other side near the window, trying to distance herself from the three advancing men.

"What's going on, Lucien?" Ashton demanded.

"A magistrate and another man are riding down the road and will be at the door any moment. Godric thinks Parr must have told the authorities and they've come to take Emily back to London."

"Finally!" Emily cried out, a little too triumphantly. There were three men plotting to hide her, after all. She threw herself under the bed, just as Cedric's arms enclosed around the air where she'd stood moments before. Sliding on her belly, she moved further under the bed, praying she was out of reach.

Lucien's well-polished boots stepped in front of her, and Ashton's on the other side.

She was surrounded.

"Come on, Emily, we've no time for this!" Cedric growled as his hands scraped at her ankles.

Emily kicked out at him, but in doing so, came too close to Lucien's side of the bed. He latched on, hauling her out like a kitten by the scruff of the neck. A cloud of dust billowed out, and both she and Lucien sneezed. He nearly dropped her as the sneeze wracked his body.

"Can't you stay clean for even half a day?" Lucien pushed her down onto the bed.

Emily kicked him hard in the stomach. He doubled over with a pained moan, clutching his abdomen and leaving her an opening. She slid off the bed and bolted towards the door. She had to get downstairs and reach the magistrate. He would save her from this madness, get her back to London, and perhaps Anne could help salvage a marriage to a man who didn't care about scandal.

She took the stairs two at a time, and skidded to a halt just in front of the entryway, heart lurching high up into her throat, the pounding sound of boots behind her.

Godric came into the hall from his study, no doubt hearing the commotion. His eyes fixed on her, then the men rushing down the stairs, then flicked to the unguarded front door. The blood drained from his face.

"No! Emily, no!"

"Oh, go to blazes!" She spun and wrapped her arms around the door. She flung it wide so that it crashed against the wall, rattling a nearby mirror. The rush of fresh country air was a blessed relief. She'd made it, as soon as the magistrate saw her she was as good as delivered.

Two figures on horseback were close by. One she was certain was the magistrate.

"Here! I'm here!" Emily shouted, waving her arms to attract their attention. One of the men, a more rotund looking man sat up straighter in his saddle and craned forward. She would know that man anywhere. Emily dashed back inside and slammed into Godric's chest. "Quick! I've got to hide, he's coming for me!"

Godric stared down at her in anger and confusion. "Now you want to hide? Perhaps I'm too busy packing a valise since you've so politely informed me I'm to leave for Blazes."

"Quit being so stubborn and help hide me or we'll both be in serious trouble."

Godric reached around her and slammed the front door shut. "Who's after you?"

"There isn't time to explain. Can you find a place to hide me or not?" Emily demanded.

He gestured to the stairs. "This way."

They returned to her room where the rest of the League joined them.

"You have to hide Emily. I think she might have been seen. I must see to the magistrate." Godric stalked off, shooting a dark glance over his shoulder. Emily gulped.

"Bloody hell." Ashton muttered. "Well, does someone have a plan?"

"I do," Lucien pulled Emily over to the huge armoire in her

chamber.

It was only half full of clothes and plenty of spare room remained in the bottom. They would be easily concealed.

"Get in, I'll join you." He tucked himself into the bottom of the armoire then pulled her onto his lap before the others shut the door to cloak them in darkness.

Godric couldn't believe it.

This man—Thomas Blankenship—possessed the nerve to come into his home armed with a representative of the court.

What Blankenship didn't know was that Mr. John Seaton, the magistrate, had known Godric and his family for years. In fact, Godric's father turned down the magistrate position when the Crown offered it, and recommended Seaton in his place.

Godric asked Simkins to put the two men in the drawing room while he spoke with his friends.

"You three go to Emily's chamber at once and see that every bit of clothing, every stocking, is taken below stairs, and hidden with the maids. I want no evidence that she was ever here. Send me her maid, have her dress in one of Emily's gowns. I'll require some way to explain this if they saw Emily."

Ashton, Charles and Cedric nodded, then bounded back up the stairs.

Godric stood alone, fists clenched at his sides. It was time to deal with the magistrate and this Blankenship fellow.

Seaton, the magistrate, was a wizened old man who possessed the refined features of a country gentleman. He flashed an apologetic look at Godric, and Godric reassured him with a nod before he turned his attention to the other man.

Thomas Blankenship was tall, but his wide girth and sour face took away any chance of decent appearance. Beetle black eyes and a sharp hawk nose contributed to the man's predatory state, one that unsettled Godric. Blankenship was older, perhaps in his sixties, but the sense of power in him left Godric uneasy.

Godric gestured for them to sit. "What brings you here, gentlemen?" The magistrate gratefully dropped into the nearest chair. Blankenship, however, watched Godric for a long moment, studying him, before he finally sat.

"My deepest apologies, Your Grace. I had no wish to disturb you, especially not here—"

"It's no trouble, Mr. Seaton."

"This man, Mr. Blankenship, insists that you are holding a young lady captive. I refused to listen to such nonsense and he said he would come here anyway. Your Grace, I do not come here in my office's capacity, but merely to assure you that I know his assertions are groundless. I will not be making any inquires or searches of this home."

"What is the name of the lady?"

"He says her name is Emily Parr."

"Who?" Godric masked his reaction to Blankenship's face. A possessiveness had taken root there, a look Godric didn't like.

What was Blankenship's relationship to Emily?

"Miss Emily Parr. She is the niece of a gentleman named Albert Parr. I believe, if my facts are correct, you and he know each other?"

"Ahh, Parr. Yes. I have done business with him. I haven't seen him in a few months, however." Godric stretched his legs, seeking to look calm and collected. "Now you say you are here about his niece? What's happened to her?"

Blankenship sat at the edge of his chair. A dark shadow passed across his face. "Don't play the fool, Essex! I know you've taken her. We saw her come out of the door, she was shouting and waving at us."

"Sir!" the magistrate snapped. "Restrain yourself in His Grace's presence."

"Why the devil would I wish to take Parr's niece? What would I do with her? I have no need of some young chit just out of the schoolroom. I certainly don't have to kidnap a lady if I desire one."

"You took her because you believe Parr is indebted to you. We saw the girl ourselves and I showed the magistrate your note."

"My what?" Godric laughed softly, genuinely amused.

With a weary sigh, Seaton pulled a note from his pocket and handed it to Godric.

He scanned the note he'd written and contained a smile. "This is not my handwriting."

"Of course it is," Blankenship said. "Parr recognized your hand."

"Well, that is easily put to rest. Come, I shall show you." Godric stood and quickly walked to a writing desk in the far corner. Both visitors followed.

He grabbed a sheet of paper and inked his quill. Holding the quill deftly with his right hand he scrawled a few sentences, blotted the paper and handed it to the magistrate.

Seaton pulled out his quizzing glass and examined the two works side by side. "Mr. Blankenship, take a look for yourself. This handwriting is not at all like the original note."

"Nonsense!" Blankenship snatched the two notes out of the magistrate's hand and studied them.

Godric fought the devious smile tugging at his lips. He'd written both notes, of course. The real one with his left hand and this one with his right. As a child, he'd had few friends. To occupy himself, he'd learned to write with both hands. The effect was two very different writing styles. Neither of his guests knew that he only wrote a few notes to Parr, always using his left hand—something he had never done in his normal correspondence. There was something he had never fully trusted about Parr and therefore he had never left much evidence by way of letters.

"But...that's not possible. I know he wrote this. He's tricking us. He had a servant write it for him." Blankenship tossed both notes back at Godric.

"Mr. Blankenship, I believe it is time for you to leave. You have disturbed His Grace and as magistrate here, I'm telling you there is nothing to see here." Seaton put a hand on Blankenship's shoulder, but the man thrust him away.

"I am not satisfied. You and I both saw the girl on the road. I know it was Miss Parr. I wish to see every room in this bloody place."

Godric gave a dramatic sigh. He could easily send the man packing, but he'd rather just show him the rooms and be done with it. He didn't want the man skulking around his home. "If that will ease your concerns for the lady, then I will happily open my house to your inspection. I daresay you'll be disappointed. I'm sure she's merely run off."

The three men left the drawing room.

"Run off? That little chit wouldn't know where to go." Blankenship frowned. "Besides, no one would take her in."

Godric scowled. Blankenship spoke as though Emily hadn't an intelligent thought in her head. Emily was nothing if not clever, and possessed two heads worth of knowledge.

"This way, gentlemen." Godric gestured for the two men to follow as he led them about the house. He opened every door, and not one contained a sign of Emily. Her chamber had been immaculately cleaned. Emily's maid, wearing a gown similar to Emily's, sat on the bed, reading a book. The maid blushed when Godric and the two men noticed her.

"Ahh, sweetheart, there you are. I'm sorry to have upset you, we must never quarrel again." He bent to press a kiss on the maid's hand, and she ducked her head bashfully. Godric turned back to two men.

"Excuse me, gentleman, this is a dear friend of mine, Libba. She is the lady you saw when you arrived. I'm afraid we had a row. But all is well." Godric flashed a quick look at the maid. "You ought to go to the kitchens. Cook is preparing those pies you like so much."

The maid gratefully escaped the watchful gazes of the three men and departed.

When they finished their inspection, the magistrate seemed convinced that Blankenship was destined for the nearest madhouse.

"I'll show you out now. I have estate matters to attend to today and tenants to visit. I can't delay any longer."

"Of course, Your Grace." Seaton walked outside and took the reins of his horse from the waiting groom.

Blankenship whirled to face Godric, bringing himself far too close for his liking.

"I know you took her. But know this. She is mine. Parr gave her to me. I will get her back and she'll be punished for staying here with you."

"You would punish a woman for leaving home?"

"I would punish her for trying to escape me. The girl belongs on her knees before me and I'll have her there, soon. And you, with all of your bloody arrogance and pride, I'll tear you down before this is done."

Godric laughed. "Tear me down? You, my dear fellow, have no idea whom you're dealing with. Your insolence is matched only by your stupidity. It's you who should worry. I've destroyed greater men for less than the insult of your presence in my home. Even if I did have Miss Parr, I'd keep her just to spite you."

But Blankenship was not easily cowed. "You might want to ask your friend Lord Rochester, what happened to Lord Pitherington.

Terrible bad luck can befall even the mightiest of us. Bear that in mind."

"And you bear this—I don't like men who abuse women. When you threaten me, you threaten four more men far above you in intelligence, power and fortune. Should I wish to tell them about your hasty words, you might not wake up tomorrow morning. Good day to you." Godric finished with such a menacing growl that Blankenship staggered back, then hurried to his horse without looking back.

"Pleasant journey!" Godric hollered as the horses left a trail of dust in their wake.

"And good riddance," Ashton echoed from behind. The others, save Lucien, were with him.

"Are we in the clear then?" Charles asked.

Godric turned to face his friends. "I wish I could say otherwise, but the truth is no. We aren't the only ones with an interest in Emily. I believe our interest in the lady is far better than the alternative."

Chapter Six

Only a tiny beam of light cut through the keyhole of the heavy wood armoire.

Emily tried to remain absolutely still, focusing on the noises of the manor. Several minutes later, the door opened and Godric entered, followed by Blankenship and the magistrate. Emily bit her lip so hard she tasted blood. Her uncle's business partner moved through the room, studying it. She held her breath, terrified he would hear her panicked gasps for air. Finally the inspection of the room was over and the men departed. She sagged against Lucien in relief.

"Christ, that was close," Lucien muttered. "But they might be back. Keep still."

After a quarter of an hour, Godric and Ashton's voices grew louder out in the hall. Lucien loosened his grip on Emily as the armoire door swung open. Ashton and Godric stared at the pair for a second before Godric snatched her out of Lucien's lap and tossed her over his shoulder. Sadly, she was getting used to the treatment. It was easier for him to carry her about whenever she couldn't be trusted to walk. She wasn't a valise that needed to be carted about by a servant.

"Good thinking on the armoire, Lucien. That one fellow was insistent on seeing the rooms." Godric shifted Emily and she grunted in discomfort.

"You could put me down, now," she stated, but it went ignored.

"Thank you," Lucien said. "I have been known to have the occasional stroke of genius. Now who was that other fellow? That wasn't Parr, was it?"

"He introduced himself to me as Mr. Thomas Blankenship. Supposedly, he and Parr are friends."

Blankenship. Why was he here? Why hadn't her uncle come looking for her? She froze, too terrified to move. He'd probably convinced her uncle to let him marry her...a thought so abhorrent she was sick to her stomach. Emily huffed.

"Blankenship?" Lucien growled. "That devil owes me three thousand pounds, he belongs to a group of investors who purchased a bit of property from me."

"Do you know anything about what happened to Lord Pitherington?" Godric asked. "I read about the accident of course, but Blankenship suggested there was more to it."

Lucien's brow furrowed. "Yes. The man was broken by debt earlier this year. Some of my interests were tied in with his, and I took a small hit as well. There were whispers about Blankenship's role in the matter. Pitherington...well...he put a pistol to his mouth when he couldn't pay, I'm afraid. It was reported as an accident for the sake of the family."

"Well he sounds like an absolutely fantastic fellow, we ought to invite him to our club," Godric drawled sarcastically.

The news that someone hated Blankenship as much as she did gladdened Emily's heart. *The enemy of my enemy is my friend...I hope,* she thought grimly.

Despite the fact that Godric still had her slung over his shoulder, the men talked on as if she didn't exist. With an irritated grunt, she kicked out to remind them. Godric moved over and dropped her onto Lucien's bed.

"What would Blankenship be doing here?" Ashton asked. "Why didn't Parr come?"

Godric shrugged.

"You wish to know why Blankenship came?" she asked sharply. "Perhaps you should consider asking the one person here actually involved?" They watched her now in surprise.

"You know that man?" Lucien asked.

"Oh, yes, I know him. He's despicable. He's been haunting my uncle's doorway ever since I moved in with him. He's even—" She choked on her words she was so angry.

"He's even what?" Godric's eyes were sharp as jade daggers.

"He's even taken liberties with my person, liberties I have not given him, nor ever will. He's been courting me with the intention to marry me. My uncle thinks I don't know that, but I do. I'm not daft."

All three of the men looked justifiably horrified. At that moment Charles and Cedric joined them. Charles took one look at their faces and his eyes widened.

"What's happened? Did someone die?"

"Someone just might..." Godric muttered under his breath.

Lucien grimaced. "We're fine," he said. "We've just received some unpleasant news."

"Oh?" Cedric held his cane like a sword, his hand resting firmly on the silver lion's head.

"Apparently, Mr. Blankenship believes he has some claim to my Emily," Godric said with disgust.

Emily blushed at Godric's possessive tone, though it still offended her.

"Oh for heaven's sake, stop speaking of me as if I'm an ornament for your shelf." Still, to belong to Godric, it was a thought that gave her pause.

"What? That old toad? Why he'd—" Charles began, but Cedric tapped him on the shoulder with the tip of his cane. Charles decided to not finish.

"He is a vile toad and I hate him," Emily spat with such loathing that her captors exchanged looks of concern.

"But you don't hate us?" Lucien asked, noting her omission.

"What reason would I have possibly have to hate any of you? Aside from being kidnapped, that is." She allowed a small reluctant smile. "I suppose I like you all well enough." It made little sense that she trusted them as much as she did; she could barely explain it to herself, let alone to them. Of course the alternative, which had come within a foot of her while she hid in the armoire, was so much worse.

"Well, despite how you may take our actions, keeping you here has been a most amusing challenge." Godric laughed.

Emily narrowed her eyes to slits. "I'm glad my value is based on how much I amuse you."

"Well," Ashton sighed. "At least we escaped a potential disaster. I suppose it's safe enough to resume our day." The others agreed.

"I have some work to do. Emily you will accompany me."

The command in his tone made her bristle but she didn't protest. She wouldn't have won that argument.

Godric escorted Emily down the stairs and gestured for her to sit on a red velvet settee while the others vanished. She took the opportunity to examine the study, richly decorated with bookshelves and odd trinkets. He must have traveled the world. Watercolor paintings of distant locales hung above the chairs, and unusual things—like elephant tusks, no doubt from Africa—had been pinned alongside them.

Godric sat at the large rosewood desk, perusing papers and letters.

She envied him the freedom to get up and leave, not just from the settee, but to go on adventures. If she was forced to marry Blankenship, there would be no chance of adventure ever again.

She scanned the walls again, noticing a small portrait of a raven-haired woman seated on a swing. The cut of her gown was old enough that Emily knew the portrait must have been commissioned years ago. Bewitching eyes glinted at her from the layers of paint. Godric's eyes, save for the color.

"Godric..." she began. He glanced at her warily. "Yes?"

"Who is the lady in that portrait?" Emily leaned against the armrest nearest his desk. "Is it your mother?"

Godric's gaze darkened. "Yes."

"She's very beautiful." Emily saw how much the late Duchess of Essex's son took after her. Godric had the harsh beauty of a Greek sculpture, but each feature held traces of his mother's softened beauty. No wonder he captivated her. Ashton had been right. Godric had his father's power, but his mother's gentleness and compassion.

Godric rose from his chair and walked over to the portrait. "She was a great woman. She never spoke a harsh word to anyone, nor raised a hand against me. I..." Emotion roughened his voice. "I used to climb onto her lap each evening after supper and she would read to me. She always smelled of lilacs. Even now her room still carries the scent."

Emily's chest squeezed around her heart. He was lost in memories; she saw it in the distant focus of his eyes.

"And your father?" She was afraid to break the spell, but she wanted to understand him.

"He loved her in a way he never loved me. I remember the way they danced together. When my mother held her annual ball here, I'd sneak out of the nursery and watch from between the spindles of the stairs. My mother would float across the floor, laughter shining in her eyes. And Father? He would hold her close, smiling like the clouds had opened to reveal the sun. They could waltz for hours, spinning in delicate circles, and I'd watch, enraptured by the sight."

"I am sorry she died," Emily said. Thoughts of her own parents crashed against the walls of her heart and fought to break free. She drew in a deep breath, strengthening herself against the battering.

Godric laughed, but it held no mirth. "We're both orphans, aren't we?"

"I suppose we are." A slight shiver trespassed over her skin. She hadn't realized before now that they had something in common. A long moment of silence passed. Finally, Godric sighed and returned to his desk. His weary expression pained her. She hadn't meant to hurt him by inquiring about his mother. Emily stood up and walked towards his bookshelves.

"Is this the world's slowest escape attempt? If so shall I order tea before pursuing you this time?"

His sarcasm prickled her pride. "I simply wish to find a book to read. It would help to pass the time."

His eyes stayed on hers. She let her honest intentions shine from her eyes. She truly did just want to read.

Her mother had taught her the pleasure of books. As a child she'd been a wild hoyden. Her father had indulged her in every boyish entertainment from riding to climbing trees and fishing. But as much as she loved to catch a perch and haul it into the boat with her father, something magical overcame her while reading with her mother. They'd curl up on the worn couch, find one of the larger illustrated tomes about the natural sciences, and study the renderings of each exotic creature. For a moment, Emily lost herself in that memory, and with piercing agony was pulled back to the present.

Godric went over to the shelf on the right side of his desk and selected a book for her. All her senses sharpened when he sat next to her on the edge of the settee. Godric placed the book in her lap, then took her hands in his.

Her eyes shut for the briefest moment as she enjoyed his touch. Godric stroked her wrists, gazing down at her.

"Emily, I demand a payment for this. Should you refuse, I'll take the book back." He reached out and tucked a lock of loose hair behind her ear. His fingers lingered on the sensitive spot below her ear. A sharp tingle shot down her spine at the touch.

Emily bit her lower lip. What payment he would demand for so small a pleasure? She was afraid that his price would be something she'd pay without hesitation. When his gaze fixed on her, like emeralds pulled from blazing fires, she felt his hands already upon her body. "What is your price?"

His eyes fell straight to her lips, and she did the same. The soft lines bracketing his mouth often turned hard when she frustrated him. It was one of his flaws, that hardness that could turn his sensual features so cold.

"I want you to kiss me." His voice was a hoarse whisper.

But his phrasing didn't make sense. She was to kiss him?

"I have kissed you, but you've never kissed me back. I want your full participation."

"But I don't know the first thing about kissing." Until now, she'd just enjoyed the rush of sensations he thrust upon her, contributing nothing, only taking. But it was improper to talk so openly of physical intimacy.

Godric just smiled, a gentle twist at the corners of his mouth. "With enough practice you'll learn. A few minutes with me as a tutor and you will be a master." His grip tightened, as though their talk had excited him.

"One kiss? You won't demand anything more of me?"

"One kiss, but you won't get away with a saintly peck on the cheek, Emily. I demand a real kiss."

"Demand?"

"Request," he amended.

"Request or you'll deny me my book? Still sounds like a demand."

"God's blood, woman, you are trying my patience." He seemed to be suppressing a smile.

Could she accept a devil's bargain? Godric's kisses robbed her of rationality. But if she didn't prove she could best him, even at a kiss, then he would win. But this question transcended a game. Kissing him was a dare she wanted to accept. Part of her yearned to show him she was a woman who desired him and that she could kiss as good as any woman he'd been with before.

Heart waltzing in her chest, she spoke: "I agree then. One kiss." She felt compelled to offer her hand to shake on the deal but she knew he'd only laugh, so she refrained.

Emily took the book and set it aside. Godric rested his palms on the tops of his muscular thighs. He ceded control to her, allowed her to take action. For some reason this both comforted and aroused her, and she found the courage to reach up and take his face in her hands.

The ghost of a beard that shadowed the line of his jaw was rough beneath her palms. Her skin tingled and her breath quickened. His eyes fixed on hers, lacing a spell around her with their magic. He was too far away, and she needed him closer. Her fingertips slid back to curl around either side of his neck so she could pull his mouth down to hers. He dipped his head, the tendons of his neck taut beneath her hands, vibrating with tension, energy, all focused through one single place—his mouth.

Just before they kissed, his warm breath danced over her lips, mixing with her own. The intimacy of that instant seared her inside. No wonder women were compromised so often, it was impossible to resist something like this. The excited breaths, that delicious moment right...before...a kiss.

Godric's lips met hers in a soft yielding blossom of tender heat. He didn't respond right away, but let her explore his mouth without resistance. She grew bolder, wanting more from him than she really understood. She mimicked some motions he had used on her. Her tongue teased his lips, enticing him to open his mouth to her, and when at last he did, a thrill of triumph struck deep in her belly.

She gave into the pure physical senses. That masculine aroma of sandalwood and spice, uniquely his, imprinted itself in her. Emily's heartbeat doubled as his tongue finally danced back with hers, but he did not invade her as he'd done by the lake. It seemed he meant to keep his promise that she was to kiss him.

She moved her fingers into the roots of his hair at the nape of his neck, ruffling the dark glossy hair, enjoying the breathlessness that it stirred in Godric as his mouth mated with hers. He shivered beneath her touch and excitement flowed through her to discover she'd found a weakness in him.

Ashton's stories about Godric's abuse at his father's hands added tenderness to her kiss that she hadn't expected. Leaning into him, she raised herself up, pressing her chest against his, wrapping her arms tight about his shoulders to hold him. She spoke without words, telling him she wished she could erase the darkest of his memories.

When Emily's kiss changed, it shook Godric to his core. He felt something beyond curiosity and innocence. A storm of emotions flowed from her—tenderness, protectiveness, ferocity, but also another emotion, one that ran deeper than the seas.

Something impossibly wonderful was born between them in that breathless kiss, and it terrified him. His heart thudded painfully as her fingertips caressed his neck again. His body tensed with desire, but her lips stilled him.

She tempered his impulse to take her with primal violence with a mere swirl of her tongue and her body pressed against his in a way that meant to comfort and not entice. Somehow, his hands wound around her, fingers digging into her lower back to urge her closer. How could a kiss soothe and excite all at the same time? That had never happened before in his life, and it scared him. He had to free himself of Emily, had to sever the invisible gossamer strands that connected his heart to hers. He couldn't do this, couldn't fall for her. It was wrong. They were wrong for each other.

He reached up, disentangling her hands from his neck, and pulled his lips out of reach. Emily's eyes fluttered open, as startled as a butterfly caught by a sudden breeze.

He wanted to apologize, but words were beyond him. He'd been struck speechless. That kiss was more dangerous than she could possibly know. It had cut him open, exposed his soul. If she ever kissed him like that again, he'd be lost...

"Godric?" Worry tainted Emily's beautiful face.

Something had to be done before he lost himself in the storm that brewed in her violet eyes. Before he sought to calm it and return to the comfort.

"I'm sorry. I should not have asked a child to kiss me." He stood and turned his back on her, leaving her alone in the room with her book.

A child? Godric's words had wounded her, a clawing pain in the center of her soul. Tears sprang to her eyes and she buried her face in her hands, burning with shame.

She looked up to the sound of soft-booted footsteps across the carpet.

Ashton stood at the doorway, eyes dark as sapphires. He came to her without a word. Silent sobs wracked her body as Ashton held her close to his chest.

How could Godric just walk away? He thought she was a child still? After everything? She was a woman, with a woman's heart and woman's pride and she was trying to learn—she wanted to learn everything from him—but he'd scorned the first true kiss she'd ever given anyone. The agony in her heart was so great she felt sure it had shattered into a thousand glittering pieces.

Emily cursed her foolishness, her belief that she could be desired by a man like Godric. She was the last woman on earth someone like him would ever love.

Love... Did she want his love?

Did she love him? When had her anger and frustration with him changed into something deeper and softer? Lord help her, she couldn't love him.

But surely only love could cause pain like this.

Ashton wasn't sure what transpired between his friend and Emily, but her tears moved him more than anything had in years.

Since Emily had come into their lives, parts he had thought long dead were reawakening. The urge to protect was the strongest now, to punish the source of her tears, even if it was Godric who paid the price. They had all vowed to ensure her well-being and that, in his eyes, included this.

Despite her tender years, Emily was a strong woman, and until now he hadn't seen her cry. Godric must have done something terrible to leave her so inconsolable.

"Hush now, my dear, shh." She quieted at his words. "There, now. Can you tell me what happened?" Ashton cupped her chin and lifted her face up towards his.

"I don't know if I can say..." Her cheeks warmed with a soft peach blush.

"Please, Emily. I don't want to see you hurt again, so I must know what to protect you from."

Emily drew in a slow shuddering breath. "I asked Godric if I could read a book. He said that if I wanted to, I would have to kiss him as payment."

Rising fury darkened Ashton's heart.

"But I'm not very good at it, and he said he'd teach me."

Ashton's animosity grew.

Lauren Smith

"Did he...did he force you? Did he get rough with you?" he asked, a dangerous edge to his words.

Emily shook her head.

"Then why are you crying?"

"It was what he said to me afterwards... He said he shouldn't have asked a child to kiss him. *A child!*" She buried her face in his chest again.

Ashton was confused. He couldn't understand what had gone wrong. What could lead Godric to say such an odd thing? Women were always natural kissers and caught on quickly. It was men who needed practice to master the art.

There was no reason for Godric to have said such a cruel thing, not when she'd done as he'd asked. "Emily, look at me, dear."

She did.

"What did you do when you kissed him? Can you tell me?" Perhaps he might learn what had bothered his friend.

"I just kissed him. I thought about what you had told me about him, about his childhood and his father, and I kissed him. Did I do it wrong?"

The shadows underneath Ashton's eyes lightened a little. "I'm sure you did not."

"Then why?"

Ashton put a finger to her lips. "I believe you have done something to Godric that no one has done before. It scared him. He needs time to sort his feelings out. Can you be patient with him?"

"But what did I do?"

"You really don't know, my dear?"

Emily shook her head.

"You kissed him from the depths of your heart."

Her brows drew together as she considered his answer. "Isn't that how everyone is supposed to kiss?"

It pained him to realize that she was as sweet and innocent as she appeared. No man under this roof was worthy of such a heart as hers. Ashton held her hands together, kissing them softly before he spoke.

"If everyone kissed as you do, men would never leave their lovers to go to war, fathers would never beat their children and wives would never worry about unfaithful husbands because there would be none.

More of us should kiss with our hearts. No matter what Godric said, remember this. What you've shown in your kiss is priceless."

And Emily had reminded Ashton that he'd once wanted something more from life. He silently thanked her for this epiphany by kissing her forehead. He helped her up and escorted her out of Godric's study and back to her room.

"I have a matter to settle with Godric. May I ask you to stay here unguarded until tomorrow? Charles has wagered twice our previous amount that you'll escape before dawn, and I would very much like to see him lose."

It wasn't the first time her escape attempts had been compared to sport, but how Ashton said it made Emily laugh. "In fact we were discussing giving you a ten minute head start tomorrow," he added.

"You are?"

"Oh yes. On foot, of course. Then we'll use horses and hounds to chase you."

"You cannot be serious."

Ashton grinned. "Of course not. But it made you laugh. Now, will you give me your word of honor as the daughter of a gentleman not to try and escape until tomorrow?"

Emily nodded, weary from the emotional onslaught she'd suffered but warmed by Ashton's odd humor. "On my father's honor."

"Thank you." He stroked her hair and pressed his lips to her forehead before he left her alone. He paused at the door, watching her as she fell back onto her bed and lay still, counting her breaths.

"I must always kiss from the depths of my heart..." she murmured to herself after he'd gone.

Godric stormed into the boxing room where Charles and Cedric had gathered to engage in a bit of pugilism. Charles, an expert boxer, loved to go a few rounds in the ring when in London. Of course, the rings Charles often found himself in were often less than reputable. Though he spent hours training at Jackson's Salon, he preferred the rougher rings, in which he proved himself.

Cedric danced back as Charles attacked. "Godric? You look murderous."

"The little brat twisting your trousers?" Charles joked as he swung a loose punch in Cedric's direction, missing by several inches.

Godric tore off his waistcoat and started to roll up his sleeves. He nodded to Cedric who left the lined ring in the corner of the large leisure room.

"Shut up and fight me, Charles."

Charles smirked, always ready to throw punches in Godric's direction when the occasion arose.

They had only been at it for a few minutes when Ashton and Lucien walked in, both visibly upset. Lucien looked nervous while coldness burned behind Ashton's face.

Godric was so startled to see that expression that Charles caught him off-guard and planted a facer. Ashton peeled off his jacket and vest, handing them to Lucien as he rolled up his sleeves.

It was then that Godric realized all five of them were without Emily.

"Wait a minute... Who's watching Emily?"

Lucien answered. "She's in her room. She gave Ash her word she would not escape anymore today."

"And you believed her?" Godric shouted. "She could be miles away by now!"

"If she promised, then I believe she'll stay put," Lucien said with a coolness that left Godric more anxious than before.

Ashton, who'd been silent, came to the ring and spoke to Charles. "Mind if I step in?"

"No, you may not!" Godric didn't want to fight Ashton when he looked the way he did, not if he didn't even know from whence his friend's anger stemmed. Godric had every right to be angry with Emily for what she'd dared to do, the way he felt as a result. What was Ashton's excuse?

Charles looked between Godric and Ashton and, knowing any place was better than here at the moment, he bowed and fled the ring.

"Scared of a little competition, Godric?" Ashton's words teased, but Godric sensed the veiled threat.

"You've never beaten me in the ring, Ash. Today will be no different." It would be a pity, but he'd bloody his friend's nose to prove his point.

"Good, glad to hear it." The cold smile on Ashton's face promised pain. He raised his fists and waited for Godric.

Godric danced a few steps to the right, Ashton mirrored him to the left, and so it began. But rather than box defensively, as he usually did, Ashton seemed eager to meet Godric's every blow. It caught him off-guard and Ashton landed a blow to his stomach. Godric doubled over with the pain.

Ashton didn't wait for Godric to right himself before he charged and knocked him so hard that Godric flew back several steps. Charles moved to intervene, but Lucien stayed him with a hand.

Adapting to Ashton's ferocity, Godric retaliated. He snuck in a left-handed hook and caught Ashton in the right eye. It would blacken nicely by the next morning. But his victory was short-lived as Ashton returned the favor.

The fight continued for another five minutes. Ashton fought as though possessed. His relentless pursuit wore Godric down. None of the others interfered. Some things could only be resolved in a ring.

Godric fell back again, finally finding his breath.

"Dammit, man, why are you trying to pound me into oblivion?"

"Why?" Ashton punctuated the word with a blow to Godric's lower cheek. Blood dribbled down from Godric's split lip. "If I ever find out that you've made that dear woman cry even one more tear, so help me, Godric..."

Ashton spoke with such venom that Godric's fists dropped. Ashton finished him off with an uppercut. Godric toppled backwards, landing on the mat with a loud groan. Ashton lowered his hands to wipe his bloody knuckles on his trousers.

"Well, I think my point has been made." He took a few deep breaths, approached Godric and held out a hand.

He took it and Ashton pulled Godric onto his feet. "Point taken, friend. I've done her a great harm and needed to be reminded of my vow."

Ashton clamped a hand down on his shoulder in approval. "Sorry, Godric, but I knew there was no other way to get through to you."

"Just answer me one question. Was I off my game or have you always gone easy on me in the ring?"

"You will never find that out, I'm afraid." He turned on his heel and retrieved his clothes from Lucien. Once they'd cooled off and were fully dressed, Ashton turned back to Godric.

"Now that this matter is behind us, I believe you owe a large stack of books and an apology to a certain lady."

"She told you about..."

Ashton smiled. "She told me everything. She's so traumatized by your cruelty that she's convinced she was a wretched kisser. You know that is the worst thing men like us can do to a woman. We're rakes, not bastards. We seek to love women, not spurn them."

"What on earth did you do to that sweet kitten?" Cedric demanded.

When Godric didn't reply, Ashton sighed. "Godric demanded a kiss, and when she did he dared to chastise her for kissing like a child. You'll be lucky if she ever forgives you."

Shame heated Godric's face, but he reminded himself that he'd walked away for her sake and his. He couldn't allow Emily to fall in love with him, but that was exactly what her kiss threatened.

As if reading this thoughts, Ashton put a hand on Godric's shoulder. "I think she has feelings for you, Godric."

The men left the boxing room and moved into the main hall. Simkins passed by and froze at the sight of his bruised and bloody master. "Your Grace?"

"Don't worry, Simkins, just having a bit of fun."

"Very good. I'll send a maid to clean up, Your Grace." Simkins looked over Godric into the boxing room. "Perhaps two are in order? And one of the larger buckets?" He bowed and departed.

Godric decided Ashton was right. For that one kiss Emily had earned a stack of books.

Emily was curled up on the window seat when someone knocked on her bedroom door.

"Come in." Her eyes were focused on the gardens below. The faint ghost of her face reflected in the thick pane of glass. Emily put her hand on the glass and let the sun's warmth heat her cool palm. For a moment she lost herself in the sensation, letting everything else drift away, before the world demanded she face it again.

"Emily?" Godric's voice played like a forbidden symphony. She turned her head just enough to present him with her profile but didn't look at him. She couldn't bear it. She wanted to go back to despising him for his pig-headed nonsense.

Loving him would be the greatest mistake of my life. He'd break my heart. I'd be left with nothing.

"Emily, I've brought you something." A rustle sounded from behind her, and items fell on her bed. The door settled in its frame as Godric shut it.

"Please, just go," she said. But her heart ached to beg him to stay, to take back his cruel words.

"If that is what you want—"

She nodded.

"But I have something to say first. Will you please look at me?" Footsteps came closer, that scent so uniquely his, so close behind her.

Emily turned. Her lips parted in horror at his bruised and bleeding face.

"Godric, you've been hurt!" She reached up to his face but did not touch, afraid to harm him further. He patted her hands and she winced at his bruised knuckles. For a long second neither of them spoke. Something between them had changed. She was forced to admit she cared about him and he was revealing a tenderness she hadn't thought he was capable of. His eyes met hers, a spark shared between them and a blush heated her cheeks.

"What happened?"

"Ashton and I had a discussion. A rather thorough one."

He kissed her hands and released them then pointed to the bed. A stack of books had toppled over in a small literary heap. There had to be at least eight. Curiosity got the best of her. She climbed onto the bed to peruse the titles. It was an unexpected pleasure to find that he'd brought her more than she'd asked for. Emily dared not look at him, her eyes still red from the weight of tears. Instead she turned her attention to the gift he'd brought and what it might mean.

When she climbed up onto the bed, Godric wanted to catch hold of her from behind. She looked irresistible with the loose curls of hair on her neck and the sway of her bottom. She moved with the grace of a wood nymph. He knew she would be a playful bed partner, eager and delightful in her moments of rapture. *What the blazes is wrong with me?*

He fought off the heady rush of desire and focused on her. Emily's hands caressed the covers of each book, her eyes roving over the selection, oblivious to him. Godric feared he would ruin the moment if he joined her, but decided to take the chance. He eased himself on the edge of the bed nearest her while she sorted the books into piles.

"I brought a little of everything. I was unsure as to your preference."

Emily tucked up her skirts around her knees as she folded her legs to sit more comfortably.

"Philosophy, art, gothic romances, sciences." She scanned the piles with such delight that Godric expected snow to fall outside, for her eyes lit up like a child's during Christmas. He wished in that moment he was a poet or an artist, so desperate was he to capture the beauty of Emily's soul. Her eyes flicked up to meet his, a blush coloring her face. In the afternoon light he could make out the faintest smattering of freckles across the bridge of her nose. Most women would have hidden them with powder. Not Emily, she bore them without a thought. He adored that about her, she did not dwell on what other women would have seen as flaws.

"I'm intrigued by your choices. What makes you think I would be interested in science or philosophy?"

"You struck me as an intellectual reader, not one prone to frivolous reading such as books on sewing or manners."

"Manners?" Emily scoffed. "A rather bold claim coming from you. But these are all excellent choices. However, you've brought me too many." She pushed them all away save one, *The Iliad and The Odyssey*.

Godric leaned over and with the sweep of his arm brought the books back. "Consider the rest a prelude to my apology." He caught her chin in one hand, his thumb sweeping over her chin and up to outline the bottom of her lower lip.

"You are apologizing?"

"Yes, and not just for what I said earlier, but for everything—the abduction, the lake and the laudanum. All of it." He meant it too. Hurting her seemed akin to stabbing his own heart and he couldn't bear it. She was weakening him, and he should send her away before she destroyed his solitary life. But the thought of not seeing her was equally incomprehensible. She leaned into his caress, like a cat seeking affection. That simple action seared him with a heated pleasure.

"Don't apologize for everything." Her lashes fluttered as she looked at him, a secretive smile on her lips.

"I've not wronged you by all my actions then?" He laughed.

"Not *all* your actions." She studied the book she held, then opened the pages and sighed.

"My mistake: I forgot you could not read Greek." Godric reached for the novel she held. While the title was typeset in English, the text itself was entirely in Greek.

"This is one of my favorite stories. My father never cared for novels, but he loved the classics and would read this one to me often." She held it out to him. "Would you read it to me?"

"But you won't be able to understand it. I suppose I could translate it for you." He took the book from her curiously.

"I know the story by heart in English, and if you just read it aloud to me in Greek, I can imagine it myself and follow along. Consider it another part of your apology."

Godric stretched out on the bed and Emily joined him, curling her body up against him, her head on his shoulder. He let the book fall open to the first page, took a deep breath, and began to read.

The next hour passed in soft sunlight and the murmur of a foreign tongue. He was a child again, reveling in the pleasure of a well-told tale and the comfort of Emily's presence. He cherished the innocent fall of her head on his shoulder and tucked her against him by wrapping one arm around her waist.

When he reached a good stopping point, he marked his place with the purple satin bookmark and set it aside, turning his attention to Emily. How long had it been since he'd spent time with a woman on a bed, sharing an intimate moment that didn't end in the shedding of clothes? Too long. This moment contained a fullness, a ripeness, that gave him a bottomless sense of peace. But something this grand and enchantingly perfect could never last.

He didn't deserve her.

He wasn't worthy of love, especially not Emily's.

She'd return to her uncle and be married to that horrible Blankenship fellow just to settle a debt. Surely there had to be a way to save her from such a fate, but he couldn't think of one. It was impossible to make her his mistress. She'd find him unworthy and her disappointment would kill him. Could he marry her? Offer her a life uncertain of love? Godric forced himself to stop thinking of something so wretched and tried to turn his mind elsewhere.

"Shall we go to dinner?" His breath stirred her hair.

She tilted her face up, lips brushing his so lightly it was more a memory of a kiss. "Yes."

Emily moved away and in that moment Godric's heart leapt to follow her. What if she was his, not just now, but always?

A potent yearning gnawed deep in him for such a life. The despair that followed required Godric to quiet the unfamiliar urge to rage and cry all at once, and master himself again.

He still needed to make sure she would not fall for him. It shouldn't be too hard—he just had to be himself.

Chapter Seven

Ready to return to her room after dinner, Emily rose from her chair. "Do I have your permission to retire, Your Grace?"

Godric caught her by her right arm, tugging her right onto his lap. She ought to have struggled, she knew that, but she found it nearly impossible to summon any will to get away. It seemed her heart had finally decided to fight against her head.

"Will you stay in your room as you promised?"

"I promise I won't escape tonight." She tried to remove herself from his lap. "I gave my word."

He grunted softly and grabbed her by the back of the neck, bringing her mouth towards his. He kissed her deeply, almost primitively, with a harsh penetration of his tongue. Her body melted against his fire.

Ashton cleared his throat.

Emily wrenched her face away, embarrassed he would treat her like this in front of the others. She tried to slap Godric, but he caught her hand.

"I've had enough bruises for one day. I won't let you slap me. Remember that, Emily."

"I am not a fast lady. You cannot go about manhandling me."

"She has you there." Ashton snickered into his wine glass.

Godric ignored him, his full attention on her, her hand still raised, and his still holding it back. There was something in his gaze, a wildness born of his desire to chase her.

"May I go now, Your Grace?"

"You may." She started to pull free but he prevented it. "If you give me another kiss goodnight."

He flashed her that smug grin, and she really did want to hit him. Emily was beginning to despise her confusion when it came to Godric.

"Very well, although in my opinion you've had far too many kisses today, Your Grace."

She leaned down to kiss his forehead. He caught her chin and brought her mouth further down to meet his. Her raised hand dropped to his shoulder as he delved into her mouth with his tongue. It was so easy for the world to fade when he kissed like that. *Damn him.*

Godric's arm around her waist tightened, but that called her back to reality, and she wriggled free of his grasp.

"Fine, go."

His treatment of her only reaffirmed her belief that she would be nothing more than a mistress, a body to warm his bed. He didn't respect her the way he would a wife. Then again, there was no guarantee he'd respect a wife. His reputation was shadowed with tales of seducing married women away from their cold marriage beds. Obviously, he had no concern for the sanctity of marriage. Which meant even if he married someone like her, he'd most likely continue on with his affairs. The thought was sickening.

But something teased at the edge of the realm of possibilities. What if...what if she could get him to fall in love with her? If she found a way to make him realize she wasn't like other women, that she was perfect for him. She'd be with a man who wanted her.

She passed Simkins in the hallway on the way to her room. "Mr. Simkins? Could I trouble you to send up a maid to help me undress?"

"I shall have Mrs. Downing send someone up," the butler said, and Emily thanked him.

Her room was dark in the purpled evening light as she sat at her vanity table, planning. The question was how did one seduce the master seducer? The chase. He loved the chase, and if she was honest, she rather enjoyed it as well. Was that the answer?

Minutes later, Libba knocked and entered with a broad smile. "Evening, Miss."

"Libba, please call me Emily. I should like to be friends." She rotated in her chair to smile at the maid.

"But it wouldn't be proper, Miss."

"There is nothing about this situation that is proper, Libba. Now, please, let us be friends. I have no one here to talk to."

"Talk? I can certainly do that, Miss...Emily. Now, let me get you out of that dress." Libba's hands were nimble as she helped Emily rid herself of her clothes and step into a white muslin night rail, which flared out past her calves like the petals of a moonflower. More of her figure was outlined than she would have liked due to its thinness.

Being around a woman her age made Emily feel more comfortable. She grinned at the maid.

"What gossip is there downstairs? I'd love to hear more about His Grace and his friends."

Libba's cheeks reddened. "Well, I heard from Bethany, who heard from His Grace's valet, Jonathan, that Lord Lennox beat His Grace something dreadful over a slight he made against you this afternoon."

"But...you mean to tell me they were fighting over me?" She recalled Godric's bruised knuckles, beaten face and split lip. She hadn't forgotten Ashton's knuckle bruises, or his black eye, but it was clear Ashton had been the victor.

"Jonathan also said he heard Lord Lennox threaten to kill His Grace if he ever made you cry again!"

"Really? That seems to be a bit of an overreaction, but Ashton is sweet."

Libba chuckled. "All of those men are sweet on you. You best watch out or His Grace will act on his desire for you to share his bed, just to keep the others from winning you away."

"Thank you for the warning, Libba." She hadn't considered that. If she were to play the men off each other, she might end up in Godric's bed quicker than she intended.

"I'll go now." Libba shared a conspiratorial smile before she left.

Alone again, Emily crossed to the window and gazed out at the view below. The garden stretched out below it. Mazes of hedges and flowered bushes still clung to their blooming petals despite the approaching fall.

A vine-coated trellis had been constructed six feet below the lip of her window, and next to the trellis, on the ground floor, a window that looked into one of the parlors.

"Admiring the view, or contemplating escape?" Godric's voice drifted through the room behind her. Her blood heated at the very rumble of his sensual voice.

How long had he watched? Attempting to conceal her surprise, Emily didn't turn around. He was too quiet; she'd have to remember that.

This time his steps padded barefoot across the floor.

"I made a promise, if you'll recall. I was admiring the view, unless that isn't allowed?" She turned to face him.

"That is allowed, so long as admiring the view doesn't entail you falling out of the window. The height is too great to make a safe leap. It would be a nasty way to snap those beautiful legs of yours," Godric said, in a mockingly tragic tone.

"A few broken bones might be worth my freedom." She raised her chin, hiding the urge to smile.

"I'd like to see how far you got on broken legs. Quite painful, I'm told." He stared at her seriously.

"Is...is that a threat, Your Grace?"

"What?" His eyes widened. "No! Of course not. I would never... I was simply trying to protect you..." he trailed off she when she laughed lightly. She was teasing him.

Godric chuckled and came towards her. He'd lost quite a few layers of clothing since dinner. Gone were the waistcoat, boots and cravat. He stood in her bedchamber clad only in breeches and a white lawn shirt, the sleeves rolled up past his elbows. He approached her and leaned casually against the wall a few inches from her, warmly surveying her body from head to toe.

With a flush she remembered she wore nothing more than a night rail. Hands flew over her chest as she turned her back to him.

"Avert your eyes, sir!"

He didn't obey. "Took you long enough to notice...and might I say that this view is just as delightful as the front," he purred, a step closer, one finger tracing the curve of her spine.

Emily repressed an achy shiver. "You made it very clear earlier that you had no interest in a kissing a child; and if that is what I am, then don't mock me with threats of your lust." Her irritation had returned, pressing against her chest.

Her harsh reply brought Godric's temper to the surface. "Bloody hell, Emily, I apologized!"

She whirled on him, jabbing a finger in his chest. "And I accepted your apology, but that doesn't mean you can change your mind and waltz in here!"

"Like hell I can't!" He snagged her wrists with one hand, forcing them up over her head as he pinned her against the window with the length of his body.

"Let go of me or I'll scream!" She tried to break his hold on her wrists, but his hand ensnared them tightly above her head.

"Scream. I dare you. Who will come?"

In mere hours he'd gone from prince to villain. She wasn't frightened, only furious. He thought he was entitled to her, but after the way he'd treated her in his study, he deserved no cooperation, not unless he groveled...on his knees...for at least an hour.

She tensed as he pressed himself against her. His other hand dug at her chemise near her thighs, dragging it up so he could push one of his own muscular thighs between her legs. Emily fought to keep her knees together, but he was too strong.

"Oh!" she gasped as he thrust his thigh hard against the soft melting core between her legs. Her head fell back against the wall as her body shivered.

"Godric, please...please, I..." She tried to speak but he wasn't in the mood to listen. She wasn't even sure what she was trying to say. His mouth came down on hers, rough, unyielding and brief. He kept her against the wall, his forehead falling against hers as he took a deep breath.

"Would it be so bad for you to just enjoy your time here? Why keep looking for ways to escape?"

He lifted his eyes up to hers. The two were so close; bodies almost entangled. The hand that held her wrists pinned above her head tightened a little as he shifted his body, trying to move even closer.

"Let me show you a reason to stay..."

Godric nuzzled her jaw until his lips found her neck, planting seeds of heat with his faint kisses. Emily raised her chin, providing Godric a better angle to torture her with the sensation of his lips on skin. His arousal dug into her belly, to which she responded with a sharp, throbbing need.

"It isn't fair. You're distracting me," she gasped as he cupped a breast through her thin chemise, toying with her hardened nipple.

"Nothing in life is fair, my sweet. Shall we continue on?" He flicked his head towards the door that led to his bedroom, and that single gesture killed all the helpless desire in her.

"No," she said firmly, expecting him to release her. When he didn't, she looked at the doorway of her bedroom, wondering the length of time it would take someone to break it down if it were locked.

"No? Are you sure?" He raised his thigh between her legs, increasing the pressure on her aching core. She stifled a moan as he did it again, quicker this time. "I said... Are you sure?" A crooked smile crossed his lips when he realized he had robbed her of the ability to speak in clear words rather than moans. His hand on her breast slid down along her belly towards the juncture between her thighs, coiling the fabric of her night rail up again. The instant his fingers reached the aching spot between her legs she cried out, her voice carrying loudly.

Her shout shocked some sense into Godric. He released her immediately and stepped away just as Ashton burst into her doorway. He took one look at the scene and spoke to Godric in Greek.

"I thought you had yourself under control. You said you could manage this." Ashton took a step towards Godric, who dug his hands through his hair.

"She... I may not be as in control as I thought."

Ashton looked at Emily's firmly closed window and her state of undress with narrowed eyes. "If she resisted you?"

"No, she hasn't..." Godric lied.

"I did not agree either," Emily said in flawless Greek.

Both men looked at her, mouths agape.

"You lied about the Greek?" asked Godric.

"*Erre Es Korokas!*" She snapped out. *Go to the crows.*

Godric wrenched her away from the wall. "What else have you lied about?"

Ashton took a sharp step forward, his hand raised, as if to say, *No, Godric, let her go.* But he seemed to have his own issues with her deception. "Emily, you lied to me, the one person in this house who stood up to Godric for you. I asked for the truth and you repay me with lies?"

"That was before I trusted any of you...when I still felt myself to be at risk!"

Ashton's eyes were as dark as the sea at night. "Did you ever think you were truly in danger? We never meant for you to feel that way."

"You abducted me, drugged me. What did you expect? You may not be my enemies, but forgive me if I don't consider those the actions of friends." Her eyes burned but she didn't cry. "What would you do in my position?"

"Were you... Did you lie to me this afternoon, when you gave me your word?"

"No. That was the truth, on my father's grave, wherever in the sea it may be. I shall not try to escape tonight."

Ashton was silent for an eternally long moment.

"I believe you. But I can no longer stand between you and Godric, not tonight at any rate. Please...don't call for me again." Ashton turned and left, shutting the door behind him.

Emily's knees shook. Her only protector had abandoned her.

Godric jerked her towards the small door that led to his room. Emily dug her heels into the floor and tried in vain to stop him.

"Go ahead and fight me! I'll take your rage and turn it into passion!" Godric cast her to the floor and locked the small door, sealing her inside his chamber.

Would he really force himself? She didn't expect cruelty, but Godric had changed. This wasn't the man who read to her this afternoon.

The duke gripped her upper arms and yanked her to her feet. She looked at him, cold and unflinching even as she shook in his arms.

"Go ahead, Godric. What are you waiting for? Prove to me what sort of man you are. Prove to me that you are just the same as Blankenship." His fingers dug into her arms.

"I am nothing like that old cretin, you hear me?"

"Taking me by force would make you the same as him in the eyes of the law and God."

Godric's eyes changed. "Take you by force? Emily...you may be shaking right now and confused, but that's desire, not fear. Blankenship could never stir those feelings you have at this moment."

She knew it was the truth.

"The man I want is the man who read *The Odyssey* to me this afternoon." She softened her tone. "Find that man again and I'll reconsider."

His eyes were like the leaves of English rosebushes. "There's a darkness in me that I can't always fight." His voice was barely above a whisper, as if he didn't fully understand it himself.

Emily saw that understanding was within reach. "I'm not asking for a saint, Godric. I'm asking for time... Time for us both to understand what we are to each other and what we want."

His grip on her arms loosened and he finally let go. "How is it that you are so young but so wise?"

"I was raised by two loving parents who educated me well."

"So you are correcting more of your lies then?"

"Yes, I am very, very well educated. I speak fluent Greek and Latin. You didn't know about the Latin, so I am telling you now, out of good faith. I've ridden horses all my life and am an excellent swimmer."

At that Godric started. "About that... I may have faked my drowning at the lake." He waited for her to explode into a rage, but she didn't. "You knew?"

"Your eagerness upon your recovery had raised my suspicions. The recently drowned are not usually so lively." She sighed and eased back, to sit on the edge of his bed.

He came over and sat down, then casually slid his hand over hers, lacing their fingers together. He raised their joined hands and held them against his chest. This was not an attempt at seduction. Somehow, in the midst of these confessions, they had reached a kind of understanding.

"Sleep with me tonight?" he asked. Emily started to shake her head but he added, "No. Just sleep, that is all. Just let me have you near. I want to hear you breathing, feel your warmth. Please..."

The word 'please' shuddered on his lips and Emily nodded in agreement, even though she hadn't meant to. How could he always do that?

He cupped her shoulders in his palms and gently guided her back to the edge of the bed. Pinning her with his hips, he claimed her surprised mouth in a kiss, a long, exploring one that bore no resemblance to earlier.

Ashton's words replayed in Emily's mind, and she let the emotion she'd held back flood through her, into him once more. His arms wound around her lower back, pressing her tightly to him before he stopped.

"It's going to take me some time to get used to that way of kissing..." he murmured against her lips.

Emily almost smiled. "Maybe if you adjust to me, I can adjust to you." She thought of his rough caress with dark fire behind it, and she realized she wanted it no matter how overwhelming.

"It seems we will both learn."

Godric swept her up into his arms, and settled her on the far side of the bed.

Emily felt a brief flare of concern, but Godric merely shut his eyes. "Goodnight, my little vixen."

She lay still for a long while before she rolled on her side for comfort. Feeling strangely protected, she drifted asleep.

Well past midnight, Godric woke to Emily talking in her sleep. She shifted restlessly, her murmurings soft and pitiful.

"Stop...please. I beg you... Let me alone..." Godric's stomach churned in response to the helplessness that underlay her tone. She was dreaming and he hoped to God it wasn't about him.

"Emily?" He moved over to touch her shoulders. She flinched, and struck out at her unseen assailant. "Emily!"

"I'll die before you touch me!" she snarled. Godric almost released his hold on her but he wanted to wake her from that dream.

"Emily, it's Godric. Please wake up..." He wrapped his arms around her and slid her across the bed more fully into his embrace.

"Godric..."

"Yes, it's me. You're safe." He kissed her lips, trying to kiss her the way she had him in the study. He wanted to promise her that no harm would come to her. Those long dark lashes flared out on her cheeks as she opened her eyes. "Emily? Are you awake?"

"I am now... Why..." She stared confusedly at his mouth; her little tongue darted out to lick her lips.

"You were talking in your sleep. Who were you dreaming about?"

"Blankenship. He haunts me even in my dreams."

Godric exhaled in relief.

"Did you think I was dreaming about you?"

"After my recent behavior, I feared you might be." The admission filled him with concern. In the darkness of his room and the warmth of her body in his arms, he wanted only the truth between them.

"You would never really hurt me, Godric, I know that now. But I won't surrender to you." Emily paused as if a plan had occurred to her. "I could compromise, though."

Godric was genuinely surprised. "Your terms?"

"I can promise not to escape between the hours of ten in the evening to six in the morning. That way you and your friends will have your beauty sleep with no fear of disruption."

"Beauty sleep? Why, you little..." He pinched her waist and she offered a mock indignant gasp. "And you expect me to agree? What do I get in return?" His hand slid lower down over the curve of her hip. He relished the breathless sigh that escaped her mouth when he tightened his grasp.

"You get sleep and I promise an escapeless eight hours. That is a fair bargain," Emily said.

He groaned. "And an escape-filled sixteen hours."

"Well, if you insist on being a pessimist that's not my concern."

Godric shifted closer, pressing against her. "Sleep with me every night. Promise that, and I'll agree."

"And by 'sleep' do you mean innocent and harmless sleep?"

The mischievous gleam mixed with moonlight in her eyes fascinated him.

"Hmm...yes, but if you want things to change, I'm ready to oblige you."

"Of that I have no doubt," Emily murmured, yawning, her fist covering her mouth. She tried to roll onto her back, but Godric rolled her so that her body spooned up against his. He buried his face in her hair, the scent soft and floral as a garden. The long ago day when he'd first seen her returned—the woman kneeling in the garden, flowers ringed around her, a butterfly dancing about her head while she weeded. Godric's lips twitched. He felt like that butterfly, seeking the comfort of her presence.

"I can't believe I'm allowing this..." Her voice was barely a whisper.

"Give me time and you'll never want to leave." He kissed the soft skin on the nape of her neck and she sighed, almost entirely asleep. Godric wanted her so badly, but he kept control and counted backwards from a hundred in Greek. *Ekato, eneida enia, eneida okto, eneida efta...*

Chapter Eight

Godric was having the most wonderful dream. Emily lay curled up in his arms, finding warmth and protection from her nightmares. He had rarely slept with his former mistress, Evangeline. While she was a wicked temptress in bed, she was an awful partner to lie next to at night. She kicked, snored and stole the covers too frequently for him to enjoy the experience.

His dream was too real and perfect. There was nothing carnal about the act, only the comfort of Emily's body entwined with his. Her face was pressed into the groove between his throat and chest, her body halfway on top of him, lounging asleep with that feline grace only women possessed.

The coils of her hair were a russet waterfall against the pillow, and sunlight slid down the waves in enticing patterns. One of his arms curled around her waist, keeping her close. In this world Emily was his. She belonged to no one else, and he didn't have to share her with the world.

Unfortunately, Emily didn't want to belong to him. Why did she have to be so damned independent? If she'd only surrender herself Godric could make her the most satisfied women in the world. He'd buy her the most expensive gowns, the richest jewels, and all the horses she could ever desire. He wanted her more than anything in his life.

He wished she wouldn't fight him with such determination. Emily didn't seem particularly protective of her virtue. It was her freedom she clung to. He'd caged her in his manor, and the thought irritated him. Even if it was a cage, it was only a temporary one, and a gilded, luxurious one at that. Why couldn't she be happy?

Emily would never be satisfied unless she was the sole controller of her destiny. But as a young, unmarried woman, she stood no chance of that. A man held the reins over her fate, the only question was which one.

But if she let him take control, he'd promise to make her happy.

Godric was still thinking when Emily started to wake. Her breath quickened and her chest rose faster beneath his palm. Her legs tensed slightly as her muscles came to life. Emily rested her chin on his chest as her lashes fanned open.

"Good morning, Emily." He brushed her loose hair back from her face, absorbed in the sight of her fluttering lashes and parted pink lips. Her sleepy expression warmed him right down to his toes as she snuggled against him.

She blushed, shutting her eyes. "I actually slept here, didn't I?"

"Don't be sorry. Enjoy the fact that we spent an innocent night together. It is something I have never been able to guarantee any other woman."

One of her brows arched. "Is that because I'm no temptation or because you've learned some self-restraint?"

"It's because I respect you enough to not break my promise. But now you're awake, so all bets are off, my dear."

"What do you mean by that?" She started to push away from him.

"I'm allowed sixteen hours of seduction in order to distract you from escaping." Godric grasped her tightly and rolled over, covering her body with his. "Let me kiss you good morning, Emily—just one kiss?" He'd shared no moment like this with any woman before and he wanted it with Emily. He needed to thread his fingers in her sleep-mussed hair and feather kisses on her eyelids.

Eyes wide, she flushed but nodded. "One...one kiss, Godric," she whispered.

He didn't need any urging. His mouth found hers at the same time his hand slid inside her night rail. The delicious heat of her skin beneath his palm doubled the throbbing between his legs. He prayed he could hold himself together long enough to see to her pleasure.

Emily flinched as Godric's hand glided up between her thighs. His fingers touched her sensitive folds and stroked the hot wet flesh. When the pad of his thumb skimmed her swollen bud, she jerked. The sensation terrified her. It was almost too much for her.

A sweet tension built there, mirroring the rough possession of Godric's mouth on hers.

She focused on the movement of his tongue in her mouth and tried to imitate it, learn the savage play he sought to teach her. But she was distracted by the hardened length pressing down against her right hip.

His fingers continued to gently brush over her sensitive mons.

"Do you burn for me?" Godric whispered against her mouth.

"What? No..." She tried to deny it.

His lips curved into a smile and he sank his teeth into her bottom lip.

Emily whimpered, straining against him. "Please..."

"Please what?"

She choked down a little sob as tension continued to pool between her legs. "I don't know..."

Godric's other hand wound into her hair and pulled her head back. He exposed her throat as his mouth moved to her neck, and his fingers rubbed on that tender bud. Emily couldn't stop her hips from rolling in small circles against his hand. Blood pumped through her as the pressure and tingling turned to sharp pangs of physical excitement. Like gliding higher and higher on a swing, until she succumbed at last to the breathtaking drop. She cried out.

His laughter warmed her neck. His kisses returned to her startled lips when he withdrew his hand from between her legs and laid it on her bare hip. The touch was both possessive and sweet. His thumb smoothed tiny circles on her skin just below her waist and she resisted the urge to laugh at the ticklish sensation.

He rubbed his cheek against hers, his night beard scraping her skin. "How did you like your little kiss?"

Emily breathed in his scent, completely sated. "I liked it very much, but I think you cheated, Your Grace." She gave him an advantage with such an answer, but right now, she couldn't think clearly enough to lie.

"I cannot deny cheating was involved." The devil had the nerve to wink at her. "Every night and every morning I will kiss you."

Emily opened her mouth but he pressed a finger to her lips. "Now don't protest. You will be safe each night in my arms. I have enough restraint to stop." He sat up and released her. Emily should've scrambled off the bed but she couldn't. Her legs would give out and she'd fall right back into his arms.

He chuckled. "I thought for sure you'd flee my bed the moment I let you up."

"I...I see no need to hurry." Emily attempted to hide her unsteadiness. She tugged her night rail down to cover herself and looked at him, hoping he'd let her go.

After what she'd just experienced, she needed a good, long time alone.

Godric allowed Emily to slip into her own room. He shut his door to offer some privacy.

Even though he had not found his own release, there existed pleasure in knowing he had been the first man to touch Emily in that fashion. It put a spring in his step as he dressed for the day and made his way down to the breakfast room. He caught Simkins in the hallway and gave him instructions to send a maid to Emily.

"I trust Miss Parr is well?"

Godric didn't miss the concern in the elderly butler's face. "Yes, she is well. I take it you heard her cry out last night. Well, be at ease Simkins. The lady is fine."

"That is good, Your Grace. I trust nothing shall make Miss Parr angry or scared enough to call out in such a fashion again." A soft admonishment hid behind the butler's tone. Only Simkins could take that tone with him.

"I can't promise she won't call out again. Her temper and independence make her a feisty creature. Tell the servants they mustn't go to her, except for Libba who will see to her personal needs. Emily is my responsibility."

"But, Your Grace—"

"No buts, Simkins. If Emily is shouting, she is getting whatever she deserves, good or ill." Godric was firm on this point. Emily's seduction required daily doses of wickedness. He didn't want her to clear her head. Logic always ruined passion's best moments.

"Very well, Your Grace. Lord Sheridan and Lord Lonsdale rode to London last night, and they returned early this morning. I believe Lord Sheridan wished to speak with you about a present he brought for Miss Parr?"

"What the devil is he playing at?" Regardless of Rule Four, the thought of any man trying to woo Emily with gifts boiled his blood. "Trying to outdo me? I bought her a bloody wardrobe."

"Perhaps, Your Grace, you ought to wait and see what it is."

Was Simkins smiling as he left? Godric scowled as he followed the butler into the breakfast room. Cedric, already eating, still seemed possessed of boundless energy, despite the fact that he'd only slept for a few hours.

"Did Simkins tell you about my gift for Emily?" An irritatingly hopeful gleam in Cedric's brown eyes left Godric distinctly uncomfortable.

Godric crossed his arms over his chest. "What did you buy for her?"

"A puppy. An English foxhound."

Godric didn't know whether or not to laugh. "A dog? What good will a foxhound do her? She's not going to be hunting." What was a girl to do with a puppy, especially a hunting dog at that? Didn't most women prefer cats? A kitten would have been a smarter choice if Cedric wanted to woo the young lady. Then again, as she was fond of pointing out, Emily wasn't most women.

"I know what you're thinking, Godric, but this is more than just a present. The dog will bark and yip and follow her about. She may stop trying to escape if she doesn't want to leave the dog behind."

Godric considered this. "You might have a point there, Cedric."

"Wonderful!" Cedric jumped out of his chair eagerly. "May I bring it to the breakfast room when she comes down?"

"I suppose." Godric took a seat and started to prepare himself a plate as Cedric vanished.

Ashton arrived at the table without a word. It troubled Godric deeply to see his friend's usually vibrant eyes so muted and dark, his healing black eye aside.

"Ash?" Godric asked.

Ashton set down his coffee cup, folded his hands and looked up at Godric. "Well?"

"Well what?"

"Did you finish what you started with Emily or did you find some mercy in that black heart of yours?"

His friend's accusation wounded him, but much like their boxing match, one he knew he deserved. "Ash, I did not harm her after you left. There was a bit of yelling, I admit, but I cooled off, or rather she cooled my temper off."

"Why do I find that hard to believe?" Ashton muttered.

"I swear it. She is still as innocent as the day she was born... Well, more or less."

Ashton's eyes narrowed. "Swear to me on the stones of Magdalene College." The stones of their college at Cambridge were the foundation of the League's relationship. An oath upon them was tantamount to swearing on the Bible.

"I swear on the stones."

Ashton's shoulders slumped with relief. "Thank God. I lay awake all night worrying that I'd done the wrong thing, leaving her with you. You had that glint in your eye."

"She worked me up into a good temper but calmed me just as easily. We have worked out a bargain."

"Oh?" Ashton slid a tray of toast in Godric's direction.

"Emily vows she won't make any escape attempts between the hours of ten at night and six in the morning."

"And what did she get out of that arrangement?"

"My solemn promise not to seduce her between those hours. The rest of the day is fair game."

"My, my, Godric, you came out on top of that bargain, didn't you?" Ashton had returned to his usual lighthearted countenance.

The door to the breakfast room opened once more as Lucien strolled in, Emily at his side. Ashton and Godric rose to their feet as she took a seat next to Godric. Her green dress, the shade of summer grass, lit up her lilac colored eyes. The gown's sleeves were loosely puffed about her shoulders, and gathered at her back in gentle pleats that were not severe on her form, as other dresses might be. It displayed Emily's natural beauty by accenting her curves and the maid had pulled Emily's hair into a loose tangle, gathered back by green ribbons.

"So, did everyone have a good evening? I thought I heard sounds of a party..." Lucien watched Emily and Godric as he sat next to Ashton on the other side of the table. "In fact, if I didn't know better—" Ashton kicked him sharply, and Lucien winced. "I've been informed that I do not."

Emily reached for a plate near Ashton's elbow. He immediately passed it to her; she blushed. Godric noticed her look and rose from the table, catching Lucien's eye.

"I say, Lucien, have you spoken to Cedric? I thought we might go see what has become of him...and rouse Charles, no doubt still asleep." Godric started for the door.

Lucien sighed and followed him. "I suppose."

"May I...may I have an audience with you, my lord?" Emily tried to keep her voice from shaking, but failed.

"Of course, Miss Parr," Ashton replied.

She bit her bottom lip. How Ashton must hate her, if he refused to call her by her given name.

"My lord, about last night..." She swallowed hard. She hated apologizing, especially for something she felt she'd done right. But an apology was worth her new friend. Somewhere between her capture and this moment, she'd grown fond of the cool, collected baron. He was kind and courteous and had defended her honor.

"Please, Miss Parr, don't distress yourself on such a small matter." His tone was reassuring, but she needed him to understand. She needed to know he wouldn't abandon her again.

"I...I am sorry that I lied to you. I shouldn't have."

I should hate them. I should wish them dead for what they've done. But the rage wouldn't come. The short span of time she'd been in their company, she had been strangely happy. Godric had shown her passion, the others companionship. She couldn't let lies, even lies to secure her freedom, ruin her bond with them. How such a thing was possible she did not know.

"Miss Parr, it is I who seeks forgiveness. You did what was necessary to protect yourself from unscrupulous rakehells." Ashton pushed his chair back walked over to her. He grasped her hands between his, holding them against his chest. "I would have acted no different in the same circumstances. I daresay I'd have done worse."

"Then...then you are not angry, my lord?"

"Miss Parr—"

"Please, don't call me that!"

"Emily, you were forgiven the moment I left your room last night."

Her heat lilted, confused. "Then why were you so quiet this morning?"

"I feared you'd not forgiven me for abandoning you. Did he harm you?" Ashton pulled Emily up on her feet and spun her around, as though inspecting her for obvious signs of harm, but there were none.

117

"He yelled dreadfully, but he didn't hurt me. My lord—"

"Ashton."

"Ashton, if you ever ask me for the truth, you shall have it."

Ashton smiled. "I have but one question, my dear."

"Yes?"

"How many other languages are you fluent in?"

Emily was overcome by the surge of happiness. He appreciated her intelligence where her uncle had not. "I am fluent in Greek and Latin... I am passable in French, German and Spanish."

"Not Italian?" His lips quirked into a crooked smile.

"Italian? No, I suppose it's similar enough to Latin that I might make out some of it, but not enough to be fluent."

"Ah, good, a language I can use against you, should I need to." Ashton chucked her under her chin as Godric and Lucien returned to breakfast.

Accepting the hot chocolate Godric once again served her, Emily settled herself back into her seat and relished the dark, exotic aroma. The kindness presented here was genuine and because of the rapport between them, she grudgingly forgave the kidnapping, and all that had come after it.

Despite the sometimes-rough treatment, Emily was still better off in the League's care than under her uncle's suffocating rule—or, worse, the fate she'd face with his business partner.

After breakfast, Emily rose but Godric put a hand on her arm.

"Stay. Cedric will be down soon, and he has a gift for you."

Lucien and Ashton both looked up in surprise.

Emily's eyes filled with shy disbelief. "Cedric brought me a gift?"

"Yes, he has." Godric found a smile, but not without difficulty.

It was strange that he should be angry with Emily's excitement. Godric knew her uncle had been less than kind when providing for her, but he had begun to notice just how poorly Albert treated her in the past year. The young woman deserved fine gowns, and embroidered pelisses, not threadbare dresses or worn slippers. He should be glad to see this childlike curiosity flare up in his Emily. But it hadn't come from him.

Five minutes later, Charles entered, followed by Cedric, who held a large blue hatbox. Charles shot an impish grin at Emily as she nearly bounced in her chair.

She looked to Godric. He nodded and she leapt up.

Cedric bowed and held out the large box, setting it down at her feet. "A gift for you, kitten." The box shook and Emily stepped back. Godric wrapped one arm around her waist to comfort her.

"Did it just move? What have you brought me?" Her hands rested lightly on Godric's arm.

Godric put his lips to her ear. "Open it and find out."

The men watched with fascination as she untied the loose string that held the box lid.

The lid popped off and a puppy's head peeked out, a blue satin bow around its neck. Its tail wagged so hard its little body shook. The puppy's fur was white, its ears a warm reddish brown, and its muzzle white, tapering into an elegant line up the puppy's nose and between her furry eyebrows. It was far too chubby now, but it would grow into a lean white-legged hound.

Emily didn't say a word, but she dabbed at her eyes. His friends looked aghast at her reaction.

"You don't like her?" Cedric knelt across from her, his fists clenching against his thighs, as though he fought off a wave of frustration and disappointment.

"Not like her?" Emily scooped up the wagging pup and shoved it toward Godric, who barely had time to grasp the puppy before she embraced Cedric.

Godric glowered as she placed a light, excited kiss on Cedric's face. The poor rake was blushing deeply by the time she released him and reclaimed her gift from Godric. The puppy's pink tongue lapped her chin as she held it up to her face. Never in all of Godric's life had he been jealous of a dog.

Cedric ruffled his hand through the puppy's fur. "She's an English foxhound. She'll need a lot of daily exercise, but she'll be the best hunter and the most loyal companion you'll ever have."

"You are utterly darling, my little Penelope." Emily bestowed a kiss on the puppy's head.

"Penelope?" Charles asked.

Emily shot Godric a bashful look. "Yes, Odysseus's loyal wife."

He blinked in surprise. She'd chosen a name from the story they'd shared yesterday afternoon. An odd warmth settled in his chest.

"Do you want to take her out for a walk now?" Cedric asked.

"May I, Godric? Please?" Emily freed one hand from Penelope to tug on Godric's sleeve.

"If Cedric and Charles join you." She missed his wink at Cedric as they shared a mutual triumph over the gift.

The pup had curbed Emily's urge to flee. It was clear she wouldn't bear to leave behind her Penelope. The puppy squirmed in Emily's arms and she looked upon it with such happiness that Godric wanted to buy her a thousand more to ensure that look would never leave her face.

Other women might not have been so sweetly lost in joy over such a simple gift—they would have wished for jewels and gowns, but Emily treasured books and faithful animals, not glittering trinkets and fine silk gowns.

"Shall we go?" Cedric asked and, with a delighted "yes" from Emily, the three left the breakfast room.

Lucien and Ashton stayed and turned their attention to Godric.

Lucien smirked. "Leave it to Cedric to buy Emily's affection and trick her into staying." The others chuckled.

"Yes, I wonder if he's tried that little trick with Anne Chessley yet," Ashton mused.

"He'd have to buy that woman a horse, a good one, before she'd even begin to take him seriously," Godric said.

They chuckled at the idea of Cedric trying to woo a woman who knew more than him about horses by buying her one. It surely would end in disaster.

"Well, onto more pressing matters I'm afraid," Godric said. "I have to return to London for at least the rest of the day."

"Oh?" Ashton's brows arched. Godric understood his friend's reaction. He loathed leaving Emily alone.

"Yes, I need to tidy up some affairs with my properties. I must visit my solicitor, and I thought I might pay a discreet visit to Albert Parr."

"What do you mean to say to him?" Lucien asked.

"You ought to be cautious, Godric, now that Blankenship is on our trail," Ashton said. "They're surely both trying to prove you abducted Emily. Keep what you say about Emily veiled. We can't have another unexpected visit from the magistrate."

Godric tugged the edges of his waistcoat, already irritable at the mere thought of the man. "Ash, would it be a terrible imposition if I were to ask you to come with me? Knowing how Blankenship fits into this business, I fear I may need someone to help me rein in my temper."

"Yes, of course I'll come. Lucien, would you mind taking charge here? We all know how impulsive Charles is and how Cedric can get so easily distracted. I think we'd all be wary of trusting them with a bag of sand under the circumstances. Emily will need a third adversary as much for her sake as ours."

"You don't think she'll run? Even with the dog?"

Both Godric and Ashton nodded.

"She'll try, or she'll plot. It's in her nature." Godric hadn't ignored what she told him last night, that her freedom was vital to her. No, it wouldn't change Emily's escape plans, only alter them.

"I'll watch all three of them."

Godric nodded. "Excellent. Expect us back quite late. We'll probably miss dinner. Oh, and Lucien, remind Emily of her promise to remain here between the hours of ten and six."

"You got that little fox to agree to some terms?" Lucien asked. "Did you use thumbscrews or the rack?"

Godric's face darkened.

"Just remind her of her agreement before you leave her alone, but...and I must press this warning—" Godric and the other two men walked out into the main hall, "—don't let Emily out of your sight for even one minute before ten."

"Don't worry." Lucien slapped Godric's shoulder. "She'll be here for you when you get back."

"She better be because there will be hell to pay if she is not."

Chapter Nine

The day was exceedingly fine with sunny skies and a light breeze. Emily leaned down to let the knee-high silky grass brush under her palms. Cedric and Charles walked on either side of her, carrying on a conversation while Emily listened. Penelope, not tethered by a leash, moved about several yards ahead. The small puppy worked to jump through grass, a good five inches above her head. Emily smiled at the pup's black nose trained to the ground. She sniffed and then bounded over the grass only to resume sniffing again.

"So then," said Cedric, "I said to the sheikh, 'Bet you eight hundred pounds I can win this hand,' and the sheikh, the haughty bastard, replied, 'Let us make the wager on something more valuable. How would a pair of Arabian mares suit you?' And I told him I would accept that wager."

"Are these the mares you mean to breed with Anne Chessley's stallion?"

"The very pair!" Cedric laughed.

"You won the horses from the sheikh then?" Emily asked in amazement. "Wasn't he angry?" She envisioned Cedric playing the winning hand before an olive-skinned sheikh whose eyes flamed when he lost his horses.

Cedric swung his cane low over the grass as he strolled.

"Was he angry? The man was livid! But I won fair and square in front of a dozen pairs of eyes. Honestly, foreigners don't know how to play whist. Too much impulse and bravado."

A wry smile creased Charles's lips. "I take it he was fond of his horses?"

"Fond of their lineage," Cedric clarified. "The mares were both sired by his best stallion, an Arabian called Firestorm. Even I couldn't afford to make an offer to buy them."

Emily was in awe. She'd seen an Arabian once, at a country fair, which had performed jumps and pawed the ground and danced. Its coat had been white, like the first snowfall.

Unlike most horses, the nose of Arabians curved up a little at the end. Their equine beauty was alluring and mysterious, and their trim legs lent them an air of delicacy while providing much strength. Their unique build also contributed to fast runs.

"Why aren't there more pure Arabians in England? I've only ever seen one in my life." Many Englishmen boasted that they owned fine Arabians, but those horses had been bred in England over countless generations. It was rare for Arabians fresh from the Middle East to arrive on English shores.

"The sheikhs jealously guard their horses. People have been killed over them."

"I'm rather surprised the sheikh let you walk out alive," Charles said.

"He let me leave the card room, but he told me one day I'd die a horrible death and he'd get his horses back."

Emily gasped, but the men only chuckled. Emily saw nothing humorous in a death threat.

"What did you say to that?" Charles asked.

"I told him if he wanted revenge for an honest game of cards he'd best wait his turn because I've done far worse to better men." Little in the world scared either of these men.

"But surely you don't mean that, Cedric. You have your flaws as all men do. But you are also kind. You wouldn't do something to a person undeserving." Emily hoped it was the truth. She knew they were capable of kindness, but an impish curiosity drove her to learn whether these two men would admit to their wicked pasts.

"Are you claiming then that women have no flaws?" There was a merry twinkle in Cedric's eyes.

"Hmm. I know of a flaw she has..." Charles spun and caught Emily about the waist, tickling her so that she dissolved into giggles and gasps for help.

"We try to be kind to you, kitten, because you are so helpless and sweet."

Cedric crossed his arms and laughed as she struggled to escape Charles.

"Oh help! Cedric, make him stop!" She tried to free herself, but Charles would have none of it. Cedric gave a well-placed whack of his cane to the back of Charles's legs. Emily broke free and skirted around Cedric using him as a human shield, as Charles did his best to stalk her like a jungle cat.

"Enough!" Cedric dodged Charles's reaching hands and fended off Penelope as the pup joined in the fun. Finally Charles relented and let Emily catch her breath.

Cedric held out a hand. "Come along, Emily." She darted forward, sliding her hand in his, laughing as Charles told an amusing tale about his latest boxing match. It was a perfect day. Almost. Only one thing was missing. One person.

Whitechapel was a despicable area. During the day, carts and people selling cheap wares littered the streets. By night, the area transformed into a haven for prostitutes, degenerates and murderers. Side streets cut and slashed their way through the area, weaving a deadly maze of filth and danger.

Blankenship kept to the shadows. Though a large man, more than able to protect himself in a fight, he'd never believed that any such fight should be fair. He kept his palm tucked inside his jacket on a Manton-made pistol.

A sharp cry above was his only warning to sidestep as a chamber pot was emptied overhead. He moved into a yellow pool of light, bumping into a ragged whore.

"Care for a quickie, love?" The woman's painted face was a mask of disease and hardship. Blankenship cursed and ducked back into the shelter of the shadows. Something squirmed under his boot. He kicked out, sending a rat scurrying. The next turn he took was down Dorset Street, his fingers curled around the handle of his pistol as he approached a tavern called The Black Boar's Head.

The scrap of parchment in his pocket he'd received this afternoon had born the name of this tavern and a time for a meeting. Someone had known he needed help in acquiring the Parr girl and had suggested he come here to discuss an alternative to the legal means he had attempted and failed. He was too desperate not to try any method, even if it meant meeting a stranger here.

The moment the door swung open the scent of gin and unwashed bodies assailed him. His eyes watered and Blankenship nearly tossed his accounts.

He dodged a number of serving wenches, their breasts nearly toppling out of thin muslin bodices. Such low, dirty creatures held no appeal to him any longer. He craved soft, creamy skin, burnished gold hair and pale pink lips.

He craved Emily Parr.

Blankenship started to slide into a table near the door when something caught his eye. Near the back, a well-dressed man lounged at a table, one hand curled around a glass of gin. The other hand was fisted in the tangled mess of a woman's hair as he urged her head up and down over his groin. Blankenship stifled a moan, then shifted uncomfortably, and adjusted his trousers. His greatest desire was to have Emily at his knees, wrapping her lips around his length and taking him so deep she gagged.

The man at the table arched his hips in release and shoved the woman away. She wiped her mouth with the back of her hand and slunk away into a corner. The man held Blankenship's gaze, fixed his trousers and smiled. It was a cold expression, one of frozen metal. A flick of his hand indicated that Blankenship should join him.

"You've been watching me."

Blankenship was unable to hide his scowl. "You put on distracting show."

The man laughed again. Soft. Dangerous. "Sit. I believe you need help."

The chair Blankenship took creaked in protest. "So it was you who sent me the note? Who are you?" He studied the other man. His long fingers were manicured, his hair styled, his clothing immaculate. A lord perhaps?

"Hugo Waverly."

He'd heard the name before but couldn't recall where.

"What interest do you have in my affairs?" His hand still rested on the gun tucked in his coat.

Waverly fixed cold brown eyes on him. "We share a common adversary, do we not?"

Blankenship's gut twisted. Any man who knew of his affairs was a threat, yet a man like this might be a potential ally.

"I assume you mean the Duke of Essex?" Blankenship leaned back in his chair, crossing his arms over his chest. "What do you have against him?"

"It's personal. Suffice it to say I'd like to help. I know a man." Waverly's fingers danced on his shot glass as he swirled it in front of him, his eyes fixed on Blankenship. "He's highly skilled. Eyes and ears everywhere. He specializes in retrievals of a delicate nature. If you pay him well, he can retrieve what is rightfully yours." Waverly smiled. "And I'll have the pleasure of knowing something was taken from Essex, something he loves."

"You think he loves her?"

"I know nothing of any woman." His sly gaze met Blankenship's. "To my knowledge this involves a misappropriated piece of property, nothing more. Essex thinks he's entitled to this property and you and I both know it isn't his. That doesn't change the fact that he cares for this...property."

"Who's this man?"

Waverly reached into his pocket and withdrew a slender slip of paper. He slid it across the table. Blankenship took it, stared at the name and address.

"I should add there is someone else you might find useful. Someone who is intimately familiar with Essex's habits. You need only to consult *The Quizzing Glass Gazette's* Lady Society column to determine her identity."

Satisfied, Blankenship stood up to leave.

"Blankenship?"

His shoulders stiffened, but he stood facing Waverly.

"Essex especially hates it when the things he cares about are *broken.*"

Once Godric concluded his meeting with his solicitor, he and Ashton walked to the little jeweler's shop on Regent Street he'd frequented in his earlier years. Godric examined the glittering trinkets from the window display—mulling, picking, debating. After an intense study, he chose a gold comb adorned with a butterfly, with an opal-colored body and mother-of-pearl wings.

Emily reminded him of a butterfly. She flew to her freedom each time he sought to capture her, but when he sat very, very still, she rewarded him with the most enchanting kisses meant for him alone.

Godric brushed his thumb over the smooth opal and pearl,

imagining it nestled in the waves of auburn gold hair. He would savor the moment of removing it at night when she climbed into his bed. Her hair would cascade down in a waterfall of color.

He was acting like a young man again, uncertain as to how to win a woman. How many years had passed since he and his friends had schemed about the best way to capture a girl's heart?

Godric selected a hairbrush to match the comb, then handed the shopkeeper a leather dog collar with a silver name plate to have it engraved for Penelope. Once the items were ready, he and Ashton departed.

It was time to pay a visit to Albert Parr.

Parr's sallow-faced butler showed them in with the stiffest and most unwelcoming behavior. He merely stepped aside for them, then lead them down the hall. Godric frowned at the unkempt surroundings. He ran a gloved finger along the nearest banister, and his brow creased at the smudge of gray dust that marred his glove. The house was only a few streets away from Park Lane, yet it was clear that the employment and supervision of servants was not Albert Parr's primary concerns.

"Poor Emily," Ashton muttered under his breath. "Not exactly a warm place to live."

Godric growled. "My Emily belongs in a palace, with silk sheets and a thousand servants."

Ashton cocked an eyebrow at him. "You mean she belongs in a place like Essex House?"

Godric's silently contemplated the comment. "For the moment, yes."

"Why not longer? Say...forever?"

"What would I do with her, Ash?"

"Woo her. She'll not long be an unplucked fruit, my friend. Wouldn't you rather it be you than some scoundrel like Blankenship? She deserves a man who would be tender and passionate with her."

"But what then? I've ruined her reputation. Am I to marry her and live happily ever after? You know better than that." The people he loved had either left him or betrayed him. He didn't want either with Emily.

"Isn't that what reformed rakes are supposed to do?"

"Who said I was reformed?"

Ashton merely smiled.

Neither man said anything more as the manservant led them to Parr's study. Emily's weasel of an uncle was reading some letters, bent over his desk. He glanced up, and then did a double take.

Rather than treat a duke and a baron with deserving deference, Parr rose reluctantly to his feet.

"What took you so long?"

Godric stared him down until the man added, "Your Grace."

Godric's fists clenched sharply at his sides. He had the oddest sense he was being played. "I would like to discuss my investment with you." He and Ashton approached Parr's desk, bearing down on him with scowls that would have sent any other man fleeing, as though the devil himself was on his heels.

Parr settled back into his chair, eyeing them. "Is that what you call my niece, Your Grace?"

"Oh? You have a niece?" Godric smiled but the warmth of it did not reach his eyes. "Ashton, did you hear that? Parr has a niece. How lovely."

"You are a terrible liar, Your Grace. I know that it was you who spirited Emily away." He stepped to his right, as if he planned to come around the desk, but then thought better of it. "Mr. Blankenship had no luck finding her, I understand, but I am sure you stuffed her in your cellar, or perhaps a cupboard. I imagine you had no reservations about doing so." Parr's thin lips stretched into a smile, one as cool as Godric's.

"Where's my money?"

"Your money is gone. I spent all of it paying off creditors, which you are well aware. There is nothing left for you to seize and sell in this house or I would give it to you. I also owe Mr. Blankenship a great deal more. Emily was my last bargaining piece. But of course, you already knew that as well, which is why you took her."

"She's not a piece to be bargained. She's a woman!" Godric slammed his hand flat on Parr's desk. Ashton put a steadying hand on his shoulder.

"If she's not something to bargain for, then why did you take her? If there has been some guileful behavior in my use of your investment, let us at least be honest and admit this dishonesty now runs both ways." Parr replied.

He wanted to leap across the desk and strangle the life out of

Parr. But the urge had to fight with his own guilt. It was true. He was no better than Parr. He had not cared one wit that his actions would destroy her reputation. He'd counted on it. He'd laughed at the idea, thinking it all a game.

He was as much a villain as her uncle.

Ashton intervened. "Mr. Parr, just how much of a claim does Blankenship have on Em...uh...your niece?"

Parr's business demeanor returned. "Ironclad. I exchanged her for my debt. He agreed to honor his end of the bargain by marrying her. Unless, of course, she is no longer a maiden."

"And then she's free of him?" If so, Godric had victory within his sights again.

"No. Should she come to him devoid of her innocence, he'll keep her as his mistress."

"And you agreed to this?" The blood drained from Godric's face, not with horror, but rage.

Parr looked down, no longer able to mask some sense of guilt. "I did...and it was a devil's bargain. But what choice do I have? If Blankenship demands payment, I will be destroyed. I am not without sympathy for the girl, but if you knew Blankenship as I do, you would understand."

"We are not unfamiliar with his influence," said Ashton.

"Are you? The financial ruin of his enemies is only part of the man's reputation."

"And what of Emily? Has she no say in the matter?" Godric interjected.

"She'll do whatever is necessary. What other use is she?"

Godric planted him a facer and Parr fell back in his chair, clutching his mouth.

"That won't happen."

Parr's tongue probed his teeth, showing blood. "Oh? Why not?"

"Emily is no longer your concern. You won't have her to settle your debts."

Albert relished the pain with a small amount of satisfaction. Essex did have Emily, and what's more, she had caught his fancy. Who knew how long the Duke would enjoy her, but at least for now, she was under his protection. Blankenship would be hard pressed to find a way to get to her. Perhaps it was for the best. Blankenship certainly couldn't hold him responsible for this. He might be able to work this to his advantage and remind his niece of the kindness he'd shown her by being her guardian. Perhaps Essex would forgive Albert's debt for his efforts to take care of Emily.

The blow to his jaw proved that Emily was in far better hands than his. A man simply did not hit other men in polite society unless their emotions ran a thousand leagues deep.

Albert smiled, winced, then smiled again. It seemed Emily's sweet temperament was paying off. But for her sake he hoped Blankenship's ambitions for her were not as obsessive as they seemed to be.

Jim Tanner scouted the darkened street ahead of him. It was one of many clever routes in St. Giles where he could slip away into the impenetrable darkness, evading any who might pursue him. It was also the perfect place to meet a new client. Evening was drawing closer and shadows stretched over the maze of the rookery, darkening pawnshop windows and hovels. He had received a note through his connections that a man wished to pay him highly to recover a young lady from the clutches of a group of dangerous noblemen. The prospect had intrigued him enough to agree to meet the potential client an hour after sunset.

Scuffling steps in the darkness ahead had him reaching for the blade he kept tucked in his coat.

"I say...are you there?" A low rumbling voice demanded. "I brought the information and a down payment." The voice softened to a rough whisper as a tall, wide man stepped into a pool of fading light only a short distance away.

Tanner revealed himself, enjoying the gasp and the jump from the potential client. He'd been only four feet away, and the man never noticed.

"So you need me to acquire a lady?" Tanner clarified.

"Yes. She's currently hidden at the Duke of Essex's estate. Five men are guarding her at all times." The man said as he handed over a scrap of parchment with directions to the estate.

Tanner read the paper and then ripped it to pieces, discarding them in a pool of dirty water where the ink would smudge beyond readability.

He'd never crossed paths with the Duke of Essex, but he was sure to be like every other pompous aristocrat. Bored, rich and allowed far too much power.

As a young man, Tanner had felt such loyalty towards these men, especially his master, a middle-aged viscount. As a footman, he'd seen to the man's every need, expecting no extra kindness or treatment for his hard work. There had been pride, great pride in one's duty to his master.

At least until his master had discovered Tanner's sweetheart and violated her. Lacy. Tanner's blood boiled at the memory of finding her bent over his master's bed, skirts up around her hips, taking whatever his master wished to give her. She hadn't protested, no woman in the service ever did. To refuse their master was cause for dismissal.

Rage had destroyed Tanner's sanity. He'd killed his master, killed the man with his bare hands and then fled. Now, seven years later, he'd established himself as a professional thief for hire, one of the finest. The deft of hand talents, and the ability to go unseen by everyone, a footman's trade, worked even better for him as a specialist in acquiring items desired by paying clients.

The man, Thomas Blankenship, was certainly able to pay him well. His sources had confirmed it, though they also warned he was dangerous and deceptive.

"I want five hundred pounds upon delivery of the girl. Crossing a duke will require a time away from England."

His client huffed and tossed a leather bag at him. "Here's a hundred up front as your note required."

Tanner caught the bag and tested the weight. "Good. Here is what you must do for me. I need to have someone access the inside of Essex's estate, a friend, a confidant, a servant, anyone you can buy off to enter the house and give me details of schedules of watches and habits. These are things I cannot learn but need to know in order to acquire your *possession*."

Blankenship shifted on his feet and then nodded. "I know of someone."

"Excellent, send it to the address you sent your previous note and it will find its way to me." He waited, curious to see what the client would do. The man obviously didn't like to take orders, but for the money he was paying, it was better to leave Tanner to do his job without interference.

"Very well. I will write to you when I have details."

Neither man shook hands, they simply met gazes, sealing the deal with a nod. With a soft little chuckle, Tanner pocketed his money and slithered into the darkness of the secret alleys of St. Giles.

Emily turned from the window. "When will Ashton and Godric return from London?"

"Sometime late tonight," Lucien said. "He guessed they would miss dinner."

Emily's heart pitched south in disappointment.

She missed Godric, missed the heated glances, the tenderness of his lips, the rough weight of his body, those hands that drove her to madness. But she also missed the rich timbre of his voice, the way he saw to her every need. She even missed his desire to sleep beside her, just to hear her breathe.

"Looking forward to his return?"

Emily nodded. A dark, vast emptiness had rooted itself inside her heart. Despite the pleasant time these men were providing her, the same darkness to her future remained. A tremor shook her body as panic and dread threatened to overtake her.

"Cheer up, my sweet." Lucien brushed a hand on her waist, tickling her just a little.

Unable to help it, a little laugh escaped her. She glowered. "It is ungentlemanly to use my weaknesses against me like that."

"Then it is fortunate that I don't often count myself a gentleman."

Simkins entered the room and announced dinner.

Emily settled down in the dining room between Lucien and Charles with Cedric across from her. "May I ask a question?"

"That depends." Lucien's eyes glinted. "We are not about to regale you with tales of our legendary adventures in the arms of our lovers. We do not kiss and tell."

Charles shot him a glance. "I thought that's all we did."

"Well, not to other women." Lucien rolled his eyes.

Cedric shrugged. "My mistresses always ask about my past...er...indiscretions with an avid curiosity."

"I cannot believe I am the voice of reason for once," said Lucien.

"Emily is a proper lady. Neither of you will share one word or I'll box your ears."

Emily's giggled. "I only meant to ask, how is it that you all came to be friends? Surely that does not include tales of your lovers?"

Cedric and Charles exchanged an amused glance.

"No, no, our meeting is more adventure than romance," Lucien said.

"Will you tell it to me?"

Charles answered. "The tale is best told when all of us are here, but perhaps we can tell you how we each first met Godric. Those are stories in themselves."

"That would be wonderful!" There was nothing she loved better than a good story, and these five men had been at the center of many.

"Then I ought to go first." Cedric finished his plate and looked about the table for approval to proceed. "I was the first one to meet Godric, in 1807, when he and I were seventeen. I convinced him to sneak out of the dormitories of Magdalene College. We had dinner at a local pub and got into a brawl with an upper year named Hugo Waverly over a woman. I beat Waverly to a bloody pulp and took his cane as a matter of honor." Cedric's fingers gently twined about the stem of his wineglass.

Emily's gaze fell onto the silver lion's head of the cane that was propped up against the table. "Is that his cane you carry now?"

He held it out to Emily, who took it as though she held a precious artifact from ages gone. "Yes," he said.

She sensed by the strained look on Charles's face that there was something more they were not sharing with her. "Did Hugo Waverly ever exact his revenge?"

Charles dropped the bottle of wine he'd been examining. It hit the floor with a sickening crash and a spray of crimson ruined his clothes. He dove to pick up the pieces.

"Charles, are you all right?"

Lucien knelt to assist him.

"So what did happen to Hugo Waverly?" There was something about his name, or perhaps his memory, that had caused Charles to react. It was clear there was far more to this story than just a brawl and the acquisition of a cane. There had been reasons, and there had been consequences.

"It is as you said. He vowed revenge." Cedric's answer evaded her inquiry but she knew she would hear no more about the mysterious villain.

She gave the cane back, a shy wistful sigh escaping her lips. "I should have loved to have had adventures like that."

Every mouth was agape, as though her announcement had been a shock.

"What on earth do you call this, Emily? Abducted, fending off the advances of shameless rakehells... Nothing about that is for the faint of heart," Cedric said with mild amusement.

"I know...but it isn't really dangerous, though, is it?" She ran a fingertip over the surface of the white tablecloth then stifled a shudder. "Aside from Blankenship's visit here."

"Between riding like an Amazon and jumping walls you've put our lives in danger, and that should count for something," Lucien said.

Emily's lips changed to a disappointed frown. It was no use to explain to these men that she hungered for travel to foreign lands, for sights unseen, and art not yet made by painter's hands. There was so much she was missing.

If her uncle married her to Blankenship, her life would be over.

Stifling a yawn, Emily wondered when Godric would return. The conversation at dinner had distracted her for a short while.

"It is late. Perhaps you ought to retire for the night, Emily," Cedric said.

"I suppose you are right. I am fatigued." She bent down to retrieve Penelope, who rustled against her skirts. The little dog licked her chin and wriggled in excitement, and Emily couldn't help but take comfort from such innocent affection. Cedric escorted her upstairs, a shadowy reminder of her status as prisoner.

"You have your books and Penelope. Will you be all right the rest of the evening?"

"Yes."

"All right then, kitten. I'll have Simkins send up bowls of food and water for Penelope."

"And a basket? Wouldn't she need one to sleep in?"

"I'll see that she has everything her little heart desires."

"Thank you, Cedric."

"You are most welcome. We will be downstairs, should you need anything."

Once alone she settled down on her bed with Penelope in her lap and pulled one of the novels off the side table. *Lady Viola and the Dashing Duke.* She wanted a good story.

As she read on about the plucky heroine and her first encounter with the dashing hero, she saw Godric, and her heart ached. Was he thinking of her now, or even at all? What if she fell asleep before he returned? Would he still come to collect his kiss goodnight?

She should not have wanted him to but, Lord help her, she did. She wanted him to sweep into her room and kiss her senseless. Godric's kiss was a wildfire on a dry meadow, and she craved that inferno like nothing else. It was madness to want him so much. Logically she knew the danger he presented to her heart, yet she couldn't seem to resist him.

Emily eased onto her bed and daydreamed of Godric. Penelope curled up against her chest, the dog's brown eyes drowsy as she fell asleep. Emily remained in that delightful state of partial wakefulness, picturing Godric's hands on her, his mouth on hers, soft words of love tickling her ear. But they were dreams and nothing more.

Chapter Ten

Godric had never been so anxious to return home.

He rode his gelding so hard that twice Ashton shouted out to him over the thunder of hooves to slow down or his horse would throw a shoe. Then they would really be delayed. The trip had taken longer than they planned and they wouldn't arrive at the estate until an hour past midnight.

Emily's gifts were tucked away in his riding coat pocket, and he was desperate to see her, to hold her in his arms, to kiss her, to tickle her just to hear that breathless laugh. He hungered to taste her lips, to watch her eyes sparkle with delight or sear with the first blush of passion. He wanted to speak to her in Greek, to see how much she really knew. He longed to test her mind and taste her lips. She was an enigma to him, a woman unlike any other he'd ever met before.

The pearly moonlight broke over the distant manor's pale stones, taunting him like a mirage in the desert. Would Emily wait up for him? He hoped so. He wanted to tuck her into his bed and kiss her goodnight, and to his surprise, his desire to do so was not purely carnal.

How on earth had he come to care for this young woman in a way he never cared for anyone, save his closet friends?

Ashton had been right. She'd enchanted him, and he hoped the spell lasted forever.

When he and Ashton reached the manor, they abandoned their horses to a groom and went inside. A servant had dimmed the candles and the hall lay silent. A bloom of distant gold light brightened the path to the drawing room. Cigar smoke wafted down the hall towards Godric and Ashton.

Emily was not with them. Even gentleman such as themselves never smoked in front of a lady.

Godric and Ashton headed towards the room and found Cedric, Charles and Lucien lounging in wingback chairs near the fire. A gray cloud of cigar smoke hovered above their heads as they spoke in hushed tones and played cards.

"You're back." Cedric looked relieved to see them.

"It seems we have been missed." Quiet concern laced Ashton's tone.

Godric didn't like the sudden pitch of panic in his stomach. Had something happened to Emily?

"I am almost afraid to ask, but where is Emily?" Godric's heart was tight in his chest.

"Don't worry, Godric. She's in her room, asleep. She has been since ten o'clock."

"Thank God for that. Excuse me." Godric bid the others goodnight, desperate to reassure himself she was still there, still his.

He sprinted up the stairs but slowed at Emily's door. He tested the door handle of her room. It was unlocked. The fools! She could have snuck out without their knowledge.

Stray beams of moonlight lit Emily's room. The dark form of the young woman lay outlined on the bed. She was still fully dressed and looked as though she'd collapsed in exhaustion. Had she meant to wait up and fell asleep? A flicker of hope burned in his chest. He wanted it to be true.

Godric hesitated before he summoned the courage to enter and lock the door. He reached down, removed his boots, and left them near the door.

Padding softly to the bed he examined Emily. She seemed to be dreaming of happier days, with that soft expression on her face. He bent down carefully and brushed his lips over hers, not wishing to wake her, but she stirred all the same.

"Godric?" she murmured, her eyes still shut.

"Yes?" He knelt next to the bed as she opened her eyes.

"You're really back?"

"Of course, my dear. I do live here, you understand."

She tried not to laugh. "Do you? I had no idea." She flashed him an impish smile. "I wanted to be up when you returned, but I must have fallen asleep." She reached out a hand to touch his cheek.

Godric turned his lips towards the center of her palm, kissing it. "What did you do while I was away?" He wanted to know everything that she did and whether she missed him. He'd hated every minute he spent apart from her, and he wanted Emily to reassure him he wasn't alone.

He crossed his arms on the bed's edge and rested his chin on them as she told him of her day, his chest filling with an odd warmth. Emily was an open book to him at times, but tonight her eyes were mysterious pools. He sank deeper and deeper into them, entrapped by the wondrous emotions reflected there.

She wrinkled her nose and then smiled. Her hand toyed with his cravat absently as she gazed at him, wide eyes dark as diamonds, veiled by midnight shadows.

"And you? How was your trip to London?" Her question left Godric with a smile.

"Pleasant enough, but..."

"But?"

But I missed you terribly, he wanted to say, but the words choked and died somewhere between his throat and his lips.

"It doesn't matter. I bought you some presents while I was there. Would you like to see them?"

"Presents?" A smile bloomed on her face, an irresistible enchantment that stole his breath. He'd waited all day to see her look at him like that, as though he'd ridden up upon a white charger, ready to fight for her heart.

But Godric couldn't trust himself to read that thought in her eyes. He wanted it to be true, but how could she want him? Him, the man who'd taken so much from her?

"Of course I brought presents. Cedric couldn't be allowed to have all the fun."

He pulled the parcels from his riding coat pocket, and Emily took them. Godric joined her on the bed. She unwrapped the dark purple paper and found the first two items, the brush and the comb adorned with butterflies. The pearl of the butterflies' wings channeled the moonlight, and the opal gleamed darkly, like the sea at midnight. She stroked a fingertip over the surface of the comb's butterfly and turned her face towards Godric, not realizing how close he was. Their noses brushed and she smiled before giving him a kiss on the cheek. A butterfly's kiss, so faint he wondered if he'd imagined it.

"They are so beautiful. I have never owned anything this lovely. Thank you."

Godric flushed. He'd never seen a woman take such simple gifts with such reverence and joy. He could have thrown the Crown Jewels at Evangeline's feet, and she would not have expressed the same gratitude. The thought humbled him in a way he hadn't thought possible.

"I chose them myself. The butterflies reminded me of you."

She kissed his other cheek and looked up through smoky lashes. "I remind you of a butterfly?"

"Yes, you do. They are beautiful, mysterious, alluring, easy to catch if you bring a big enough net..." His voice was low and husky as he gazed at her lips.

"Godric, I believe you are trying to seduce me." Her words teased, but the heat in her eyes was no joke.

"Always, my dear. Always." His lips were so close to hers. He ached to kiss her, he needed to kiss her. He had to blind her with the light of the fire in his heart just as she'd blinded him with hers.

"Are you going to kiss me goodnight?" Her question was innocent, but her tone held something more.

"Not yet." He pointed to the parcel in her hands. "There is still one more present for you."

Emily dug deeper into the wrapping and found the leather collar with the silver engraved nameplate.

"Penelope," she read in an excited whisper and leapt from the bed.

She crossed the room to the small little basket near the vanity table. The puppy was fast asleep, unaware of the world around her. Emily slid the collar underneath and around her neck. She fastened the buckle and patted Penelope's head before coming back over to Godric.

"I am sure she'll be excited in the morning when she wakes."

Godric almost laughed. "I imagine she will be." He stood, taking Emily by the arm.

"Shall we go to bed, my dear?"

A flash of panic marred her beautiful face.

"What's wrong?"

Emily's cheeks reddened. "I..."

But Godric realized her fear and sought to reassure her.

"We will sleep, and nothing more. I care for you too much to want to do anything but hold you tonight." From the bottom of his black heart, he truly meant it. Tonight he wanted to reassure her of his honorable intentions.

Honorable intentions. What madness was this that ran through his soul like quicksilver? Godric was incapable of love. How often had his father told him that? Told him that if he was capable of love, his mother would never have died. Rationally Godric knew his father had tried to ease his own grief by putting the burden of her death on him, but he couldn't help but agree. Had he been older, or stronger, he could have ridden to town to get the doctor, while Father tended to her. But he hadn't. He'd hidden in the dining room, his little knees tucked up beneath his chin, listening to his mother's screams. And then that dreaded silence, how it had pounded against his ears.

My fault. Always my fault.

Maybe he was capable of love, but he'd stopped himself because the risk was too great. He'd lost his mother, his father, the sibling who'd never had a chance to breathe its first breath. What if he lost Emily? His insides recoiled at the thought. He mustn't care for Emily, mustn't feel anything for her. It was better this way.

But it was all a lie. He did feel for her.

Strongly.

Emily's worries vanished in the wake of excitement as he led her through the adjoining door into his bedroom. He pulled back the covers of his bed but prevented her from crawling in. His hands fell heavily on her shoulders.

"Let me undress you." His voice was rich and dark.

Emily should have refused, but his heavy-lidded gaze robbed her of speech.

She gazed, it seemed, into the eyes of the captivating marauder-turned-duke of her novel.

Godric accepted her silence as consent and turned her back to him as he undid her laces. The gown wilted at her feet.

His fingers deftly untied her stays, plucking them free like a skilled harpist.

Emily shivered, nervous at the intimacy of being undressed. "Have you had much practice at this, Your Grace?" She realized at once what a silly question it was.

"You know my reputation, darling." He continued after her intake of breath. "But I've never been so pleased by it before."

Emily was certain she would melt into a puddle.

He leaned forward and kissed her, nibbling where her shoulder met her neck. She sagged helplessly into his embrace. Godric caught her before she crumpled to the floor.

"Easy. We aren't done yet." He pushed her back so that she leaned against the edge of the bed.

She was down to her chemise and stockings.

Godric knelt before her and patted his right thigh. "Put your left foot here."

She did as he asked, faint with inner hunger as his hands roved up to her thigh, unfastened the garter, and caught hold of the top of the stocking. He slid it down her leg and placed soft, hot kisses on each inch of skin he bared until he freed her foot entirely. Godric then repeated the ritual with her right foot.

He slid his hands back up her leg and pushed the chemise out of the way so he could lean forward to kiss her on the inside of her leg, near her knee.

Emily shivered. She was not prone to swooning, but when Godric sucked on her skin and flicked his tongue, she wavered.

"Are you all right?"

She half-laughed. "If you keep kissing me like that, I'm bound to forget my name…"

"That's a sign that I'm doing all the right things," he teased. "I believe you have had enough for one day. Even I am not so villainous as to demand more tonight." Godric went back into her room and returned with her night rail. Emily turned her back and removed her chemise, and slid the night rail down over her body. When she turned back around, she found Godric watching her, fists clenched.

He nodded towards his bed. "In you go, before I change my mind about only sleeping."

She slid between the sheets and watched in fascination as he undressed himself.

"Will I ever get to undress you?"

He stared back for a long moment, an unreadable expression in his eyes. "Tomorrow night." He bared his chest, removed his breeches and donned his night shirt. Emily, suddenly self-conscious, slid away

141

from him as he joined her under the covers, but the mattress dipped with his weight and she rolled into him.

"Now, about that kiss good night." He wrapped her in his arms and kissed her.

Emily never wanted that kiss to end, the soft movement of their lips, the dance of tongues, the straining breaths shared in the quiet darkness... She could never leave the bed, and forever be content, so long as he kept kissing her.

Godric molded her body to his as he kissed her with both fire and gentleness. Undressing her had been a bad idea. All he could think about was the taste of her skin, the shivery sighs she made when he removed each piece of clothing. It had been her gift to him, and she hadn't even been aware of it. Now he had Emily in his arms, kissing him back with her sweet, inexperienced mouth. He couldn't wait to teach her all the things his years of experience taught him. Would she like it when he put his mouth between her legs? Would she want to do the same to him? For her to torture him in such a way would be glorious. Desperately, he reined in his hunger and focused on her soft insistent mouth meeting his with wild abandon.

What was it Ashton had told him? Emily kissed him from the depths of her heart.

Could he do the same? Tonight he wanted to try...

I missed you today, I thought of nothing else, I...I think I love—

The last thought had come unbidden, but he was too weak to deny what felt so strong and true. He wanted to claim her, but also protect her. He'd do anything to keep her, just like this. Sweet. Innocent. His.

Had he, Godric St. Laurent, finally become a fool in love? God help him.

The gilded grandfather clock in the upstairs hallway chimed seven, waking Godric. The fire crackled, twigs and bits of logs snapping. He lay on his back with Emily, still asleep, curled up against his side. The feel of her in his arms was wonderful. A perfect fit. He wanted to hold her more often, keep her close so he could smell the flowery scent in her hair, relish her satiny skin beneath his palms.

They could always be like this, he realized. He and Emily could grow old this way, spending years exploring each other. He craved that elusive, impossible future. To want something, to know you could have it, and once you had it, lose it. He wasn't ready for that, might never be ready. But what could it hurt to pretend, for at least a few days, to have what he wanted? Godric slid a hand under the covers, seeking the edge of her night rail. His fingers met bare skin near her calves, and he slid the fabric up to expose her hips to his hand. Emily's head twisted a little. She nuzzled his chest, and Godric stifled a groan.

Seducing this woman was an infuriatingly slow process, but he didn't dare rush it. He wanted to savor Emily's first time and know without a doubt she was well and truly pleasured at his hands. He'd become too accustomed to the deliciously rough tumbles during which he unleashed his primitive urges and freed his lover from her own inhibitions, but with Emily that would come later. The question was whether he could restrain himself that first time. The last thing he wanted to do was hurt her.

Godric rolled over onto his side, facing Emily, as he moved his hand farther up to cup the smooth rounded globe of her rump. The satiny skin beneath his palm gave him a small rush. He rubbed his hand up and down over her bottom, enjoying a little purr of sleepy pleasure that rippled from her throat. Godric pushed his hand harder, urging her to press herself against him.

She stirred, arching her hips into his, allowing his arousal to meet her. "Hmm..."

Godric rubbed his hips against hers, simulating the pressure and rhythm as if he were actually inside her. His eyes nearly rolled back in his head as his erection rubbed against her building wetness. She finally woke. He kissed her open lips, silencing whatever protest she'd been about to make. Emily raised her arms but he trapped them into the pillows on either side of her head as he mounted her. She wasn't going to escape, not just yet. Godric nudged her knees apart and he slid between her thighs. He paused in his kiss to glance at her.

"Godric, what are you doing?" Emily asked breathlessly.

"I'm trying to teach you, at great cost to my personal satisfaction, how it feels to make love." He kissed her lips again, slowly sliding his tongue in and flicking it against hers before retreating and nibbling on her lower lip.

"You never give up, do you?" She tried to sound irritated but was already surrendering from need.

"I'm a St. Laurent. We never give up once we set our minds on having something, and I want you, Emily. I want you desperately. Now lie back and enjoy." He hoped his firm tone would cow her into submission. Her lips parted, and those dark lashes fluttered against her cheeks. He ground his hips against hers. Emily moaned, a loose, deep wild sound that aroused him beyond rational thought.

"Do you feel how much I want you? How much I need you, Emily?" He brushed his lips along her jaw down to her ear; he bit her lobe and then kissed the soft sensitive skin behind it.

"Yes..." Her voice was barely more than a strangled gasp as he ground against her. She arched her back, her legs tightened around his hips.

Keep control, damn you! But with her next moan, it was almost impossible. He moved against her, and she came apart in his arms with a great cry of surprise. He spent his seed in his nightclothes like a damned inexperienced youth. Emily was limp and gasping for breath beneath him, gazing up at him in wonder.

Godric tried to calm down, his entire body weak with the rippling aftermath of his release.

"Bloody hell."

"What did you say?" Emily pushed herself up on her elbows. "You're shaking."

She had no idea. He never lost control. What sort of man was he if he couldn't perform better than a mere boy with his first girl? The Duke of Essex, firing off a warning shot across Emily's bow. God, if the others ever found out, he'd never hear the end of it. Godric tried to disentangle himself, but he was desperate to hide his embarrassment, and practically ripped himself from her arms. He rested his elbows on his knees, ducking his head to run his fingers through his hair. Emily moved towards him, but he waved her off.

"Godric, what's wrong?"

"Nothing. Go, before the maids come looking for you." He tried not to sound cold, but failed.

"Did I... Did I do something wrong?" She reached for him, but he rose and darted over to his armoire to fetch his dressing gown.

"Godric?" Her eyes welled with tears.

He cursed silently and came back to her, cupping her face and kissing her tenderly.

"You were perfect, Emily. It was me. It's...complicated. Go now and get dressed if you wish." He traced her lips with a fingertip.

"You're not mad?" The catch in her voice made him all too aware how his behavior affected her. She didn't know anything about men, and she wouldn't understand he was angry with himself and not her.

"I'll be mad if you cry, my little hellion." He dropped his hands to her waist, tickling her until she was laughing helplessly.

"All right! All right, I surrender," she gasped.

"Now, go on back to your room." He lifted her off the bed, onto her feet and swatted her rump, urging her towards her door. She went, but looked back at him, her face a mixture of emotions he couldn't puzzle out. There was curiosity blazing behind her eyes, as though she'd sensed she'd conquered him somehow. God help him if she ever discovered how right she was. He could have laughed. Emily's hold over him was so potent that he might agree to anything she asked of him. What a horrifying thought that was—to know he was a prisoner to her kiss and touch, when he'd never been anyone's captive before.

Emily shut the door to her room and leaned back against the frame, taking a long deep breath. Her body still convulsed with little spasms of pleasure. Was that what it felt like to make love? What sort of sinful god was Godric if he could make her feel that way without being inside of her? Emily shivered. She'd changed too much in the past few days. Her resistance to his charm was crumbling. Just after a few heated kisses, wicked caresses, she'd lost every ounce of self-control.

It wasn't fair that she fell too easily for him, that she thrilled just to hear him speak her name, to hope that, at any particular moment, he would think about her. Caring for Godric was a dangerous weakness. She needed to reclaim her pride, relight her inner fire, if she was to survive this captivity. She'd not be reduced to a meaningless mistress to be cast aside and forgotten.

Her mind replayed what they'd just done, the way he'd shaken above her, the way he'd pulled away, like a wild animal. The flash of vulnerability on his face had shown her something incredibly important. He'd lost control as well...with her. Was it possible? Had she made him want her as much as she wanted him? Would it be enough to get him to fall in love with her and marry her? If it was at all possible, she needed to play this game the way she played chess—passively with some subtle aggression. Then make the necessary sacrifices to reach checkmate.

There was a soft knock on her door and Libba entered. "Good morning, Libba."

"Good morning." The maid went to select a gown for her to wear and then joined Emily at the vanity table. She studied the maid through the reflection in the looking glass.

Emily watched Libba tidy up her vanity table. "What made you come to St. Laurent manor? To work I mean. Surely being a maid wasn't your dream."

"I've been raised in service, but I'd always dreamed I would be a singer. Mama says I have a wonderful voice."

"Would you sing for me?"

Libba chuckled. "Perhaps later, Miss."

"So why here? Why choose to work for His Grace?"

"My mother was a lady's maid to a countess. She raised me to be prepared to go into service since I was five years old."

Emily knew only too well what that was like, to have a world that belonged entirely to one's self. Sometimes leaving that private world was frightening. Moving in with her uncle had been terrifying. But Godric's world was a dream unlike any other.

She reached out to touch Libba's arm. "I'm glad you're here."

"You're sweet. None of His Grace's other mistresses were ever sweet."

"Mistresses? But I haven't—I mean, we haven't...well, not exactly. Not the way you mean. I mean..."

The assumption made her stomach pitch. She couldn't be his mistress...his wife, yes, but a mistress...no. She couldn't let that happen.

Libba blushed and pointed towards the door and a pair of black boots...Godric's boots.

"I'm sorry, Miss. I saw His Grace's boots and—"

"Never mind that, Libba. That man has an awful habit of throwing clothes about and leaving them places he shouldn't. It's no surprise he left them in my room."

Managing the duke and getting him to value her above a mistress would not be easy. In order to make him fall in love with her enough to marry her, she'd have to figure out what made him tick.

Chapter Eleven

Rather than Godric, Ashton waited outside Emily's door to escort her to breakfast. Today the baron looked exceedingly fashionable in a dark blue coat, biscuit-colored breeches and an immaculately tied cravat.

He smiled and took her arm. "Emily."

"Good morning, Ashton." She couldn't resist the urge to smile back.

With Ashton alone she felt like a queen. It was a pity Charles lacked his subtle charm. He'd be truly dangerous to every woman in the *ton* if he accomplished that skill.

She proceeded with Ashton down to the dining room, with only Cedric present. He rose, bowed and sat back down as she took her seat.

"Lucien and Charles left for London about ten minutes ago. I believe they'll return tonight," Ashton said.

"Is Godric coming down?" She couldn't forget the tension that had passed between them. Emily had the jarring sense that he might try to avoid her.

"Yes, he's trying to find an old hunting coat."

"A hunting coat? He doesn't have one?" Every sensible man had at least one hunting coat.

"Yes, of course he does," Cedric said. "He's trying to find one for you."

"For me?" She was delighted they would let her come on such an outing, to which women were usually unwelcome.

"Yes, kitten. You're coming on our outing today. Why do you think your maid set out a twill gown and black boots for you?" Cedric asked with a small smile.

Emily glanced down at herself. She barely asked questions anymore when the maids pulled out clothes. She was dressed for a day of walking, not riding.

"We aren't hunting foxes then?"

Ashton laughed. "Lord, no, you are the only fox we've hunted lately. We want something less bothersome, so our prey will be pheasants."

Emily sat up on the edge of her seat. "Will I get to shoot one?"

Cedric's brows rose in surprise. "I would never have taken you for a hunter, Emily."

"It seems I never cease to amaze you. Will I get to shoot?"

"If you think we are stupid enough to give you a firearm—"

"I've handled one before! I know how to hunt."

Ashton steepled his fingers. "Our fear is not that you haven't handled a gun..." The unspoken words revealed his true concern, and it wasn't for the pheasants.

Emily eyed the men reproachfully. "You honestly think I would shoot you? Any of you? Well, perhaps Charles, but only if he tries to tickle me again."

Cedric sat up in his chair, leaning towards her. "You will be in charge of Penelope. She has to learn to retrieve the fowl once we've shot them. Best to start them young, you know."

"I suppose I won't mind that." Emily nibbled at a scone. That they would limit her enjoyment out of some silly fear that she would shoot them irritated her. Well, perhaps it wasn't too silly. The thought of her out in the grass with five men whose arms were raised in surrender did put a smile on her face.

A few minutes later, Godric joined them, looking virile in his hunting jacket and buckskin breeches. He held out a black coat for her.

"It is my old coat, Emily. Let me put it on you."

Emily stood away from her chair and put her arms into the coat he held for her, and then he spun her around to face him so he could button it up. She wanted to swat his hands away and do it herself, but knew she'd lose that battle.

"There." He patted her shoulders so roughly that Emily staggered. The jacket hung loosely over her, hiding her figure.

Godric pressed her back down into her chair and took a seat next to her. "Now, finish your breakfast."

Emily felt a childish retort on the tip of her tongue but for once restrained herself.

After everyone ate, Ashton and Cedric fetched the guns while Godric lingered in the hall with Emily. He seemed indecisive about something, but finally spoke.

"You know, I don't think I had my proper good morning kiss from you." His eyes heated as they fell on her.

"You're mistaken. You stole a fair number of kisses from me this morning." Something in his face had changed, the dark part of him seemed to have returned, meaning to restore his control. She couldn't allow that, not if she wanted him to fall in love with her.

"This morning was an introduction to another type of pleasure."

"Well, I hate to disappoint you, Godric, but you are out of opportunities." Emily took a big step back, putting herself out of his immediate reach.

He advanced.

"That is the beauty of holding you captive. I don't need to worry about opportunities."

Oh? He thought she couldn't play the game back? Well, he was about to earn his kisses. She bit back a grin and glanced about the hall. Could she make it up the stairs to a room? No, he'd snare her halfway to the top.

She bolted, thinking only to get the first doorway she could find, his study. She slammed the door, turned the key in the lock and braced herself against the door.

Godric beat on it from the other side. "Emily, open this door at once! I am in no mood to hunt you down."

She huffed. "But it's such a fine day for hunting, don't you think?" Let him make what he would of that.

"Simkins, get me the spare key!"

"Oh, blast." She studied the window. A sash window. The view beyond the windowpane revealed a small side garden on the left end of the manor.

She lifted the sill until the bottom half was wide open. Gathering her skirts in one hand, she tucked her legs up and dropped over the edge into a flowerbed.

Emily's hopes of evading Godric unseen were hampered. A gardener tended to a row of nearby yew bushes with a pair of shears— a stunningly handsome young man in his early twenties. He ran a hand through sandy blond hair that cast shadows above his eyes as he stared at the bushes he was working on. Hoping to sneak past, she started to move, but he turned just as she raised one foot. His gaze caught hers, a bewitching emerald trap she was intimately familiar with.

Her gut clenched, and realization dawned—this man had to be related to Godric. This man before her was a golden haired replica.

But Godric had been an only child—

The man dropped his shears and removed his gardening gloves. "You, I am guessing, should not be out here alone. His Grace must be looking for you."

"I...I was taking a bit of fresh air."

He studied her with amused interest...his eyes that same bewitching green. A distant cousin, perhaps? Surely, he had to share the same blood.

"Fresh air, eh? You couldn't have just walked out the front door, like a proper young lady? Scampering out of study windows is highly suspicious."

She waved her hand airily. "Oh, it's all the fashion in London, I assure you. Excellent source of exercise if one cannot go on a walk in Hyde Park."

The man smiled. "All the fashion? Be that as it may, I am afraid I must escort you back to His Grace."

He could have just taken her arm, politely escorting her back to her captors, but he didn't. He grabbed her by the waist and hoisted her up over his shoulder. It seemed they had that in common as well.

"Good heavens! Put me down at once! I assure you it is just a game I am playing with His Grace. He would have found me soon enough."

"I'm sure he would, Miss. Nevertheless..."

He even talked like Godric. If not for his sandy blond hair, she would have sworn that...but that was impossible.

The young man carried her around to the front of the manor. Cedric and Ashton stood waiting, guns in hand.

Cedric chuckled. "Afternoon, Jonathan. I suppose we're fox hunting after all."

"And the hound's already got her," added Ashton.

Emily knew she must be offering the rogues an excellent view of her backside and kicking legs. Jonathan put a firm hand on her rump and Emily growled indignantly. Would no man in this world treat her with the respect she deserved?

"Put me down at once!" Emily balled a fist and pounded it into Jonathan's own rump. "How do you like it?"

Jonathan jerked in shock. "She's a spitfire!"

Ashton laughed. "You have no idea."

Despite being a servant, this one seemed at ease with Godric's friends, even more so than Simkins. Emily filed this away for further contemplation.

"How did you catch the vixen?" Cedric walked around behind Jonathan to look at her. Emily scowled as the blood rushed to her head.

"She was climbing out of His Grace's study window. I thought His Grace might have misplaced her."

As if summoned, Godric came storming around the corner. No doubt he had climbed out the same window. Relief softened the anger in his eyes.

"Ah, Helprin, you found her. I wasn't sure how far she'd gotten."

"Not far. She barely put up a fight. Just stood there staring at me." Jonathan slid Emily off his shoulder and into Godric's waiting arms.

Godric held her firmly in place as she looked away from all of the smiling men. They had yet again wounded her pride, and things continued to worsen.

Godric loosened a coil of rope from his arm.

Cedric and Ashton kept her rooted to the ground while Godric secured her. With a complex knot about her waist Emily found herself anchored to Godric, separated by only six feet. His friends released her. She plucked at the rope and then looked up at Godric, her lack of amusement evident.

"This isn't humiliating at all," she said, her voice laced with sarcasm.

"Don't pout, Emily. You can't run from me now. I always get what I want, and it is time for you to accept that."

"If we are discussing things that we must learn to accept, you ought to accept that I won't cower and just melt in your arms whenever you command! I have better things to do with my life than become your plaything!"

Godric didn't seem the least bit perturbed. He grabbed her by the arms, tugged her to his chest and covered her mouth with his. Godric's tongue shot straight between her lips, and Emily's body reacted as it always did, with weak knees and a heat that defied rational thought entirely. Damn her senses.

She was still on her feet only because Godric maintained a firm grip on her arms. Otherwise she would have collapsed like a newborn foal, shaky and untested.

"What was that you were saying about not melting in my arms?"

Dimly Emily remembered their audience, staring at Godric's eyes was like being swallowed up in a meadow of tall grass, a personal paradise for her and her alone.

"I..." Coherent words weren't possible. Godric smiled with the grin of a cat sated on a bowl of cream. She bristled with indignation. He enjoyed destroying her resistance. If he meant to toy with her, just use her the way he would any woman... Well! That wasn't going to happen.

"You bind me as if I am a dog on a leash, then take what you desire with no regard to me. Touch me again, without my permission—" her voice dropped into an icy hiss "—and you will lose a body part, the one you favor most. Think about that. I have not asked to be here. I am not some lightskirt, and when you treat me like one, it is humiliating."

Godric blinked. He'd clearly not expected this reaction. "But, darling—"

"Do not 'darling' me, Your Grace." Emily dragged her index finger in a dangerous line down his chest to his waist and scissored her fingers. "I will geld you like a horse if you continue to treat me so."

Her words might have made more of an impression if the other rogues hadn't been laughing so hard.

"Are we ready to leave?" asked Cedric. "As much as I enjoy a good kissing, if I'm not on one end of it, I tend to lose interest. We are wasting the day away watching you two have all the bloody fun."

Godric studied Emily's face for a long moment, then brushed a loose coil of her hair back from her cheek. "We're ready, Cedric. Lead the way."

The hunting party set out. Penelope bounded ahead of them, her young instincts guiding her. Cedric, the most avid hunter, cradled his gun in the crook of his arm, scanning the fields and woods. They climbed over the stone wall and moved into the forest. The weather was fine. A cool breeze tugged playfully at Emily's loose hair.

She'd not used Godric's butterfly comb. Libba told her that it wouldn't match her outfit. She'd been right, but Emily brought it with her to put her hair up later.

As she trudged behind Godric and Ashton, Emily slipped it into her hair. She plucked it from the hidden pocket of her skirts and gathered her hair back into a loose bun, and then slid the comb's teeth in to secure it.

Godric walked ahead of her. The length of rope tightened between them before she could catch up and the rope jerked her forward. He spun around as the rope tugged, just in time to catch her stumbling into his arms.

He pulled her up against him with ease, saving her from a nasty fall.

"What were you up to, little vixen? Escape again?"

"And give you a reason to chase me? Not a chance." She hoped he'd notice the comb, but wasn't going to point it out to him. She didn't need to inflate his oversized sense of self further.

Ashton walked past the pair of them. "That is a lovely comb you have in your hair, Emily." He hurried to catch up with Cedric.

Godric, gripping Emily's arm, turned her around. "You weren't wearing that when we left."

Emily's lashes dropped. "Libba said it didn't match my outfit, but I expected there to be wind, so I smuggled it out."

Godric smiled with such warmth and pride that Emily tingled. He gripped her waist again, pulling her against him, his body warm and hard, unlike the cold air that danced, shifted, celebrated around them. Emily didn't mind at all.

"You do find ways to get what you want, even if you continue to act like you don't." He chuckled.

"Minor victories, Your Grace, are not worth counting."

"Everything you do is worth counting."

He didn't move to kiss her as she'd expected him to. He merely moved his hands up and down her back over the loose hunting jacket.

She shivered beneath his touch.

"Are you warm enough, darling?"

"I am warm whenever you touch me." Realizing she'd admitted too much, she hastily added, "When I wish to be touched, that is."

"Hmm, I shall remember that." He released his hold on her waist and put an arm around her shoulders as they walked after the others.

Emily realized Godric wasn't carrying a gun. "Are you not shooting today?"

"I don't need to hunt. I've already caught you." He kissed the top of her head.

"It is highly unfair that Penelope is running around free while I am leashed."

Godric considered this. "You're quite right. Cedric, tether the pup so she doesn't wander off." He looked back to Emily. "There, my dear, fairness has been achieved."

Cedric grumbled. "Would you two kindly stop cooing at each other like a pair of doves? You are scaring away the pheasants."

"Jealous, Sheridan?" It was the first time Emily had ever heard one of the five men call another by his last name. It sounded like a schoolboy challenge, and she nearly laughed. Men would always be boys on some level, that much never changed.

"Jealous of you?" Cedric snorted. "You think I want to constantly chase and tie down a little fox like her? Not on your life, St. Laurent. It is far too much work. No woman is worth that."

Emily lifted her skirts as she stepped over a large stone. "Not even Anne Chessley?"

Cedric froze, his foot braced on a fallen log, watching the dog.

Penelope sniffed around the log's opening and then dove inside.

"Penny, come!" Cedric commanded, tugging on the leash.

The little hound crawled out from under the fallen log, looking alert and ready.

"Penny, sit." Her haunches dropped, her tail wagging on the grass, stirring leaves with its energetic swiping.

"Good girl." Cedric pulled out a biscuit from his pocket and tossed her a piece. Penelope caught the crumb, licking her lips.

"She's a fast learner. You should have no trouble with her, Emily."

"Cedric, you didn't answer my question."

"I had not planned on doing so."

"But—"

"No, Emily." He made a show of checking his gun and jumped over the log, walking away from them. Emily watched his retreating back with disappointment.

Ashton bent to stroke Penelope's head. "He's a bit stubborn when it comes to women."

"Really? When he told me about how he met Godric—"

Godric and Ashton looked at her.

"He told you that story?" Godric's face was red. Emily couldn't contain her grin. It was nice to see him flustered for a change.

"Oh, yes. He told me you got into a fight with an upper year over a woman."

Godric stumbled a step. "He did?"

Emily thought of the man with the cane. "Did you know Waverly very well?"

"Hugo was an older student and an unpleasant fellow to say the least," Ashton said. "He made a lot of trouble for us, but if it hadn't been for him we would never have met Charles."

"How did you meet Charles?"

Godric and Ashton laughed. Their reaction contained no humor, only a strange coldness.

Ashton answered vaguely. "What a night that was. Suffice it to say we rescued him from a rather prickly situation that Waverly put him in. Rescuing him was how the League was formed."

"Oh, but you must tell me more than that, Ashton!" Emily tugged on his sleeve, annoyed that he would deprive her of what was sure to be a grand tale.

"Perhaps at dinner. It is better if Charles is there. It is after all, more his story than ours."

There was another log ahead of them. Ashton casually stepped over it. Emily tried to lift her skirts, but Godric merely scooped her up and stepped over the log before setting her back down on her feet. She shook her skirts, trying to resume some sense of dignity, but none of the others had noticed. They took their hunting very seriously.

Far ahead, a crack of gunfire sounded as Cedric felled a pheasant. Emily, startled by the sound, took a step closer to Godric. She wasn't frightened of guns, but there was something about those first few shots, when the shooter was out of sight, which made her nervous.

"Can't stay away from me after all, eh?"

"Actually, your height and build are excellent for a shield."

Ashton chuckled but Godric recovered quickly and threw an arm back around her shoulders, keeping her tucked against his side.

"Cedric is fine shot. He won't hit me, no matter how much you might wish for him to shoot my black heart."

She gave him a wicked smile. "If he managed to hit your backside, that would be well enough for me."

"Careful, darling, my temper is all over the place today."

She had a retort ready, but silence was probably best.

"Well, look at that." Ashton pointed to Penelope. Too small to carry her prize, the pup had resorted to dragging the pheasant along, growling with the effort. Cedric followed the dog, flashing a black look in Emily's direction.

"Here, Penelope." Emily patted her thighs. She dropped the bird and ran to her, bright eyes fixed intently on Emily. She rather looked like she was smiling, with her tiny pink tongue lolling out between her white little teeth.

"Good girl." Emily picked the dog up, hugged her and set her back down.

Ashton picked up the pheasant and dropped it into a burlap sack.

Cedric fixed a surly look at Penelope. "Little Penny here is just as willful as her mistress. She broke away from my grip, then refused to bring the bird I shot back to me." He continued to scowl at the dog, but without real malice.

Godric grinned. "She's loyal. You can't fault her for that."

Cedric frowned as he reloaded his flintlock. Emily figured the irritation of loading a gun was one of the reasons Cedric had learned to be a good shot. A man could grow old reloading his gun.

"I think I'll try my luck." Ashton hoisted his gun and walked off. Penelope followed at his heels.

Now alone with the duke, Emily wondered about a different matter.

"Godric, may I ask a question?"

He nodded.

"What is Mr. Helprin to you?" She phrased the question carefully, in case the answer proved upsetting.

"Jonathan? He's my valet."

"Valet? I haven't seen him attend you..."

Godric pulled her to a stop and cupped her shoulders. "Why the sudden interest in my valet? Not thinking of making me jealous, are you?" He grinned below stony eyes.

She couldn't resist teasing him. "Would you get jealous? I assumed with your hundreds of mistresses, you wouldn't worry if I turned my attention elsewhere."

"Don't you dare joke about that, Em." He growled the new nickname. "I want only you. I have no other women."

He didn't declare his love, didn't promise a permanent relationship, but it was a start.

Emily leaned against him, hugging his waist briefly on impulse.

"Will you untie me now? I'm not in the least inclined to run off."

"No. I like you tied to me." His words seemed filled with a deeper meaning.

The forest was quiet and beautiful. A fullness settled into the air and woods, as though a sleeping god dwelt within a tree close by. The trees sighed and swayed with the pull of the breeze. Magic coated the forest floor, and leaves fell every few moments in a storm of gold and red.

Everything was perfect. She owned a loyal hound, and walked in the presence of a man who wouldn't let her leave his side, albeit in a far too literal fashion, and the company of new friends built inside her a peace and joyful fervor. Words were unnecessary. Instead she spoke to Godric with smiles and the clasping of his hand in hers.

Life with her uncle had been cold. There were no jokes, no laughter, not even tears; just awful silence and the scratching of quills on paper. Why couldn't time stop for just a few days? A few weeks? She could stay here forever with Godric and the others.

"What are you thinking about?" Godric asked. Emily came back to herself, trying to dissolve the sudden melancholy.

"It's nothing." She tried to wipe away the evidence of her tears.

Godric's brow furrowed. "You are unhappy? Does the rope hurt?"

The caring tone clashed with his words in such a way that it made her laugh but it came out as a sob. "Unhappy?"

He massaged her waist, but she shook her head, and turned away, ashamed. She tripped on a broken branch but Godric caught her. He pulled her fully into his arms and held her tight to his chest.

"What... What can I do?" He couldn't know what she wanted or needed, but his intentions warmed her heart.

"Please, Godric, just hold me for a moment." Her lips brushed his throat as she snuggled against him.

He walked them back to the nearest log and sat down, cradling her in his lap. From the moment her parents died, no one had held her, comforted her. She'd been forced into her uncle's household, where her heart withered and died.

Godric wasn't offering love, but at least he cared, and that was a thousand times purer to her then anything her uncle had provided.

At that moment, Emily needed Godric's warmth, his strength, his embrace, more than she needed the air in her lungs.

It finally hit. Her parents were dead, and they would never come back. She was alone.

Tears came. Harsh, painful tears, but she let them flow, let them rule her. Soon enough they faded, and she was empty, a skeleton on the inside.

"Emily, are you all right?" Godric's warm lips caressed her ear.

"I'm...I will be all right. I am sorry to have cried. It must be annoying to listen to me."

"The only thing that upsets me is knowing I've made you cry."

"You? Oh, Godric, this was not... My tears were for my parents. It's finally sunk in that my parents are dead...that they're never coming back." Her voice shuddered. "I can't help but wonder what their last moments were like. My mother never learned how to swim... She must have been so frightened." Emily couldn't breathe, thinking about the cold, dark waters. A tightness gripped her mind, clenching around her head, making it hard to think.

"Breathe, Emily. Breathe." Godric's arms tightened about her body as he held her closer to him. Rather than feel suffocated, his embrace cocooned her with strength. She felt his mouth against her temple as he kissed her. Emily drew in a slow, painful breath.

"My poor darling," he murmured between gentle kisses that traveled down her from her temple to her cheek. He nuzzled her neck, and his scent flooded her nose. It was soothing, dreamy, and yet enticing.

"I know what I can do to make you smile again."

"What? No, not that!"

"Oh yes."

Emily threw her arms around herself defensively, but it was too late as Godric began to tickle her.

In seconds she was laughing again. It was too odd to believe, she and the infamous Duke of Essex were entangled together, laughing and teasing. It was how she'd always believed love would be like.

The stormy passion in his eyes softened when she smiled at him. "Come on. We ought to catch up with the others."

Emily climbed off his lap.

They started to walk, and without a word, Godric slipped his hand into hers, their fingers lacing as if the world had always meant them to be together.

Chapter Twelve

Thomas Blankenship stood in the parlor of Evangeline Mirabeau's townhouse, admiring the woman. She reclined on a chaise and watched him through hooded eyes painted an unusual, rich, honey-colored hazel. Her curves—large breasts and shapely legs, revealed through a dampened muslin gown in thin blue—could easily harden a man. Her pale blonde hair curled in perfect ringlets down her neck and back.

Blankenship smiled. It was no surprise that this courtesan had been the Duke of Essex's lover for a year and then some. If Blankenship didn't contain such a hatred for whores, he would be tempted to sate his desires between this woman's thighs. Evangeline had the body of a siren, one that beckoned men to perish upon the rocks at sea, but she lacked Emily's innocence and sweet nature. He craved that, needed to bathe in it, let it soothe the beast which rampaged in his head.

"*Monsieur* Blankenship, we have not met, have we?" A lilting, sultry French, Evangeline's accent alone would have swayed most men. She must have entertained Essex in his bed in ways innocent little Emily Parr never would, unless the duke took the time to teach her. Blankenship certainly hoped he would. It would make his own claiming of her all the sweeter.

"No, Miss Mirabeau, we have not yet had the pleasure. But we share a mutual acquaintance—the Duke of Essex."

Evangeline's eyes narrowed. "Oh? And how did you come to meet His Grace?" She spit out her words with all the friendliness of a viper. The duke had burned this lovely bridge and Blankenship would benefit from the destruction.

"He and I crossed paths when he stole something that belongs to me."

She laughed harshly. "His Grace, steal? Impossible, *Monsieur*. Whatever he wants, he acquires, either by charm or money. Steal? *Mais non.*"

"Ahh, but he has changed, Miss Mirabeau. What he stole from me is the reason I have come to see you."

Evangeline lifted a hand to idly gaze at her nails, but the faintest blush in her cheeks revealed her interest. "*Moi? Pourquoi?* I have not been with His Grace for the last six months. What has he stolen from you, *Monsieur?*"

"A young lady."

Essex's ex-mistress started.

"He has stolen a young lady from me."

"A young lady?"

"Yes. Her name is Emily Parr, and her uncle is in debt to me, as well as His Grace. Essex decided to abduct Miss Parr from her uncle, who has refused to pay him. Since she is my property, I want her back."

She moved to rest her hand on her hip, smoothing the silk as she did so.

"How do you know he stole this girl?"

"He wrote her uncle a note." Blankenship approached her and passed her a piece of paper, which she studied.

"This is Godric's handwriting, written in his left hand. A school boy trick."

"Yes. I took the magistrate to his estate, but we were unable to find her. They must have hidden her."

"They?" Evangeline raised an eyebrow.

"He had his League—" he choked back the urge to spit "—with him."

"Did he? Then it is no surprise. Those men are stubbornly loyal to one another." Her derisive tone and the flare of bitterness in her eyes was a pleasant surprise.

She would be an excellent ally.

"What do you want from me, *Monsieur?*"

"I would like to employ you in a scheme that would return Miss Parr to me, and perhaps give you the chance to win Essex back."

"Win him back? I never lost him!"

"Ah, yes, of course." He resisted the urge to smile. She'd revealed her weakness. Pride.

Evangeline pouted a moment before she spoke again. "What is

this scheme of yours?"

"I give you this letter, written to mimic Essex's hand, which invites you to come to his estate and spend time with him. It implies that he is not finding satisfaction with Emily. You will confirm my suspicion that Emily is there and send me a letter by post to this name and address. It should not raise Essex's suspicion in case he monitors your correspondence. Provide me with any details as to her exact whereabouts in the house, where they are keeping her, the routines of the serving men, anything you can tell me that will help me retrieve her."

"And once you know that she is there?"

"I have in my employ a most dangerous man, one who will stop at nothing to get the girl. Assuming the duke and his friends stay out of the way, they should not be harmed. Once I have the girl, Essex will be free and clear for you to take back." Blankenship's smile held no warmth.

A hint of wariness betrayed the Frenchwoman. "This hired man... Would he kill Godric?"

"If Essex tries to stop him from bringing back the girl, then yes. He is very skilled. I have more men to back him, just as ruthless in their means." Should someone pry the information from her, better that she lead Godric's men to believe he had an army at his disposal.

For a long moment, Miss Mirabeau did not speak. He had no doubt she still cared for Essex. It only made her more likely to help his cause if she could spare her lover and get him back.

"Your plan is ridiculous. His Grace will know he did not write this note. How will I explain my sudden appearance?"

"Tell him it must have been a prank played on you. Show him the note, say you've given your servants a vacation and it would be a hardship to return so soon. He's a gentleman and no doubt he'll let you stay. I will pay you handsomely for this little mission."

Greed lit up her eyes. "How handsomely, *Monsieur*?"

"Very."

She plucked the cheque he held out, eyes widening at the sum. "*Monsieur!*" She smiled, but at the same time, it wasn't a smile at all.

"And more when you return," he added.

"Consider us partners."

Soon Emily would be in Parr's house and Evangeline back in

Essex's bed. Blankenship would graciously forgive Parr his debts the moment Emily was his. He would have Emily, and Essex would be out of the way.

The hunting party had nearly reached the edge of the gardens, bags full of pheasants, when Emily tripped on a loose stone and rolled her ankle. The men turned at her cry. It hurt like the devil, and she couldn't stifle her whimper. Godric instantly assessed the injury, his fingers pushing her skirts up. He touched her stocking-covered ankle with gentle but firm fingers.

"Does that hurt?"

Emily answered with a wince. She fought to stand upright.

"Don't be silly. I'll carry you." Godric slid an arm behind her back and the other under her knees, lifting her up. Penelope followed close by, whining softly. Ashton and Cedric stayed ahead to help open the garden gate and the door back into the manor.

"Your Grace! What's happened?" Simkins approached, his wrinkled face lined even further.

"Emily sprained her ankle. Have dinner for two brought up to my chambers. I don't want her to aggravate it."

He glanced from her to Godric and said, "Of course, Your Grace," before he departed.

"What's all this, then?" A familiar voice called from the stairs. Charles and Lucien were back from London, it seemed.

"When did you return?" Ashton asked.

"Half an hour ago. Simkins told us you were out hunting." Lucien glanced at Emily in concern.

"Odd looking pheasant you have there, Godric. Did you shoot her in the leg?" Charles, unfortunately, was as brash as always.

"Hardly. I tripped on a stone on my way back into the garden."

"You're not hurt?" Lucien asked.

Cedric picked up Penelope, who was now sniffing Charles's boots. "She may have sprained an ankle."

Godric ignored the conversation and carried Emily up the stairs. He lay her down on his bed and untied the rope from his waist but did not free her. He took the loose end of his rope and tied the same intricate knot to his bedpost.

"Godric, honestly, is that necessary?"

Godric caught her chin in one hand, tilting her lips up to his as he kissed her.

"It is not yet ten, and I don't believe in taking chances where you are concerned. I'll be back soon." He kissed her again, a lingering pull of her lips, a tease of his tongue against hers, before he finally left her alone.

Emily rubbed her ankle and rotated it slowly a few times in each direction, working through the pain. As a child she'd often rolled her ankle. The pain never lasted long. The stiffness had already begun to fade.

Godric was smart to keep her restrained, but foolish to think she was powerless. Emily studied the knot of the rope around her waist. It was a multi-looped creation that she could eventually undo. Struggling with the knot for a few minutes, she managed to loosen it, but upon the sound of footsteps outside, she dropped her hands into her lap. Godric, Simkins and Libba bore two trays of food, a bottle of wine, and a pair of glasses. The maid gave Emily a conspiratorial wink as she and Simkins left.

Godric pushed one of the trays nearer to Emily, pointing at the dishes before he untied the rope at her waist. She supposed now that he had returned he could watch over her himself.

"Hare soup, lark pudding and," he grinned, pointing to the small chilled bowl covered with a silver lid, "ginger ice cream."

"Ice cream?" Emily's stomach growled. Ice cream was a delicacy only those with an icehouse could afford.

Godric smiled. "Perhaps I should have used ice cream earlier to bribe you into being a good captive..."

Emily reached for the small bowl, eager to feel the cool treat melt in her mouth. Godric swatted her hand away with a tisk.

"You must eat your other food first. Simkins would have my head if he learned you'd seduced me into letting you eat your dessert first."

"Would he?" She couldn't imagine that.

"Well, no, he'd simply look at me in disappointment, which is somehow rather worse."

"Can you even be seduced over ice cream?" She curved her lips in a small but suggestive smile. His answering grin nearly melted her insides.

"You'd be surprised."

Godric handed her a knife, fork and spoon. Emily smiled ruefully as he went to shut and lock his bedroom door, closing them in together.

"Am I going to eat here on your bed?"

"*We* are going to eat on my bed," he corrected as he sat down next to her.

"But..."

It was too nice, too sweet, to think that he wanted to share a meal so privately with her. Emily shied away from him, knowing if he touched her, she'd lose her tenuous grip on control. Half of her wanted to toss the food off the bed and taste him instead. The other half knew that each moment she spent with him, she drew one step closer to losing her heart.

"Eat, my dear, or you won't get to the ice cream."

Emily sighed and started on the soup and pudding.

Godric ate alongside her, the silence surprisingly pleasant. It was a simple joy, to have him so close, just existing in a space so near her.

"How is your ankle?" Godric set his tray down on the floor and reached for her leg. He pushed her skirts up past her knee. Shivers shot up Emily's spine.

"It is much better. I think it will be all right soon enough. I often hurt myself that way as a child. I never sat still long enough. My mother said I was quite the hoyden. That's why she started to educate me in all of those languages." Emily settled back into the pillows of the bed, shifting her shoulders for the best position of relaxation. Memories of her childhood unfurled like brightly colored flags in the wind.

Godric's palm moved over her leg as he listened to her talk. Emily knew she ought to be ashamed for letting him touch her so boldly, but they'd done so much together already that she couldn't bring herself to resist such a simple, sweet touch.

"Learning was the only way she kept me still. We used to hole up in the library for hours, reading stories in other languages. She challenged me, rewarded me when I did well." Emily smiled. That her mother persuaded her to abandon the outdoors for at least an hour so she might read was miraculous. "We used to hide from Father when he came to look for us at lunchtime. I will never forget when we hid under the table by the door and snuck out the door past him. He came into the dining room and found us already eating. I don't think he ever figured out how we did that. Mother was so clever." She batted away a tear.

"I imagine she was a wonderful woman." Godric caressed Emily's leg again, toying with the edge of the stocking near the knee, as though he longed to slide it off her. Emily felt her breath quicken but she struggled to remain calm.

"She was a great woman. My father said the world always needed more women like her. He wanted me to be as intelligent as she was." Tears prickled Emily's eyes, but they didn't sting. They were tears of acceptance from remembering happier days. Would she ever feel that way again?

Godric stole her attention as he pulled her onto his lap, picked up the bowl of ice cream, and held a spoonful to her lips. He'd abandoned his cravat and waistcoat, the white lawn shirt molded to his frame. He rested his chin on her shoulder as he watched her eat. To sit on his lap, to feel him as he held her close, shot Emily onto a plane of wonder.

"I want to know everything about you, Emily. Tell me the story of your life."

"The story of my life? There isn't much. I've spent more time dreaming about a life yet to be lived than actually living it. My father was not ambitious and had no love of town. We rarely went to London and I've never set foot off English soil. My parents, however, were often gone. My father had part ownership of a shipping company and he would travel to the various ports to see how the business was getting on. He always took my mother...they were so in love."

Flashes of memory, her father's fleeting smiles at her mother as she donned her traveling cloak. The brush of lips on her chubby child cheek as they headed for their hired coach, leaving her behind, clutching Mrs. Danvers' skirts. If only she'd known this would be their last trip. When her parents had left, she'd been deep in the woods behind their cottage, sketching wildflowers and birds for an essay she was writing. She'd arrived an hour too late to say goodbye and this haunted her.

Emily would have given her soul to go back in time and make herself leave her sketching for another day and return home early. She would have held her mother tight, clung to her father, and begged them not to go. One never knew the mistakes one might make, nor the price to be paid until it was too late.

Godric seemed to sense her distance and brushed a lock of hair back from her face. "You wish to travel?" His free hand dipped his spoon into her bowl and stole her ice cream.

"More than anything, I want to..."

"You want to what?"

"It's silly."

Godric abandoned his spoon to stroke her cheek with the back of his hand. "Tell me."

It was so easy to give in, to surrender to anything he asked of her, when he touched her like that. "My father left me his interest in the company as my inheritance. A fair amount of money came with it and would have gone to my husband upon marriage. I'd hoped to marry someone who'd allow me take over my interest in the company and manage the books. I could travel, see the world when I had the chance. Wouldn't it be glorious to have an opportunity to live? I want to bathe in the Mediterranean Sea, I want to feel the Egyptian sun on my skin, and I want to throw a snowball in the Pyrenees. I want to taste the Indian curries, and see the temples of the Orient..."

Godric's eyes softened.

"Those aren't silly wishes." Godric's hand against her cheek moved down her neck, a fingertip drawing a line down towards her collarbone. Emily wanted nothing more in that moment than to live her dreams with him.

"Perhaps not, but I am silly for hoping they will ever happen." She set down her spoon and bowl.

When it was clear he would not release her, she settled back in his arms. He wrapped himself around her, burying his face in the groove between her neck and shoulder, his lips pressing into her skin. Emily's head fell back against his shoulder as he moved his mouth up her neck towards her ear, nipping her lobe.

She sighed, a haze of warmth coiled around her body. She could have slipped into sleep, safe in his arms. The grandfather clock in the hall chimed nine times. The distant pings roused Godric and he eased her off his lap.

"I must go down and see to the others. I shall be back soon and we'll go to bed." He didn't wait for her to protest but left her alone to sit and wait.

The five men stood around the billiard table in the drawing room. Cedric lined up his shot while Lucien and Charles told the others about their time in London.

"We ran across Blankenship in Hyde Park," Charles said, swirling a glass of brandy.

Ashton's eyes flashed. "Really?"

"Yes, I took the time to remind him of his debt to me," Lucien said. "It seems, he's quite clever in his financial practices. He takes investments from men like me and uses them to break men like...Albert Parr. I asked around today and it seems that there are hints here and there which point to Blankenship having masterminded Parr's money troubles."

Godric picked up a cue from the wooden stand up against the wall. "I wonder if Blankenship bankrupted Parr just to obtain Emily..." He studied the billiard table then looked at Lucien. "How did Blankenship's debt to you come about?"

Lucien took his time in answering. Once he pocketed two balls, he answered Godric's question. "I've only met him once. I sold him one of my smaller properties in France, the little cottage near the Château de Chenonceau."

Charles sighed wistfully. "I rather liked that place..."

"Well, Blankenship has the deed to it. He's only paid me the down payment." Lucien's face darkened, his features stilling into coolness. "He hasn't sent me the remainder for the property."

Godric almost pitied Blankenship. Those who dared to cheat Lucien of anything could end up on the wrong end of a dueling pistol.

"You don't think he'll try to swindle you?" asked Ashton.

"No, I am far too careful to fall into such traps, as is he to be caught using them. He's simply delaying payment to the last possible moment for the sake of interest."

"What was he doing in Hyde Park?" Godric's turn was up. He gripped his cue and took his shot, and missed pocketing a ball by an inch. His mind was decidedly elsewhere and his game suffered for it.

"Not sure. He seemed awfully smug when he saw us, the blighter." Charles growled.

Godric smothered a laugh. They all hated Blankenship for the sole reason that he believed Emily belonged to him. Godric tried not to dwell on the thought. It only reminded him of his own less than respectful behavior.

"That does not bode well. I had my concerns about him since he came here with the magistrate," Ashton said.

"He won't rest until Emily is his," Cedric said.

"Then he will be a very tired man indeed." Godric fought the urge to pace through the halls of the house until all his energy was spent. "We must be vigilant," he said, and the others agreed.

Cedric grinned. "Besides running into Blankenship, I assume you enjoyed yourselves?"

"Indeed we did! Lucien has quite a knack for picking out women who like to experiment. They had these splendid toys imported from—"

"*Ahem.*" Ashton coughed. "As much as we all enjoy tales of your and Lucien's depravity, Charles, there is an innocent young lady under this roof who should not overhear you boasting of your conquests."

Godric stifled a laugh. Once again, his thoughts were drawn to Emily. He'd left her in his bedroom, unable to trust himself with her a moment longer. But he did not simply seek the pleasures of her flesh. He wanted to be with her completely, body and soul. Had he ever been with a woman that way? If he had it must have been years ago... He set the cue down on the table, drawing the attention of the other men. The time for waiting was over. He wanted her and if he was any judge of women, she wanted him just as much.

"Excuse me. I have to check on Emily."

"Of course you do..." Charles chuckled. "I imagine you'll need to check on her all night."

Godric ignored the laughter that followed him as he left the room.

Emily was stretched out on her stomach, reading a collection of essays about philosophy when Godric entered. Her eyes lifted from the pages as he shut his door and leaned back on it, arms crossed. One dark brow rose, as did one corner of his mouth. Her heart leapt. She had the urge to bolt and hide in the underbrush like a startled fawn. The embers between them had smoldered beneath the surface far too long, and would finally be tended to. There would be no going back. Did she trust him?

Yes. Far more than she ought to, but it was too late to question that part of her heart that gave itself over to him.

"Come to me, darling." Like the serpent offering her an apple, his tone promised to educate her with all of the things an innocent young woman shouldn't know.

The book fell from her hands and she eased up into a sitting position. Her mind was clouding with heady desire. He had to be as desperate for this as she was. Emily let her legs dangle over the side of the bed and leaned back, hands behind her hips and chin raised, offering him what she hoped was a come-hither look.

"If it's me you want, then come."

The wolfish gleam in his eyes told her he knew she was trying to control the situation. Finally, he pushed away from the closed door and came to her.

Godric cupped her face with one hand, his eyes flicking to her lips. "Emily, you're driving me mad."

"You think this has been easy for me? You know how I feel, but for you the choice is easy and free of consequence. For me? I'm giving up so much to be with you. Please tell me you understand that..." She didn't want to beg, but the tremor in her voice betrayed her.

"I do..." Godric moved his hands from her shoulders to the neck of her shirt, gripping its edges. In one swift movement he ripped it clean in two, then slid it off her arms and tossed it away. It fluttered to the ground, a white symbol of her surrender.

"You will never regret this choice. I vow it." His voice was ragged as he cupped her shoulders.

"Godric..." She tried to put a hand out to steady him. His whole body shook as his fingers quickly untied her stays.

"Not another word, vixen. The hound has come, and there is no escape." Her mind flashed with the image of a red-coated fox caught between the teeth of a hound. She had always been the fox to him, and he had won.

Godric's hands moved down to her feet, unlacing her boots and dropping them to the floor. He peeled her stockings off next. Emily lay still, watching as he worked on the hooks of her skirt before he slid it to the floor. He stood back, slowly taking off his shirt and casting his boots aside. He started to remove his breeches, but stopped when she shifted uneasily on the bed.

"Now you fear me?"

Emily thought she heard a hint of concern in his tone. *Of course I fear you. You take control of everything, demand I give you everything, not just my body.* Fear danced through her insides, pulling her back. Breaths became shallow, her heart tapping an unsteady, faint rhythm. Would he accidentally hurt her?

He'd taken her from her carriage by force and subdued her. But as their days together passed, he'd also shown a gentleness he was unable to hide. Would the heartless rake or the wounded soul take possession of her?

The determined look in his eyes told her the rake had control, but the shadow of that gentle soul peeked out from beneath his long, dark lashes.

Any remnant of her fears faded, but a nervous tension just as heady to her senses took its place. She didn't know how to be with Godric as a lover.

"I...I'm not afraid." Her insistent tone didn't convince either of them.

Godric took in Emily's appearance; a startled creature in a light, filmy chemise, her hair pulled up. He reached for her but only to remove her hair comb and set it on the bedside table. Her hair spilled around her shoulders. He ran his hands through it, admiring its silkiness.

She mesmerized him like an ancient goddess. He'd been with some of the most beautiful, sought after women in all of England, yet never in his life had a woman held him captive like this. It had everything to do with the way she whispered his name, the way she smiled, and the things that ran through her head as she talked of her dreams. She was not just a warm body to bed. Emily was infinitely more to him. She was real.

He moved his hands up to cup her face, then tilted her head back and plundered her trembling mouth, then dragged her closer to him.

He held her, the heat of her both arousing and soothing. The last thing he wanted was to frighten her, yet here he was ripping her clothes and growling like a damned wolf. His need to have her, to make her his was fast overriding rational sense. But his actions were also rooted in a new fear—losing Emily. She'd become impossible to do without. Godric's arms tightened around her, as though letting go would erase his protection.

The scent of her hair, like fresh-picked flowers, enveloped him, soothed him. She was here, in his arms, safe.

"Don't be afraid," he murmured. His mouth brushed along the line of her jaw to her neck.

Emily sighed, reaching her arms up around him, trying to pull him closer. He took advantage of her distraction by sliding her chemise up. He continued to kiss her until the thin cloth was near her neck, then pulled it up over her head. A gasp escaped her as she tried to cover her breasts. Godric caught her wrists and slowly lowered her back against the bed. He pinned her wrists near her waist.

"Godric... I don't think I'm ready to do this."

"I'd never hurt you, darling. Please believe me." He placed a soft kiss at the corner of her mouth, teasing her. He wanted only to keep her safe, keep her happy. He wouldn't dare risk losing her now.

Emily writhed in mounting pleasure as he slid his hips into the cradle of her thighs. His mouth descended on hers. The heat of his kiss sent thrills through her. She heard in the tone of his voice that he wouldn't hurt her, but her heart was reluctant to believe it.

"Please, Emily, trust me to take care of you. I need you."

Emily pushed at his chest. "You need my body."

Godric pulled back, his emerald eyes drowning her in the endless glints of light. "It's more than that. It has always been more. From the first moment, I knew you were mine, body and soul. Forever."

He twined a loose lock of her hair about one finger, spooling the gleaming coil in a mixture of playfulness and tenderness that undid her. "You've bewitched me, Emily. I'm under your spell and I never wish to wake. Don't deny me the right to worship you, goddess mine." He sealed his plea with a soft circling of his lips over hers, leaving her desperate for more.

Her body sparked to life. Every nerve, every muscle twitched in anticipation of that pleasure she'd yet to experience. It was a gift for which she dared not ask. All that mattered now was Godric. The power of his body, the dance of his tongue, and the ache that built between her legs.

Godric nestled his body against hers, rocking forward, pressing himself against her. Emily struggled to breathe, her lips still his prisoners as he slanted his mouth over hers. His teeth nipped her lips while his hands slid up the length of her outer thighs, pressing down with slight pressure. When he finally gazed down at her breasts, he moaned at the sight of the rosy nipples budding for him.

"I've been waiting to taste you for so long." He laid a trail of kisses from her neck down to her breasts. When he took the breast into his mouth, Emily arched into him as it sent violent tingles down her spine.

His mouth encircled her nipple, tongue laving the taut tip until Emily dug her hands into Godric's hair, urging him to continue. Godric abandoned her breast and reached up to catch her hands, returning them back to the bed near her hips.

"I am not going to give you what you desire just yet."

"No?" she gasped.

He chuckled as he kissed her collarbone. "No. It is time I punish you for your escape attempts."

His tongue flicked out and licked her skin. Emily groaned. "If this is punishment, let me admit to other sins, so I might atone for those too." His heated laugh captivated her with its burning sweetness.

Godric moved his mouth down between the valley of her breasts, past her belly and towards the dark triangle between her legs. He slid off the bed, kneeling between her legs, using his shoulders to keep her knees open as he kissed her inner right thigh. Emily's vision blurred as he moved slowly towards her wet core.

"Godric..." she whimpered as, at last, his mouth moved between her legs. As his tongue swirled sinful patterns into her throbbing flesh, she cried out his name again. He growled, loving the sound of his name as it ripped from her lips in desperation.

Godric was so tight in his breeches he could barely think. He knew he shouldn't bed Emily. He had to stop tasting her, had to stop before he went too far and pounded himself deep into her. She was a virgin, an innocent, and the first time would be painful. She needed the calm, sweet kisses of a lover, not the violence of a man possessed. Godric was on the verge of regaining control when Emily moaned loudly urging him to continue.

He nipped at the sensitive bud of her arousal, gasping himself as she cried out with pleasure. Godric released her hands as he stood to free himself from his breeches. If he wasn't inside her soon he'd lose himself as he had this morning.

Her eyes widened as he kicked his breeches away and stood before her completely nude.

Emily stared at his arousal, eyes glowing with fascination. "Godric, are you going to—"

"Emily, I know this will hurt, but I'll be as gentle as I can." His voice was strained as he parted her knees gently.

Emily wriggled as he settled over her. "Do you promise?"

"I promise." He had never meant any promise more in his life.

He slid his hands down under her bottom and lifted her hips. In one slow motion he thrust deep inside. The wall of her maidenhead tore against the force of his entrance. Emily's sharp cry of pain followed the rise of her hips as she tried to pull free, but the motion only forced him deeper.

Godric froze at the sound of her pain.

"Should I stop?" His voice was raw, scraping over his own ears.

She feathered kisses on his jaw and lifted her hips in encouragement. "No, don't."

Leaning down, he caught her mouth in a deep kiss. Her tension lessened. He urged her to move with him, and match his rocking rhythm. He was soon lost in the tight squeeze of her inner walls and the rise and fall of her breasts as she breathed, and each time a soft sound mewed from Emily's lips. Her legs moved up to wrap around his thighs as he stood at the edge of the bed, bent over her, driving himself into her. Never had he felt so consumed by a woman before, so desperate to brand his soul into the very core of her being.

Mine. You are mine, he said in the rough play of his tongue against hers, his hands clenched her hips tighter as her breasts rubbed against his chest.

A crimson sea of desire enveloped Emily as Godric pushed himself deeper and deeper into her. Each time he withdrew she felt the depths of her own emptiness. Only Godric's returning thrusts eased the ache. Nothing existed, held shape or matter, beyond the mating of her body to Godric's. She tightened her legs, claiming him as hers as her tongue fought its way into his mouth, tasting the ginger from their ice cream and the remnants of brandy.

The ache and flashes of pain turned to bolts of pleasure. She was careening towards a cliff, and once she fell, there would never be a way back up to sanity. The pleasure of this union between them was beautiful and devastating.

"Take me deeper," he urged in her ear as his teeth grazed her neck.

Emily slammed her hips as hard as she could against his. All of him reached, straining towards her womb as the pressure within her crested. Emily swam on a foreign shore of desire, a scarlet sunset splashing her world in shades of fire and pleasure. Godric was there with her, his hand stretched out to grasp her, making her his forever.

She was his. Fire burst out of her body from that single point of connection and rippled through her in crashing waves. Emily cried out again, this time with sheer pleasure and Godric thrust twice more, harder than before, and collapsed onto her with a groan.

She fought to regain her breath. His heat spread out deeply between her legs as he rocked out of her a few inches before he slid back inside. Emily moaned, her inner walls convulsing around him, still welcoming him. Their bodies were damp as he slid against her, nuzzling her neck. Emily wrapped her arms around his body, the muscles of his back shifting with his movements beneath her hands. He reached under her and lifted her up a little, sliding her farther back onto the bed so he could lie beside her.

When he finally pulled himself off her, Emily shivered, and tried to reconnect to him, wanting to be held. Godric drew her against him, hands stroking her back, her bottom, her thighs, back up to her hair, holding it in place at the nape of her neck so he could kiss her. Emily rested her cheek against his chest, savoring his heat and the steady beat of his heart.

"Are you all right, Emily?" Concern roughened his voice.

She shut her eyes, enjoying the warmth of his skin beneath her cheek. "Yes." She loved to feel him breathe, to know that life flooded through him, and that he was hers and hers alone, even if for a brief time.

He kissed her hair. "I didn't mean to hurt you, my darling. The first time always hurts, but I should have been gentler."

"Shh..." She raised a hand to cover his mouth. He kissed her fingertips tenderly and she smiled.

"And to think you meant to punish me." Emily gave a soft, sultry laugh that stirred his desire.

"Don't tempt me to be more creative. Lucien has some fascinating ideas from the Far East involving bondage with strips of red silk—"

"You wouldn't dare!" Her head snapped up, eyes darkening, and gasped as he pinched her. She beat a loosely balled fist on his chest.

"You rogue!" she hissed, but only laughter filled in her eyes now.

"I've never claimed to be anything else." Emily relaxed, burrowing into him, absorbing his warmth. Godric, rather than continue to hold her, disentangled himself and pulled back the covers of the bed.

"Get in," he whispered. He tucked her in and started to dress himself. She looked up at him, the covers pulled tightly to her chin. He had just made a woman of her and yet he was abandoning her.

"Where are you going?" The quiver in her tone shamed her.

"Downstairs. I'll be back soon." He threw his shirt on, waiting for her reply.

Emily opened her mouth but the grandfather clock in the hall outside chimed.

"Ah, ten o'clock." He leaned over and kissed her forehead.

She lay still in his bed for a long minute. She wanted to laugh, to scream with joy. She had never felt so wonderful before. For a time she and Godric had been a single living entity without end or beginning. He'd been lost in her, and she in him. As soon as she realized this, she realized something more important. She never wanted to leave him.

"I love him..." The epiphany brought both thrill and heartache.

She was in love with a man who would never love her back. He was not the sort to love. Men like him never did.

Her plan to seduce him was ever more crucial. She had to do the impossible and win his heart. It was the only way they could both be happy.

Emily snuggled deeper into the covers, Godric's scent wafting about her and comforting her as she dreamt of that oneness.

Chapter Thirteen

Godric returned to the drawing room, where he found all four of his friends overly interested in their billiards game. They glanced at him, then all looked quickly away, and for a long minute no one said a word.

Charles tossed his cue carelessly on the table, ruining the game as it knocked balls out of place. "Bloody hell, if no one is going to ask, then I will. How was it?"

"How was what?" Godric pretended innocence.

"We all know that you and Emily..." For a man who never failed for words, Charles certainly came up short now. "Well, you know... Oh, for God's sake, we have ears, man!"

Cedric hissed, "Good God, do you want to get us shot?"

Godric wasn't the least bit upset. In fact, he found it rather amusing, the image of his friends scrambling like school boys in the hallway just for a glimpse through a keyhole... How could he not laugh?

"There will be no shooting of anyone, unless any man here dares to try seducing her now. Remember Rule Four. She has chosen me. Is that understood?"

Curt nods followed all around.

"You didn't hurt her?" Ashton asked after a moment, his face a little red.

Cedric mirrored Ashton's concern as he leaned back against the billiard table.

"She is fine now. I was not as gentle as I should have been... But I know how to distract a woman from pain and replace it with pleasure. She was brave, my Emily." He'd only slept with two virgins in his long life of conquests. They'd both cried the whole time and he'd sworn off innocents since then. No man liked to spend the entire night cajoling a woman back into some semblance of acceptance.

But Emily had met him with surprising passion, one that rivaled his own.

Ashton fixed him with a look. "She loves you, Godric. A woman in love can endure more pain and suffering than the strongest man. Their hearts are unique things, sturdy and loyal, but susceptible to one great weakness."

The sudden warmth in Godric's chest surprised him. Emily loved him. He liked knowing that she loved him. He struggled to retain his composure. "And what weakness is that?"

Ashton frowned. "It is easily broken if she is not loved in return. You must find it in your heart to love her, Godric, or you will have done her a great injustice."

Godric sighed and ran a hand through his hair. "You may be right, Ash. I've ruined her, at any rate and she deserves to be cared for. We certainly can't return her to her uncle."

Lucien's face darkened. "That would be as good as handing her to Blankenship."

"It is settled, then. At the end of the week I will return to London to tell Parr that Emily is no longer his. Her remaining here with me will be the settlement of his debt to me, and all contact will be severed between us."

"And what about Emily?" Cedric asked.

"I'll keep her here."

"Is that wise?" Lucien asked.

"She'll be bound by her honor. Besides, I doubt she'll try to leave, not after what happened tonight." Godric tried to stop himself, but his lips curved up regardless.

"That good, eh?" Charles chuckled.

Godric shook his head. "As if I'd tell you." What she lacked in experience she made up for with confidence and enthusiasm, and if Ashton was right, love.

He wondered if that emotion, one so elusive in his own heart, had filled the moments with fire and tenderness. He'd lived a life of pleasure, and in that life, love had no part. His lovers enjoyed him as he in turn enjoyed them, but there was nothing more to it than that.

Emily... That had been something else entirely.

"Godric, you will take care next time, won't you?" Ashton said after a minute. "I would hate to see Emily burdened with a babe so young,"

Godric winced. He hadn't even thought about that. Christ! She could be with child now this very minute because he hadn't controlled himself.

"I will take the necessary precautions." There were a few ways, but the best was a French letter, an old favorite of his. He would be prepared next time. Of course, the next month would be a nerve-wracking one as he prayed to God that the first time with Emily didn't result in disaster.

Even as he thought it, he knew a child born from that singular moment of wondrously tender pleasure would be a beautiful one. With his dark hair, and its mother's expressive violet eyes. Her ticklishness. His boldness. What a child that would be. The image of this enchanting nonexistent child shocked him. A child? Eventually he would need an heir.

He needed to clear his thoughts of Emily and that imaginary child. "Shall we start a new game?" The other men joined him at the billiard table.

When Godric finally returned to his bedchamber, he carried a sleeping Penelope under one arm and her basket in the other. He set the basket down near his bedside table and fluffed the blankets for the puppy before setting her down. Penelope licked his hand with a sigh of contentment.

"Good girl." He stroked her sleek head and scratched behind her ears. Her eyes drifted shut and Godric quickly undressed, dropping his clothes in an untidy pile at the foot of the bed, before he slipped under the covers. His body warmed instantly as it came into contact with Emily's.

"Godric..." Emily murmured as she rolled over to face him.

"I'm here, darling." He slid his arms around her waist, tugging her against him. She sighed, rather like Penelope, not really awake. He took advantage and kissed her lips. In the darkness, with their bodies entwined, with no witness but the moonlight, he almost thought himself capable of loving her. Emily almost read his thoughts as he freed her lips and nuzzled her neck.

"I love you," she whispered, speaking to a dark prince in her dreams. She didn't seem to expect a reply.

"I know," he whispered as she fell asleep in his arms. Godric followed her into the land of dreams not long after, into a place surrounded by fields of exquisite butterflies. He could not catch a single one...

Emily woke to a new world.

Her body was languid and loose, flush with a new understanding of herself. No longer did a barrier exist between her and the elusive state of womanhood.

The man who changed everything lay next to her, his skin warm against hers. Before now she'd only ever felt embarrassed and shy about her body, but Godric had seen and tasted every part of her. He too had shared himself. She'd felt the passion in the tenderness of his kiss and the vulnerable glimmer in his eyes.

Emily pulled her hair into a loose coil at the back of her neck as she shifted closer to Godric. His chest rose and fell in a slow pattern of sleep, and she couldn't resist him, as exposed as he was at that moment.

She kissed his chin and trailed her lips down his chest until she reached his left nipple, her mouth teasing it. Godric moaned groggily as his sleeping body responded.

Emily had one leg wedged between his, and his manhood stirred against her thigh.

She sucked harder before moving down over his abdomen.

A hand clasped her head, holding her mouth to his body. He was definitely awake now. "What are you up to, little vixen?"

"I thought I ought to wake you. I desire my good morning kiss."

"Your kiss? My darling, we are far beyond kisses now." His husky tone lit a tingling fire between her legs.

He didn't wait for an invitation but slid her upwards and rolled her beneath him. Catching her mouth in a tender, sinful embrace, his left arm reached for the small drawer on his bedside table.

"What are you doing?" she asked between kisses.

His hand returned to their bodies under the covers. "Don't worry, darling. I'm protecting you, that is all."

The heat of the next kiss stole away all rational thought.

Some time later, she and Godric panted in each other's arms as pleasure flooded their limbs. Godric's body trembled and Emily cradled his head to her breasts, stroking his hair. She couldn't help but admire the deep shades of brown caught by the morning light in his thick mane.

"Why do you tremble?"

"Making love to you..." Godric's voice was barely above a whisper.

"Yes?" She kissed his dark hair, inhaling his masculine scent.

"I feel like a boy again."

Emily was not sure what to make of this. "Is that...a good thing?"

"It is a wonderful thing, Emily. Every sensation, every kiss... It feels new. I never thought I could feel that way again." Godric raised himself onto his elbows as he lay on her, still deep inside, the connection intense between them. His long lashes fanned out over his cheeks as he shut his eyes. The confession seemed to open him, make him vulnerable. She knew that tortured and hesitant look too well.

"Emily, there is something I would like to discuss with you." He gently withdrew, and sat up close to her.

"What is it?" Suspicion clouded the sunny warmth in her heart.

"Because of this new development—" he waved a hand over the rumpled bed sheets "—returning you to your uncle is out of the question. I won't hear of it. But you must decide what you wish to do now."

Emily sat up, bringing the sheet up to cover herself. "You wish to send me away now?" Grief settled over her like a thick wool blanket, smothering her.

"What?" His brows drew together. "Send you away? Are you mad? I want you to stay here, stay with me. You need never concern yourself with your uncle again." His thumbs stroked her cheeks. The gesture calmed her, but her chest still twinged, anticipating the death blow she knew he'd someday deliver to her heart.

"You want me to stay here with you? For how long?" She had to have some answers, even if they were painful ones.

"Yes." The first question he answered without hesitation, but the second question he lingered over. "You will stay as long as you like once this business with your uncle is over."

Emily tried to banish the burn of tears. He was not offering marriage or love, but time. If this was all she could have of him, she would take it, for now.

I will think about the consequences tomorrow.

"Then I will stay." Her agreement brought him back down on her again with eager kisses.

The grandfather clock outside chimed nine times. The morning hours slipped away as they lay amid the destruction of pillows and sheets.

"What about breakfast?" she asked in a sated daze.

"Breakfast?" Godric's hand traced designs on her collarbone. She lay back against his chest. One arm lay wrapped around her upper body while fingers danced across her skin. She watched as one formed a decisive pattern over and over again.

"What are you doing?"

His lips curved into a smile against her cheek.

"Writing my name on you."

"If you're claiming me, then I deserve fair turnabout." Emily caught his hand and turned his palm up until it faced her. She held his hand still and used her right index finger to draw her own name in an invisible signature, then she brought his palm to her lips and sealed her name with a kiss. Godric covered her hand with his and nestled their paired hands on her waist. The soft silence between them was warm and secretive. Beyond Godric and their bed nothing else existed.

Was there ever a moment better than this? Nestled in his strong arms, she felt strong herself. She couldn't help but imagine what life could be with the handsome, brooding Duke of Essex, who broke into smiles just for her and made her laugh and cry out with pleasure. Each breath, each kiss shared between them, tied her heart with strings and connected her to him. She'd always feel that cosmic pull towards him and fall into the gravity of his being. Whatever else happened, this moment, this perfect single instance, would always exist. A sunny memory bathed in love and bottled in her heart. It would never be enough, but she would take whatever came her way until it ended.

The rumble of Emily's stomach broke the silence.

"Right! Breakfast! You must be famished!" Godric flew from the bed in a flurry to dress. Emily gathered her torn garments, heading to her room.

When they finally made it to the dining room the others were finishing their meals. Emily read at once their knowing gazes, and she flushed, eyes falling to the floor as she remembered her cries of pleasure. The entire manor must have heard her and Godric last night...and this morning.

Godric greeted them without a hint of embarrassment. "Morning."

"Morning." Lucien had his usual paper, but he folded it down over his fingers to glance at her and Godric before flipping the paper shield back up. Emily decided Lucien was less interested in his paper than in hiding his expression. She had glimpsed a smirk before the newspaper blocked him from view.

Charles stifled a yawn, running a hand through tousled blond hair. He was such an odd man. His clothes always neat, trim and finely cared for, but Charles himself was always sleepy-eyed and rumpled, as though he'd just emerged from bed.

Cedric kept busy by feeding Penelope crumbs of his leftover toast. A servant must have come up and fetched the pup before she and Godric woke.

Ashton regarded Emily with the same intense scrutiny she had given the others. "You look very lovely this morning, Emily."

The compliment startled and pleased her. "Thank you."

Ashton smiled then turned to Godric and—damn the man!—spoke in Italian. Whatever Godric replied seemed to ease Ashton, and amuse the others, except Cedric. He looked more than once in her direction with a mingled look of pity and concern. Emily's stomach knotted. She ate her breakfast, but chewing became a task. Out of the corner of her eye she watched Godric talk and eat with his friends.

After nothing else distressing occurred, she relaxed.

Cedric eased back into his chair. "I say, Godric, how is the fishing in that lake of yours? Anything worth catching this time of year?"

"It's been months since I've been there with the intent to fish. Be my guest, and feel free to take the others with you." Godric put his hand on Emily's knee under the table. Did he want her to go as well?

Emily bit her lip a moment, debating what his touch meant before speaking. "May I go too? I used to love fishing as a child."

Cedric and Charles exchanged amused looks. Godric's hand tightened on her leg.

"May I, Godric?"

"You want to spend the day fishing?" Displeasure darkened his eyes.

"Well, if you'd rather that I didn't..." She wished she understood men better. They were such secretive, guarded creatures, and entirely unpredictable in what they wanted. They were frustrating.

"Let her come, Godric. Fresh air is good for a woman like Emily,"

Cedric said.

"You truly desire to sit about in a boat for several hours in the sun?" Godric's eyes widened in sheer disbelief.

"You'd be there with me, wouldn't you?" Emily's hand underneath the table settled lightly on top of his hand. "And if you fall in and pretend to drown, I can pretend to rescue you again."

Godric sighed in defeat and shot a rather mutinous glare at Cedric. "Fishing it is then. Give me one hour in my study. I've a few things to attend to." Godric got up from the table and left Emily alone with the other four lords.

Emily finished her hot chocolate before jumping up to follow Godric.

Charles half rose, ready to follow her but Ashton put a hand on his forearm.

"Rest easy, Charles. She is not going anywhere."

"How can you be sure? The little sprite has run us ragged over the past few days! How do you know she's not giving it another go?"

"It is obvious you've never been in love before. Emily doesn't want to let Godric out of her sight. She's attached to him now more than ever."

Charles sat back down. "You're saying that she won't run because she's infatuated with him?"

"Some people spend their entire lives falling in love again and again, over and over. Others fall in love that first time, and it is a true spark of love rather than a passing fancy. What Emily has shown towards Godric is not infatuation." Ashton sighed and took a long sip of his coffee. "And that's what worries me."

He prayed to God that Godric knew what he was doing. If Emily was harmed physically or emotionally it would hurt them all.

To think that the infamous League of Rogues hung on the happiness of one young woman.

Emily paused at the open doorway to Godric's study. He was seated at his desk, pouring over ledgers and letters. She took the opportunity to memorize his features, paint them on the canvas of her mind, and burn them into her heart—the way his dark hair fell into his eyes, the strong hands that gripped the pages, the lean muscled legs stretched out and crossed at the ankles.

With a tentative step she crossed study's threshold. The wooden floor creaked. Godric glanced up at her, smiled and resumed his work. Perhaps another woman would have been upset that she hadn't been addressed. But Godric's polite acceptance of her trespass had a wholly different meaning. It represented trust. She didn't wish to ruin the moment by being bothersome and distracting. She selected a book from the shelves, a botanical discussion of plants native to Kent, and settled herself on the couch near him.

After a quarter of an hour she looked up to find Godric glaring down at a ledger before him, his teeth gritted in a silent snarl. Emily set her book down and got up from the couch, coming behind Godric and studying what had upset him. It was a messy book of accounts, very ill-kept and confusing. But Emily's keen eye located instantly where the numbers were incorrectly calculated.

She put a hand on his left shoulder, her fingers curled into his shirt. "Oh dear. May I help?"

He turned his head in surprise as though not even aware of her presence.

"What?"

She gestured to the books. "Is this how you keep all your books?"

"It's how I was taught."

"But it's so confusing the way you've set up your columns of numbers."

Godric grinned. "It's how business is done, darling."

This time she arched a brow. "Yes, I know, I've seen it before. *In businesses that have failed.* Your structure is wrong. It's a wonder I can even follow the entries."

"You know about accounting?"

"Yes, in fact, I do. Would you like me to fix the errors for you? I can tidy it up in a new book if you have a spare one—"

He gaped at her. "You're serious?"

"I helped my father with his." Emily shooed him out of his chair and sat, pulling the ledger closer and taking an empty book when he fetched it for her. She turned the old book back to the first page and started his accounts over. "Numbers are far less confusing when you arrange them correctly," she said. "Let the sums add themselves, as it were."

In less than an hour she'd corrected all of the miscalculations as well as highlighted the weaker investments he'd made, her uncle's mine scheme included. Godric leaned back against the desk next to her.

"Just when I have myself convinced that I've learned everything about you, you surprise me." He twined a lock of her hair about his fingers, eyes warm on her face.

Emily preened. "Then you're pleased with me?" She wanted to be sure she had not injured his male pride. Men were such fragile creatures.

"What do you think?" Godric pulled her up and into his embrace. He laid a languid kiss on her, fingers digging into her lower back as he pushed her closer to his body.

"I suspect that is a yes."

Godric kept his arms about her waist, nuzzling her neck, the embrace sweet rather than sensual.

"Do you really wish to go fishing, darling? We could empty the house of the others and have it all to ourselves." He flicked his tongue inside her ear.

Desire sparked through her like a lightning strike. As much as she wanted to be right back in bed, uniting herself with him, she worried he might tire of her. She needed him to spend time with her outside the bedroom.

She had to keep him wanting her because, the moment he stopped, her heart would shatter and she'd have to take Penelope and leave. She'd never want or love another man as she did Godric. He hadn't just drawn his name on her body, he'd carved it into her heart.

"I do want to fish." She toyed with the folds of his cravat. He caught her hands, lifting them up to his mouth for a kiss.

"I could certainly make you change your mind." The rich timbre of his voice warmed her.

"I know you could, but we mustn't neglect your friends. They are so kind to keep you company while you hold me captive. You ought to repay them with your presence at least during the day."

"You still see yourself as a prisoner?" asked Godric.

She considered this. She still felt caged by the situation, but the in last day, she had felt distinctly less a captive and something far more.

"No. But, we do need to be more social. I cannot lie in bed with you all day." No matter how enjoyable that might be.

Godric smiled and tucked her arm in his. "You, my dear, have a resolve made of stone, and a silver tongue." He sighed as they left to rejoin the others.

Cedric and Lucien held the fishing poles and Charles a box of lures. Penelope sat patiently at Ashton's feet, her little black nose upturned as she looked from man to man, waiting and watching, knowing something was afoot.

"Ready?" Cedric made no attempt to conceal is boyish excitement as he brushed his chestnut hair back from his forehead. His brown eyes glowed with the fervent expectation of their future fishing expedition.

"Yes, we are." Emily left Godric's side as she caught up with Cedric and Lucien.

"Did Emily join you in your study after breakfast?" Ashton asked Godric, as they watched Emily and the others.

"Yes, and wouldn't you know it, she helped me sort out my investment ledger. You know how dreadful I am at it. She's an excellent mathematician. She got me well sorted out."

"It seems she is still keeping secrets from us. Emily told me she had no head for business."

"Indeed." Godric nodded. "But your choice of Italian this morning was smart. She caught none of what we said, I am sure. She would have certainly blushed."

"I meant what I said. You have to be careful with her. She's too young to be a mother."

"Ash, not today, please. I've heard enough of your scolding. Can't I just enjoy Emily? She is happy, I am happy, you ought to be happy."

When Ashton's gaze did not subside Godric continued. "No matter if Emily was to have a dozen babies pulling at her apron, she would never lose that innocence. It is something not even time in bed can cure, and I am glad for that. It makes each moment precious." It was the first time he'd admitted such emotion aloud, but Ashton only smiled.

"As long as you see the value of it for what it is, that Emily is indeed precious, there is still hope for you." Ashton's blue eyes were grayer today and filled with contemplation and concern.

Godric patted his friend's shoulder. "I'll not do wrong by her, Ash. You have my word on that."

"I am glad to hear it. So long as you treat her kindly you will both be happy."

"Perhaps." Godric knew Emily more and more each day, and while she was gentle to a fault, her rebellious streak was not so much a streak as an impossibly deep river, a river that would never dry up, and never turn its course.

The truth was, he could not do without her. Being with her was like winning the right to breathe. He had to have her, all of her, for as long as he could.

The outing had been an enjoyable one. Cedric was delighted at their catch of perch and wanted to stay out longer, but when the skies above the manor darkened, the group decided to return to shore.

Lucien studied the clouds. "Nasty turn in the weather."

Emily glanced at the marquess. "Do you think it will storm tonight?"

"We could certainly use the rain, but it will make the roads dreadful for any sort of travel"

A low rumble of thunder rippled across the meadow as they walked back to the manor. The sinister crash from the skies churned Godric's stomach. Deep in his bones he sensed something was amiss.

Simkins met them in the hallway, his face strained. "Your Grace, you have a visitor."

"A visitor?" Godric nodded to Cedric and Lucien to take Emily to the drawing room. "I'll only be a minute."

Simkins struggled to maintain his composure. "Yes, Your Grace. She is in the parlor."

"She?"

"It is Miss Mirabeau to see you."

Godric cursed. What the devil was she doing here? He made it clear she was never to darken his doorway again.

Godric patted Simkins's shoulder. "Thank you, Simkins. I'll see her now."

They had once been lovers, but she hadn't understood him and the way he approached his servants. He'd suffered her bad attitude towards his household. Having been born to a family of exiled French aristocrats, she had different expectations of relationships between the classes. Godric viewed a few of his servants like extended family and Evangeline had most vehemently objected to such closeness. The memory of their final fight over her treatment of Simkins left a bitter taste in his mouth.

Evangeline sat primly on the couch near the fireplace, but her demure expression did not fool him one bit. She loved to play at being a lady, but during their time together, Godric hadn't wanted a lady.

"Miss Mirabeau, good evening." She stood up, offering her hand to him. He ignored it and bowed stiffly.

"Why, Godric, we are friends. You mustn't be so formal." She laughed as though amused at his cold reception. Her French accent was softer when she spoke with him. He used to love hearing her breathe his name in the heat of passion.

"I'll be happy to drop formalities. In fact, let us be brief. You're not welcome in my house. What are you doing here?" He wanted her gone, now. She'd no right to come here and disturb his life. Godric especially didn't want Emily to find out about her.

Evangeline turned away from him as she retrieved her fan, swaying her shapely hips. Her dampened salmon-colored gown revealed too much of her body but the sight did not move him.

She dug a letter out of her reticule and handed it over to him. Her eyes ran up and down him as he read.

He placed the letter back into her hands. "I never sent this."

She looked confused, and reached out, putting a hand on his forearm, "But...but *mon amour*, this is your hand. After all of those letters you've written to me, how could I not recognize it? Do you remember...? How you used to tell me all of the wicked things you wished to do to me?" She pushed her chest forward, though it was hardly necessary.

The thought of bedding this woman no longer held any appeal. "Those days are long past and I wrote no letter asking you to come here. I will instruct your coach to come around." It must be some new scheme of hers. Likely she'd forged it herself in attempt to create a reason to come out here and rekindle their relationship.

"*Mon dieu.* I didn't bring mine. I came on a hired coach. It only just left before the storm started. I could not possibly leave."

Godric opened his mouth, closed it. What the devil was she playing at?

"Besides, I've sent my servants away for few days. It would be impossible to find suitable replacements before they return."

He pulled away from her. She was a black stain on his life that he wanted desperately to erase. "You may stay the night and dine in your room. I expect you to leave no later than tomorrow at noon. Do not trouble me or my guests."

She fluttered her lashes. "Trouble? *Moi?* Godric, since when have I ever been troublesome?"

He clasped his hands behind his back to resist the temptation to strangle the damn woman. "When? There was the time you spilled tea on my entire collection of cravats when I wouldn't buy you that emerald necklace you wanted."

"An accident, as I told you then."

"Or perhaps the time when you demanded to have your own carriage made with my family crest on it."

"*Oui.* I admit that was a *petite* bit presumptuous."

"And let us not forget the reason I made you leave. You demanded I put Simkins to pasture."

Her lips formed a *moue.* She had nothing to say to that.

"Shall I be staying in my old room?" Her hopeful tone made his skin crawl. Something wasn't right about her here, but he couldn't put his finger on what.

"No. I have friends visiting, as you must have guessed."

"Indeed. I met with Lord Lennox and Lord Lonsdale earlier when they returned from *qu'est-ce que c'est*...fishing trip?" She seemed to be resisting the urge to laugh at him for enjoying his lands in such a rustic fashion. That was nothing new. "Don't tell me you are forcing a lord to sleep in my lovely little room?"

"A guest."

Evangeline raised an inquisitive eyebrow. "A guest?"

"Yes. A friend of mine from London. She's staying here a while before continuing on to Scotland."

"Very well. If you won't tell me, and you clearly do not wish to entertain me. I suppose I should retire." She was smiling as he showed her out of the parlor. Godric gave Mrs. Downing instructions to settle her and her things in the room at the end of the upstairs hall. The farthest room from his and Emily's.

With Evangeline gone, Godric headed for the drawing room and found Lucien, Cedric, and Charles around a rosewood table playing Whist. Emily was cuddled up next to Ashton on a couch, listening to him read. She put a fist in her mouth stifling a yawn, and stroked Penelope. Jealousy shot through Godric. He wanted to be the one she cuddled against, his shoulder offering her a resting place. Emily glanced up as Godric took a step into the room.

The look in her eyes melted him. He relished that simple joyous expression and tucked it away in the most sacred part of his heart.

She immediately put Penelope down and slid off the couch, going to him.

"You've attended to your visitor?" Ashton rose and came to stand behind Emily. She looked at the two men curiously. Godric knew it must be killing her to not ask for details.

He glanced at Ashton. "She'll dine alone. She knows she must be gone by tomorrow at noon."

A growing sense of unease clenched his insides. Emily raised an eyebrow, and he sighed.

"Miss Evangeline Mirabeau, a former acquaintance of mine. She mistakenly thought I'd invited her here."

Emily blinked rapidly. Her violet eyes darkened with an unreadable emotion. "Evangeline? Your lover is here?" Emily's voice came out a little louder and sharper than she would have liked.

Godric flinched. "How did you know she was my lover?"

The other three men turned around to stare at her.

Emily hesitated, then said, "Look at the company I'm keeping. It was hardly a gamble."

He cupped her chin, tilting her head up. "Former lover," he admitted. "She is no longer welcome here."

Emily wrapped her arms around Godric's arm, searching his face for the faintest hint of deception.

He kissed her forehead. "Trust me, sweetheart. She's nothing to me. There's only you." To his astonishment, he meant it. For him there was only Emily. Only her laugh, her smile, her sunny daydreams and her fierce passion. Everything beyond her was inconsequential, irrelevant.

Emily didn't relax. She was innocent, but she was not without her natural feminine instincts to defend and protect what was hers. Godric, at least for now, was most certainly hers. If Miss Mirabeau decided to declare war over him, Emily would prove herself to be a dangerous foe. The grim determination in her face warmed him. He held her more tightly against him.

Ashton's brows drew together. "You said she thought you'd invited her?"

"Yes. She showed me a letter she'd received. It certainly looked like my handwriting. She claimed someone must have played a prank on her."

Ashton's frown deepened. "Perhaps. But the timing could not be more suspicious. We'd best be on guard for mischief."

Charles nodded. "I agree. Evangeline is an ungrateful little—"

Lucien stamped on Charles's foot to silence him.

"When is dinner?" Emily asked Godric, still leaning into him.

"In a few hours, I imagine. Why?"

"Might I have a bath? I didn't have a chance this morning." She squeezed his arm.

Godric's lips twitched in a smile.

"Of course, I'm sorry I forgot. Come with me." He walked her out of the drawing room, leaving behind four men who knew far more about her personal life than was proper. But nothing about the League was proper, and that was the way it should be.

Emily had calmed down after the scare of Evangeline's unexpected arrival before they reached the stairs, but her relief was short-lived. A door at the far end of the hall opened. Godric's arm tightened beneath her grasp.

"Ah *bonsoir*, Godric!" The most attractive woman Emily had ever seen walked down the hall. She was radiant with her salmon-toned gown, large breasts and wide hips. Blonde ringlets danced down her back in perfect proportions.

Emily's chest tightened. She expected Godric to have taken a gorgeous woman as his lover, but to see this Aphrodite in the flesh was too much to bear. By comparison, she was young and inexperienced. She could never match Evangeline in looks or mimic that lusty gaze or sway of hips. To Emily's mortification, she realized she was no competition. If Godric wanted a real woman he could take Evangeline back without question.

Godric frowned, clearly uncomfortable with the required introduction. "Return to your room at once." The sharp tone in his voice made both women flinch.

"But, Godric..." Evangeline began in a breathy lilting French accent.

Emily was thankful she didn't have to exchange pleasantries with this woman. She wanted to toss her out the nearest window, preferably one overlooking a prickly rose bush. That would mar her perfect complexion nicely.

Evangeline put a well manicured hand on his arm. "I was about to seek some entertainment. Godric, are you sure you will not join me?"

Godric slid his other arm under Emily. "I have matters to attend to. My other guests are in the drawing room. I suggest you seek their company." There was a command rippling out of those words. A command Evangeline ignored.

"You would not throw me to those wolves you call friends?"

Emily almost growled. "Wolves? Those four men downstairs are some of the most generous and charitable men in all of England. Don't dare insult them." Emily delivered her speech with such venom she hoped Evangeline would wither on the spot. Instead, she laughed.

"I speak in jest." The gleam in her eyes belied her words. She turned to Godric again. "Wherever did you find such a charmingly naïve creature, Godric? Children can be so sweet when they misunderstand things."

Child? Resentment tore through Emily's insides. Had Godric not been standing there, she might have done something truly childish...such as pull the woman's hair out, ringlet by blasted ringlet.

Godric rescued Emily from any further embarrassment. "You must excuse us." As rescues went it felt more like a cowardly retreat.

Alone in the safety of her room, Emily pulled away from him.

"Why didn't you defend me? Why didn't you...do something?" Emily fought off the urge to shout at him. His lack of action felt like a betrayal.

Godric sat at the edge of her bed while she paced. "I wanted more than anything to take you in my arms and kiss you senseless, prove you were my woman."

Emily's blood heated at the thought. "Then why didn't you?"

Godric seemed bemused. "Because she can be jealous and when she is people get hurt, my dear."

"Are you saying you want to protect me?" This was amusing coming from the man who'd destroyed her reputation.

Godric's lips twitched but he continued. "I don't want her to go to the magistrate and tell him I've been secretly keeping you. Not before I visit your uncle once more. It could bring Blankenship back down on our heads."

"Surely she doesn't know why I'm here."

"At the moment, no, but she is clever and might guess. It would be best for you to avoid her."

She knew it was risky bringing up the truth of her feelings, but she did so anyway. "Godric, I no longer care about my reputation. I care about you."

Godric's arms curled around her waist. Emily surrendered, leaning back against him. He kissed her neck lightly, teasingly.

"You really mean that?" His breath stirred her hair.

"Yes. I don't care what she thinks about me."

He spun her around in his arms and leaned his head down, touching his forehead to hers. "No, little vixen—I meant, did you mean that you care about me?"

"Of course I care for you." Emily's cheeks heated. She'd admitted it once, when half asleep, but now was different. She wasn't blinded by passion. This was her heart, exposed and aching for him to return her love.

Godric's hands settled on her lower back, pushing her tighter to him. He kissed the corner of her mouth, and then the tip of her nose, then her chin.

"Do you love me, Emily?" He clenched her harder, the pleasure of his touch making her lightheaded with desire.

"I..."

"Answer my question." It was a sensual rumble, not a command.

Emily shivered. "Yes. Yes, I love you!"

Sweet amusement shown in Godric's emerald eyes. He was a sorcerer, casting love spells over her heart, stealing her soul with honeyed kisses and whispered dreams.

He lifted her chin and fixed his eyes on her. "Then rest easy. So long as you love me, you need not worry about any other woman. Do you understand?"

"I understand." But she didn't. He hadn't said he loved her, but he'd promised to be faithful so long as she loved him... What on earth did that mean? Could she trust the word of a rake?

Godric released her and started towards the door. "I'll send Libba up to prepare your bath."

"Godric..." Emily shouldn't have spoken. She'd set herself up for disappointment. He paused, hand resting on the door handle. He looked back at her.

"Do you love me?" God, she sounded pitiful.

The sweet, pleased expression which had rested so comfortably on his face withered. "Emily..." Her name escaped his lips in a heartrending sigh. "For me, it is not an easy question."

I must not cry... I will not cry. She tried to remind herself that this was the man who had abducted her and seduced her. She focused on these darker memories, or else the pain in her heart would surely strangle the very breath from her body.

"You demand an answer from me, but cannot answer in kind?" When he didn't reply, she threw herself against him, kissing him. Emily curled her fingers into his cravat, pulling him down so she could better reach his mouth.

Pinning him against the door, she plundered his startled mouth. It hurt that he didn't love her, but she couldn't help loving him. Come what may, she truly, deeply loved Godric St. Laurent.

Emily broke the kiss and turned away, putting distance between them. The floorboards creaked as he took a step towards her, but came no further. Emily's head fell, her eyes fixed on a spot on the floor, and she waited for him to say or do something.

"I...I care for you, very much." And then he was gone, taking her heart with him. She knew with painful certainty she could never get it back.

Chapter Fourteen

Dinner that night was a far more formal affair than any other since Emily's abduction. Prior to Evangeline's arrival, all propriety and formality had been banished where the five lords were concerned. Now they observed every single point of etiquette, even though Evangeline wasn't present. Libba had told Emily that Godric had ordered his former mistress to take her meals in her room. That, at least, gave Emily a tiny sense of comfort, knowing that Godric wouldn't allow her to dine with them.

He sat at the head of the table with Emily directly to his right. The rest of the men ranged down on either side according to titled order. Well turned out, each gentlemen wore black knee breeches and well-tailored black coats. Emily wore an ice blue silk gown overlaid with a layer of silver netting. Pale stars were embroidered on her matching slippers and pearls threaded her hair like frozen dewdrops. She couldn't believe the results Libba had wrought. She'd never looked so beautiful, never felt so beautiful before. The butterfly comb was nestled amidst the pearls in her hair. Godric's eyes had flashed when he'd come to escort her to dinner. A proud smile had crossed his lips, which made Emily smile.

Conversation hummed all about the table as they dined on roasted pheasant and carp. The finest Wedgewood was used and the best bottle of Bordeaux filled their glasses.

Emily had Godric and Charles as her partners for table conversation. Godric said little, his eyes lingering on her only briefly before they danced along the table to the other guests.

Charles however was in his element as he regaled Emily with humorous tales of other adventures. He set his fork down and reached for a glass of wine. "Have you visited Vauxhall Gardens yet?"

"Not yet. My coming out was cut short. You may have heard." She raised a sardonic brow.

"Well, I shall take you, my dear. It is quite the sight! Fireworks, galas, and they have the best arrack-punch—"

A low chuckle interrupted Charles. Godric speared a piece of pheasant. "There is nothing in this world that could convince me to let you take Emily to those gardens alone. Don't forget I was present the last time you had too much arrack-punch."

"You're ruining my fun." Charles wore a smile, but a low edge sharpened his words. A challenge. "Emily would have a wonderful time with me. Wouldn't you, Emily?"

"I imagine so, Charles, assuming you remained a gentleman."

"For you, I would endeavor to be the perfect gentleman. I might even succeed."

Emily blushed and tried to change the subject. "You flatter me, Charles. Now, do tell me what happened when you had too much arrack-punch?"

Godric answered her. "I believe Charles left more than one disappointed young lady alone that night under the delusion they would soon be wed to an earl."

Charles set his wine glass down. "It's not my fault I become overly romantic when I am a bit foxed. Every woman looks prettier, tastes sweeter, and even the dreaded prospect of marriage doesn't sound as awful as usual."

Godric laughed. "I'd love to meet a woman who could last one day married to you."

Charles theatrically mimicked being stabbed in the heart. "That hurt, Godric!" He moaned, and feigned death.

Emily bit her lower lip to stifle a giggle. "You've never felt enough affection for a woman to want to marry her?"

Instantly resurrected, Charles said, "I'm an active man, my dear. I need a woman who could keep up with the fast pace of my life and as of yet, I've never encountered such a woman. I'd only marry a woman if she could understand that I, in all truth, can't settle down."

"I'll find you a woman, Charles," Emily promised. In brief moments she had glimpsed a startling melancholy in his expression.

"I thank you, Emily, but I'd much rather steal you away from that odious duke there." Charles nodded his head in Godric's direction.

Under the cover of the table Godric's right hand settled on Emily's knee. The heat of his large palm warmed her skin through the thin silk, but his hand merely patted her knee before vanishing again. It took her all her self-control to prevent a sigh upon being robbed of his caress, the warmth of his touch.

After dinner the party retired to the drawing room where the men poured glasses of port. Choosing then to retire, Emily made her excuses and left the men to drink.

Emily had reached the stairs when a whisper of silk on wood froze her in her steps.

Evangeline emerged from the shadows behind the staircase. "Tell me. How do you find your stay here? Your captor treats you well?"

Emily, unprepared for this remark, blanched. "Pardon?"

"Don't look so surprised. I know Godric and his friends have abducted you."

Emily recovered quickly. "I have no idea what you are talking about."

"Lying does not become you, Miss Parr." Evangeline smiled, and Emily knew that the fear in her chest reflected in her features.

"I'm here of my own free will."

"Of course. No doubt you are enjoying the warmth of Godric's bed. You would not be the first. He does love to seduce innocent little creatures. It fans his pride, you see." Evangeline's words dug under Emily's skin.

"You're wrong about him," Emily said, but the words felt thick and heavy on her tongue.

"May I offer some advice, Miss Parr? Leave here and return to London. Godric will only break that delicate little heart of yours, or leave you with child. Even if he did care about you...I fear that would not stop *Monsieur* Blankenship from pursuing you. He is a very dedicated man."

"What?" How could Evangeline know about Blankenship?

Evangeline hesitated, and the first hint of genuine emotion trespassed across her features. "I will be honest with you, I believe it would suit us both better. *Monsieur* Blankenship came to my residence. He told me of your abduction. I sensed right away he was... I forget the word..." A tiny crinkle furrowed her brow.

"Mad?" Emily supplied.

"*Oui.* Mad as Robespierre. He paid me to come here and provide information on you. He has more power than you would expect. Consequences do not matter to him, only getting what he wants. But then you know this."

"Yes," Emily admitted.

"What you do not know is that he's hired men to retrieve you. Mercenaries, I am told. They are the lowest, vilest of men. Men who would happily murder Godric and his friends if they tried to protect you."

Emily felt the blood drain from her face. "How do you know this?"

"*Monsieur* Blankenship boasted of his scheme. I do not wish to see bloodshed. It is vile and even I do not want to see Godric or his companions harmed. You *must* leave this place and convince *Monsieur* Blankenship you have left, or I am certain he will harm Godric and the others." Evangeline plucked at one of her white silk sleeves but the woman's hands trembled slightly. She was telling the truth.

"He... No... I can't leave, even if I wanted to," Emily said, more to herself than Evangeline. She knew that, between her love of Godric and his own iron hand over her freedom, she could never leave. It would be impossible.

"It is not an easy decision, I understand. You are a pawn in other men's games. Although I am loath to admit it, at the moment, I am as well. Pawns are always sacrificed. It is not fair, but that is our lot, *n'est pas*? If you do not go, Godric will die."

Evangeline was right. Godric would only get himself killed trying to protect her. What choice did she have? She was a pawn.

"The thing about pawns," Emily said, almost to herself, "is if they reach the other end of the board, they become a queen."

A smile flitted across Evangeline's lips. "You play chess. *Très bien.* *Monsieur* Blankenship expects you to come to him at once, and though it is not my place to say, I think you should not go to him. I wish you gone from Godric's life, but I do not wish you to fall into the hands of a madman. Find someone to take you in. You are a beautiful girl, and I believe you are no fool. You can find a protector." Again, she paused, as though lost in memories. "It is how I survived. I am still crossing the board, as it were."

Emily wasn't sure how to react. She was taking advice from Godric's former mistress and finding she reluctantly admired the woman. "Th...thank you, Miss Mirabeau."

Evangeline nodded and left her alone.

Emily couldn't let Godric or the others get hurt, which meant she would have to leave immediately. But she needed to find Jonathan Helprin first. Jonathan was driving the cart to Blackbriar for supplies, that much she knew. Jonathan's open friendliness with Godric's friends was improper, even rebellious after a fashion. It was that hint of rebellion she was pinning her hopes on. If she could convince Jonathan to help her escape, for Godric's sake she might have a chance.

She turned and ran straight into Godric's butler.

"Simkins!"

He bowed and stepped back. "A thousand pardons, Miss Parr. I did not expect anyone to leave the drawing room so early."

"Don't apologize, Simkins! The fault is mine. Could you please tell me where Mr. Helprin is?"

The butler's white brows winged upward in surprise. "His Grace's valet?"

Emily nodded. "Yes."

"I believe he is in the servants' quarters." He seemed suspicious. "Has he incurred your displeasure?"

"No. I merely wished to see him briefly." If Simkins didn't trust her, her plan for escape would unravel in a matter of minutes.

"Well then, good night, Miss Parr." Simkins smiled, bowed, then slipped into the drawing room, leaving her alone in the hall.

Emily dashed towards the servants' stairs. After getting directions from a footman, she found Jonathan's room and flung open the door. He sat on the edge of his bed. His white lawn shirt was half unbuttoned, and in his lap rested one of Godric's fine hessian boots, which he was presently polishing.

He glanced up in surprise. His green eyes narrowed as he took in the sight of her alone. For a second Emily regretted the decision to come to him for help. She hadn't forgotten the way he'd tossed her over his shoulder and carted her off to Godric when she'd crawled out the study window.

He set down the boot and stood. "You should not be alone, Miss Parr. I am obliged to return you to His Grace."

"No, wait! I need to speak with you..." She started strong, but her tone became uncertain. Her heart skipped a beat as Jonathan advanced towards her. Had she made a mistake in thinking she could trust him, that she could persuade him to help her?

"With me? What would a proper young lady have to say to a valet?" He gave that same devastating half-smile Godric often flashed at her. He moved one arm around her body to swing the bedroom door shut behind her. She was trapped now, in more ways than one. Drawing a deep breath, she forced herself to remember that this man cared for Godric and it was that loyalty which she hoped would save Godric's life.

"I need your help." She realized that if she spoke with Jonathan alone like this, she might give him the wrong impression about her. Too late to go back now. His body already leaned slightly towards her. He even loomed like Godric. Even though she hadn't been successful in getting Godric to talk about Jonathan, she was no fool. Some looks simply ran in the blood. He claimed he had no siblings, and he never talked of cousins so few options remained. Who was Jonathan to him?

"I'd be happy to help you." He raised his other hand, trailing it down her bare arm. Goose bumps erupted in the wake of that slow, forbidden caress. Lord, if he wasn't Godric's kin then she wasn't a woman. She smacked his hand away.

She kept his attention on the matter at hand. "Can you take me to Blackbriar tomorrow? I have to escape. I'll be dressed as a maid and you need to give me a ride in the cart, nothing more."

"Are you asking me to betray my master?" Rather than look scandalized, like she'd expected, the sandy-haired devil had the nerve to grin.

Emily drew in a steadying breath. "As far as I am aware, he never forbade you to take me to Blackbriar, did he? If need be, I can elude you in the village and hide so you can honestly say you couldn't bring me back."

Jonathan eyed her critically. "Very well, Miss Parr. But first you must tell me why you are leaving. I've seen the way you look at His Grace. I can't begin to fathom why you would want to run off."

Emily drew a deep breath, praying she was doing the right thing. "I have to leave to save his life."

Jonathan's brows rose. "What?"

"It's Blankenship, the man who came here with the magistrate. He plans to kill Godric and anyone else in his way to get to me. If I leave, he won't have a reason to hurt anyone here."

Suspicion narrowed the valet's eyes. "How do you know this?"

"Godric's mistress, Evangeline. She warned me, told me what would happen if I didn't leave. Blankenship is mad. He's already hired men for the job."

"You're serious, aren't you? His Grace is truly in danger?"

Emily nodded. "I can't risk anything happening to him."

"Have you considered telling him what Evangeline told you?"

"Of course I have. But you know the man he is. Do you think he'd sit idly by under this kind of threat? No matter how matched they were?"

The valet considered her words. "No, the damned fool would rally his friends and go charging off to get killed."

Emily's shoulders sagged. "So you understand why I have to leave. He cannot know the truth or he will do something foolishly noble."

"You do realize this is an extremely bad plan. The man has a temper that makes even angels quake with fear. He won't be happy if you leave."

She didn't need Jonathan's warning, she knew the risk she was taking. "It's a choice between hurting him and killing him, and that isn't really a choice is it?"

Jonathan deliberated a long moment. "Very well. I'll take you to the village if you agree to my price." She was trapped against the door, unable to escape. His warm breath fanned her face.

She raised her chin a little, hoping it would strengthen her resolve. "What price?"

"Hmm..." He studied her, looking for what she didn't know. "I'll decide later. Be ready to depart tomorrow." He gently shoved her out into the hallway.

She hastily walked back up the servants' stairs, then the main staircase as she headed into her bedchamber on the second floor and ducked inside.

"There you are, little vixen! I've been waiting for you to turn up." Godric's voice made her jump. "Thought you could slip away from me?" Godric chuckled, his hands encircling her waist.

The tension in her body relaxed as she realized he hadn't overheard her conversation with Jonathan.

"No, of course not. I merely had to fix my hair, a few pins felt loose." Her hand rose to her hair as though to show she'd fixed the matter.

The predatory gaze he gave her made her ache inside. "I don't believe you, my dear. I thought we came to an understanding."

It irritated her that he didn't believe her, even if she was lying. "We have. Let me go, Godric."

"Now, now, I've had to play the gentleman all evening and I'm not able to last another minute behaving like a bloody saint." His hands on her waist curled around her back and slid farther down over the curve of her bottom and clenched hard, lifting her into him.

Emily gasped.

He pressed her back against her door. The corded sinews of his muscled arms were taut beneath her hands as she tried to push him away. She had to keep her senses unclouded if she was to escape tomorrow, but it was nigh impossible to do so.

Godric thrust a thigh between her legs, the pressure flaming to life. Emily's head fell back, offering him her throat. He dragged his mouth down from her jaw to her shoulder.

Emily barely had time to prepare herself, before he robbed her of her control, assaulting her mind and heart with a deep kiss. They moved away from the door and he turned her so the back of her knees bumped the bed and they toppled over, Godric on top. With a soft laugh, he nuzzled her cheek and rolled them over until she lay sprawled across his chest. He gazed up at her, his eyes warm, fingers gentle as he traced her spine in soothing strokes.

"What's that look for, darling? You seem concerned." He laughed and moved his head up to nip her collarbone affectionately.

He fascinated her. One minute fiery and possessive, and the next tender, and heart-breakingly sweet. Emily's heart skipped. Would this be the last moment she would have with him? If she escaped tomorrow, it would be.

Tears stung her eyes and she bit her bottom lip, hoping that pain would distract from the stabbing wound in her chest. There would never be moments like this again.

"Don't cry...please don't cry. We'll go slow. I didn't mean to scare you." Godric sat up, keeping her straddled on his lap. His thumbs brushed away her tears and he eased the ache with feathering kisses along her cheeks, the tip of her nose, her forehead.

At last he tucked her against him, and Emily surrendered, burying her face into the groove of his neck and shoulder. They remained locked this way for a moment, the mere touch enough to calm her.

When she finally wasn't falling apart on the inside, she placed a kiss on his shoulder. Then, despite her tears and sadness, craving him desperately, she nipped him. He groaned as she flitted her tongue against the spot she'd bitten.

"You little imp!" He laughed and cupped her chin, raising her face to his. "You know I'll get back at you for that." He palmed her breast and when her nipple budded beneath his hand, he tweaked it. "Shall I start here? Or—" he slid his hand down her side over her thigh and onto her bottom "—here, perhaps?" He tightened his hold on her buttocks and Emily squirmed as desire flooded between her thighs.

Emily raised her eyes to his, eyes challenging him. "I think you are all talk, Your Grace."

"I am, am I?" He growled and rolled her beneath him. Rather than undo her gown he flipped her onto her stomach, grabbed a pillow from near her head and lifted her hips, settling the pillow beneath her pelvis. Trembling, Emily looked over her shoulder at him, confused at what he meant to do. He knelt between her spread legs, and unfastened his trousers. The wicked smile he flashed her when he caught her looking sent new shivers down her legs.

Godric slid his palms up under her gown at her knees, raising the gown and petticoats out of the way, until she was bare to him. He stroked her bottom, his fingers drifting down until they reached her sex.

"So hot, you're so wet, darling. You undo me. I can't wait another second." He placed himself at her entrance and, bracing one hand next to her shoulder on the bed, thrust home.

They shared a mutual cry of bliss at the connection. Part pleasure, a hint of pain as he slid out and rammed deep. Emily cried out at the ecstasy. Godric continued, dragging the tip of his arousal along her inner walls, striking a spot deep inside her that made her mindless with passion. Desperation tore through her, she needed him, more than she needed his body, this clash of bodies and souls could be their last time. Panic forced a sob from her throat, yet pleasure stole her breath.

"Em...oh Em. Darling...I love the way you feel...push your hips back...YES!" Godric's ragged panting and rough praises unraveled her heart and soul. She came apart, blasting into a million pieces around him.

She was vaguely aware of his echoing shout, and the heavy weight of him on her back. His huffing breath against her neck was a sensual reward.

After a few moments, he recovered, his breathing more controlled as he fell onto his side. He reached for her, and Emily fit her body to his, for perhaps the last time. Tears burdened her cheeks, but Godric didn't see them. His eyes were closed, dark lashes spiked across his cheeks.

"I love you. No matter what happens. I love you," she whispered. He didn't stir.

She kissed his chest where she felt his heartbeat strongest. If he'd heard her, she didn't want him to say anything back. If he didn't love her, the reality would wound her. If he said it, it would kill her.

Godric held Emily's body loose against him. One of her bare legs stretched over his abdomen, and he rested a possessive hand on the soft skin of her outer thigh. Her head rested on his chest and her faint breaths betrayed her deep state of sleep. He'd worn her out tonight, she was still adjusting to his voracious appetite. She was bolder too, but she still made love with that strange mixture of wanton innocence.

It would be a lie to deny his joy at the enthusiasm and boldness in her responses. She loved him, he heard her breathe it once while asleep, and today, she'd said it without the influence of passion. She'd not taken it back, and for that he was glad.

No one had ever claimed to love him before, no woman besides his mother. He was loved by Simkins and the League, but Emily was different. He'd always assumed a woman's love would be a burden, but it wasn't. Her affection and loyalty strengthened him. She knew him for who he was, but she loved him anyway, loved him enough to declare her reputation worthless, but it mattered to Godric. The thought of anyone speaking ill of Emily churned his stomach.

He would do whatever was necessary to protect her honor, even if that meant giving her up. He'd told her she could stay as long as she loved him, but the truth was she could never leave him. There was only one option left for her, and for him.

Marriage. He had to marry Emily to salvage her reputation. In return, she would have a life she wished to live, and he would give anything to see to her happy.

In the bright light of day, he knew that marriage to Emily was a terrible idea. His reputation in society was far from unsullied and while it had never mattered to him, it would affect her. Would she ever be accepted as the wife of a duke, or simply be seen as a glorified mistress? At night, though, he couldn't help but wonder how happy they might grow to be.

He allowed himself to imagine a lifetime of nights during which Emily wound her warm body around his, and her hair spilled across his pillow like amber wheat. In his dreams she would always be there, his cunning little vixen. In a few years, babes in cradles would fill the empty ghost-ridden corners of his life, and he'd possess a family he'd never expected. He'd buy Emily a stable full of horses, a thousand hounds, whatever she desired.

Emily shifted against him, stirring slightly. Godric pulled the covers up about them to keep her warm. Only when she was asleep could he savor her—the full breasts now pressed against his chest, and the smooth muscular thighs and calves. Those legs gripped him tightly about his hips whenever he mounted her. She was sweet...and real. Nothing like the sculpted perfection of Evangeline who never liked a hair out of place or a gown rumpled. She did not really live, not like Emily. He adored the way she embraced life.

His hand slid up towards the juncture between her thighs. He slid a finger inside her, and she stirred again. Godric smiled, gently toying with her. She made that adorable sound of drugged pleasure. It took all of his willpower to stop teasing her and torturing himself. She needed sleep after the day she'd had.

Emily nuzzled his chest, rubbing herself against him as she settled down again. It struck Godric then that this moment felt right, frighteningly right. Everything he'd ever known had changed when he'd put that unconscious young lady on her bed that first night. How could it be that she'd only entered his life less than a week ago? What would happen when they were forced to accept their situation? He didn't want to think about it. His chest tightened and his fists clenched.

The abduction of Emily Parr hadn't changed just him. The League's bond epitomized the hard love men shared with each other, but when it came to Emily, they were all helpless. Ashton admired Emily's purity of soul, Charles her playfulness, Cedric her love of the outdoors, Lucien her cleverness, and Godric—he loved *everything* about her.

The thought shocked him. If he could love all the things within a person, did that not mean he loved the person? The question plagued him.

He ran a hand through Emily's hair, coiling a silken tendril between his fingers. Never in all his years could he have expected such a creature, so different from him, to make him so happy. He lived to see her smile, to make her laugh, to kiss her. He wanted to spend all day reading with her, all night loving her. Find every ticklish spot and every place that made her moan and sigh. He wanted a life with her, but it wasn't possible.

"Godric?" Emily's voice cut through his brooding. He hadn't realized she was awake.

"I'm sorry, darling, did I wake you?"

"I am a light sleeper." She raised her head a little, her violet eyes pale and silvery in the moonlight. "May I ask you something?"

Godric fought the urge to smile. "Oh, I suppose."

"Ashton mentioned your father, and how he—"

Godric's smile faded. "How he disciplined me?"

"Yes."

"What is it?" His tone was harsher than he meant. The ache of that old wound still stung.

Emily put a hand on his chest, right above his heart. "I am sorry he hurt you."

"That is not a question."

Her forehead creased. "No, I suppose not, but...but I wish he hadn't hurt you. I don't know how anyone could want to hurt you." She pressed her lips down on his chest, in an enticing kiss. It was so pure in its affection, in its tenderness, that Godric's throat tightened. He didn't know how to tell her that her words meant everything to him.

Instead, he wrapped his arms about her waist and slid her up several inches, to his mouth. Her lips parted. Her fingertips stroked his jaw, and she sighed contentedly.

"I have another question," she said at last. "A real one."

He was amused by the shrewd gleam in her eyes. "All right then, my dear, let's hear it."

"When you and the others abducted me, how did you know I was in the carriage? I thought I'd fooled you with the false bottom of that seat..." She laid her palms flat on his chest and pushed up a little, which gave him a pleasing view of her breasts.

"You had me quite fooled. Ashton, however, noticed a piece of your evening gown sticking out. He devised a plan to wait for you." Godric grinned as the memory of that night flooded him, the adrenaline, the sheer exhilaration of chasing her, fighting her, capturing her...

Emily frowned. "And what if I hadn't gotten out of the carriage? I might have suffocated."

"I dare say it couldn't have been airtight." Godric tried to lift his hips, but Emily slid an inch out of reach.

"Did you really have to use laudanum? I despised that." She scowled now, which somehow resembled a puppy growl.

"We used it at Ashton's recommendation. We were worried you might scream for help."

"Why didn't you just gag me?"

"And have you squirm in my lap the entire way? You could have fallen and injured yourself."

"Your lap?" Her eyes were warm, but her nose wrinkled in consternation. "You carried me?"

Godric tugged one a lock of her hair, winding it around his finger. "Absolutely. Once I set eyes on you, I refused to let any other man have responsibility for you. I wanted you all to myself, which, let me assure you, was quite a battle. I had to endure nearly an hour of Charles's grousing. He's a dreadfully sore loser." Godric chuckled.

Emily digested all of this in silence.

"Did you plan on seducing me before you saw me?"

That was a volatile question, and Godric decided the truth was best.

"I only meant to ruin you by bringing you here, I didn't really intend to physically er...ruin you. There was no thought of seduction until I put you on this very bed. You were so dirty and dusty from your attempts at escape, but when I set you down... I was entranced... I had to touch you...so I did."

"You did?"

"Only a touch, I held your face in my hands. Your cheeks were covered in dirt and I rubbed it away. It took every bit of my self-control not to kiss you. That was when I knew you had bewitched me."

Emily was surprised, pleasantly so. She remembered little from that first night, but she had a vague memory that a handsome prince had stroked her face and nearly kissed her, a fanciful, fairytale dream, she'd thought.

Emily slid off Godric and tucked herself up in the warmth of his embrace. Sharing a bed with him now made her realize how lonely she'd be tomorrow. There would be no good morning kisses, nor more quiet afternoons in his study. There wouldn't be any warm masculine body to cuddle up to at night when shadows lengthened across her bed.

Her love for him burned hotter and brighter each hour she spent with him, but that love would kill him if she didn't leave. Blankenship's men would arrive and there'd be bloodshed on all sides.

She considered telling him the truth, telling him what Evangeline had said, but she couldn't. He and the other lords were nothing if not prideful and stubborn. They would vow to defend her and someone would get hurt or killed. Their blood could not stain her hands, they had become like family. She had to leave. Perhaps she could send Blankenship a letter when she reached Blackbriar, tell him she escaped and he would have no luck at the Essex estate. She could only hope it would work and keep them all safe.

Godric's hand gently stroked her hair, the sensation so soothing and calming that she could barely stay awake. She needed a moment longer.

"Godric..."

"Hmm?" His response vibrated her body in its soft rumble.

"Thank you."

"What have I done now?"

"You showed me a part of life I might have missed otherwise."

The back of his knuckles brushed along her cheek. "If you were a chance, my dear, then it was my good fortune to take you."

Her eyes burned. She couldn't cry, not now.

"I know I shouldn't say it, since it ruins our moments...but I love you." She might never see him again after this and she wanted to know she was brave enough to say it to him, one last time.

"You could never ruin anything, darling."

Godric raised her head to his and slanted his mouth down over hers. It didn't matter how he kissed her, chastely or lustily, she came to life at his touch. Her tongue danced between his lips. He groaned softly, fisting his hand in her hair. His fingertips massaged her scalp, and Emily's hands slid along his chest, reveling in the hot skin beneath her fingertips.

"Make love to me," she pleaded between deep, languid kisses.

"As you command."

Chapter Fifteen

The house was rid of Evangeline Mirabeau long before breakfast was even set. Someone had seen to her early departure, and the rest of the house was none the wiser as to who it was. It would seem that, having played her role, she had wisely chosen to leave lest she still be around when Blankenship's men arrived. The relief among the lords was tangible. Breakfast became a cheery affair, and despite Emily's plans to depart, she took advantage of these last few hours with her friends. For they were just that. She'd miss Ashton mothering over the others. She'd miss Lucien's attempts to hide behind his newspaper while teasing the others. She wouldn't get to fish or hunt with Cedric, nor listen to Charles's outlandish tales.

And Godric... She would miss *life* with him, but she had no choice.

"Toast, Emily?" Charles offered a plate of toast as it came her way, breaking through her dark thoughts.

"Why, thank you, Charles," she said.

"You're welcome." The earl winked, and when she fetched a slice of toast, he passed the plate over her head to Ashton.

"What has everyone planned for today?" Ashton asked the table at large.

Charles precariously balanced on the back two legs of his chair. "I've got some correspondence to catch up on."

"Oh? You actually answer your letters, do you?" Lucien commented from behind his newspaper.

"Of course I do. Just because I never answer your mother's letters doesn't mean I don't answer any of them"

Lucien folded his paper and gave Charles a stern look. "My mother writes you letters and you don't answer them?"

"Hang on—" Cedric cut in. "Lucien, your mother writes to Charles?"

Lucien's darkening scowl made Cedric laugh.

"Go on, Charles. What does she write to you about?" Godric prodded.

"It is of a private nature."

"Nothing ever stays private with you, Charles, so you might as well tell us." Ashton's lips twisted into the faintest essence of a smile.

Charles scowled. "You want to know? Fine. Lucien's mother has convinced herself I am the perfect husband for Lysandra."

"My sister!" Lucien choked out. "God in heaven, man, you had better never reply to those letters or so help me—"

"Easy! Lysandra is not my type, as you well know." Charles glanced around the table. "Besides, we have our rules, don't we?"

"Rules?" Emily shook her head, confused.

Ashton looked over at her. "Even the so-called League of Rogues has rules, my dear."

They had rules? The thought made her laugh.

"Even rogues must draw the line somewhere," he added.

"And in this case no League member shall seduce a sister of another member," Lucien said.

Charles nodded. "Rule Eight to be exact."

"I am still wondering why you call yourselves the League." Emily giggled. She'd heard of the name before, of course, whispered between society matrons, often followed by gasps of horror.

Godric grinned wolfishly. "That curious moniker was actually thrust upon us by *The Quizzing Glass Gazette* in the Lady Society column. It regales the *ton* with stories about our exploits, or what they believe we've done. They exaggerate quite often, but we found their name to be accurate. We wisely accepted it and now use it, with much pleasure, I might add."

"It does have a rather charming ring to it," Emily said.

Ashton turned the conversation back to the events of the day. "So Charles is writing letters. What about you, Cedric?"

"Thought I'd go for a ride."

Emily straightened up in her chair. Perhaps she could go for a ride before she had to set her final escape plan in motion. One last good memory...

"And what about you, Lucien?"

"I've a small matter in London to see to. I should be back by nightfall."

Emily didn't miss the glance made towards Godric. She doubted he was aware of it.

"Perhaps I ought to accompany you?" Ashton suggested.

"I wouldn't mind the company."

It was as though they were speaking in code. Emily wondered what the two men were up to.

With breakfast over, Emily followed Cedric out of the room, eager to watch him ride. But Godric caught the back of her dress and pulled her to an abrupt halt.

He nuzzled her neck playfully and said, "Now where are you off to?"

Emily sighed, watching Cedric's retreating back. "I thought I might watch Cedric ride." Godric wound his arms about her waist from behind. His lips brushed her right ear and he nipped her lobe. She stifled a little moan.

"We could stay here..." Each word hung heavy with the promise of passion.

It was so hard to resist, but the second sigh that escaped her was one of defeat and Godric noticed.

"Everything all right, my dear?" He stroked her chin with the pad of his thumb. The truth of her fears lay on the tip of her tongue, but she bit it back.

He studied her silently. "Do you really miss riding?"

Emily brightened a little. "I do, oh, I do."

"I would let you ride..." he paused as her eyes lit up with hope. "If you ride with me."

"Oh, Godric, thank you!" She threw her arms about his neck and covered him with kisses.

Cedric was just trotting out of the stables when they caught up. The dappled gray mare he rode looked eager to be galloping, as did the rider.

Cedric called down as they walked past. "Shall I wait for you?"

"Could you?" Emily asked.

Godric went inside to fetch his gelding while Emily waited.

Cedric gazed down at her. "Emily, when you return to London, may I introduce you to my sisters? Horatia and Audrey would adore you."

"I'd like that very much. I know so few people in the *ton*. We have mainly country connections."

"Not to worry, kitten. My sisters are level-headed creatures for the most part. I think you'd like Horatia especially. She is very much like you." Cedric grinned as though remembering some private joke. "Audrey...is a bit of scamp. Always in trouble for one thing or another."

"Do they love the outdoors like you?"

Cedric nodded. "Horatia loves to ride almost as much as I do. Audrey loves fresh air, though she's not fond of horses. Got bit by a rather nasty tempered pony when she was eight. Hasn't forgiven the equine genus since, poor dear."

Emily stroked his mare's charcoal mane. "My father always said they had a propensity for biting, so I was fortunate never to be subjected to a pony's temper. Horses though, were a different matter. He had the best pair of thoroughbreds which he taught me to ride."

"Your father was a smart man." Cedric reached down to smack the mare's neck affectionately.

Godric came out that moment, his magnificent black gelding in tow, one hand resting on the horse's neck, the other threading fingers through the dangling reins.

"Hold him for me, Cedric?" Godric handed him the reins. Godric gripped Emily at the waist and hoisted her up onto the saddle then hauled himself up behind her. He looped an arm about her waist, pulling her back into the cradle of his hips.

They trotted away from the stables, Cedric a few paces ahead. The horses settled into a natural rhythm.

They rode for an hour before Godric decided the chances of them getting caught in the storm were too great. Emily fixed her attention on the sky, where storm clouds still hung. Not a single drop had fallen the night before, but she could taste the thickness of the air, and the delicious clean scent of a thunderstorm teased the air with a hint of danger. Emily did not protest ending their ride. She'd need to be back at the manor soon to see to her preparations.

Charles joined Godric, Cedric and Emily for a light luncheon an hour later, but Emily could barely eat. Her stomach churned fitfully and she said little.

"Are you feeling well?" Godric put the back of his hand to her forehead.

Emily shut her eyes, enjoying the warmth of his hand. This would be the last time he touched her. Pain tore through her heart, rending it in two. She'd remember him like this, gentle and concerned. A tender rogue, hiding his heart from her for fear of being wounded. But it was she who'd suffer most. At least he did not love her, it would be easier for him to accept her leaving.

"You feel a bit cold." Worry darkened his tone.

"I fear I'm rather under the weather." It was an opportunity to excuse herself.

Godric started to rise from his chair. "Shall I send for a doctor?"

"No! No, don't trouble yourself, please. I think I'll take a nap. That may put me to rights." Emily rose from her chair, put a hand on Godric's shoulder and gently forced him back down.

"I'll come and check on you in a few hours then, darling." Godric kissed her hand resting on his shoulder. Her heart bled with the knowledge that this was her last kiss. It couldn't be the last... Not something so inconsequential and chaste as a kiss upon her hand...

Emily bent and captured his mouth. She couldn't breathe...couldn't think. There was only this last, eternal and yet ephemeral kiss. It was her last memory, one that would have to last her the rest of a lonely lifetime.

I'm letting you go because I love you and it's the only way to save you. She begged silently with all her heart that he would understand. It nearly cleaved her heart in two when he smiled against her mouth and brushed a hand over her cheek as she left.

What would he think when he came to her room and she was gone? Would he wonder why she'd abandoned him? Would her leaving be worse than the abuse Godric suffered at the hands of his father?

Someday he'd understand. She'd find a way to tell him the truth when it was safe to do so. But even then, she doubted he would forgive her. Until that day, she'd slowly die inside from a bleeding heart.

With a strength she hadn't known she possessed, she raised her chin and departed from the dining room with grace.

Once in her room, she leaned back against the door. Her chest surged as she swallowed silent sobs. Her entire world shrank into that single moment of loss. Her throat closed and she struggled to swallow.

Sinking down the wood panel of the door, Emily curled her legs up beneath her chin, tears sliding down her face. She'd been such a fool to fall in love, but she'd never make this mistake again. Her heart would harden and she'd live on alone without Godric and without love. She had to.

Years from now she'd be somewhere in the world, remembering this final day, this final hour of losing her first and only love. The memory would rush in on her like a thief in the night and leave a raw, aching pain in her chest just as fresh as today. Tears formed salty tracks down her cheeks and carved trails like mighty rivers on stone.

It was the right thing to do. If she left, Blankenship wouldn't have a reason to harm the others. That was more important than her tears. This resolve strengthened her. She remembered something her father used to say. "Fear is only as strong as the weakness within you."

Her choice was clear, had always been clear. Deep in her bones, she's always known she'd have to go at some point. The sooner she could accept it, the sooner she could move on.

Once her eyes had no more tears to shed, she mastered her grief and summoned Libba to her chambers.

Waiting for the maid, she wrote a note to Godric. She couldn't afford to tell him the truth, but she had to say something.

When Libba arrived, she was shocked by Emily's tear-stained face. Before the maid could say a word, Emily took her into her confidence.

"That man you saw before with the magistrate, he's going to come back, with armed men. Too many of them. They will hurt anyone in their way. I have to leave. His Grace's life depends on this. You must trust me. I need to borrow your serving gown. I'm going with Jonathan to Blackbriar."

To Emily's surprise there was no protesting from the maid, only a nod of understanding. "When that man saw me in your room, he thought I was you for a moment. I know how he looks at you, Miss." Libba twisted her hands into her skirts. "I'll find my extra gown."

"After I'm gone, stuff some pillows in my bed. Make it look like I'm sleeping. Once they discover I am not, tell them you saw me cross the meadows, it may buy me some time. Whatever you do, don't tell them I've left with Jonathan. Promise me, Libba. Godric's life depends on your silence."

"I promise. But...Miss...you want to stay here, though, don't you?"

Even though she thought she'd spent her tears, a dry sob escaped

217

her. "Some people aren't fated to get what they want, Libba."

Lucien and Ashton crouched beneath an open window of a townhouse on Bloomsbury Street, just out of Mayfair. The two men shared a concerned glance as they eavesdropped on a conversation, in the parlor just past the window.

They'd arrived in London an hour before and rode straight to Evangeline's townhouse, intent on speaking with her. She'd departed for the day, but the scullery maid next door told Lucien which direction she'd seen her go after he loosened her lips with a none-too-innocent kiss and a few well-placed caresses. The poor girl wanted to tell him everything after that, if only he promised to stay and entertain her. Only Ashton's polite cough reminded him of their mission.

The forged note Evangeline offered suggested to Ashton that she was not a helpless pawn but an active player in this game of deception, and it was imperative they determine the puppet master in order to protect Emily.

Lucien argued against Emily as the root of Evangeline's appearance, but as always, only Ashton saw the larger game being played. He didn't believe in coincidences and Evangeline's appearance had little to do with chance.

When they tracked Evangeline's carriage down to this particular address, Ashton found his suspicions confirmed. The moment they turned onto an intersecting street, Lucien paled and then turned scarlet with fury. "I know where she's gone." He growled. "Blankenship lives not far from here."

They slipped down the side street and crouched below Blankenship's parlor window.

"Miss Mirabeau, back in London so soon?" Blankenship's voice carried into the alleyway.

Ashton lifted his head up a few inches over the sill, catching sight of Evangeline and Blankenship. She was facing him and her eyes widened as she saw him. His breath hitched as he feared she would give his presence away.

She did not. Her eyes flicked back to Blankenship's as if nothing had occurred.

"I was turned out in less than a day, *Monsieur!* But since you have paid me, I brought you the information you seek."

"And?"

A brief moment of silence gnawed at the air.

"Your lost lamb is there as you suspected. I met her. *Elle est très jolie!* You did not tell me that, *Monsieur.*"

"Does it matter?" Blankenship snorted rudely.

"*Pour moi*, of course. Essex is too attached to her. He watches her every move."

Blankenship's voice lowered. "Is she unspoiled?"

Evangeline chuckled. "No, *Monsieur*. I believe His Grace has long since plucked the fruit of that vine. She is helplessly in love with him."

"Her love doesn't matter to me. One does not need that in a mistress."

Lucien's mouth twisted into a snarl, and Ashton's fists clenched, but both mastered their tempers.

"Very well. Here is a bonus payment, as agreed, Miss Mirabeau. I will handle the matter from here." Blankenship paced away out of sight.

Evangeline met Ashton's gaze and gave him the barest hint of acknowledgement before speaking again.

"You should know, *Monsieur* Blankenship, I convinced the lamb to leave. I told her that if she did not return to London, you would kill Godric and his friends."

"Why the devil did you do that? The last thing I need is for them to be warned."

"I only wished to save you the trouble of retrieving her by force as you had planned." Her voice was all sincerity, but Ashton knew better than to take that tone at face value. She was speaking too loudly for the words to be meant only for Blankenship.

"You know nothing of my plans. Still you may have saved me some effort if she obeys." Blankenship hummed, as though pleased, with a cruel note along his throat.

"I have no doubt she will, *Monsieur*. None at all."

When the conversation's volume decreased, the pair crossed the street, hailing a carriage back to Lucien's townhouse.

"We have to get back to Godric immediately," Lucien said.

"I agree. Emily will make another run for it, and I suspect this time she might manage to succeed. Godric won't stand for another attempt. He'll be furious."

"I know, and I'd prefer we get there before he punishes her."

Ashton glanced at him, then away. "You think he'd harm her?"

"Strike her? No, but his temper... We all know how hard he fights it. I worry about what he'll say to her. She doesn't know him like we do. Words can strike deeper than any blow, and he'll say things he doesn't mean to protect his heart."

"Don't we all?"

Lucien pulled a pistol out from the inside of his jacket.

"Same old Lucien," Ashton said under his breath.

Lucien grinned. "Old habits die hard."

Ashton laughed. Old habits indeed...

"Do you think we'll get back in time to stop Emily?"

Ashton bowed his head. "For now I'm more worried about Blankenship's men, whoever they are, and what he intends to do with them." He watched Lucien check the pistol. "Before long we might all need to carry one, old friend. I've never been a religious man, but I believe now is the time to pray."

Emily spent her last hours collecting her few possessions into the small cloth bag that Libba left under her bed. Tucked away were her butterfly comb and brush, her night rail, and a spare set of clothes to change into once she could remove Libba's uniform. The trickiest part would be Penelope. She couldn't leave the puppy behind. Libba would fetch the dog and bring her out to the cart. Soon she would be Emily's only companion.

Libba returned and helped Emily into the extra maid gown. Emily tucked her small bag of possessions in her arms while Libba fixed the white cap over her hair. If she kept her head down, she might yet escape.

Libba peeked out the door, then waved to Emily that the halls were clear. There was no sign of anyone; the upper manor hall was quiet. She walked briskly, head bent to the floor, her ears pricked for the slightest noise.

In the parlor, Cedric and Godric laughed about something. She lingered for a brief painful second.

Goodbye, my League of Rogues.

She slipped down the servants' stairs and out a door that led to the stables. The urge to look back just once was strong, but she resisted. She would take only memories. On cold nights she'd sink into those blissful moments and find herself here again, even if it was only in her dreams.

Jonathan sat impatiently on the cart seat, his face dark. He scowled when he saw her, as though he'd hoped she wouldn't have come. He raised his hand, motioning for her to hurry. A basket lay next to him. It contained a drowsy Penelope.

"What's wrong with her?" Emily hissed as she climbed up into the seat next to him.

"Nothing. When Libba brought her down I fed her warmed cream. It'll keep her quiet until we reach the village."

Emily relaxed, but the pup was more than just drowsy. "Just warm cream?"

"Well, there might be a pinch of something stronger to make sure she didn't run off. Needs must as the devil drives, as they say."

Emily knew that only too well.

Jonathan slapped the long reins against the bay's back and the cart jerked into motion. When they reached the road, Emily breathed a sigh of relief, one shadowed by sadness.

On to Blackbriar…

Rain pelted Emily's face, soaking her clothes. She cursed herself for not bringing a wool hooded cloak to wear.

"How much farther is it?" The heady scent of wet grass and wool surrounded her. She shivered, and her skin iced over with the rain.

"Not far," Jonathan said. "We'll have to get a room at the inn. You can't travel in this weather, and I can't return tonight. The food might spoil." His beautiful mouth twisted in an unpleasant frown.

She trembled again. "I suppose you are right."

Jonathan put his arm about her shoulders to pull her closer. He was just as wet, but much warmer.

"Th-thank you." Her teeth clicked together as a bone deep chill sank into her.

"Don't mention it, Miss Parr." His eyes were on the road, not on her.

Emily relaxed a little and Penelope stirred beneath Emily's black

221

skirts. She dropped a hand down near the hound and the pup anxiously licked her fingers.

"There, there, darling," she murmured.

They rode in silence the rest of the way. The drive to the village stole much time, since the road skirted around Godric's lands and the lake.

The village itself seemed nearly deserted. The cart creaked and groaned as it rode over the rough uneven stones of the main street, echoing in the midst of the storm's rumblings. Jonathan guided the horse towards the tall barn next to an inn called The Pickerel.

"Take Penelope inside. Wait for me near the bar." Jonathan didn't wait for her to protest.

She took the hound and her cloth bag, and dodged through the rain into the inn. Oil lamps were lit on the tables and several villagers huddled around the main fireplace, warming their hands. They all turned their heads at her entrance. A plump woman wiping the bar with a cloth smiled, then seeing her, drenched and shivering, immediately changed to concern.

"You poor lamb!" She rushed around the counter to get a better look.

"M-May I wait here?" Her teeth chattered so sharply that her jaw ached.

"Of course, dear!" The woman took a fresh towel and dried Penelope. "Caught in the storm without a proper coat? Here, let me help you."

"Th-thank you."

Jonathan came in, shaking his sandy hair.

"Jonny, love!" the woman greeted him.

Jonathan raised his arms. "Lucy, you're prettier every time I see you."

The middle aged woman blushed, "Oh, hush, you scoundrel." She swatted his shoulder.

"Could we have a room, Lucy?" Jonathan tilted his head in Emily's direction.

"Ahh, so she's yours, is she?"

"It is not what you think, Lucy."

"It never is, love. But it always is." Lucy winked, but said nothing else. She grabbed a set of keys from a nail on the wall, then led them up a set of narrow stairs and down a hall of four rooms. She picked the last one on the right and opened it for them. Inside stood a narrow bed, a small table and basin of water next to some towels.

Emily set down Penelope and her bags, while Jonathan ripped off his dripping cloak and outer coat.

"I'll send up some soup for you both." Lucy left them alone.

Emily stood indecisively for a moment, cold and wet, and watched Jonathan warily. "Should we share a room?"

The handsome devil just laughed. "It is part of my price...and one room is cheaper than two."

"But you never told me your price."

Jonathan, still not looking at her, ripped off his white lawn shirt and hung it over the edge of the single chair near the table to let it dry. Roped golden muscles cut his broad chest. Where Godric was an inch taller, Jonathan's muscles seemed larger, presumably from the years of labor on the estate. She was struck by the similarity all the same.

He crossed the distance between them and without a word plucked the silly white cap off her head. Her hair spilled down in a tumble.

"Better." He reached out to touch her.

Emily backed up another step.

"What are you doing?"

"My price, Miss Parr. I'm collecting it now." Jonathan's green eyes burned.

Emily nearly panicked but a knock interrupted them. Jonathan opened the door and took the two bowls of soup from Lucy before shutting the door in her face.

"Sit and eat, then we'll discuss payment."

It seemed her fears about the method of payment weren't unfounded. The soup warmed her up considerably, but the wet gown didn't prevent the chill that crept over her. *I ought to change*, Emily thought, but she wouldn't undress with Jonathan in the same room. She let Penelope lick her bowl and eat the crust from her bread. All the while Jonathan watched her.

"Mr. Helprin, may I ask a rather odd question?"

Jonathan waved a hand in the air, urging her to continue.

"Are you related to Godric?"

Soup spewed across the table. He froze, then carefully wiped a napkin over his mouth. "What makes you ask that?"

"Are you?" She pressed.

"Of course not."

Emily set her spoon down. "I'm sorry to have offended you. It's just that...well, you look so much like him. You even act like him."

When she raised her face, his eyes locked with hers.

Jonathan propped his elbows on the table, resting his chin in his hands. "I take no offense, you merely startled me. No one has ever said that before." He paused, eyes resting on her face, yet his expression was unreadable. After a moment he shoved his chair back, scraping it against the wooden floor. Rather than approach her, he paced away, the lithe grace of his movements every inch identical to his master's.

When he turned, she was struck by his profile, the long-limbed muscled body of a man who'd worked in the service, but there was still a refined quality to him. Half the *ton* lacked the innate well-bred features and manners that came so naturally to Jonathan. Something in his very breaths set him apart from his fellow servants.

"You are so like him," she half-whispered. "The way you move, talk."

"I suppose that is because I grew up wanting to be like him. I was born and raised in that house. My mother was his mother's lady's maid. I used to follow him about when I was a boy. He is eight years older than me."

Could it be that simple? She supposed it could, and she felt like a ninny for thinking otherwise. They weren't related. He merely mirrored his master the way any man would reflect someone he admired. But still, her instincts shouted otherwise. But she just had to be sure...

"Did your mother have green eyes?"

"No."

"And your father?"

"I never knew him." An answer that wasn't really an answer, just like Godric. It was time to change the subject.

"What will you do after I've left? Will you return to the manor?"

Jonathan's lips pursed for a moment. "Assuming His Grace hasn't discovered it was me who helped you, then yes, I shall return."

"Libba promised she wouldn't tell anyone how I got away. I'm sure you will be safe."

Jonathan laughed, the sound rich, dark, dangerous. "Concerned for me?"

"I'm concerned for all of us. Blankenship is not a man to be taken lightly." She stood and looked about the small room. "May I have some privacy to change?" It was probably safer not to undress around him, but her wet clothes were thick and suffocating on her skin.

"That won't be necessary, Miss Parr. I will be happy to aid you." He started towards her.

Emily stepped back, the wood wall striking her from behind. "Mr. Helprin, please, don't come any closer."

"I know this is a game, Miss Parr. It's not the first time I've performed dramatic roles for a woman. Just like His Grace's last mistress you seek to sate yourself with a younger man now and then. Evangeline liked to pretend the Revolutionaries had captured her. But you didn't need an elaborate ruse to have me. I know Godric really isn't in danger." He reached for the buttons on the front of her gown. She was suddenly very aware of the large size of his hands, the breadth of his shoulders and the power of his muscled frame.

She bared her teeth like a cornered animal. If she had to fight him, she would. "Let go of me."

"Shh...Calm down, Miss Parr. It will be enjoyable, I assure you. I know that's why you asked me to help you. It's obvious, you are here to be with me. I've never had complaints...and we shall be very, very warm afterwards." His voice oozed with honey.

Emily exhausted and distressed, pawed at his hands, trying to push him away.

"I tell you your master is in danger and that I'm fleeing to save his life and you assume it's part of some elaborate ruse for you to take me to bed? Do you possess that thick of a skull that logic cannot penetrate?" What she had hoped would have been a bitter tirade ended in a most unladylike sneeze and a sudden headache.

The sound of horses riding up outside in the rain could be heard.

"Hark!" he gasped. "It's Blankenship's men. We're surrounded! It's only a matter of time before they catch us. We should steal this one brief moment while we can."

"This is not a game, Mr. Helprin!"

Emily swayed as a wave of dizziness struck her. Her hands fell on his shoulders when she struggled to stay upright.

Jonathan lifted her up off the floor, and carried her to the bed. "Just close your eyes. I'm sure I'll feel the same as my master."

Emily struggled, muscles straining as she fought to keep Jonathan at a respectable distance.

"Get off me, you stupid oaf! I cannot believe you are such an addlepaited twit! I don't want you!" Her protest was lost on him and she sneezed again.

Jonathan pinned her down on the narrow bed, wedging his hips between her legs.

"That is what Evangeline said, but then she kissed me and all but dragged me to her bed. She said she liked to play games, that most women did. You cannot be all that different, Miss Parr."

He slanted his mouth down over hers.

I swear when I have the chance, I will kick him right in his manhood, she vowed. Emily clawed at his chest, but she was so tired and her head felt thick with a fogginess that frightened her. Tears pricked at the corners of her eyes.

Jonathan's mouth moved to her neck and the second her lips were free a small pitiful sob escaped Emily's throat.

Jonathan froze when she sobbed again. He pulled back, startled.

"My God. You really don't want me." The look of sheer shock on his face relieved her. He seemed completely horrified at his actions.

Emily sank limp into his arms, but managed a weak nod and then sneezed again.

"I'm so sorry, Miss Parr, I thought...it doesn't matter. Did...I hurt you?" He moved off her and sat back. Emily rolled onto her side away from him and burst into tears. Jonathan awkwardly patted her back. He couldn't understand the rending of her heart from her soul, the shattering of her essence into a thousand pieces. She wept for the life she left behind, the love she'd never know again.

"There, there." He tried to comfort her.

She slowed in her tears and only hiccupped once or twice, quivering. "I...don't think I'm well..." she started to say. A rough knock at the door cut the string of words from her lips.

"We're busy!"

The knock turned into a furious beating. Jonathan rose to his feet with a grumble, still shirtless as he moved.

When he opened the door, an absolute silence fell for all of two seconds before someone roared, and Jonathan hastily begged to explain. A fist flew through the door's opening to catch Jonathan square in the jaw.

Chapter Sixteen

Godric left Cedric alone in the drawing room to check on Emily. She'd looked decidedly pale and he was worried.

I'll read to her! She'll like that.

His eagerness surprised him, the temptation to abandon his friends and seek her out was great. But she probably needed some time alone—women often did; they were quite mysterious creatures. Knowing this didn't make him miss her any less. He snatched a book from his study and hurried upstairs.

On his way to her room he passed by a chamber he'd not entered in years. Strangely tempted, he opened the door. The nursery was a lovely room, even when muted by afternoon shadows and warm with its buttery yellow walls decorated by various painted scenes. Scenes painted by Godric's father a month before Godric was born.

He remembered his father pointing to a mighty frigate, guns blasting at a pirate vessel, deep voice rumbling as he spoke of age-old tales.

Godric's gaze fixed on another scene, one of a babe in a basket nestled against a wall of reeds as an Egyptian woman knelt to investigate her discovery. The tale of Moses—his mother's favorite story. A misplaced child loved by two mothers.

His throat tightened as he approached the empty crib. The faded blankets were perfectly folded, dust collecting on the crib's smooth edges. He ran a fingertip along the white wood, admiring the craftsmanship. His parents' ghosts were so alive in this room, in a way they hadn't been in a long time. Even though his father had lingered longer than his mother, Godric always felt his father died with her, at least on the inside.

The memories were bittersweet. How different his father became after losing her. The man whose talented hands had created such vivid dreams turned those hands to fists with which to pummel his only child.

No child should ever choose between wanting his father to leave and fearing actual abandonment. For half his life, a nightmare kept him trapped in a crumbling relationship with his only surviving parent.

Godric wondered whether he could recapture the soft magic of those early days, his mother still alive, his father's eyes joyful. Could those sacred hours of love and security return? It seemed impossible.

He couldn't erase the stark, empty plight of the days after his mother's death. He used to stare out the nursery window, waiting for his father to leave the distant grave. With the quiet patience of a frightened child, he lingered by his father's door each night, hoping for reassurance. A hug, a smile, any sign of affection, any sign he wasn't forgotten. A few months later, his father's indifference turned to violence.

Then Godric was desperate to hide, to pretend he never existed. It had been easy enough, living like a ghost in the lonely manor.

A vision burst before him, splitting the dark memories with its ray of light, the room lit by oil lamps. A lady with auburn hair peeked over the edge of the crib and cooed softly. She turned to face him, her violet eyes wide with wonder at the miracle of the babe before her. A miracle they'd brought to life together.

The vision faded. Emily and a child. A dream he might yet make real. He fingered the soft cotton of the baby blanket, hungry for the reality of the child he dreamed about. He would love it, whether boy or girl, cherish it and raise it to be perfect, just like its mother. The woman he loved. Loved.

He was in love with Emily.

The realization didn't shock him as he'd expected it would. Rather, his love grew the way seeds do, slowly, first planted the night he held her in his arms. Emily's laugh, her smiles, her dreams and soft touches, had nurtured it, until love covered his heart like a wealth of rich ivy. All these years he'd been convinced loving someone would leave him vulnerable. What a fool he'd been.

Love strengthened a person. It fortified their heart until they could defeat any enemy, survive any hardship, achieve any dream.

Godric tucked the baby blanket back into place and left the nursery, a look of joy on his face. He'd tell Emily right now. Confess his love and demand she stay and marry him, no matter the scandal. He had to have her, had to spend the rest of his life at the altar of her love, worshipping the woman who'd taught him to trust in himself and his heart.

He rapped his knuckles lightly on her door. It was half past three in the afternoon. Surely she'd slept, or at least rested, since lunch. He knocked louder when no one answered. Godric frowned, put his hand on the doorknob and turned it. Emily's door swung open, revealing a darkened room, curtains pulled shut. She looked to be buried deep into her covers. "Emily? Are you well?" Still no answer. "I thought I could read to you..." He rushed to her bed and tugged back the covers, his lips moving—"Emily?"—as his voice increased in volume.

The sight he beheld cooled his blood.

Someone—Emily—had lined up pillows beneath the covers, mimicking the presence of a body. She'd pinned a white piece of paper to the pillow. He picked it up with numb fingers, not even feeling the sting of the pin as it pricked his thumb. Godric blinked, opened the paper and read her letter.

Godric, I'm sorry to have left like this, but there was no other way. You must believe me. We are two different people, our lives worlds apart. I love you, but I cannot stay with you. I'm so sorry.

Emily was gone.

Rather than crumple the note in his fist, he set it down on the pillow. It was the last thing he had of hers, the last thing she touched in his world. He couldn't bear to destroy it and was too weak to remove the painful reminder.

He stumbled, faltering, as reality set in.

"Oh God...Emily!" She couldn't be gone... She couldn't have left him...

Cold rage engulfed him in icy flames, returning strength where love had rendered him weak.

Never again.

"Cedric, Charles!" he bellowed, wrath building in him. It crushed the despair that blackened his heart and gave him purpose.

Godric ran from the room and found his friends shooting up the stairs towards him.

"What? What's happened?" Cedric asked.

"Has anyone seen Emily?" He quivered with rage and, strangely, fear.

Charles shook his head. "No..."

"I haven't seen Penelope either..." added Cedric. "You don't think—"

Godric growled. "Find Simkins and Mrs. Downing! Tell them to have the servants search the manor from floor to ceiling. Charles, search the stables and the gardens. Cedric, you'll search the meadow with me. We'll take horses and go around the lake as well."

Charles raised an eyebrow. "And if we find her?"

"Subdue her by whatever means necessary. Cedric, bring the laudanum."

Charles balked. "But she hates—"

"I know. It was a mistake to grant her even one measure of freedom."

Godric scowled and neither man dared argue with him, not while fury lit his eyes like the fires of Hell.

Ten minutes later Godric and Cedric galloped across the meadow under a threatening sky. Cedric stopped well ahead of the wall and made to climb it, but Godric dug his heels into his horse's side. It cleared the wall entirely. He turned his horse to the left abruptly, as he'd seen Emily do, and spared himself another unpleasant dunking.

He didn't wait for Cedric.

His eyes scanned the ground for any sign of her passage.

Nothing... It was as though she had vanished into thin air.

Cedric studied the meadow. "Has she been planning this for a long while, do you think?"

"I do. I think she was biding her time for this moment, lulling me into a false sense of security."

"Then she fooled us all." Cedric's voice darkened with disappointment.

"What now?"

Godric raked a hand through his hair. "Where would she go?"

Cedric shrugged. "She could be anywhere. She must have quite a head start."

"No, she won't get far with a storm coming. We will find her, no matter how long it takes. I will track her down."

Cedric's voice was quiet. "Maybe you ought to let her go."

"Go?"

A tic worked in Cedric's jaw but he didn't back away. "You and I both know that clinging to things we don't deserve isn't healthy. Perhaps it is better this way."

"I don't care what is better!" Godric roared. "She is mine." He couldn't do without her. She was imprinted upon his heart, his soul. She had said she loved him. He wouldn't let her walk away.

When they returned to the manor, Charles appeared in the doorway, a flicker of apprehension crossed his features.

"No sign of her?"

Cedric frowned. "No. She wasn't in the gardens, I take it?"

Charles shook his head. "No. Nor the stables, and all the horses are accounted for."

They returned to the house, helping the servants search room by room. Rain lashed at the windows and lightning laced the skies with white fiery streaks. The clock in the hallway read half-past four. One more precious hour gone.

Godric stood on the landing, scowling as he gazed out the tall window to the view across the meadow, towards the lake.

"Why did you leave me?" His voice wavered. If he hadn't been in such pain, he would have laughed. The Duke of Essex had found his heart, only to have it broken.

Her leaving him was infinitely more painful than any blow his father ever struck.

His darling, sweet, innocent Emily had betrayed him. She was no different than Evangeline. Yet he would drag her back here and imprison her for as long as he liked. Society and law be damned. She'd wounded his pride, wounded his heart. She'd pay dearly for it.

"Your Grace?" Mrs. Downing cut through Godric's dark thoughts.

He spun to face his housekeeper at the foot of the stairs. One of the serving maids cowered behind her, avoiding Godric's glare. "What?"

"This young lady has information regarding Miss Parr." Mrs. Downing sidestepped and exposed the girl to Godric's wrath.

Godric descended the steps and grabbed the maid by the shoulders. "Speak, girl!"

The maid cast a furtive glance towards the housekeeper, seeking some aid.

Godric shook her. "Speak now, or you will find employment elsewhere."

"Sh-She's gone off with Jonathan Helprin to Blackbriar village. She wore my extra serving gown. She said your life was in dan—"

Godric released her. "Silence!" He turned to the others looking for his butler. "Simkins! Have the grooms ready three horses. Charles! Cedric!"

They emerged from the rooms they'd been searching.

Godric strode to the door. "She's gone to Blackbriar village. We leave immediately. If we ride hard we can be there in an hour." Godric slung himself up into the saddle. "I'm on your trail again, little fox." He was going to catch Emily Parr one last time, and she would never escape him again.

Jonathan stumbled backward, a hand to his jaw as Godric stormed into the room.

Emily scrambled off the bed, realizing how the situation must appear to Godric, she in her undergarments crying and Jonathan only half-dressed.

"What have you done to her? You bastard!" Godric threw himself at Jonathan.

Jonathan put up his hands. "Nothing! I've done nothing, I swear!"

Godric threw another vicious punch, and that was it.

Jonathan crumpled to the floor unconscious.

Penelope snarled at Godric, lunging for his Hessians as he turned on Emily. The little hound was determined to protect her mistress.

Cedric and Charles rushed into the room. Relief lightened their faces. "Emily, thank God we found you!" said Cedric

"Wait outside, and take that filthy hound with you and Penelope as well." Cedric scooped up the pup while Charles dragged out the valet.

Godric slammed the door behind them, turned the lock and faced her. Water streamed down his clothes, and his dark hair curled against the collar of his neck.

The world ceased to move. Stars winked out in the distant cosmos, the wind and rain outside paled into mist. Emerging from the gloom, Godric was her beacon of light, the shelter from her storms.

Emily realized she could never do without him, never leave him again. Without him she would have faded into a shadow of her true self. It had already begun before he'd found her.

Emily choked back a sob.

But she'd abandoned him. Despite her reasons, the love that drove her, the hope that carried her, he wouldn't forgive her now, perhaps ever. The pain in his eyes told her just what her departure had cost him.

All she had to do was explain. He'd listen, and maybe, if she was lucky, forgive her. He'd have to, once he knew what Evangeline had said.

He removed his cloak, overcoat and shirt, then took slow deep breaths as he stepped towards her. Emily's heart quickened. She saw the animal lust in his eyes, and she knew her own gaze answered his.

Without a second thought Emily flung herself at him, pressing tight against him, arms banding about his neck. But he didn't return her embrace. His arms hung at his sides. He was coiled tight, rigid and so impossibly cold.

"Godric, I'm so glad you're here, but..." Godric pried her arms from around his neck and set her firmly away from him, the distance between them a vast ocean, dark and bottomless. She needed to explain. There was no other option. "You shouldn't have come. I can't protect you like this."

"Do. Not. Speak."

A rabbit trapped against a serpent's gaze, Emily stood mesmerized and unable to move. He backed her into a wall, pinning her shoulders with his palms.

"You left me. You lied to me."

"Listen to me! I had to."

"You *abandoned* me. So much for your love." His voice harsh, his teeth gritted.

"You don't understand, Blankenship was going to—"

He caught her chin with one hand and took her mouth with his. Took everything she offered. He left her no time for breath or thought. Emily gave in. The hard kiss turned soft and deep. His touch was full of tenderness as he stroked her body. He had forgiven her, he had to, otherwise he would not have been so gentle now.

Her breasts grew heavy, aching for his touch and the silken heat of his mouth. Everything she swore she could live without rushed back to her. No sooner could the moon abandon the earth than she could leave him. He would take her back, forgive her for breaking his heart. It was there in his kiss, that sweet emotion she craved.

"Godric, please... I need you." Her plea was an aching whisper against his neck.

His breath grew ragged as he dug at his breeches, freeing himself. He thrust a hand between her legs, finding the wetness that pooled there for him, and sank two fingers deep between her folds. Emily moaned. He pleasured her with his hand, and each time she tried to shut her eyes, he demanded she look at him, so she did. His face was dark with shadows.

"You left me. Your room was empty. Do you have any idea what that did to me?" The growls vibrated against her throat as he nuzzled her. "You are mine. Do you understand? I'll never let you go. Never."

Finally, when Emily was weak-kneed from desire, he snagged her left thigh and wrapped it around his hip. He was poised at her entrance, the tip of him barely inside. For one tense second, their breaths mingled, their eyes locked, and then he plunged inside. Emily cried out. Her head fell back against the wall and Godric fisted his free hand in her hair at the nape of her neck, holding her still. The fingers of his other hand sank into the skin of her thigh as he impaled her against the wall. He kissed her again, taking her lips, a conquering warrior.

Emily accepted it all, moving her hips into his, craving this new wildness. Her own hands scraped his back, marking him. Waves of pleasure rolled through her body as she neared her climax.

Emily raked a hand through his hair. Godric dragged his lips away from hers so he could bury his face in her neck. He pounded harder into her and his thrusts sent her careening over the edge of bliss. Crimson spirals of dark rapture flashed over her eyes. She whispered his name like a midnight prayer, weakening in his arms. With a roar of primal satisfaction, he came. His seed spilled deep into her.

Gasping for air, he sagged against her, keeping them both upright against the wall. Emily finally shut her eyes, stroking his hair, smoothing back the dark silky strands from his temples down to his neck, soothing him.

"God, I'm such a bloody fool." He shrank away from her. Emily's knees buckled and she braced against the wall for support.

"What do you mean?" His tone worried her and fear gnawed at her insides. He wasn't holding her, kissing her. This was not the reunion she'd imagined. Panic began to trickle through her, and her vision blurred with tears.

Godric was still muttering, not looking at her as he fixed his clothes. "You don't love me. You never have." The self-deprecating laugh which followed sent chills through her. "If you love someone, you don't abandon them. You don't hurt them."

"I didn't abandon you, Godric, but I had to leave. I'm so sorry about the note I—" He silenced her with a wave of his hand before tossing her clothes at her feet.

"But you're in danger!"

Godric ignored her. "Get dressed. We have to return home at once."

"But why?" Emily froze, gown half up her shaking calves. She had an eerie sensation of dread, as though she was climbing the stairs in the dark and thinking that there was a last step, her foot fell through the empty air, taking her body with it.

"I think perhaps your uncle and I finally agree on something. You've outlived your usefulness, and it is time I returned you to him."

A slap across her cheek would have hurt less.

I've outlived my usefulness?

His affections had been merely a momentary attraction built on nothing but lust, just as she'd feared. Now he'd destroy her in return by delivering her back to her uncle and the marriage that would seal her doom.

She blinked, dazed to find Godric holding a silver flask, no doubt filled with the water and laudanum she hated so much. The day couldn't worsen, of that she was sure.

"That won't be necessary I promise to come quietly." She stumbled. Thunder rattled the inn and lightning sparked outside the windows, a reflection of the turmoil in her heart.

Godric studied her before pocketing the flask. "Very well, though your promises mean little to me."

She finished dressing, hastily shoving buttons in all of the wrong slits, but it didn't matter. Nothing mattered anymore. She'd lost him. What she'd believed had been forgiveness, had merely been a final goodbye. Her own stupid actions had destroyed her precarious grip on his affection.

An unfamiliar despair seized her in its grasp. Her lungs slowed, breath coming shorter and shorter. Black dots spotted her vision. She took a shaky step towards Godric, but the movement sent her vision spiraling out of control. Emily pitched forward as darkness descended and the floor rushed up to meet her.

Godric caught Emily a second before she hit the floor. He cradled her to his chest, savoring the feel of her in his arms, then chastised himself for doing so.

Her escape had proven her intentions well enough. Her whispered words of love were nothing more than lies, a clever ruse to lower his guard.

He retrieved Emily's small cloth bag where she'd set it down by the door. Her head lolled sideways, bumping into his chest. God, he was a fool.

He was even more a fool for threatening to return her. He knew what life awaited her there—marriage to Blankenship, a lifetime of misery. He wanted her to deserve that after what she'd done to him, but revenge seemed the farthest thing from his heart.

Emily needed to go. That was all. If she stayed, he'd do something he'd regret, like beg her to love him. He'd relive his boyhood all over again, seeking love, knowing it would never come. The self-loathing that coiled about him increased with every step as he finally opened the door and came out into the hall.

Cedric and Charles were there, Cedric holding the struggling pup and Charles holding up a groggy but conscious Jonathan Helprin. All three men looked at Emily with deep concern.

"Is she—" Charles began.

"She's fine. She fainted." A nasty bruise had already formed on Jonathan's jaw.

"Your Grace, I swear nothing happened to her."

"I will deal with you when we return to the manor." If he tried to talk to the man now, Godric would strangle him.

His friends followed him as he carried Emily down the inn's stairs, past the shocked guests, and back into the rain where Cedric held her until he mounted his horse. Once Emily was tucked into his arms, he relaxed, but only just.

As night fell, they rode back toward the manor, the thundering skies heralding their return.

When they arrived, Simkins took Jonathan and Penelope away to see to their care. Charles and Cedric followed Godric up to his bedchamber, where he lay Emily down. He stripped her of her wet dress and undergarments after the other two men stepped out into the corridor. He pulled back the covers and tucked her into his bed, then he called his friends back into the room.

"Check the windows, Cedric. Charles, you lock the adjoining door." They both scrambled to do this, no doubt fearing his black mood. Godric leaned down over Emily and tucked the blankets more firmly about her, right up to her chin. He gently brushed back the soft damp locks of her hair, then he motioned for his friends to leave with him. Time to deal with another traitor.

They returned to the drawing room where Simkins and Jonathan were waiting.

Godric turned to his butler. "Simkins, send someone to light a fire in my bedchamber. *Not* Libba." Simkins bowed and disappeared.

Charles started to edge towards the door. "Shall we...er...go too?"

"Stay. You might need to keep me from killing this bastard," Godric said as his gaze fixed on Jonathan. "But don't try too hard."

Jonathan stood up, defiant. "Nothing happened, Your Grace. She asked for my help. I gave it. We only took the room at the inn to avoid the rain."

"You lie!" Godric's fingers dug into his palms as he clenched his fists. "She was half-naked, as were you!"

Jonathan kicked the chair between them away. "You want to kill me? Then kill me! If you think you can."

Cedric and Charles each took a step forward, ready to intervene.

"So be it!" Godric lunged for him and grabbed his shirt collar, shaking him.

"Unhand him at once!"

Godric and Jonathan stopped and turned, shocked to see who would dare address Godric that way. Simkins stood in the open doorway, as if he were the master of Essex House. When he had their attention, he returned to his usual self and added, "Your Grace."

Godric recovered himself. "Don't interfere. It is a matter of honor."

Simkins raised a pistol from under his coat and aimed the barrel at Godric's chest.

"You will step away from your half-brother, Your Grace," Simkins said, voice surprisingly calm.

"Brother?" Godric asked, letting go of Jonathan's shirt.

Simkins lowered the pistol. "I vowed to your father that no harm would befall him. It puts me in a difficult position. I will of course tender my resignation after this, but I am firm in my decision to protect Jonathan."

Jonathan glanced sharply at Godric as the news sank in. "I'm his what?"

Godric was not as surprised. Ever since Emily had mentioned it, he'd half suspected there was more to his valet's past than he knew. He'd even warmed to the idea, but that was before tonight. Tonight was bad timing. Right now he wanted Jonathan dead.

"I don't care if he's the king of England! If he harmed my Emily—"

"Then we will deal with that problem, but only if Miss Parr confirms your belief that he has, in fact, harmed her."

Godric groaned, his shoulders hunching forward as he pressed the heels of his hands into his eyes so hard he saw stars. Right now he didn't even feel like the master of his own house. Not with his butler pointing a pistol at him.

"How...how are we brothers?" Jonathan demanded.

Simkins lowered the pistol but didn't put it away. "The late duke sought comfort in your mother's arms. He cared about her, as he did you. When he fell ill I vowed to care for you as I have His Grace."

"So I really am—"

"A bastard," Godric supplied.

"No. Jonathan is a legitimate son of the former Duke of Essex. He married her in secret ten months before Jonathan was born. His birth was recorded in the parish registry under your father's name, Your Grace."

"If I'm not a bastard why wasn't I raised alongside him?" Jonathan jabbed a finger in Godric's direction.

Heavy lines creased Simkins eyes. "The former duke told me, on his deathbed, to keep Godric an only child. He never wanted the truth of your heritage to be known, unless Godric died without an heir."

"Why would he do that?" Jonathan's anger began to overshadow Godric's. "Why would he take from me my right as a duke's son?"

"Your father realized he'd been terribly cruel to Godric and that admitting he'd found love with another would only make matters worse, and he feared Godric would be jealous of you."

Godric couldn't believe it. The stupid man! Godric would have preferred a brother over solitude. That his father chose to love a lady's maid made no difference, but to be denied his brother all these years did.

Jonathan looked to his brother, uncertain what to say. "Well then... Where does that leave us?"

Godric frowned. "You're still a bastard."

"If you think I'm ever polishing another boot of yours, you're mistaken. I am not a bastard and you cannot treat me like one."

"I didn't mean that kind of bastard, you imbecile. You're a bastard for touching my Emily!"

"Your Emily? Such devotion you must have instilled in her if the poor thing was crying her eyes out."

Charles sighed and leaned against the mantle. "Ah, brotherly love. Reminds me of home."

Cedric stifled a chuckle. "For you, perhaps. Didn't you challenge your own brother, to a duel over a woman?"

"Yes, bit of rotten luck that. Mother found us counting paces in the garden. That woman can still wield a switch to make a grown man cry."

"Well, Jonathan certainly has the St. Laurent temper, eh, Godric?"

How many times had Godric hated being an only child? Now he was blessed, or rather cursed, with a sibling, just like the rest of the League.

Godric and Jonathan shared murderous looks, but a sudden commotion outside scattered their attention.

"Godric!" someone yelled.

Lucien and Ashton burst into the drawing room, knocking Simkins out of the way in their haste. The pistol fell from his grasp and hit the floor, setting it off and shattering a vase not three feet from where Godric stood.

It took a moment for the panic everyone felt to subside and return to normal. If anything about today could be called normal.

"Godric!" Lucien noticed the butler and the weapon on the floor. "Why was Simkins holding a gun?"

Charles waved a hand for the newcomers to get comfortable. "My dear Lucien, it's just like you to start a conversation at the most boring part."

Ashton looked between Godric and Jonathan. "What? Boring?"

Godric threw a pointed look at Jonathan. "Ashton, Lucien... Meet my half-brother, Jonathan."

Lucien looked more than a little confused. "Brother?"

Ashton checked his pocket watch. "But we've only been gone one day..."

Cedric crossed his arms. "Lessons in recent ancestry can wait. Now what's happened with you two?"

Ashton said, "We were able to follow Evangeline in London. Blankenship hired her, Godric. She came here to spy on you, to make sure you did in fact have Emily."

Hearing her name ripped Godric's gaze from his brother to Ashton.

"What? She was Blankenship's puppet?" Godric blinked in shock. It would explain everything. Her strange story, showing up at his home with a forged note. That crafty bastard.

Ashton nodded. "Not exactly. Say what you will of her, but I think we all know that woman is no one's puppet. Evangeline told Blankenship that she convinced Emily to escape or else Blankenship's men would show up and kill all of us to get to her. Emily must be stopped before she does something foolish."

Godric choked. "Too late..."

Christ, he'd done the worst thing possible. He'd hurt her for the crime of trying to save him. He had repaid her devotion by locking her in his bedchamber yet again. If there hadn't been a circle of hell reserved for him before, he'd just qualified for an entire realm.

The blood drained from Lucien's face. "What do you mean?"

"She made it to Blackbriar village with the aid of my brother. We've only just returned."

Ashton frowned. "And Emily?"

"Upstairs."

"Well, have her come down. We need to discuss what to do about Blankenship."

"That is not exactly possible," said Cedric. "He left her somewhat...indisposed upstairs."

"Oh, Lord," said Lucien.

Ashton pinched the bridge of his nose. "Godric, listen to me. She only left to protect you. She does not know how capable you are of defending yourself. She did it because she loved you and couldn't bear to see you hurt for her sake."

Charles and Cedric exchanged grim looks. Jonathan's face paled and he failed to meet Godric's eyes.

"It's too late, isn't it?" asked Ashton.

Godric nodded, and turned his back on them. "I've wounded her in a way she will never forgive." He couldn't forgive betrayal so how could she? Knowing she was lost to him forever, because he'd acted rashly, let his temper direct his actions, made the agony of her loss worse.

"Excuse me." He left the room and no one dared stop him.

Godric had barricaded himself in his study, and it was up to the others to take up the mantle of Emily's care and protection.

They found her in Godric's bed.

Emily shifted slightly, still asleep. All of them were as guilty of ruining and hurting Emily as Godric was. That would change.

Ashton turned to Lucien. "See to having a fresh pair of undergarments ready for her when she wakes."

Lucien nodded and left to find her clothes.

Ashton eased himself down on the edge of the bed and bent down to press his lips against her forehead. She felt feverish beneath his kiss. If she became ill… No, he mustn't think such thoughts.

He smoothed her hair back from her brow. "Sleep, dear Emily."

Lucien returned and took a position near the foot of the bed in a chair. The nearby fire crackled and sparked in the darkness.

The League had gone too far to satisfy its pride and lust.

Emily stirred, her breath shallow.

Heavy rocks lay on her chest. It was harder and harder to fill her lungs.

Panic surged through her, making her body shudder. Glass

shards seemed to be embedded in her throat when she tried to swallow. She needed to cough, but no strength remained. The rasp of her indrawn breath sounded like an ominous death rattle.

"Emily!" A man's voice. Low, hoarse, and grating to her ears. She winced as she tried to swallow again, and finally managed a weak cough.

"Emily?" The voice was a familiar one, a warm hand on her forehead.

Where am I?

Sensations crept back on her, the soft slide of bed sheets beneath her bare skin, the aroma of sandalwood. Men were nearby. Who? Though she couldn't see it, she could feel the pulsing rhythm of a candle nearby.

"Quick, Charles, the water." Cedric, her mind finally recalled. She was at Godric's estate, in his bed. Once again a captive of the League of Rogues.

"Go...dric..."

Cedric shushed her, then raised a glass of water to her cracked lips. She drank, the cool water a balm to her parched throat. Her eyelids finally cracked open. She was in Godric's bedroom; Cedric and Charles hovered over her. She shivered and rubbed her naked arms—

She was naked.

Emily gasped, a dreadfully sick sound.

"There, there, love, You're safe," Charles said. Neither he nor Cedric seemed interested in her state of undress. She swallowed, which was still painful.

"How?"

"How?" The men shared a confused look.

"How—" but she couldn't finish.

Cedric took the glass from Charles and refilled it from a pitcher. "We brought you back from the inn in Blackbriar two days ago, kitten. You've been very ill."

He held the glass out to Emily. She reached for it, but her arms shook. Charles took it and sat down on the bed before he held it to her lips again. She emptied the glass.

"Two...days?"

Charles nodded and tucked a stray lock of hair tenderly behind her ear. "I should tickle you to death for all your foolishness."

Dark smudges beneath his grey eyes revealed his lack of sleep. Charles had always come across as the most immature, though only a year separated him from Godric and Cedric. But a lined, wearied expression was now fixed to the youthful earl's countenance. She reached up and touched his cheek. Charles shut his eyes, a tic working in his strong jaw. He caught her hand, kissed it and set it back beneath the covers where it was warm.

She looked to Cedric. He too seemed sick with worry, dark circles under his brown eyes as he hovered nearby.

"The others?"

"Ashton and Lucien are resting. We have been taking shifts to watch over you."

"And...Godric?" This was what she really wished to know. Where was he? She needed him.

"He—" Cedric paused, as though choosing his words carefully "—is not himself right now."

"Is he unwell?"

Did the others know what had happened at the inn? Did they know how she'd betrayed him? She remembered the choked sound he'd made when she tried to soothe him. A horrific sound. She'd wanted nothing more than to assure him that she loved him, that she'd only left him to protect him. But he hadn't given her the chance.

The...*idiot*. She was not sad, she was furious with him. All she'd needed to do was explain herself and he hadn't given her the chance. She wanted to slap him, then kiss him, and then slap him again. The damned fool.

"Take me to him now."

Cedric laid a palm on her shoulder. "He isn't at his best, kitten. He's—"

"I don't care! Take me to him." She could only manage a whisper that she followed with a forceful stare.

Cedric jumped up. "I'll go."

Charles nodded, pulled a pistol out from his waistband, and sat back on the bed, facing the door.

"A gun? He's...he's not gone mad, has he?" She reached for the pistol, but Charles pulled out of her reach.

Charles gave her a devil-may-care grin. "It isn't for Godric, Emily. Lucien and Ashton followed Evangeline Mirabeau to London. They learned that Blankenship hired her to find you, and what he has planned for us. Hence the weapons."

"Godric knows why I left?"

Charles nodded. "Not until after we returned to the manor. Lucien and Ashton were a bit late to the party, so to speak. Godric has had a rough couple of days. He lost you, tried to kill his brother, now he's done nothing but drink in his study. Only Simkins has managed see him without getting something thrown at his head. I nearly got beaned with the Bible he threw at me." Charles chuckled. "Don't mistake me, Emily, I quite enjoyed the irony. Reminded me of this one lady who threw a vial of holy water at me, expecting me to burn."

"In all fairness, you did smoke a little," said Ashton.

Charles scoffed. "It was winter and the water was warm."

Emily tried to smile but she was caught up by the more salient point.

"Brother?"

"Oh, of course. I suppose you've missed a lot of the fireworks. Godric tried to throttle Jonathan. Simkins pointed a gun at Godric and said he can't kill his half-brother. It turns out Jonathan is the son of the late duke and the lady's maid to Godric's mother."

Emily did smile then. She hadn't been mistaken about Jonathan after all. "I knew it."

Charles chucked her under the chin affectionately. "None of us saw it."

"You've known him for too long and simply gotten used to him, I suppose."

Cedric returned, looking pointedly at the floor. "It's as I feared. He's completely foxed. Trust me, kitten, you don't want to see him like this."

"I do and I will." She struggled to get up but remembered she was naked and clutched the sheet about her breasts. "Robe, please." Cedric hesitated but Emily's glare had him retrieve Godric's red velvet robe straight away. Emily studied Cedric and Charles, weighing who she trusted more to keep his hands to himself. Neither were good choices, but one was most certainly worse. She chose Cedric.

"You help me."

"Ahem," Cedric said to Charles, who waited outside with a huff.

Cedric averted his gaze as he pulled the covers back and then eased Emily's arms into the robe's sleeves. She wrapped it snugly about herself and tied the cord at her waist tight before getting out of bed. As grimy as she felt, the more important thing was to see Godric. She could bathe later. Emily took a deep breath and tried to stand.

She wavered and Cedric caught her up in his arms. "I'll help you, kitten."

They must have been an odd sight, Emily in her oversized robe, barefoot, leaning against Cedric for support. Thankfully, no one saw them but Simkins, posted outside the door to Godric's study.

The butler's eyes widened. "Lord Sheridan, she shouldn't be out of bed!"

Emily held up a hand and pointed to the study door.

"Open it."

Simkins shook his head. "I'm afraid he's not fit to see anyone."

"I don't care." Emily growled.

"Very well, Miss Parr, but I will intervene if he grows violent." Simkins fumbled with his set of keys.

"Yes, he might shoot another vase," said Charles.

"What?" Emily gasped.

"It was an ugly vase, one his mother always hated. It won't be missed," said Simkins.

Godric shouted from the other side of the door. "Simkins, I told you to leave me be!"

"Silence, St. Laurent." Cedric's voice echoed, a boom that brought silence from the study. "Emily is here. Behave, you hear me?"

Simkins opened the door and Cedric stepped inside, Emily leaning against him. Godric was at the back of the study, facing the window with his back to them, the night outside was inky black. One candle lit the room.

"Help me to the couch," said Emily. "Then leave us."

"I'm staying, Emily."

She stroked his face as she had Charles's. "Thank you, Cedric, but I will be fine."

He bent to kiss the top of her head before retreating. Simkins shut the door from the outside.

An agonizing moment of silence followed—Godric at the window, she on the couch, both still as statues. Could she make him understand that she hadn't betrayed him?

"Godric," she breathed.

Slowly he turned to face her. Her dark prince with shadows beneath his tortured emerald eyes with hair tangled as though he'd dug his fingers into it over and over again. How had it come to this?

Emily knew of the deadly calm before the storm, but she believed it was the calm afterwards which often proved worse, with century old trees ripped from the soil and birds lying dead upon the ground after being hurled through mighty winds. Everywhere lay destruction. In watching Godric's haunted eyes, she saw that same vast path of devastation.

She found a new strength in her voice. "Come to me."

He obeyed, feet dragging until he stood before her, gazing down at her, those long dark lashes fanning against his cheeks as he shut his eyes for a brief moment. His right hand was the closest thing she could reach. She caught his wrist, lifting it until she captured his palm and brought it to her lips. She kissed the inside of his hand, letting him feel her tenderness.

I love you.

Godric's legs buckled. Suddenly he was on his knees, burying his head on her lap, arms wrapping around her as he clung to her. Emily bent over him, kissing his hair, stroking his shoulders as he shook with violent silent sobs. He clenched her tight, as though he feared she'd vanish in his arms. She felt the tremors of his receding grief as he finally raised his head.

"Emily..."

She put a finger to his lips and shook her head.

"I forgive you." She found a smile, let it pull her lips up but this only made him cringe, his face that of a fallen angel. But *her* angel.

"I can't forgive myself..." He turned away from her.

Emily grabbed his chin, forcing his face back towards her and catching him in a violent kiss.

"You are a fool, Your Grace," she said then ravaged his mouth again, bruising him with her possession. He barely had time to kiss her back before she released him. Godric put a shaking hand to his mouth, startled as he felt his swollen, punished lips.

"I'm learning your way of kissing." Emily smiled at him, a wicked smile. The kiss had somehow breathed life into her.

Godric slowly got up off his knees and joined her on the couch. He leaned forward to kiss her. Emily braced herself for a return of the heated melding of mouths she'd given him, returning fire with more fire.

But she did not get it.

Godric barely kissed her at first, so faint was the pressure of his lips on hers. It was a dream of a kiss. But then he deepened it. His tongue slipped between her lips, with infinite tenderness as their lips began that slow ancient dance. Emotion flooded through that kiss. Godric had to tell her everything he felt—the relief, joy, guilt, passion, concern.

Emily Parr had to be some sort of angel. No mortal woman could forgive a man for such sins. He'd abused her trust and taken her up against the wall like some barbarian. He'd threatened to return her to her uncle and deliver her to an unhappy marriage to a man she despised. He'd terrified her to the point that she'd fainted and been senseless for two days.

Feel me, darling! Feel me. Know that I love you. This time, when the words rushed out in his mind, he welcomed them. It had to be love. Nothing could wound a soul like hurting the one you loved. How he wanted to say the words, but it felt wrong when he'd done nothing to prove it. No. He would not tell her loved her until he could prove it. He was too deep into his cups and would have been unable to get out the words she deserved. *Bloody fool I am.*

When their lips broke apart Emily's eyes were still closed. Godric trailed a fingertip down the upward curve of her nose and she opened her eyes to see him.

"Let me take you back upstairs to rest." He stood up and scooped her body into his arms when he realized she was naked beneath the robe. He almost laughed.

"Are you not wearing anything else?" Emily blushed and the sight relieved him. Her face had been too pale. "After all that I've done to you, you just keep rewarding me," he teased as he admired the way the velvet molded to her curves. Emily flashed him a mock scowl and he grinned, pressing his forehead against hers, gazing deep into her violet eyes.

"Will you promise to never escape again?"

"I was not escaping. I was saving your life. And you're still not safe. We must talk..."

"All right, my darling. When you're feeling better, we'll talk." He kissed her cheek and then opened the study door.

Charles, Cedric and Simkins all huddled about the door, faces pressed close to the frame, caught in the act of eavesdropping.

Out of the three of them only Simkins managed to maintain his dignified air.

"We were monitoring the corridor for security, Your Grace," he said.

"Security? I suppose those carpets do look most suspect, Simkins. Good idea, best to watch the paintings and statues. They could be working with our enemies." Godric hid a smile. "Now if you'll pardon us. I am just taking Emily back up to bed to rest." The three men watched him leave, no doubt wondered what on earth transpired to calm the tempest of his famous temper.

Once upstairs, Godric put Emily down on his bed and started to move to the empty chair nearby. Emily grabbed his arm, keeping him close.

"Stay." Her free hand patted the bed. Godric sat down on the edge of the bed, bent over and pulled his boots off and turned to join her. Emily snuggled deep into the covers.

Godric turned her face towards his. "Emily, about what happened in the inn—"

"Yes?"

"That should never have happened. It will never happen again." He brushed his lips against hers.

"Don't promise that. It was beyond anything I've ever experienced. Of course, at the time I thought you had forgiven me and had missed me terribly."

"Forgive you? Emily, I was not gentle with you. Why don't you hate *me*?" Fearful confusion clouded his wide eyes.

"I could never hate you. Godric, I love you. Haven't I told you enough for you to believe me? As for not being gentle... I enjoyed it. Now stay. Sleep with me." Her voice was a command. "From what Cedric said, you've not had any rest."

Godric wanted to shout, to laugh. If this was the extent of her temper, she truly was an angel. He pulled her into his arms, burying his face into her neck, kissing the sensitive spot right behind her ear until her breath quickened.

"I don't deserve you, my darling."

"You certainly don't. Lucky for you, I seem to have developed a taste for rogues." She ran her fingers through his hair, teasing the nape of his neck.

"Rogues?" He flicked his tongue against her neck, eliciting a soft little moan. "As in more than one?"

"I've lived with five of you under the same roof. Suffice it to say I've found your little League quite—" She paused as he sucked her skin, and she flushed with heat.

"Yes?" He prompted.

"What were we talking about?" One of his hands slid under the gown of her robe and palmed her breast, caressing the pink bud that tightened beneath his fingertips.

"I believe we were talking about sleep," he murmured against her lips before he slid his tongue into her mouth, barely able to think straight himself.

"Sleep?"

"Sleep...yes..." He'd barely let himself rest, let alone sleep in the past two days. Now the drowsiness was starting to catch up with him. Godric drew in a slow deep breath, his body relaxing, but his heart and soul breathed, danced and rejoiced. Emily was back where she belonged, with him. He could rest. She was safe.

"Emily," he whispered against her neck.

"Yes?"

"I'm not like my father. I have his temper, but I am not like him."

"Godric. When you were angry you made love to me. That doesn't make you like your father." Emily's eyes twinkled as she ran a fingertip down his open shirt, skimming his bare chest. Godric groaned, wishing that fingertip would keep going down.

"Can we talk about Jonathan?"

"My brother? Wish I could kill him. Can't." He moaned. "He's a St. Laurent." Godric's words scattered apart as he struggled to fight his need for Emily. She needed to rest, not make love.

"He's a lot like you."

"Oh? In what way?" Godric's hand moved around to her back, caressing her underneath the velvet robe.

"He's a stubborn, green-eyed rogue who assumes every woman secretly wants him and just needs to be convinced of it." She giggled and twisted her body so that she lay on her back.

A smile escaped his lips and he bent down to kiss Emily again. "You're right, the devil does sound like me."

"You need to rest."

"So do you, darling." He settled her deeper into his embrace.

They were both quiet for a long moment. Godric drew in a deep breath. "Promise me you'll be here when I wake up." He brushed a hair from her face. "I know you will, but I need to hear it." Emily groggily looked at him, her brow crinkling in an adorable way.

"I promise I will be here. Godric, I'm so sorry I left. I can't image how it must have hurt you." She ran a fingertip along his jaw, tracing his face.

He leaned back and ran a hand over his eyes in an attempt to erase the memories. "I couldn't think, couldn't breathe. I thought I was dying, Emily. Christ, you have no idea what that's like." His eyes were those of a boy, one who'd seen years of abuse. "I swore that, after my father, no one would ever have the power to hurt me."

"When I realized I had to leave...I came back to my room and collapsed." Emily fought to control her voice. "I wanted nothing more than to run back down to the dining room and into your arms. But I had to protect you. I would do anything to protect you." She leaned up to brush a kiss on his brow before settling back down, resting her head on his chest. "I will be here tomorrow morning. I promise."

Relief filled his lungs. She was his world, his everything.

"Goodnight, Godric." Emily's voice was sleepy and soft. The intimacy of this moment was perfect. Life could have stolen everything else from him, but as long as he had Emily, he could survive.

"Goodnight, darling." He fell asleep with his lips pressed into her hair. Guilt still lingered, but Emily—angelic, loving Emily—had erased so much self-loathing.

How had he lived without her for all these years?

Chapter Seventeen

Ashton woke the next morning with a horrible crick in his neck. He had fallen asleep in a chair outside Godric's door. He yawned and rubbed the tight muscles on the back of his neck. What a night.

Ashton dared to peek into Godric's room and found his friend cuddled up with Emily as though the two would never part again.

He shut the door and returned to his chair. *Godric, you will marry her. There's no other way to keep her safe and yourself sane.*

No one had woken him to change the guard as scheduled. Rather than let anger rise up in him, he merely smiled.

How strange it all was that an act of abduction born of Godric's wounded pride would end up like this? With Godric hopelessly smitten by a singularly unique young lady every bit his equal.

Simkins came up the stairs carrying a tea tray, which meant he must have wanted to have a private word with Ashton without the other servants overhearing.

"Would you care for a cup of tea, Lord Lennox?" Simkins asked.

"Yes, thank you." He took the offered cup of steaming tea. "What hour is it, Simkins?"

"It is a little past nine in the morning."

Ashton ran a hand along his chin where pale two day stubble already shadowed his jaw. "Nine, you say? Lord... We've slept too long." He took a sip of tea. "Is anyone else awake?"

Simkins smiled. "No, my lord, you are the first. The entire house is quite exhausted from the previous day's events. I let the staff sleep in until eight-thirty this morning. I hope His Grace won't mind."

Ashton flicked his head towards the closed bedroom door. "I'm sure he won't. He has other things to concern himself with at the moment."

The butler grew serious. "May I speak with you, my lord? I have a favor to ask."

"Name it," Ashton said, without hesitation.

"Much has occurred these past few days. His Grace has endured many things." Simkins kept his voice low. "Stability is needed in his life."

"Stability?" Ashton took another sip. The hot liquid felt good on his throat. "I suppose you have a suggestion?"

"I hope—that is to say, I wish—for you to suggest to His Grace that he should do the right thing by Miss Parr and marry her. It wouldn't do for me to make such a suggestion."

"Because you had to give notice over the matter of the pistol."

"Oh no, my lord. His Grace forbade me from leaving his employment until I had paid for the hideous vase I broke. Then proceeded to drink so much he forgot I had ever offered my resignation in the first place. No, though I did what I could to tend to His Grace's needs growing up, I'm afraid when it comes to matters of the heart my instruction was quite lacking. You are the better choice."

He put his cup down. "Let me ask you something, Simkins. Why do *you* think he should marry her?"

Simkins stood erect and regal, still holding the tray. "I have never seen His Grace so concerned about another soul in his entire life, except perhaps for you and your friends. But that it is a love he knows and understands. Comradery, if you will. With Miss Parr, he may not recognize that his passions are fueled by a deeper yearning. Perhaps you can help him see that."

The butler's words, the weight of importance he'd placed on his duties to Godric and the St. Laurent family, moved Ashton deeply.

"Rest easy, Simkins. I quite agree with you. I'll speak to the others and we will raise the matter with him."

"Thank you, my lord. It comforts me to know he has chosen well in his friends." Simkins bowed his head and retreated down the stairs with his tea tray.

Ashton finished his tea in the quiet silence of the empty hallway, contemplating their other problem. The threat of Blankenship had never left his mind. It was unwise to remain at Godric's estate while Blankenship plotted Emily's capture.

The man was more foolhardy than Ashton could believe. Had he actually hired thugs to attack the duke's estate? It had to be a bluff, but Blankenship was capable of almost anything. He had destroyed more than one rival in a completely legal manner through financial disasters. Yet those had been over issues of money. With a woman involved, Ashton couldn't help but fear Blankenship would resort to more violent measures. Well, if that was the case, Ashton would not underestimate him.

Perhaps the best solution was to play a game of thimblerig with Emily in London. They could move her from residence to residence, since the League members owned several. It would be impossible for Blankenship to find her.

In the meantime they needed to convince Godric that he ought to marry Emily. If he did, Blankenship would have no claim to her. Emily would be infinitely safer and a scandalous kidnapping would become a romantic elopement in the eyes of society. A door opened down the hall and a bleary-eyed Cedric came out, shirt and breeches wrinkled as though he'd slept in them. He yawned and then caught sight of Ashton.

"How go the sentinel duties?"

Ashton chuckled. "Intolerably dull. I had expected much more entertainment, but the love birds haven't moved an inch. Godric is finally getting some rest, though."

Cedric heaved a sigh. "Thank God for that."

"Cedric, are your sisters at your house in London?"

"Yes, they've been there for two weeks." Cedric eyed Ashton. "Why?"

"Would you mind if we brought Emily to London and hid her in your house? If your sisters are present they might make for a confusing scene if Blankenship's men end up looking there."

Cedric's brown eyes narrowed. "Are you asking me to use my sisters as bait?"

Ashton held up his hands. "No! But I think that Blankenship won't expect us to take Emily to London. She might escape notice there. Meanwhile, we will spread ourselves out into the other residences about London and scatter Blankenship's men until—" Ashton paused here, hesitant to reveal his plans fully.

"Until?"

"Until we can convince Godric to marry Emily."

Cedric was quiet for a long moment. "You think he will?"

"I think he must. He cares about her to the point of self-destruction. She loves him. There can be no other answer."

Cedric frowned. "He's the one who always insisted that matrimony was folly. What if he doesn't agree?"

Ashton raised his chin. "Then he is a fool. But Emily must be protected. If Godric won't marry her, then I shall. She'll be free to live and love as she chooses, as will I. It is not an uncommon arrangement, so long as both parties use discretion. But she needs the protection of marriage." He couldn't forget the greed in Blankenship's eyes, the monstrous coldness that overtook his nature when he'd searched room by room for the girl. "Otherwise, Blankenship will hound her steps until the day she dies."

"You can throw my name onto the list of marriage options. We can let her choose between us, should Godric refuse."

This surprised Ashton. He thought he would be the only one willing to endure matrimony for Emily, but it appeared he'd been mistaken. "And what of Anne Chessley? If Emily chooses you, you could never make Anne a mistress, not when you've married her friend."

Cedric's face transformed into such a state of despair that Ashton set his cup aside and rose from his chair in concern.

"Perhaps not, but I would give Anne up, if Emily chose me. For my sins in this affair, I owe her. I'd do everything in my power to protect her."

"Let us hope that Emily won't need to choose anyone besides Godric."

Godric heard every word from behind the door. He'd been content to let Emily stay nestled up against him, but at the sound of Simkins's voice, he'd forced himself up. He paused at the door and absorbed the conversation between his butler and later his friends, moved by their views and touched by the sincerity of their wishes.

However their offers hadn't been necessary. Godric had decided last night he'd marry Emily. As soon as they reached London, he'd start immediately on wedding plans. But, to maintain Emily's safety, the ceremony would have to be hasty.

With an excited smile, he splashed his face at the washbasin before he changed for breakfast.

He adjusted his cravat in the mirror when Emily stirred. He

moved to the bed, leaned down and kissed her forehead. "Stay in bed awhile, darling. I'm just going down to breakfast."

She sighed, shifted under the covers and drifted back to sleep.

For a long moment, he simply enjoyed the sight of her. Soon they'd have a lifetime to share, and for the first time in Godric's life, he looked forward to the idea of one woman till death did he part.

And, to think, if Albert Parr hadn't been of such low moral fiber, Godric would never have met Emily, never known her the way he did now.

On an irresistible impulse he bent down to kiss Emily's lips. Her mouth opened sleepily beneath his and he savored the sweetness. An eternity would not be enough time. He would always yearn for her, all of her, body and soul.

The League of Rogues convened in the dining room that morning to discuss the upcoming London trip while Emily slept.

Godric sipped his coffee. "Once we reach London..." he paused, enjoying the strained looks of his companions. "I have decided that Emily and I shall be married."

The dining room was silent for several long seconds before Ashton and Cedric exhaled in obvious relief.

"I was worried I would have to twist your arm to convince you to marry. I will be happy to procure a marriage license for you."

Godric nodded. "Yes. See to it we have everything necessary to arrange a quick ceremony." He turned to the marquess. "Lucien, it's up to you to lead Blankenship down a false trail, lest he try to interfere."

Lucien grinned.

Charles scooted forward in his seat. "And me?"

"You'll be with Cedric, as part of Emily's protection. Never let her out of your sight, unless one of us is with her."

Charles had always viewed himself as a protective knight, and now he would play the part.

Cedric tossed a piece of crust to Penelope, who sat at his heels, tail swishing back and forth. "You know, Godric, you could just whisk Emily away to Gretna Green. It would save you the trouble of having to confront Parr. For all we know he might warn Blankenship of your plans."

Godric frowned. That was not the wedding she deserved. He didn't want his future duchess marked by further scandal. No. He would meet and speak with Parr, and get the wretched man to accompany him to the church for the marriage ceremony. Bound and gagged if need be.

"I am the Duke of Essex and I will not run off with my tail between my legs. We will avoid Blankenship if possible, and if we cannot, he will be dealt with."

There were nods all around the table.

"Ashton, can you arrange for the ceremony to be at St. George's in Hanover Square?" That was all the rage in London now. It was a lovely church, well known for its impressive front portico supported by six tall Corinthian columns and a tower just behind the portico, near enough to the League's various residences that the trip would not prove risky.

Ashton grinned. "I suppose. I do have some pull with the bishop. He owes me a favor ever since that incident last year, during Michaelmas, you know." The other men laughed with him, knowing what trouble the bishop had gotten himself into.

"When are you planning on telling Emily?" Lucien asked.

"Not until after we have all our plans settled and her tucked away in Cedric's townhouse. I want her to be at ease and feel safe when I propose. She has endured too much these last few days and a rushed proposal will not make her happy."

Suddenly the dining room door opened and Jonathan entered. An awkward hesitancy marred his steps. He'd never dared to intrude on Godric or the others before.

Godric watched him silently, curious to see what he would do.

Jonathan cleared his throat, "I know you and I have not spoken of our new situation...as...brothers, Your Grace, but—"

"If you are my brother, then you can stop addressing me as Your Grace. Now what do you want?"

"I wish to go to London with you and help with Emily."

The newly discovered brothers stared at each other for a moment before Godric said, "Very well. She is to be your sister-in-law soon enough. You ought to have some say in all of this. You shall accompany Cedric and Charles. Three is better than two for Emily's protection."

Godric didn't smile, but his tone was calm and accepting. If Emily could forgive him, then he could certainly forgive his brother.

Jonathan visibly relaxed. Clearly he'd expected a fight.

"Sit down and eat." Godric gestured to the fine breakfast on the sideboard.

Jonathan flushed, but bravely filled a plate and chose a seat next to Ashton, who smiled and gave a warm nod.

"You any good with a pistol, Jonathan?" Charles asked.

"More so with a flintlock rifle, but yes." Jonathan swallowed a bite of jam-covered toast.

"Excellent. We'll make a fine team, the three of us," Cedric said.

"What time are we to leave?" Jonathan asked.

"By noon, we hope. Emily needs as much rest as we can manage to give her. The carriage ride will be unpleasant enough, as ill as she's been."

"Well, I suppose the rest of us should be packed and ready." Ashton rose from his chair with the soft but firm suggestion in his tone that the others follow suit.

They left Godric and Jonathan alone. This was why he loved his friends. They followed his judgment and accepted Jonathan. They had always treated him nicely before—a man's valet was sacred, after all—but now he was one of them.

"Have you had enough to eat?" Godric asked after a few minutes. Jonathan flicked a glance to his empty plate and nodded. "Good. Join me in my study?"

Godric's study was still a bit untidy after his self-imposed exile. But Simkins had removed the trays of untouched food and the broken glass, and put back all the books Godric had ripped from the shelves in his rage. Godric sat down and motioned for Jonathan to do the same. Jonathan eased back into one of the chairs facing Godric's desk.

"There are some matters to settle between us." Godric leaned forward a few inches. "I want you to move your things out of your current quarters once this business with Emily is settled."

Jonathan's eyes dropped to the floor. "I understand, Your Grace. I lost my temper with you, and I put Miss Parr in danger. I should like to make my apologies with the young lady before I go, however."

It struck Godric how blinded he'd been, never suspecting for a moment they shared a father. It made him wonder what he else he'd missed by simply not looking.

"Jonathan, I'm not forcing you to leave the manor. I only meant for you to choose a room on the upper floor, a room more suitable to your new status in this household."

"My new status?"

"Yes. We're brothers, by blood and by law. If you think I'll toss you to the wayside, you're mistaken. Unless of course you wish to leave. I wouldn't insist that you stay. But I'd like it if you would."

Jonathan's face flushed. "You really would not mind my staying on here, Your Grace?"

"I've always despised being an only child. We are brothers, and that is all that matters to me. Even in my anger I doubt I could have killed you once Simkins told me. I might have throttled you a bit."

"Your Grace." Jonathan cast his eyes down again. "I don't mean to make things more uncomfortable between us, Your...Godric. But how do we go on from here? I've been your valet for nearly six years and a servant since I was born. What happens now?"

"Enjoy yourself. You've studied nearly as much as I have. You know the proper manners, it's merely time to employ them. All you must do is raise your head, not look down at the floor and wear different clothes, and learn how to dance, of course. I'm considering settling one of Father's unentailed estates upon you. I'll put it in trust. It will be an easy competence. Whenever you are ready to settle down and marry I will turn it over to you."

Jonathan blinked, eyes round as saucers. "My own estate?"

"As the second son it would be your due. I daresay you've worked hard enough for it."

Jonathan's eyes began to glisten, which made Godric uncomfortable.

"Damn it, Jon, smile for heaven's sake. No need to turn into a watering pot," he said, hoping to raise his brother's spirits.

Jonathan scraped the heel of his hand over his eyes, blinked rapidly and nodded.

"When I was a child I used to envy you, Godric. But Simkins told me what life was like for you. I was kept safe in my mother's care, but Simkins never let me forget what you endured. I thought he did it to prevent jealousy."

Godric's eyes darkened as they fixed on a spot on the wall. He could still hear his father say, *I need a reason to beat a servant, but not to beat my own son."* There was only one bastard in their family, and it certainly wasn't Jonathan.

"I suppose what I'm trying to say is, I wish I could have shared the sting. I hate knowing you suffered that alone."

Godric leaned back into his chair and started to smile, really smile.

"Would you have any interest in joining me and the other lords once a month at our club, Berkley's, in London?"

"They wouldn't mind the intrusion?" Jonathan had been there many times as his valet, but not a member.

"They've always liked you, and blood is blood. I want you to join our League. What do you say?"

"Absolutely."

Emily clung to Godric's side, nervous as they entered Cedric's townhouse. His sisters, Miss Sheridan and Miss Audrey, were inside. It was strange, but she wanted to make a good impression.

Cedric caught sight of his sisters. "There you are! Come over here and meet Emily."

The elder, Horatia, was taller, with more classical features, a long neck and sharp cheekbones that reminded Emily of a swan. Though shorter, Audrey was just as pretty, her face rounder and more childlike, but not in a way that hid the intelligence in her eyes.

"Emily, this is my sister, Horatia. Horatia, this is Miss Emily Parr. And this is Audrey." Cedric chucked his littlest sister under her chin.

Horatia gave a warm smile. "Pleased to meet you, Miss Parr."

Emily released her grip on Godric's arm and smiled back. "Please call me Emily."

"Then you must call me Horatia."

"You have a lovely home, Horatia." Emily looked about the expansive marbled floors and gilded furnishings of the hall.

"Oh, Horatia, allow me to introduce you to my half-brother, Jonathan St. Laurent." Godric prodded Jonathan forward to bow for his introduction.

"Surely you jest, we both know your valet, Mr. Helprin. Shame on you for such a weak attempt at a joke, Your Grace." Horatia shifted nervously.

"It is a long and sordid tale, Miss Sheridan, but I assure you it is true. He is my brother."

"It's a pleasure, Miss Sheridan." Jonathan bowed over Horatia's extended hand and brushed his lips over her fingers. She blushed.

Next to Jonathan, Lucien narrowed his eyes. Emily looked back and forth between Lucien and Horatia. Was that the glitter of jealousy?

Cedric suggested they proceed to the parlor, but Horatia fixed her brother with black look. "Cedric, you and the other gentleman will freshen up first. Half of you smell like horses."

"You've never minded the smell before," said Cedric.

Horatia raised a brow. "You've never brought so many guests before. It's like a stable in here. Emily may stay, she clearly rode in a carriage."

Emily enjoyed watching the sparks fly between brother and sister, but at last Ashton interceded. "She's right, Cedric. We've ridden too long today to subject these ladies to the aromas of the country."

"As if London smells any better," grumbled Cedric, and lead the others upstairs. The women headed to the parlor, free of the men for a short while.

Audrey and Horatia surrounded Emily on the couch and assailed her with questions. It did not take long to coerce the full truth of Emily's abduction. They even knew the intimate goings on between her and Godric.

A rosy blush blossomed in Audrey's cheeks as she shyly asked, "Is it true Godric...compromised you?" It seemed the reach of their gossip exceeded those of the Lady Society column, but they vowed to keep silent.

Audrey took a deep breath. "What was it like?"

Horatia pinched her sister's arm. "Audrey!"

Audrey scrunched her nose. "It's a valid question. Cedric never tells us anything. We have to learn from someone."

Emily's face reddened, but she decided to be open with them. "It is hard to describe. It is terrifying at first, like you are about to die, but you don't. I doubt I could have been with any other man than Godric. You must trust the man you are with. Otherwise, I don't think you can feel safe enough for..." Emily trailed off.

"Dying?" Horatia asked breathlessly.

"Yes. Well, I really shouldn't talk about it. I sound like some lightskirt."

Audrey steered the conversation to a safer harbor. "So you will stay with us here?"

"I believe so. Those blasted men have all been tightlipped about their plans, even Jonathan. They barely said a word on the carriage ride over, and they made me leave Penelope behind."

"The foxhound Cedric bought you?"

Emily's smile wilted. "Yes, poor thing. She barked and bit Jonathan when they took her away. I hope I can return to her soon. Simkins must be having a dreadful time keeping the carpets clean."

Horatia leaned forward and laid a slender, elegant hand on Emily's. "Well, not to worry. There are plenty of animals running about here. We have two old cats hiding somewhere upstairs." She giggled. "Mittens and Muff."

"Mittens and Muff?"

Horatia's lips twitched. "That's what Audrey named them. She was only ten years old, and got them for Christmas as a pair. She received new mittens and a muff from Cedric, so naturally she just named the cats the same thing."

Audrey tilted her chin up. "I was a child, Horatia! You make me sound so insipid!"

Emily patted Audrey's hand. "I think they are darling names."

Horatia grinned. "While you are here, we'll keep you entertained so much that you won't have time to miss Penelope."

Somehow Emily didn't doubt that.

The gentlemen, freshly changed and far more sociable, invaded the parlor soon after the women finished talking. Even Jonathan, though rather shy at being an active part in such a social gathering, seemed to enjoy himself as he and Charles engaged Audrey in conversation.

Only two people seemed out of sorts—Lucien and, oddly, Horatia. Lucien stood in the corner of the room near Cedric and Ashton, but his gaze kept sliding back towards Horatia, who did her best to ignore him.

At first Emily assumed Lucien had an amorous interest in Horatia, but the cold, imperious glances from Lucien received shameful blushes from Horatia. Something had happened between them, and

Emily couldn't even begin to guess what. Before she contemplated the matter further, however, Godric stole up on her from behind.

"May I speak to you in private?" he whispered in her ear. He put a guiding hand on her lower back, and the pair slipped out of the room unnoticed. Godric led her to the drawing room a few doors down.

"Emily, we are to be married tomorrow." Godric announced this without so much as a romantic preamble, as though it were a contract that only required her handshake at this point. Emily stared at him. Did he really just expect her to say yes? She loved him, but she wouldn't just agree because he'd declared it. It was that very commanding, dominating attitude she hated, whether it came from her uncle, Blankenship or Godric.

"No."

"Wonderf—wait." Godric gripped her by the shoulders, looming over her, his presence more dominating than ever. "What do you mean, no?"

"No. I won't marry you." It made little sense to her heart, but her head reminded her that she could not simply agree because he'd declared it. She needed to be allowed the choice to say no.

"But you love me, Emily. What more is there for you to want?"

Emily drew a deep breath. "Godric, have you learned nothing about me at all since we met? I need my freedom, the ability to control my own life. I cannot agree to marry you simply because you decree it."

"This isn't about your freedom, it's about your safety."

Emily looked away. "I understand that you think so. But know this, I don't have to marry you. I could find a willing bridegroom who would ignore the scandal you've created and take me to wife. I would rather marry a desperate fortune hunter than you, if it was the only way I could have control in my life." It stung her soul to say it, but she meant it. There was something terrifying about the prospect of marrying a man she loved, knowing he didn't love her back, simply because he was trying to do the noble thing. It would only result in unhappiness for them both. She couldn't have it.

"You really don't wish to marry me?" He jerked back as though her words had struck him like a sword. His grip loosened, and then he dropped his hands, severing the connection between them. The loss of his touch chilled her.

"It is not a matter of wishing. I want to marry you, I do, but I won't, not at the cost of my freedom."

Godric turned away from her, a tic working his jaw.

"And you think some fortune hunter will allow you that freedom?"

"You would have me live by your terms at your whim. Any man I choose will have to agree that he'll let me be and live my life as I choose after we're married. Which would you choose?"

Emily put a hand on his shoulder from behind. He flinched and jerked away, spinning back around to face her.

"Why would you do me this great hurt? Why?" he asked, voice thick with emotion, eyes blazing.

"Because." Emily's throat constricted, burning with the pain of those awful words, but they were true. "Because you will tire of me and I can't bear to think about losing you. If I don't marry you, you will never be mine to lose."

"But you must marry me! You aren't safe if you aren't tied to me by marriage." Mere moments took him from rage, to bargaining.

"Precisely. You only wish to marry me to secure my safety. You are a true gentleman in all the ways that matter, Godric, but I can't let you suffer binding yourself to me when it will make us both unhappy in the future."

"We would be happy—"

"For a time. But it isn't enough. I need to be loved. I could stand to be married to a man who didn't love me if I didn't love him. But I love you and it would break my heart to not be loved back." Emily couldn't believe she was holding up so bravely. That she hadn't collapsed in grief.

"Emily...I love you."

Emily shut her eyes, wishing they could live forever in the past. Losing him now, even though he was never hers, might yet rip the life from her body.

"You think you love me, but you don't. I don't want to live my life under that illusion."

Her words sparked his temper. "My love for you is not an illusion!" His jade eyes flared and the darker side of Godric reared its head.

Emily backed away. Her pulse raced. "I think we should discuss this later, when you aren't so upset."

"Upset? What possible reason could I have for being upset?"

Godric's voice rose sharply. "The woman I love doesn't believe me and won't marry me!"

Emily winced, hoping the others wouldn't hear him shout.

"Hear me, Emily. You will be my wife, or you will be someone else's, but you will be married. Cedric and Ashton have both offered to wed you. Is that what you want?" He grabbed her by the shoulders and jerked her up against the length of him.

Emily's breath caught in her throat, his face was mere inches from hers.

"You speak as though I'm chattel to be traded about. I won't marry them either. Do you understand?" She tried to pull away from him. As much as she loved him, longed to say yes to him, her heart wouldn't allow it. She might have survived the rest of her life as his lover but not his wife. But she couldn't put him in a position where someday he'd betray their vows or worse, come to an "understanding" as many of the men of his standing did.

Godric captured her chin, forcing her face back towards his and growled low in his throat. "Emily, I have no patience for this—"

She stomped her foot on his boot. "I have no patience for you!"

"I swore to never let you go, and I won't. You belong with me." Godric fisted a hand in her hair, and slanted his mouth down over hers. She fisted her hands against his chest.

"And when you tire of me? When you desire someone else? I will be chained to our cold, empty, marriage bed. Will you punish me then? Will you rip my inheritance from my hands and dispense with it?" She knew she'd gone too far. Godric's eyes glittered with rage, with pain, and a dangerous lust she'd seen only once before.

He slammed his lips down over hers. His kiss was bruising, fiery, hungry and punishing. Its ferocity made Emily buckle and collapse in his embrace. He wound an arm around her waist as he assaulted her senses; his lips stole her breath and robbed her of her sanity. It was just the way every kiss should be, full of fire and light, splintering one's soul and merging the pieces with another's until theirs beat as one, mighty heart.

When he finally released her, she staggered back a step, and he reached to steady her.

"No! Don't touch me. I can't think when you do." Emily tore away from him, running towards the door. She collided with Charles, who had been loitering outside, along with Jonathan and Cedric.

Charles caught Emily's wrists, holding her still despite her frantic struggles. "Everything all right?"

Godric appeared in the doorway. "No, it isn't! Take her upstairs and lock her in a room. She needs time to calm down."

"Me?" Emily shouted back. "You are the one who—"

"Charles, get her upstairs now!"

A crowd gathered as the others vacated the parlor and came out into the hall.

Charles took hold of Emily. She fought back, not caring whether she made a spectacle of herself. Charles huffed in irritation, and then dipped down, and hauled her up over his shoulder. "This seems familiar," he said.

Emily curled her fingers into fists and struck him on the back, but his muscled back seemed impervious to her blows. "Put me down at once. I've had enough of this!"

Horatia stepped forward. "Really, Charles! Put her down this instant! I will not have my guests treated in such a fashion!"

"Sorry, I have my orders," Charles said, curt but not unkind, and headed up the stairs with Cedric and Jonathan following behind.

Horatia scowled and started to chase after them, but an iron hand closed around her wrist, dragging her back from the stairs.

It was Lucien.

"Don't interfere, Horatia. You've done enough of that already." His warning carried an undercurrent of the past, a reminder that she had often interfered where she shouldn't.

Godric growled and stomped down the hall to another room, where he slammed the door shut. He stumbled back out a moment later, a broom toppling to the floor behind him.

"Who moved the closet there?" he thundered, then entered the next room down and once more slammed the door.

Chapter Eighteen

Jim Tanner lingered in the alley just off Curzon Street, and bided his time. A blade lay in his palm, which he kept in the pocket of his long black coat, ready to sink it into the flesh of those pompous lords across the street if they interfered with his mission.

Soon, he promised himself.

His employer had urged him to wait, to snatch the girl without a fight. The order had been issued not out of any need to prevent violence, but to give Tanner time to get away before the alarm was raised. Bloodshed would shorten his exit strategy.

Blankenship was a fool to want nothing more than the little chit. The house he stared at now was probably filled with expensive items he could fetch a fair price for on Shoe Lane or Saffron Hill. The *nouveau riche* were only too happy to buy aristocratic items that would fool the *ton* into thinking they weren't the descendants of lower or middleclass men.

He'd been only too eager to steal the Parr girl away from Essex when Blankenship agreed to his hefty price. He knew what lay in store for the girl, but that wasn't his concern. This was a commission, nothing more.

Tanner's extensive connections reached from the sewers to the houses of power, from valets to night watchmen and toshers. Word had come almost immediately when Essex and his friends had arrived in London. The coach went straight to Curzon Street where Viscount Sheridan lived and the Parr girl hadn't left the house since she arrived.

From his spot in the alley, he had watched through one of the windows as the Parr girl quarreled with Essex. Unable to hear words, he read their body language, and it was clear enough that trouble brewed between the lovers.

Evening wore into night and shadows melded into black pools across Curzon Street. Tanner scanned the night sky, but clouds had blotted out the moon.

Tanner spat into the darkness of the alley. What woman was worth five hundred pounds, Tanner didn't know. The old man should have saved his money and brought a classy whore. But no, his employer wanted some innocent untrained lamb who would spend the whole night screaming in pain while Blankenship violated her. Pity. But again, not his concern.

He ran a hand through his hair and scowled. How would he get the girl out of the house with all of those men watching her every move? Jewelry, paintings, he'd even stolen a prized King Charles spaniel once. But a woman? With half a dozen guards? Tricky, but not impossible.

Tanner ducked back into the alley as he caught sight of a footman who left the side door of the townhouse to empty a bucket of dirty water by the gutter. The footman headed back inside.

Tanner escaped the shadows, flipped the handle of his blade, and cracked it over the footman's head.

The footman crumpled, bucket crashing into the marble floor just inside the doorway. Tanner grabbed the unconscious man's arms and dragged him behind a counter in the small entryway.

With the house dark, most of the other servants were no doubt asleep.

Tanner took the man's coat and pants—enough to avoid suspicion inside if seen at a distance. He stepped over the footman's body, leaving the man alive. He didn't kill servants. They too suffered under the oppression of the rich.

As he moved through the lushly decorated townhouse, his mood blackened further. A dark part of him would have been happy to slit every noble throat in this house, if he'd been paid for it.

He heard voices above him, and Tanner ducked beneath the main staircase.

"Is she finally asleep, Cedric?" a man asked.

"She cried herself to sleep, poor thing. I didn't know women were so full of tears. I thought she'd flood the upstairs rooms."

"She still won't agree to marry Godric?"

"No. She won't have him, or anyone else."

"Bloody hell. Is she daft?"

"Don't ask me to explain the workings of the female mind, Jonathan."

The first man sighed. "Where's Charles?"

"He's gone to catch a few hours sleep. Why don't you have a rest yourself? It's been a long day for all of us."

"You wouldn't mind? What about Blankenship?"

"Tomorrow we'll lead his lackeys all over London while those love birds get some sense beaten into them."

Tanner grinned. *Good plan. Pity it was too late.*

He heard only one pair of footsteps walk away and a door clicked open then shut. Tanner counted away a few minutes waiting for the second pair. Eventually he dug into his coat pocket for a spare coin. He flicked the shilling out away from him. It clinked loudly across the marble, rolling away from the stairs. The floor above him creaked, and he heard a grunt as the remaining guard resumed his position.

Tanner swore under his breath, seeking another coin. He threw it further out, and the clink resounded more deeply, almost to the point of an echo.

Someone rose, and came down the stairs, step by step.

Tanner waited in the shadows. The guard had only just reached the bottom when Tanner launched himself at the man.

But his adversary had quick reflexes. He spun as Tanner attacked.

Blood splattered as Tanner's blade slid across the man's arm.

Before the guard could shout, Tanner rammed his elbow into the his face. Blood dribbled down his face as he staggered back, fell and ceased to move.

Tanner considered finishing him off, but he couldn't waste time. He needed the girl.

Light on his feet, he sprinted up the stairs and eased the unguarded door open.

A young woman lay curled up on the bed, her knees tucked up under her chin. The curtains of the window were wide open, allowing a pale blanket of moonlight to cover her sleeping form. Her hair was loose and fanned out on her pillow. Tanner was not a man to ever think of heaven or angels, but this sweet creature was beautiful. No wonder the old fool wanted her so much.

He thought of his Lacy, of what it had been like before she'd been taken by his master. For one eternal second Tanner was tempted to take the girl and keep her for himself. He imagined her being grateful, rescued from two horrible fates. Would she feel the same as his Lacy had? But no. That was simply a fantasy. He needed the money she would bring, more than any illusions of love.

Tanner cleared his head as he stole up on the sleeping girl. He pocketed his bloody knife before he leaned down and scooped the girl up into his arms.

She shifted restlessly, murmuring to herself. "No more...please...no more."

Tanner breathed a sigh of relief when her dreams did not wake her. He didn't want her screaming or fighting. If she slept all the way down to his carriage, she'd be his easiest job yet. Far easier than the spaniel, his boots still had teeth marks on them.

He walked down the stairs, kicked the body of the man he'd attacked for good measure and proceeded out the door he came in. Once outside, he flagged down his hired carriage. The girl started to wake as the carriage rattled loudly up to them. Tanner told the coachman where to go as he hopped down and opened the carriage door. She finally awoke as Tanner dropped the girl onto the seat opposite him.

She gasped and scurried into the corner, putting as much distance between them as possible. "Who are you?"

He pulled his blade out of his pocket, leaned forward, and pointed it at her chest. Her pretty little eyes fixed on the blade's tip, still splashed in crimson. "I would say I'm your worst nightmare, but considering whom I'm taking you to—that wouldn't be entirely true."

He expected the girl to cry, to beg for her freedom, to bargain. She didn't. Slowly, she combed through the tangles in her hair with her fingers, fixed her dress and assumed a look of grace and dignity.

"Then you must be one of Blankenship's thugs."

"Thug, Madame? I am not some lowly cutpurse."

The woman shrugged. "You are no different than the others I've encountered."

Tanner was rattled by her tone. She seemed unconcerned, as though the abduction were commonplace. Such self-control. He didn't know whether to be impressed or concerned for her mental health, for clearly the woman was mad.

Emily focused on slow, steady breaths. She wouldn't scream if she kept calm.

She refused to think about how this man found her, or who he might have hurt in the process. If she knew she'd lose herself to her terror, and Blankenship would win. She forced herself to study the man, taking in his dark eyes, unkempt brown hair, footman's clothes and the sneer etched into his features.

He looked to be around thirty or so in years, and radiated with a survivor's sharpness, a razor's edge balance of sanity. This man was a professional, and dangerous.

Fear threatened to consume her, but unlike her first abduction, she had a better grasp of how to handle the situation. After her encounter with Evangeline she believed she could emulate the other woman's confidence and possibly act her way out of this peril. It was a chance if nothing else, one she had to take.

"Is he paying you well?" she asked.

The man nodded. "Five hundred pounds to deliver you to his doorstep."

Emily feigned surprise. "Only five hundred? He offered the last man he hired double that." The lie came easily as she tried to emulate Evangeline's imperious tone, albeit without the French accent.

"What last man? He never mentioned anyone else."

"Of course he wouldn't. He killed that man to avoid payment." Emily plucked at her gown by her knees as though her words didn't concern her.

"You're lying!"

"Lie?" She met his gaze with innocence. "Why on earth would I lie? You'll deliver me regardless. I just thought I should warn you. He got blood everywhere, ruined my best muslin gown and it took simply *ages* for the man to die. I merely don't wish to witness such a thing again. It's unsettling and ruins my appetite." Emily's voice was almost flippant, as she pretended that she'd experienced gruesome murders with disturbing frequency.

It was useless to expect this man to let her go, but if he and Blankenship argued, then she might have a chance to escape.

The rest of the carriage ride passed in silence. The man studied Emily and she studied him back. The silent battle of wills ended when the carriage reached Blankenship's townhouse. He gripped her arm roughly, dragging her out of the carriage with such ferocity that she stumbled and fell against him. She had clearly struck a nerve.

Blankenship's ancient butler answered the door after her kidnapper beat it for what felt like several minutes. He pulled Emily into the hall and shouted for Blankenship.

The butler gave a heavy sigh and left.

Blankenship appeared at the top of the stairs, dressed and alert despite the late hour. His beady eyes rested on Emily's face then skimmed down her body. His whole air, from his eyes to the straightness of his spine, glittered with a malevolence that terrified Emily. It felt as though a thousand beetles scuttled over her skin.

"Well done, Mr. Tanner, well done. Did you have to kill anyone to get to her?" Blankenship didn't come down the stairs. He waited for her at the top, like some high and mighty sultan whose harem girl groveled before him.

Emily's nails dug painfully into her palms. Something inside her began to burn. She was tired of being at the mercy of others, especially a man who meant her harm. Tonight she would fight. He'd regret ever looking at her.

"Possibly one. I was in a hurry and murder was not my task."

Tanner's pronouncement made her heart stop beating. Possibly one? Which one? Dear God...her vision swam and she fought to stay on her feet.

"A pity, but it's true, murder carries its own complications." Blankenship smiled at Emily. "Bring her up to me." The smile lasted as her abductor dragged her up the stairs.

"On your knees, girl," Blankenship barked.

Emily glared and raised her chin.

Tanner gripped her shoulders from behind and shoved her downward. She fell onto her knees. Blankenship's eyes darkened.

"My, my Miss Parr, I quite like you on your knees." Blankenship reached down to stroke her hair with his fingertips. "Perhaps that is how we shall begin tonight?"

Emily wanted to hide her rage, but failed.

He jerked her chin up. "So defiant. I see the fire inside you. I will enjoy beating that rebelliousness out of your screaming body. I couldn't have your mother, but I will have you."

"My mother?" she choked out. What did her mother have to do with this?

"I suppose you wouldn't know," he mused. "I almost married her, but she chose that fool you called a father. She broke my heart and so I damaged their business. I hurt them in a thousand little ways, but never enough." He continued to study her as he talked, as though enjoying finally revealing his schemes.

"You ruined my parents?" She remembered the finances always being tight, and the whispered conversations between her parents. Blankenship had caused it.

"Not just them. Your uncle too, naturally. It was the only way I could get to you."

Stale cigar smoke and brandy wafted off him, in addition to his other unpleasant smells. His fingers dug deep into her face, nails leaving curved imprints. All this time, all the heartache she'd suffered...her parents had gotten onto that ship to go to America to try and restore their company and had died. Blankenship had killed her parents. If she'd had a gun at that moment, she would have shot the man between the eyes.

"Does my uncle know you've taken me?" she asked through gritted teeth.

"He no longer matters. You are mine, per his agreement, and as far as I am concerned his debts are settled." Blankenship turned her face to the side, as though admiring her profile, while he spoke to Tanner. "Have you ever seen anything so deliciously innocent? Look at those lips."

"Yes, sir, she's a decent looking chit. But I'll have my money now, if it's all the same to you and be on my way." Tanner's eyes followed every move the other man made as though he didn't trust him. Good.

Blankenship released Emily's face and turned his fury onto Tanner. "In good time. The banks do not open till morning."

"Pay me or I take her back." Tanner latched a hand around Emily's right wrist, jerking her up to her feet, just as Blankenship coiled a hand around her throat. Both men tugged on her. Pain flashed through Emily's body and her vision blurred. Black spots dotting her eyes.

"You dare threaten me?" Blankenship, with surprising strength, flung Emily away. She stumbled, rolled and then crashed against the wall.

Stars burst behind her eyelids. The scene blurred as she tried to catch her breath. The two men grappled with each other. Emily tried to crawl away, but Tanner grabbed her by the back of her neck and once more put her between him and Blankenship. He withdrew his blade and pressed the tip of it into her neck. "One more step and I end her life."

Blankenship took another step. Emily winced, stifling a cry as the blade pinched deeper. "Be still," Tanner whispered in her ear.

"She doesn't matter to me! You want her? Take her."

"Five hundred pounds for something that doesn't matter? I suppose that might be true...if you had never intended to pay." Tanner took a step back from Emily, then shoved her forward towards Blankenship. Blankenship backhanded her across the cheek with whip-like force and she fell to the floor, scrambling out of the way just in time as the two men dove towards each other. Tanner's blade fell during the scuffle as the men turned to beating each other with fists. Emily gathered her strength, biting back the tears as her fingers curled around the blade's worn wooden handle and she hastily got to her feet.

"Where do you think you're going?" Blankenship whirled on her, barely dodging a blow from Tanner.

Emily acted without thinking and slashed at him, the blade cutting across his chest. He bellowed like a wounded bear and lunged at her, prying the blade from her hands and with a devil's fire in his eyes plunged it high into her chest. Tanner shouted in a rage and kicked Blankenship from behind. "I didn't bring her to you so you could cut her to pieces! Our bargain is ended!"

Emily staggered, shocked by the pain, as the world spun and she lost her footing. She screamed in panic as she tripped backwards down the stairs. She fell, rolling down the stairs until she reached the cold marble at the bottom with a sickening thud.

Godric came out of Cedric's study shortly after the clock struck midnight. His temper had finally cooled, and he would speak to Emily. She didn't trust him to not control her. Her immediate safety had made him take measures he never would have in normal circumstances. Now that he understood that he could explain it so she could see it from his point of view. She was a little fool, his darling little fool, for thinking he didn't love her. Godric planned to spend the next few hours in her bed, proving just how foolish her fears were.

In the dim light that came in from the street he spied a crumpled body at the foot of the stairs. He froze. Had someone fallen? *Cedric.* His heart skipped a painful beat—blood coated his friend's body. Cedric groaned, moving a few inches. Godric ran over and helped his friend up. The man's nose was bloody and there was a deep gash along his arm. "What happened?"

"Attacked!" Cedric pointed a shaky hand towards Emily's room. The door was wide open.

"Help! Someone help!" Godric yelled.

Ashton and Jonathan were the first to arrive, pistols drawn.

"Get a doctor, Ash. Emily's been taken." Godric tore out the main door and into the street followed by Jonathan. A lone lamplighter rode to check on the next street lamp nearest them.

Godric ran up to him and grabbed the man's leg, dragging him to the ground. He gripped the saddle and pulled himself up on the man's horse.

"See that he's compensated, Jonathan," Godric shouted at his brother as he rode off into the night, straight for Blankenship's home. He was never more thankful that he'd asked Lucien and Ashton where the vile man lived.

Jabbing his heels into the horse's sides, he urged it go as fast as possible. He didn't care if he lamed the beast or it threw a shoe, only Emily mattered. How could he have left her alone? God, he couldn't let himself think of her being hurt, or worse.

When he reached Blankenship's townhouse, Godric launched himself off the horse and, through the open doorway, only to stumble upon a horrifying sight.

Blankenship, at the top of the stairs, plunging a knife into Emily's chest.

A footman took up the fight with Blankenship, but Godric could only watch helplessly as Emily staggered back, lost her footing on the stairs and...

Godric couldn't breathe, couldn't cry out. Terror immobilized him as his Emily tumbled down the stairs, bleeding. She didn't move. Blood oozed from her body, slowly pooling around her on the floor.

The footman had lost the upper hand, distracted by Godric in the open doorway. He screamed something about their agreement and threw himself at Blankenship bare handed, but Blankenship still had the blade. With one swift flick of his wrist he cut the footman's throat.

The man fell to his knees, blood spurting down the front of his shirt and coat.

Godric found the ability to move and knelt down beside Emily, his own body trembling so violently he could no longer stand. He collapsed next to her before he gathered the strength to turn her onto her back.

His shaking fingers brushed over her cheeks. "Emily, sweetheart, please open your eyes." He pled with her like a dying man. "My last words to you were cruel and cold. I wish to God I could take them back." His insides churned, roiled, threatened to explode. Godric had to keep talking or he'd go mad with grief. "Why didn't you believe I loved you? You changed me, Emily. When I was with you, I didn't just want to be a better man. I *was* a better man because you were in my life. How will I endure without you?"

When his perished love did not answer, he buried his face in the soft groove of her neck, inhaling the flowery scent of her gleaming hair, and Godric, the Duke of Essex, wept. He wept for Emily, for the children they would never have, for the places he would never take her, and he wept for the pain of his own breaking heart.

"No! Dammit, no!" A cry disturbed his mourning, the sound a terrible keening that grated on his ears. It rose, fast and high from his throat, then faded, replaced by ragged breaths.

He kissed her lips, expecting the coppery taste of blood, but she was unbearably sweet, as though merely sleeping.

"Is she dead?" Blankenship's reedy voice echoed eerily down the stairs.

Godric's eyes flamed with tears; they spilled down his face as he brushed Emily's hair back from her face with shaky hands.

When he spoke, his voice was barely a whisper. "You've taken from me the one thing in this world I truly loved." The void in him grew to a dull blackening roar. Flashes of memories, glittering shards of momentary joy, pierced the swelling darkness. Emily's laugh, her shining eyes, exploring hands, whispers of her dreams and breathless words of love.

Never again.

Flames consumed him, enveloped him.

He set Emily down and stood at the bottom of the stairs to face Blankenship, then slowly walked up step by step.

"All of this work and I never even bedded her!" Blankenship

hissed as he backed away. "You were a fool to take what was mine. She's dead because you abducted her." Blankenship moved back down the hall to a small side table. He tugged frantically at handle of the top drawer.

"She was never yours." Blankenship would die. It was as simple as that. His grief outweighed reason and numbed him to all except revenge.

The glint of silver caught his eye. A knife lay near the edge of the top stair, the blade gleaming red with blood. Godric grabbed it, only to hear the sound of a pistol cocked in front of him.

Godric found himself staring down the barrel of a loaded gun, and those beetle black eyes behind it reflected a heavy fear.

Blankenship had managed to retrieve a gun from the side table. "Don't even think about it."

Godric snarled and charged as the pistol shot wide. Their bodies collided against the railing. Blankenship flailed as the pistol fell onto the carpet between them. Godric wound one fist around the other man's neck while Blankenship clawed at his chest.

The man's heavy weight unbalanced their tangled bodies, and Godric fought to break free as they both started to fall, but it was too late.

They crashed down the stairs, grappling at each other until Godric landed on top of Blankenship at the bottom of the stairs, his knife stuck in his enemy's chest.

Panting for breath, both men locked gazes, hatred meeting hatred for one brief moment before the glint in Blankenship's eyes faded, giving way to darkness. Godric released his hold on the knife and rolled off the dead body.

Lucien and Ashton were at the door, their faces ashen.

"My God," Lucien breathed.

"She's gone," Godric's tone was hollow.

Ashton's hand flew to his heart. Lucien looked away.

Emily lay stretched out across the marble, pale blue slippers streaked with blood, and one limp, graceful hand caressed the floor by Godric.

Ashton leaned down to touch Godric's shoulder when Emily's index finger twitched against the marble floor. It had to be a death spasm. But...her fingers began to curl further, into a ball. "Godric, look!"

Godric, unable to see past the tears that clouded his eyes, tried to look up at his love. Emily's long lashes fluttered against her cheeks.

"She's alive!" Godric choked out in a mixture of terror and relief. She was still alive. "Quick, check her wound." Lucien knelt down near Emily's head and helped him. Lucien examined the wound carefully and sighed in relief.

"It's a muscle wound. There are no vital organs here." Lucien ripped off one of the sleeves of his shirt. With Godric's help, they bound the wound as tight as they could. "If we get her to a doctor she may yet live."

"Is it safe to move her?" Godric asked Lucien.

"I believe so."

Godric carefully picked Emily up in his arms, and the three men walked out into the street. Jonathan arrived at that moment, with the constable and several Bow Street runners. Ashton remained behind to explain, while Lucien and Godric took Emily back to Cedric's house, to meet the doctor and pray that she survived.

Heaven. It was warm and light, the soft murmur of a low masculine voice spoke to her... No, read to her. *The Iliad* in Greek. She tried to open her mouth but nothing moved.

I want to see you, whoever you are.

Did she have a body?

She managed a small strangled whimper. The voice halted, then spoke, more eagerly.

"Emily." The voice sounded like Godric, but that made sense. Heaven was wherever he was. She tried to speak again, but only yielded another pathetic whimper.

"Shh. Rest, my darling. You've been through so much." A large hand clasped hers, its grip warm, strong, and perfect.

Lips brushed over her forehead, leaving a trail of tender fire in their wake. She forced her eyes open. Even though Godric's face was pale and his hair hung limp around it, he was still everything she'd wanted, craved. Loved. The sight of him. That was Heaven.

Emily's long lashes fanned as she squeezed his hand. She gave a weak smile. Godric choked back a sob, ghostly reflections of her own pain shimmered in his eyes.

"What happened?" She fought to sit up. Pain radiated into every point of her being, but the pain proved her life—her presence.

"You don't remember?" He squeezed her hand back. Godric sat on the edge of her bed.

"Stairs. I remember stairs?"

Godric's eyes shut at this.

"You fell."

Emily squeezed his hand again, unable to do more to comfort him. "And after?"

Godric looked at her and tucked a loose coil of her hair back behind her ear.

"Blankenship killed that other man, and then I killed Blankenship."

Emily breathed a sigh of relief, only to wince from the pain. She was free of the dark specter of Blankenship forever.

"Was anyone else hurt?"

"Cedric got a broken nose, and a gash in his arm, but he'll mend. He's more upset he can't ride or hunt for the next month." Godric chuckled.

Emily's shoulders sagged. She hadn't realized she'd been so tense.

"Emily, I had my solicitor look into the matter of your inheritance. There is the possibility that if you reached out to the trustee there might be a way get your father's inheritance without marriage."

Emily bit her bottom lip. What did this mean? Did he want her to be free, or be free of her? In the darkness of her pain after she fell, she thought she heard him speak—declare his love. Had that been nothing more than a dying woman's dream?

Godric began again uncertainly. "Emily, I know you won't marry me. I know that. But I can't live one more day without you. All I ask is that wherever you go, whatever you do, let me come with you. We can travel the world. Whatever you want, it will be yours. I just wish to be with you." Godric moved closer, tightly clenching her hands. "I can't lose you. Not again."

"You would give up your place here?" she asked.

"Emily, for you I'd give up my soul."

"What if I want your heart?"

"It's already been stolen. You, my dear, are the better kidnapper."

Godric opened the bedroom door to find five chairs stationed in a semicircle outside, occupied by his friends and brother. They sat up as he stepped out into the hall.

"How is she?" asked Charles.

Godric shut the door behind him. "She woke for a few minutes but she's asleep again. Ash, can you track down the bishop?" His words turned the men's mood from relieved to anxious before he continued. "And see if we can still arrange for a ceremony in St. George's? She's agreed to marry me!"

His friends and brother all jumped up from their chairs, shouting and cheering, slapping him on the back. A month ago, a marriage among them would have seemed to be a death sentence, but this was the best news they'd ever had. Emily Parr would be a part of their lives now, and not one man would have it otherwise.

Horatia came out into the hallway, with a tray of food. None of them had eaten or slept before now. "You'll be waking the dead with your racket," she said with a disapproving glare.

"Congratulations. I knew you'd be the first to get leg shackled!" Charles joked.

What a fool he'd been. Love had found him, saved him, and he would never let her go.

"Well, don't just stand there, gentleman!" Horatia snapped at the men loitering about around her. "We have a wedding to plan! Ashton, you will arrange the church and the bishop. I'll see to Emily's wedding gown. Charles and Lucien, you must both get all of the families here for this. I want St. George's filled with our loved ones. Jonathan, you ought to go and fetch Penelope, as Emily misses her terribly.

"Cedric, you will make sure Emily's uncle gives his consent to the match. If he's very nice about it, you can even invite him." Horatia shooed the men away from the door so they wouldn't wake Emily.

Cedric looked confused as they left. "When did she become in charge?"

Once they were off Godric returned to Emily's bedside, taking her hand in his.

He rubbed his eyes and gazed down at his sleeping lover. He remembered the young woman on his bed with a dirt smudge on her nose and cheeks, the soaking wet Amazon on the bank of the lake breathing life into him, the woman who fought with words like a swordsman, yet melted in his arms, and the angel who forgave him, who promised she would always love him.

What twist of fate had led him to abduct Emily Parr that night?

He would never know the true depth of his luck in capturing her, this woman who captured him right back. He only knew he would never let her go.

Epilogue

Lucien sat at the table in Cedric's dining room, reading the morning paper. Cedric fed Penelope scraps from his chair next to him. The dining room was large for a London home, furnished with walnut chairs and a table, all gilded with scrollwork. Lucien looked over to Ashton and Charles, who were speaking near the large wood, glass-paned window overlooking the gardens.

The lords were enjoying themselves, having successfully seen Godric and Emily off on their honeymoon, and were now resting at Cedric's townhouse after the adventures of the last few weeks.

"Well, Lucien? Anything interesting?" Ashton asked as he took a seat, leaving Charles alone to gaze out the window, lost in thought.

"There's an interesting tidbit in the society pages."

"Not Lady Society again?" Cedric chuckled. Penelope barked sharply at him. He reached down and picked her up, setting the foxhound on his lap. She was no longer a puppy.

All things grow up some day, Lucien thought to himself.

"Are you going to read it or not?" Charles asked from the window.

"Miss Emily Parr married the Duke of Essex at St. George's Hanover Square on Sunday. The bride and groom will soon depart on one of Baron Lennox's merchant vessels for their honeymoon. It would seem the eternal bachelor has embraced the shackledom of marriage at long last."

"That's all?" Ashton mused aloud.

Lucien folded the paper and set it down on the table. "Well, Lady Society spent half the column discussing Emily's wedding gown and the various guests we managed to scrounge up at the last minute to fill the church. Not that it was a challenge."

He looked out through the large windows overlooking the gardens where Cedric's two sisters sat on a bench, heads bent as they spoke. As a married lady Emily would qualify as a chaperone, which only meant more trouble for Cedric. He'd have to watch over Horatia and

Audrey, especially the latter. She was often in trouble, even when she wasn't actively seeking it out. Not Horatia though, she was always perfectly behaved, and it rankled him to no end.

Charles grinned at Lucien. "I do believe that is the first positive piece about us in the Lady Society column. Wait until my mother reads it. She'll be looking out the nearest window for signs of the four horsemen."

"Speaking of the apocalypse," Ashton began. Lucien knew from his tone trouble was on the horizon. "I heard from one of my sources that Hugo Waverly has returned from France."

Charles's smile faltered.

Lucien sat up straight. "What the devil is he doing back here? I thought we'd driven him off for good."

Ashton frowned. "Been here for a few weeks they say. It seems he didn't take our threats seriously, or does not care. I recommend that each of us be on guard until we can ferret out the truth of the matter. I doubt his motives have changed. He vowed to kill every last one of us. It is a small hope to think he's changed his mind."

"What can he be thinking, though? To take us on as young men, when we didn't know our strength, that was one thing. But now?" Cedric stroked Penelope as he spoke, but the hound growled as though sensing his tension.

Lucien thought of all he stood to lose if Hugo Waverly struck. One person in particular came to mind. If he lost her, he'd lose himself. No, the time for posturing was over. It was time to prepare for war.

The League of Rogues would have to protect themselves, and those they loved, from Waverly's fatal schemes.

Emily always preferred sunrises to sunsets. She supposed the symbolism of rebirth inspired her. But now, as she admired the tangerine glow of the setting sun, she noticed the purple hues that bled along the edges. She leaned against the deck railing, the polished wood smooth beneath her hands, feeling a little nervous about their first honeymoon night. It was nonsense of course, she and Godric had done everything already and she had no need for nerves.

A pair of strong arms slid around her waist, and a firm body pressed against her back.

Godric kissed her temple and then her cheek. "There you are, love."

"Godric?" she said as lips danced down the line of her neck.

"Yes, darling?"

"Are you glad you married me?" She leaned into him, savoring his strength. After being strong and brave for so long, she was grateful to have him lend her strength when she needed it. They would support each other, as people who loved each other should.

"Glad? I could never be happier than the day you stood with me in the church. It was the beginning of an adventure." His embrace tightened, keeping her secure in his arms.

"Marrying me was an adventure?"

Godric turned Emily around to face him. He cupped her cheeks with his palms and leaned in, resting his forehead against hers in the gold light of the setting sun. Each touch, each look shared between them, was like coming home. In him she found her life, her breath, her soul. With him she belonged in a way she'd never thought possible. Emily reached up to hold his wrists, losing herself in his eyes.

With infinite tenderness his lips met hers. Their kiss gathered life from the depths of their souls. The spark of passion that had burned so often between them was no longer. The blinding light that only love could bring had replaced it, burning them with its intensity. Their lips melded into one fiery mouth, and their racing pulses fused into one steady, beating heart. When they finally broke apart, Godric smiled.

"Loving you has been the adventure of a lifetime," he said, "and we've only just begun."

About the Author

Lauren Smith is an attorney by day, author by night, who pens adventurous and edgy romance stories by the light of her smart phone flashlight app. She's a native Oklahoman who lives with her three pets—a feisty chinchilla, sophisticated cat and dapper little schnauzer. She's won multiple awards in several romance subgenres including being an Amazon.com Breakthrough Novel Award Quarter-Finalist and a Semi-Finalist for the Mary Wollstonecraft Shelley Award.

Check her out at laurensmithbooks.com. You can follow her at Facebook.com/LaurenDianaSmith and on Twitter at @LSmithAuthor. Her blog is theleagueofrogues.blogspot.com.

Political intrigue could leave his heart the last one standing...alone.

Sweet Disorder

© *2014 Rose Lerner*

Lively St. Lemeston, Book 1

Nick Dymond enjoyed the rough-and-tumble military life until a bullet to the leg sent him home to his emotionally distant, politically obsessed family. For months, he's lived alone with his depression, blockaded in his lodgings.

But with his younger brother desperate to win the local election, Nick has a new set of marching orders: dust off the legendary family charm and maneuver the beautiful Phoebe Sparks into a politically advantageous marriage.

One marriage was enough for Phoebe. Under her town's by-laws, though, she owns a vote that only a husband can cast. Much as she would love to simply ignore the unappetizing matrimonial candidate pushed at her by the handsome earl's son, she can't. Her teenage sister is pregnant, and Phoebe's last-ditch defense against her sister's ruin is her vote—and her hand.

Nick and Phoebe soon realize the only match their hearts will accept is the one society will not allow. But as election intrigue turns dark, they'll have to cast the cruelest vote of all: loyalty...or love.

Warning: Contains elections, confections, and a number of erections.

Available now in ebook and print from Samhain Publishing.

SAMHAIN®
PUBLISHING

It's all about the story...

Romance

HORROR

www.samhainpublishing.com